THE RAVISHMENT

"No-no, it's wrong," she murmured, weakly moving her head without escaping the kisses that made her lips throb. Why was it wrong? She could not answer, for never had she been overwhelmed by such powerful and dazzling feelings.

Patrick's low, sensual laugh made her shiver even as she responded against her will to the hand that had somehow found its way under her skirts, boldly exploring where layers of silk and lace fell away under his touch. His mouth was devouring her, and her breath came raggedly as unfamiliar sensations coursed through her body.

"From the moment I saw you on the ship I've thought only of you, my love," he whispered, as he pulled her down with him onto the rich brocade of the divan. "Hilary, darling girl, don't torture me any longer. Admit it, this is where you belong."

Drowning in a sea of delight, she could not answer. . . .

LOVE'S REDEMPTION

KATHLEEN FRASER

A SIGNET BOOK

NEW AMERICAN LIBRARY

PUBLISHER'S NOTE

This novel is a work of fiction. Names, characters, places, and incidents either are the product of the author's imagination or are used fictitiously, and any resemblance to actual persons, living or dead, events, or locales is entirely coincidental.

NAL BOOKS ARE AVAILABLE AT QUANTITY DISCOUNTS WHEN USED TO PROMOTE PRODUCTS OR SERVICES. FOR INFORMATION PLEASE WRITE TO PREMIUM MARKETING DIVISION, NEW AMERICAN LIBRARY, 1633 BROADWAY, NEW YORK, NEW YORK 10019.

Copyright © 1985 by Margaret Ball

SIGNET TRADEMARK REG. U.S. PAT. OFF. AND FOREIGN COUNTRIES
REGISTERED TRADEMARK—MARCA REGISTRADA
HECHO EN CHICAGO, U.S.A.

SIGNET, SIGNET CLASSIC, MENTOR, PLUME, MERIDIAN AND NAL BOOKS are published by New American Library,
1633 Broadway, New York, New York 10019

First Printing, January, 1986

1 2 3 4 5 6 7 8 9

PRINTED IN THE UNITED STATES OF AMERICA

1

The galley fires had been put out at noon, when the hazy ring around the sun gave warning of bad weather ahead. Now the orlop deck was as dark as it was at midnight. Perhaps it *was* midnight. Hilary had no feeling for the passage of time since it seemed that she had crouched below decks, deafened by the continual buffeting of the waves and creaking of the ship's timbers, for an eternity.

Mistress Polwhys and her man thought her brave to venture out of the hold on an errand. The truth was, Hilary would have risked worse than being washed overboard by a wave to get out of the crowded, stinking hold and to escape Anna Polwhys' terrified squeals, which sliced through the fetid air like a knife and echoed in Hilary's ears. There was desperate need for the ship's surgeon, and she was glad to go above where she could not hear Anna's cries.

Hilary was not in danger of being washed

overboard, nor was there much fresh air. The orlop deck was still below the water line, a dark unventilated cave divided between the galleys and the surgeon's cockpit. Hilary groped her way forward through the darkness, holding to whatever she could reach to steady her against the tossing of the ship. A violent wave knocked something loose; she heard it rumbling toward her and jumped out of the way just in time, relinquishing her precious handhold. The deck tilted out from under her feet and she went down with her nose in the cable tier and her outflung hands touching something warm that squeaked and scurried away. Whatever had come loose crashed against the opposite bulk-head with a solid thud that suggested it was no small item; a cask full of ship's stores, most likely.

Painfully climbing to her feet again, Hilary rubbed her nose with one hand and reached blindly for a new handhold with the other. Stumbling along until another wave finally threw her against the door of the surgeon's cabin, she held onto the brass handle with one hand and beat on the panels of the door with the other. Surely he must hear her, even through all the noise of the storm. No one could be sleeping through this—he would have been thrown from his bunk a dozen times.

The ship's motion tossed her from side to side, yet she still held onto the long brass handle, yanking at it to keep her balance. With a soft click, the bar suddenly slid away under her fingers and the next heave of the ship tossed her bodily into the surgeon's cabin as the door opened. This time she put her arms up to shield her face, but what she fell on was soft enough: a tangle of dirty linens and a wool blanket stiff with salt, all rolled up together and thrust into a corner of the surgeon's bunk.

The bunk was empty otherwise. Hilary felt about her with trembling hands, babbling apologies for her unseemly intrusion. Over her head the waves crashed on deck, and beside her the outer timbers of the ship creaked with strain, but inside the tiny cabin there was only silence. Then she noticed the smell of alcohol—brandy, she would have thought—and reasoned it was something out of the surgeon's medicine chest.

Fighting down the panic that threatened to overwhelm her, Hilary realized the surgeon wouldn't be in his cabin, not in a storm like this. The crash she heard a while ago was one of the masts coming down. Men were probably hurt and the surgeon would be above, helping to cut away the wreckage, stanch bleeding, and set bones.

But she had to call him away from that work. Broken bones could wait. Anna Polwhys' child couldn't.

She imagined what it must be like on deck: at least one of the ship's three masts down in a tangle of sails and rigging, men groaning with pain while other men went up to repair the damage, climbing and swaying above the black water. If she was so tossed about here in the orlop deck, how much worse must it be up above! Better not to think of it, or she'd never have the courage to finish her journey.

The ascent to the main deck was a nightmare of slippery ladders, creatures that squeaked and twittered while running over her feet, and the ship groaning like a living thing that was pulled apart by the violence of the storm. She was unmercifully tossed and battered whenever she had to give up a secure handhold to dash across an open space. But at last, bruised and breathless, she made her way to the main deck and the open air. Holding onto the ladder with both hands and taking great gulps of the sweet cold air that whipped past her face and pulled her hair loose, she was glad for her own sake that she'd dared the journey.

While she caught her breath she hung on the ladder with only her head exposed to the storm, breathing the cold salty wind and watching the men who worked by the light of a single lantern to cut away the rigging of the broken mast. Waves flecked with fiery light foamed over onto the deck as they worked, and the wind that howled around the ship threw droplets of glowing water, so that the air seemed to be on fire against the blackness of the clouds around them. It was an eerily beautiful sight, and for a moment her heart exulted in it and she forgot her errand.

Then a wave larger than the rest rose above the deck, a menacing shape outlined with glowing lights, and when it crashed down over her it was black and salty and wanted to batter her hands loose of the ladder. When she could again breathe, she noticed that the men who'd been working on the rigging had been swept clear across the deck and there was a ship's officer standing over her, cursing and demanding to know who the devil had been fool enough to open a hatch in the middle of the storm.

Soaked and trembling from the cold wave that had drenched her, Hilary climbed up on deck and faced him with her head high. "I came for—"

The wind shrieking around them drowned her out. She took a deep breath and started again at the top of her voice. "I came for the ship's surgeon! He's needed below."

"And that's where you'll find him, the damned coward," the first mate howled back. "Dead drunk in a corner of his cabin, and me with a parcel of damned lubberly fools as don't know better than to cut off their hands when they're trying to cut through the ropes!"

The wind dropped on his last words, enclosing them in an eye of calm at the center of the storm in which every sound on deck came through with eerie clarity. One of the seamen who was hacking awkwardly at the rigging with his left hand grinned and waved his right arm at Hilary. The lantern light glowed on a mass of bandages wrapped round and round his arm and soaked black with blood. "That's me, missy," he called. "But don't you fret! Come back when it's calm and ol' Tom'll show you a better time with one hand than Captain can do with two!"

"Stow your chat," the mate yelled, "and cut lively, there!" His head froze for a moment and then slowly moved across the deck as if searching for something. "Where's Jenkins?"

"Washed overboard," the wounded seaman called back, still with that idiotically cheerful grin on his face.

"Odds but the next wave takes Seaman Tom with it," remarked a light cultured voice behind Hilary. She wheeled, startled, and saw two fine gentlemen in gold-laced coats who leaned against the outer wall of the captain's cabin, legs crossed and seemingly as much at their ease as if they had been lounging in a London coffeehouse. Although their coats and their neatly tied campaign wigs were drenched from the waves that crashed over the deck, while streams of water ran down from the curved brims of their hats, neither man betrayed the least discomfort.

"Zounds, but you're off in your reckoning there, Anthony," said one of them as she stared, openmouthed. "I'll back our able seaman to survive any danger over water. Can you not see that the rogue was born to be hanged? Twenty guineas but he survives the night, unless the ship founders under him."

"Done!" said the other. "And what'll you lay that the ship rides out the storm?"

"Not more than ten."

"Fair enough." And they shook hands on the second bet.

Hilary shook her head, bemused at the sangfroid with which these two were cracking jokes and laying wagers on the very manner of their death. She turned back to the first mate, who was already halfway across the deck to help the sailors with the tangle of rigging.

"Wait—oh, please, wait!" she called. "Can the surgeon not be roused? He must come!"

The rising wind forced her to scream out the last words, adding to their intensity. The mate turned and came back toward her. The long upward shadows cast by the lantern hanging on the rail turned his face into a distorted ogre's mask, but his voice when he spoke was kindly enough.

"Nay, lass, McTavish will be out o' it for the night now. It's his way, you see, when there's a storm up. Never knew a man so afeard of drowning who spent so much time afloat. Soon as we see the weather signs, he starts putting away the brandy. He'll be dead drunk in a corner till it's all over."

Hilary remembered the reek of brandy in the surgeon's cabin, and her heart sank. "But there must be somebody else—his assistant?" she babbled, clutching at the mate's arm.

The mate shook his head and turned back to his work. "Get below," he advised. "Wind's coming up again. You don't want to be washed overboard like poor Jenkins."

Hilary stood helplessly watching as the mate picked his way through the tangle of rigging. An ax gleamed in his hand and he chopped at the salt-encrusted ropes with short, deft strokes. If only there were someone half as coolheaded and knowledgeable to help Anna!

A yank on the hood of her cloak sent her stumbling backward, barely avoiding the yawning blackness of the open hatch. One of the fine gentlemen gave a delighted crow of laughter and fastened both arms about her waist. "Caught you, kit-cat! Never fear, we'll not let you be washed overboard! I'm not a man to waste a pretty piece like you, and neither is Patrick here. Come into the cabin, we'll warm you up."

His grip was loose, his speech slightly slurred, and there was brandy on his breath. Hilary pushed herself free without trouble and spun around to deliver a ringing slap on his ear. "How dare you!"

"Lass, I dare whatever amuses me." He reached for her again.

"Aye, it well fits you to stand here and make fun while other folk are working and dying!" Hilary cried out. In that moment she hated these two fine gentlemen for being what they were, and useless to her. Why could not one of them be drunk in his cabin instead of the surgeon? "If you were men and not painted boobies, you'd be out there helping Tom cut away the rigging!"

The first mate had come back to break up the altercation. "The devil they would," he said. "What I don't need on a night like this is a parcel of damned amateurs getting in the way! Now, if these gents want to risk their lives on deck instead of staying in their cabin, I can't stop 'em, but one thing I cannot and will not have is you trollops from steerage adding your bit to the bloody confusion! Now, get below, you—"

Hilary jerked away from his grip on her arm. "I will not!" she cried at him. "Not till you tell me who's to help Anna Polwhys!"

There was a chuckle from one of the gentlemen, and Hilary rounded on them, willing to include them in her fury. "And you're as bad!

Here's a man wounded in trying to save all our lives, and a woman like to die in childbed below, and all you can do is make bets on the outcome!''

"Well, and is it any of my affair if you folk breed like rats in the 'tweendecks?" said Anthony. His hand reached out to take Hilary's chin. She twisted away and slapped his hand, and he chuckled. "Ah, here's sport to see the night through! Tell me, kit-cat—"

His friend put one hand on his arm. "Softly, Anthony, you fool! Can't you see she's troubled?"

"Aye, so are we all." Anthony was close enough that Hilary could see the sweat shining on his forehead and the trembling in his hands. He was afraid too, she realized, and somehow the thought gave her more courage. "The ship's not like to last out the night, and I know what I'd like to be doing when she goes down."

As he leaned forward, Patrick thrust him back against the cabin wall with one hand and stepped between them. The lantern that swayed from the railing illuminated his face in unsteady flashes; one moment Hilary caught a glimpse of a grave young face with laughing black eyes; the next he was plunged in shadow. "I fear there's not much we can do to help, my dear," he said. "Is there no wisewoman or midwife below decks?"

Hilary stared at him openmouthed. "But she died," she said. "Granny Tregaren? She died of the fever when we were but two weeks out. Surely you remember?" But even as she spoke, she realized that of course he'd not have noted the death of one woman, nor have understood what her loss meant to the rest of them: what had a rich cabin passenger to do with the poor redemptioners in the hold? Why, she herself had not so much as spoken with any of the cabin passengers until this desperate night.

"There must be other women with some knowledge," Patrick insisted.

Hilary nodded, her mouth going dry with the memory of the whispered consultation the women had held just out of Anna Polwhys' hearing—not that Anna would have noticed aught that was said, after the hours of thin continuous screaming. "Yes, but they said . . . the child is turned the wrong way in the womb," she whispered. Her cheeks flamed. She'd thought to find a surgeon who would understand these matters without being told. What was the good of speaking of such things to any other man? And the fact that he was young and good-looking somehow made it worse. But he was the only person up here who'd even looked as if he might help. Desperation forced her to go on.

"They said it will have to be cut from her."

Patrick nodded, and for a wild moment she thought that he had the solution for her. "I see," he said. "Well, lass, I'm afraid there's no one here who can help you. I'm certainly no surgeon, nor Anthony either."

Hilary's heart sank at his tone of dismissal, and without thinking, she caught hold of his hand. He was warm and alive in her grasp, and the easy strength of his arm steadied her against the rocking of the boat. "No, you *must* help!"

she cried in desperation. "Please. I can't go back down there and tell them no one will come—I can't, I can't!"

Anthony stirred from the wall where he had slumped, hiccuping some advice as to where else she might go. Patrick silenced him with a curt "Not now, Anthony, for God's sake!"

He turned back to Hilary. The lantern light danced crazily across the deck and the cabin wall, and for a moment she saw him clearly: young, unsmiling, but with a warmth in his dark eyes that set her heart beating faster. "Very well, mistress," he said, so softly that she could scarce hear him above the beating of the waves against the side of the ship, "I'm all unhandy as a surgeon, but if 'twill be some help to you, I'll come with you. Though I fear 'twill be less than no help to that poor woman below," he murmured as if to himself.

"That's a true word!" Anthony flipped an elegantly manicured hand in dismissal as Patrick handed Hilary down the ladder to the lower deck. "You're more skilled at the other end of the process."

Patrick paused with one foot already on the ladder and shrugged. "I've helped mares to foal. It can't be entirely different, d'you think?"

Perhaps it was as well for Hilary's uncertain temper that she did not hear those last words.

After the cold, clean air above decks, the fetid stench of the hold struck Hilary with renewed force. The air stank of vomit and urine and fear; the cold of the night was vanquished by the warmth of three hundred close-packed, unwashed bodies. The passengers lay packed like herrings in a barrel, some clamped to their narrow bunks in terror, others praying and vomiting and squabbling in the narrow gangways. Three-foot-high partitions provided the only semblance of privacy they would know for the duration of the voyage.

In the far corner a lantern had been hung up, in defiance of the captain's ruling that all lights were to be doused below decks until the storm was past. Around it, cloths draped from the low beams overhead gave some privacy to Anna Polwhys' lying-in.

Hilary threaded her way along the narrow, cluttered gangway with the swiftness of long practice. Once, sensing that Patrick was lagging behind, she glanced back and saw him rubbing the top of his head where it had come into contact with an overhead beam. Serves him right, she thought with a flash of malice. Let the fine gentleman see how the rest of us live! Then she remembered that he was here to help, and sent up a murmured prayer of repentance between two cheerful words of greeting to the passengers who crouched at her feet.

Anna Polwhys' eyes rolled up briefly as Hilary put aside the improvised curtain made of someone's petticoat. She was evidently too exhausted to move her head, too exhausted even to scream anymore as the convulsions shook her body. Huddled in one corner, the three women who'd been closest to Anna hung onto the wooden partition for balance and whispered among themselves. One of them was clicking the beads of her rosary; another put her own child to the breast. When Patrick stepped into the curtained partition behind Hilary, she blushed and flipped the tail of her skirt forward to cover the woman's breast and the child's head.

"So . . . so. Easy, now." Patrick knelt beside Anna Polwhys' bunk, speaking in a level, reassuring tone. Hilary sighed with relief. He might not be a surgeon, she thought, but at least she'd found someone who was willing to help with whatever skill he possessed, who would not panic and increase Anna's fright. And, she thought with wry humor, he might know no more about childbirth than she did herself, but he could hardly know less!

As he asked Anna a question, Hilary stepped forward and translated in a low tone. Kneeling on the opposite side of Anna's bunk, she gripped the laboring woman's thin, big-knuckled hand in both her own and told her not to be afraid, that the gentleman was a famous doctor from London town come specially to see to her well-being. Anna, too far gone to feel embarrassment, answered Patrick's few questions in a rasping whisper that Hilary translated.

"You didn't tell me she was a foreigner," Patrick said.

"She's Cornish," Hilary snapped, slightly irritated. As if that made any difference! She felt Patrick's level, measuring glance upon her, and flushed to think what a drab she must look, with her hair torn out of its decent knot and the soaked thin gown outlining her body.

"And yourself?"

"My mother was . . . of her people," Hilary said reluctantly. One of the women in the corner came forward and threw Hilary's coarse brown cloak about her shoulders. She huddled into it, grateful for the warmth and even more grateful for the decent covering it offered. "Well?" she snapped. "Are you going to do anything, or did you just come down here to chat about ethnic groups?"

"Just surprised," Patrick said. One eyebrow, black and silky as a crow's feather, slanted upward and he smiled at her for the first time. "And wondering what's best to do. . . . She'll not object if I handle her?"

"Not if I tell her it's all right," Hilary said. She bent over Anna, holding the other woman's hand tightly and murmuring reassuring words to her, while they both kept their eyes averted from the sight of Patrick's hands feeling her belly.

"Don't be offended," Patrick said at the end of this brief examination, "but I'm thinking if she were a mare, I'd know better what to do. I'm afraid of hurting her. I've heard that sometimes you can turn the child from outside. But I'll need help. Do any of these women speak English?"

Hilary shook her head. "I'll help you," she said between the waves of faintness and nausea that had been growing stronger ever since she came into the stinking confinement of the hold. "Tell me what to do."

But when they began their manipulations, Anna cried out hoarsely and half-rose from the

bunk, fighting their hands. Not all Hilary's soothing words could calm her.

"Someone will have to hold her," Patrick
snapped over his shoulder at the praying women
in the corner. Then, as they looked back at him
with blank, frightened eyes, he raised his own
eyes heavenward. "Does no one in this god-
forsaken hole speak a civilized tongue?"

His cry penetrated the thin partition surrounding them. There was a rustle and a murmur
outside, then a woman pushed through the curtain and stood defiantly facing them, hands
planted on her hips. Her reddish-brown hair
tumbled about a sharp face, almost obscuring
the green glint of her eyes, and fell in tangled
curls over the front of the gaping shift that was
her only garment. The shift was belted tightly
at the waist with a grubby scarf that fell down
over one hip, outlining the generous curves of
her body. "I'll help you, Cap'n," she announced
with a defiant sniff and a toss of her head, "if'n
you're not too proud to let London Bet give a
hand."

Without waiting for permission, she went to
the head of the bunk and placed firm hands on
Anna's shoulders. "And it's little enough I know
of such matters," she said with grim humor,
"the children being a hindrance in my trade,
y'understand. We like to lose 'em sooner than
this. But I've been hearing this poor girl cry out
all night, and if there's aught you know can
ease her pain, Cap'n, I'll be proud to lend a
hand."

Patrick nodded with grave courtesy. "And I'll

be grateful of your assistance, Mistress Bet," he said. He bent over Anna again, while London Bet gave Hilary a saucy grin that exposed two missing teeth. "Hear that?" she said in soft tones. "Called me 'Mistress,' he did, just as if I was a lady!"

In the minutes that followed, while the three of them worked over Anna's pain-racked body, there was no time for more polite conversation. In between his brusque commands, Patrick muttered to himself; Hilary caught a few words and realized he was praying.

Suddenly the ship pitched forward, throwing Hilary against Anna's body and sending Patrick against the partition. Anna gasped and gave a long shuddering squeal like a baby rabbit caught in a trap. "Oh, sweet Lord," Patrick muttered as she writhed on the bunk, "if I've done more damage in my ignorance, forgive me." The sweat was pouring out from under his flowing black campaign wig, and his eyes were dark smudges in a face white with tension. Hilary watched his face, almost unaware of the pain in her hand as Anna squeezed down so hard it seemed the bones must crack.

"Ey! Catch it, you great booby!" Bet called.

Patrick and Hilary turned startled faces toward her. Bet muttered a curse and crawled around the bunk, holding onto the wooden partition to keep her balance. She reached the end of the bunk, put out her hands under Anna's legs, and came away holding a red, crumpled mite with thick tufts of black hair covering the top of its misshapen skull.

"Whatever you done, Cap'n," she said, grinning, "seems to've worked."

"My God!" Patrick stared unbelieving as the baby's face crumpled into new lines and it gave a high-pitched wavering squall. The howling of the wind outside dropped down abruptly and the baby's cry echoed through the hold. "We did it!"

"We did it," Hilary echoed. She and Patrick beamed at each other while one of the women in the corner came forward to wash and wrap the child. Anna raised herself on her elbow and whispered a few words, smiling.

"She says she had a small part in it too, so don't get overproud of yourself," Hilary translated. But she couldn't stop grinning in triumph every time she glanced at Patrick. His slow, lazy smile and the glow in his dark eyes warmed her like a candle flame burning deep inside her.

"I don't even know your name," Patrick said slowly.

"Hilary," she said. "Hilary Pembroke."

"It's a beautiful name," he said. "Like a chime of bells or a girl's laughter."

Hilary felt as wonderful as though she herself had been called beautiful. All her life—well, ever since she'd been left with Jephthah's people—she'd heard only that her name was wicked, heathenish, and like nothing a good Christian should be called. Since Jephthah left for America there had not even been anyone left to call her Hilary; the rest of the Saints called her Hannah.

The rocking of the boat had calmed somewhat now, and the other Cornishwomen were bustling about Anna to wash her and the baby and tuck them up comfortably. Patrick rose, head bent to avoid the deck beams, and crooked one arm toward Hilary. She laid the tips of her fingers on his sleeve, unconsciously bending her wrist with the elegant turn of gesture her mother had used on the stage.

"It seems we're no longer needed here, Mistress Hilary," he said with a slight smile and an inclination of his head. "And it seems the storm has passed us by. Perhaps you'd care to favor me by taking a turn upon the deck?"

"Indeed, an' she'll do no such thing," Bet interrupted, pushing herself between them. "She needs to rest and get out of them wet things, don't you, ducks? Come along now, dearie, I'll see you to your bunk." She glared over her shoulder at Patrick and shepherded a sleepy and confused Hilary out of the partitioned area.

"That's a fine gentleman you caught," she cautioned Hilary under her breath when they were well away from Patrick, "but when it comes to little strolls on the deck by night, there's but one thing they're all after, and it ain't fresh air!" She snickered and dug her elbow into Hilary's ribs.

"Oh, no," Hilary protested as Bet towed her along the narrow aisle. "I'm sure you are mistaken. He is not like that." But the sleeping space assigned to her was before her, six feet by eighteen inches of beautiful hard planks covered with a lovely soft threadbare blanket, and she was too tired to resist Bet's kindly ministrations. Under the shelter of her cloak she stripped off the wet dress and huddled naked into the nest of blankets. The warm scratchy wool irritated her skin, but no such minor irritations could keep her from sleep.

"At least keep him waiting a few days, bring the price up," she heard Bet mutter as she drifted off. "Fair goes to me 'eart to see a girl like you trying to give it away, when the rest of us have to work so hard to sell it."

2

The day after the great storm dawned bright and clear. The raging winds had driven them south of the normal route to Virginia, and the air was warm and soft with tropical breezes. The ship moved slowly under half-sail while a group of sailors, aided by two carpenters from the steerage passengers, worked at putting up the drastically shortened remains of the mizzen-mast that had fallen during the storm.

The rest of the steerage passengers, relieved at their escape from death and delighted by the unexpected good weather, came up in twos and threes to sun themselves and take the air. The rain-washed decks, cleared of the tangle of wreckage from the night before, were soon cluttered with groups of redemptioners. Gaily chattering women washed their laundry in tubs of salt water, children ran and screamed with joy at being let out of the dark hold for a few hours, and the men squatted on their heels to compare notes about the possibilities of life in the New World.

"My contract says I'm to serve four years, then I get fifty acres of land and the tools to work it," said Jer Polwhys, rubbing his hands together with enthusiasm. He was a little blue-jowled man whose massive arms and shoulders, incongruously bulky below a foxy, sharp-featured face, bore evidence of the mining trade at which he had worked in Cornwall. "And another fifty acres for Anna! A man could labor his life away in the mines at home and never have a bit o' land to call his own. I tell you, brothers, this is a good land we're bound to."

"Aye," said one of his friends who took a gloomier view, "if you're sold together. What if Anna's bought by one o' that sort?" He jerked his head at the forward cabin, where Patrick and Anthony were once again leaning against the wall and taking the air while they made light comments and casual bets on the sights before them. "Rich lord'll debauch y'r Anna, and then who'll help you set up on y'r land?"

"Not my Anna," said Jer Polwhys with a ring of conviction that no man in the circle dared argue with. "And even if we be sold apart . . ." His face clouded for a moment and then he shook his head decisively. "Nay, these colonials be not such brutes as to separate man and wife!"

"Then they're a better breed of men than the English lords they sprang from," said his friend with a sour sarcasm that was entirely lost on Jer.

"Aye, that they be!" he cried exultantly. "I

tell you, brothers, everything is better in this New World. The land is so fertile that a man can plant a fruit orchard and see it bearing in two years—the very grapes and grain are bigger and fatter than anything at home—stands to reason the men'd be better too, don't it?" He grinned around the circle with naive triumph in his face.

"I'd like t'know where ye heard that about the fruit orchard," mumbled another man. "Be there apples in Virginia?"

"Every kind of fruit and grain," Jer insisted. "It says so in a book."

All but one nodded their heads, impressed by this irrefutable evidence. Only Jer's sarcastic friend laughed.

"A book! What would you be knowing of books, you that had to make an X on your indentures?"

Jer nodded toward Hilary, kneeling a few feet away over a washtub full of soiled linen. "*She* read it to me. Hilary!" he called. "Come over here, there's a good girl, and read the fellows that bit as you were telling me last week. Put it into the Cornish for us."

Never loath to leave the backbreaking labor over the washtub, Hilary rose and came toward the circle of men with her eyes modestly downcast. Ever since waking this morning she had suffered agonies of embarrassment over the memory of her pert manner to the first mate and Patrick the night before. How like a wanton she must have seemed, screaming at them with her hair flying loose in the wind and her thin dress clinging to her body! This morning she'd been at pains to attire herself decently, with a shawl around her shoulders to conceal the dress that was grown so tight to her body, with her copper-colored hair firmly pinned in place and all but concealed by a muddy brown calico mobcap. And she meant to conduct herself decently, too, and not behave like the shouting young girl Jephthah would be ashamed to know in America.

Yet Patrick had not so much as glanced her way since she came up on deck with her load of clothes and bed linens to wash. Hilary told herself that she ought to be glad he didn't remember her; hadn't Bet's words last night been warning enough of where his sort of attention could lead?

It was just that she felt strangely depressed when she saw him smoking and gossiping with the ships' officers forward, with no word of greeting for her. Hilary found it difficult to keep from looking at him as she knelt and scrubbed at the dirty clothes that never did get quite clean in seawater. She was grateful for the excuse to read aloud from the little pamphlet that she had bought in London with her last shilling before boarding the redemptioner ship.

"The Fruit-Trees are wonderfully quick of growth, so that in six or seven years time from the Planting, a Man may bring an Orchard to bear in great plenty," Hilary read in a clear, carrying voice that lifted above the grumbling and gossiping on deck. "Peaches, Nectarines, and Apricots commonly bear in three years from the Stone, and thrive so exceedingly that they seem to have no need of Grafting or Inoculating. Bees thrive there abundantly, and will very easily yield to the careful Huswife, two Crops of Honey in a Year, and besides lay up a Winter-store sufficient to preserve their Stocks."

"What did I tell you!" Jer clapped his hands together and looked around the circle of squatting men with a triumphant grin. "Read us that bit about what we get on freedom, there's a good lass. A suit of clothes, en't it, and tools to work the land with?"

Hilary turned the pages of the pamphlet carefully, her lips moving slightly as she sought for the section Jer wanted. The little book, not new when she bought it, had suffered from the damp sea air and she was afraid the pages would fall apart in her hands.

"Zounds, look at that!" called a loud voice from close behind her. "A woman reading!" Hilary whirled, startled, and saw that Anthony had come down from his place on the foredeck to pick his way among the steerage passengers with disdainful, mincing steps. One hand raised a lace handkerchief to his nose as if to block out the stink of poverty; the other held a slender ebony cane with which he balanced himself against the gentle rolling of the ship.

"Ah," he said as she turned, "it's the spitting kitten. Thought so. What's the matter, kit-cat? Didn't your dame-school teach you to con these big hard words? Let me help you."

Hilary shook her head. "No, thank you." It was true she'd had difficulty in making out some of the words on the stained and water-spotted pages of the pamphlet, but she wanted no help from such as Anthony. She glanced

around for Patrick, hoping that he would restrain his friend as he'd done the previous night,
but he was absorbed in conversation with the
captain of the ship.

"Ah, don't be shy," Anthony reproved her.
With a flick of his ebony cane he twitched the
book out of her grasp, the cane tip hooked in
the binding. Hilary instinctively clutched at the
pages she still held. The binding gave way and
loose pages fluttered forth over the deck, some
caught by the sea breeze to vanish over the
side, others floating into the cold tub of washing water. With a cry of dismay she fell to her
knees and scooped up as many of the pages as
she could reach. Anthony was completely forgotten in this disaster; all she saw was the page
about the fruits and grapevines, fluttering just
out of reach, and beyond it a whole section on
the Indian tribes, and to her right—

An elegant leather shoe with a red heel came
down smack in the middle of the page she was
reaching for. The tip of Anthony's cane hooked
under her chin and forced her face upward.

"Don't fuss, kit-cat," he said with a grin. "I
can show you better ways to pass the time than
pretending to read." His heel ground deliberately into the page he was standing on, reduc-
ing the center of the page to a shredded tatter
of muddy pulp.

Tears of anger stung Hilary's eyes and blurred
her vision. She grabbed at the cane, only meaning to push it away from her, but Anthony's
hand jerked sideways and the tip of the cane
caught in her mobcap, pulling it away from her
head. Hilary felt a tug and heard an ominous

ripping sound as the soft old fabric gave way. Her fingers closed around the end of the cane and she pushed forward with all her strength as she scrambled to her feet.

The unexpected shove took Anthony by surprise. He let go of the cane and the carved ebony head hit him in the stomach. He stepped backward and his right foot came down at an angle on the remnants of the page that he had just ground into pulp. The stiff wooden heel of his shoe skidded forward and with a squawk of surprise he went down on his back. Before he could rise, Jer Polwhys was kneeling on his chest.

"You . . . let . . . our . . . women . . . alone!" he grunted out, banging Anthony's head on the deck between words. The other men gathered around the three of them in a ring, dark sullen faces glowering down at the fight.

Anthony gave a wordless snarl and reached one hand for his cane. With the other hand he struck upward at Jer Polwhys' face and used the other man's momentary recoil to upset him. Up on one knee, he twisted the head of the cane and a length of steel, sparkling in the sun, glided forth from the ebony interior. Hilary shrieked and pushed herself between the two men just as Anthony thrust. Too late to arrest the power of the thrust, he turned his wrist down. The sword blade passed harmlessly through the hem of her skirt and pinned it to the deck.

"Odds, but you spoiled my stroke!" Anthony cursed her. With a smile that flashed like the sun glinting on the length of bright dangerous steel in his hand, he yanked the sword free of the deck and jumped back, raising the blade in his hand. "Come on, now," he taunted the men who had moved back when he drew his sword, "is there one of you peasants with stomach for a fight? Dare attack a gentleman, would—"

"Odd's life! Put up, man, put up!" Patrick seemed to come out of nowhere in a flying leap from the foredeck that launched him into the ring of men around Anthony. His fine gold-laced coat glittered more brightly than Anthony's sword, but the blaze of anger in his eyes eclipsed them both. "Are you mad, to draw steel on shipboard? D'you want the captain to put you in irons?" As he spoke, one arm encircled Hilary's shoulders, giving her the support she so desperately needed. She leaned against him without thinking, grateful for his strength to supplement her trembling knees.

"Ah, they attacked me first," Anthony complained, but he picked up the ebony cane as he spoke, and slowly fitted the two pieces back together. "I was but trying to make civil conversation with this spitfire here, when she takes offense for nothing, and the next thing I know, the peasant is like to throttle me with his horny hands—if I don't die first from the stink of onions on his breath." He gave Jer Polwhys a slanting, dangerous glance, and Hilary caught her breath. Jer had made an enemy of a gentleman. It wasn't a good start for his high hopes of a new life in the New World.

Biting her lip, she repressed the sarcastic comments that sprang to the tip of her tongue. Oh, but she'd love to tell this fine aristocrat that there was a difference between civil conversation and insult, that not one of the "peasants" he affected to despise would use a woman so or destroy a book with such callous unconcern. But they were in enough trouble already. Common folk should never fight with gentry, her foster mother used to say; the earthenware pot is smashed by the iron kettle. Hilary hung her head and tried to look the very opposite of a spitfire, a meek gentle girl who could not possibly have offended the gentleman.

"I might have known you were in it," Patrick said in a low voice meant for her ears alone. His arm tightened around her shoulders. "I was looking all around the deck for my redheaded vixen, and never guessing it was you with your hair pinned under that ugly cap. I might have known to wait until the trouble started, and you'd be in the thick of it."

Hilary's good resolutions vanished and her head came up with a fighting tilt. "I?" she cried. "You blame me because this *gentleman* insults me? Oh, you gentry all stick together, don't you? Can you not leave us alone? We weren't troubling you, until he had to come and stick his big nose in." She flung out an accusing arm at the spot where Anthony had been standing, and realized with a jolt of surprise that he had quietly decamped while she and Patrick were talking. Jer Polwhys and his mates had returned to their circle, too; they were squatting not five feet away, talking softly to one another and pointedly not looking at Hilary and Patrick.

"Softly, softly, love," Patrick murmured. "I was only joking."

But Hilary was too furious to hear his apology. "You ruin everything," she cried passionately, "you throw us off your land to make room for sheep, and now you won't even let us have a few feet of deck space while leaving your country. Instead you must come in and make fun of us! And *he* ruined my book," she finished, unable to say more. Shaking Patrick's arm off, she stooped to the deck and gathered up the few crumpled sheets that were all she had left of her precious pamphlet. Unable to look up or to see anything for the tears that burned her eyes, she stood with her head down, smoothing out the pages with shaking hands.

Patrick's hand slid under her elbow, steadying her. "Faith, and I'm sorry about the book," he said. He took one of the pages from her hand and glanced at it, pursing his lips in surprise. "So, you wanted to know more about Virginia? Now, I'd be happy to tell you all I know, and as a native of the colony returning home, there's not much I'd rather talk about—especially to a pretty girl." His smile invited her to accept the implied invitation, but she wouldn't meet his eyes. "But then," he conceded with a sigh, "that'll not repair the book for you. Beverley's *History of Virginia*, was it?"

"Part of it," said Hilary. She couldn't quite keep her voice from wobbling as she gazed on the ruin of the pamphlet. "Only the last section, and rebound. I had it from a stall on the docks; it was the last copy, and nobody would buy it because it was only odd pages bound together, so I got it for a shilling."

"And your last shilling, I wager," said Patrick. The caressing warmth in his voice insensibly comforted her. Hilary looked up, blinking away the tears that dazzled on the ends of her long lashes, and wondered why Patrick looked so angry. Well, she had been rude to his friend, she reminded herself. "I'm sorry I shouted at Master Anthony," she said.

Unexpectedly, Patrick laughed. "Are you indeed? Well, I'm not! Time the fellow had his due! He needs to learn that he can't have everything he fancies just because he demands it."

"Oh, all the gentry think that way—as much as they think at all, that is. They'd demand the air we breathe if they took a fancy to it," said Hilary before she remembered to whom she was speaking. She clapped a hand over her mouth, wishing the bitter words back.

"I don't," Patrick said. The pressure of his hand was guiding her across the deck. He smiled down at her, and she found it hard to concentrate on what he was saying. "I hardly ever demand. I find it works better to ask . . . very nicely, of course. You see, all Anthony wanted was for you to pay attention to him. He just didn't go about it the right way. Now, if I'd been in his place, this is what I would have done."

He broke off, stepped back one pace, and made an elegant bow. The white lace ruffles of his shirt cuff floated about the lean, tanned hand he offered her, and he looked up at her under those dark slanting brows that always gave his eyes a laughing look.

"I," he said, "would have said, 'Mistress Hilary, would you graciously permit me to escort you to the afterdeck, where we may take a short stroll and enjoy some mutually improving conversation?"

Hilary smiled and spread her skirts in a sweeping curtsy to match the elegance of his gesture. As she rose, she saw his brows shoot up, and guessed that he was wondering how a peasant girl in a brown homespun dress had learned to ape the manners of a fine lady. "And what would you do if the lady refused your request?"

"I would say, 'Your servant, mistress,' and withdraw, like the gentleman I am." But instead of withdrawing, Patrick took her hand and tucked it under his arm. "Isn't it a fortunate thing," he said, smiling down at her, "that you didn't refuse?"

His eyes aren't black, Hilary thought rather muzzily through the mist that seemed suddenly to invade her mind. They're blue—but so dark and so intense that they might as well be black. Not the blue of the sky or the sea. "*Couleur du diable,*" her mother's voice laughed in her mind, and she had to say something to drive away the memory of that light, false voice.

"Of course I didn't," she said. "I am eager to learn of this country called Virginia. Will you instruct me?"

If Patrick was disappointed at the prosaic tone of her request, he didn't show it. Pacing back and forth on the small cleared space of the afterdeck, he spoke of the great forests and rivers of Virginia, the blue-tinged mountains past which few white men had ever penetrated, the rich plantations with their rows of tobacco plants springing from the black soil, until it seemed to Hilary that the entire colony lay spread out before her like some vast and living map. Then, leaning on the taffrail and staring at the foam of the waves in their wake, he drifted insensibly into more personal details. She learned that he was the younger son of a wealthy planter on the Rappahannock; desiring independence, he had taken up his own land in the southern portion of the state and had in the last few years built up a flourishing plantation on a river called the Nottoway. He had been in England to sue for royal patents to work the silver mines which lay in the southeastern portion of his lands.

"Silver mines!" Hilary nodded and tried not to look too impressed. Of course, this Virginia was such a wonderful rich country, it stood to reason that gold and silver were lying there to be picked up off the ground.

"Well." Patrick scowled at the waves. "As it happens, I didn't get the patents. We couldn't agree on the crown's share of the profits; they wanted so much that what was left would barely pay me for my labor, let alone I've sunk all the profits of the plantation these last years into opening up the area and building a good road to the river. I told the minister straight out that I'd have to receive a big enough share to repay that investment, else I'd not proceed with the project."

Hilary's lashes fluttered over her eyes to conceal her amusement. "That sounds like a demand."

"Well, they were being unreasonable!"

"And what was it you told me," she teased,

"about finding it more profitable to ask very nicely?"

Patrick stared at her for a moment, his blue eyes darkening, then laughed. "You're too clever for a poor stupid colonial like me, Mistress Hilary. Aye. I may have been a bit too hasty with the noble lords there. But never fear," he said with sublime confidence, "they'll come around once their assayers have had a look at the specimens of ore I brought with me. The man who tested the ore in Virginia said it was the richest—"

A streak of living silver rose to the surface of the sea, and Hilary forgot to keep her eyes politely on Patrick. "Oh! Oh, what was that?" Hilary leaned over the rail in an effort to catch another glimpse of the racing silver flash that streaked alongside the ship. It was under the surface now, an oval shadow—no, two shadows—but she couldn't quite see them. Perhaps if she leaned a little farther . . .

An ungentle jerk on the back of her dress brought her back to the deck with a thump that jarred her from heels to teeth. "Dolphins," said Patrick, still holding onto her dress, "and if you lean over any farther you'll be like to go swimming with them."

"I wouldn't mind," Hilary said. "They're so beautiful." As they spoke, the dolphins rose to the surface again in lazy, graceful arcs, effortlessly matching the speed of the ship.

"Well, I would," Patrick murmured. "I'm not such a wastrel as to throw the prettiest girl on board ship to the fishes."

Something in his tone made Hilary uncom-

fortable. And he was still holding her by the
loose fabric of her bunched skirt, forcing her to
stand within the circle of his arm. "You can let
go now," she said. She stood quite stiff, arms at
her sides, so as not to brush against him. "I
promise not to jump overboard."

He released her at once. She could move away
now, she thought. But that would be rude.
He'd only been trying to keep her from getting
hurt. To sidle away would be to treat him as if
he were no better than that Anthony. It might
hurt his feelings.

So she remained where she was, staring at
the foaming green water that swirled in their
wake, wishing the dolphins would reappear so
that they'd have something to talk about. The
longer the silence lasted, the more embarrassed
she felt. Perhaps he was annoyed that she'd
interrupted when he was talking about the
mines.

"Tell me about the silver mine," she said, still
looking out to sea.

Beside her, on the rail, she could just see
Patrick's brown hand moving restlessly, the long
fingers tapping out an unheard tune. "There's
better things than that to talk about on a fine
summer's day at sea," he said. "I'd rather be
hearing how Mistress Hilary came to be traveling with a group of Cornish peasants. For it's
plain to see you don't belong with them."

"I've no wish to belong anywhere else!" Hilary snapped. "They're good people—you've no
call to feel superior."

"Now, now. Did I say superior? Different
only. Look at me!"

The last words were snapped out like a command. Startled, Hilary raised her eyes and looked him full in the face.

"You see what I mean?" Patrick shook his head. "A commoner would have ducked her head and bobbed her knee and giggled. If you want to pass for one of the mob, my girl, you'll have to change the way you walk . . . and your elegant curtsy . . . and the challenging way you stare a man down, as if he were no more than the turf beneath your pretty little feet."

Cheeks burning, Hilary bowed her head. All these years Mother Graham had tried to teach her decent modest manners, and only a few weeks on board ship had destroyed all her teachings. She bit her lip and turned away from Patrick, wishing there were some way she could get away without running.

"Here, now, don't cry," Patrick said on a note of alarm. "Didn't we get enough salt water on the decks last night, but you must be adding your piece? Darling girl, I didn't mean to hurt your feelings. Lord knows, there's not a thing about you I'd change, save to have you a little more friendly when a man's indulging his natural curiosity."

Hilary smiled at his foolery. "I didn't realize it showed," she said. "Can everybody tell just by looking at me?"

"Tell what?" Patrick demanded. "That you were born to something better than shoveling mud and peeling turnips?"

"That my mother . . . was an actress."

This time Patrick's response was long in coming. I knew I shouldn't have told him, Hilary thought. It's true, what Mother Graham always said. No decent person would want to have anything to do with me if they knew my heritage.

She stole a glance at Patrick, and was astonished to see him smiling. "Well, say something!" she cried when she couldn't stand the wait any longer.

"I was only thinking," said Patrick slowly, in a caressing voice like warm cream and honey, "that she must have been very beautiful."

Hilary remembered red hair dressed in long gleaming ringlets, a dress of satin as green as the sea and trimmed with lace that foamed like the waves, white skin and a tinkling laugh that faded into nothingness even as she strained to recall more. "I think she was," she said, trying to hold back the lump that rose to her throat.

"And it makes you sad to think of her." Patrick's hand covered hers, warm and comforting. "Tell me about it."

Hilary shook her head and stared out at the misty horizon. "There's not much to tell. She came of what you would call a 'good family,' I believe. So did my father. But her folk were Catholic, and his were Protestant, and when they ran away together, both sides disowned them. I don't call that very good."

"Neither do I," agreed Patrick. "So did they both go on the stage?"

"No. My father . . . repented. He met a very good man called Ebenezer Graham, who convinced him that he was living in sin and that he would have to leave my mother and join the Grahamites to be saved. Then my mother . . . found work in London. Yes, on the stage. She had both of us to keep, you see. And it was hard. She could have had protectors, but they didn't want to be troubled with a woman *and* a child."

Hilary fell silent, fighting back the bitter ache in her chest that this part of her memories always roused.

"So what happened?" Patrick prompted.

"I suppose she got tired. When I was eight she met a gentleman who wanted to take her to France, but he didn't want to take me. She explained it all to me before . . ."

"Before what?"

The gentle voice might have come from inside her own mind, so thoroughly was she now reliving the memory of those frightening days. "Before she left me with the Grahamites," Hilary said, and clamped her lips shut on the rest of that story. Even now it hurt too much to remember.

She hadn't been meant to hear her mother's furious argument with Ebenezer Graham, but desperate curiosity about her own future had driven her to eavesdrop. She'd heard her mother swearing that the Grahamites had stolen her husband and left her with the brat to rear, they could damned well take the child now and let her enjoy some freedom before she was too old to make use of her beauty. The bitter words, the shock of discovering that she was only a nuisance to her gay, laughing, beautiful mother, had hurt Hilary so badly that for a long time she recoiled within herself and let nothing else matter: not Ebenezer Graham's unwilling reception of her, or Mother Graham's disapproval, or the harsh rules of the little community. And when she finally did begin to care again, there had been Jephthah.

A fist smashed into the railing beside her, jerking her thoughts back to the present. Patrick was scowling at the horizon, black brows drawn together, eyes burning darkly. He used a few words she did not recognize.

"What?" The words he'd used echoed in her mind. Even without knowing their meaning, she thought they sounded angry and ugly. Hilary frowned, trying to erase the sound from her memory.

He looked at her and forced a smile to his lips. "Nothing. I was angry . . . Why do you look so worried?"

"I was thinking," Hilary confessed, "that I have a very retentive memory. Mama used to have me help her learn her lines, you see."

"So?"

"So I'm trying to forget what you said, and I have a dreadful feeling I'll remember it next time I am very angry with someone." She raised one hand to tuck a stray copper tendril back into the tight bun that confined her hair. "It's my temper, you see," she apologized. "The Grahamites tried to break me of it, but I'm afraid the teaching didn't take very well."

Patrick threw back his head and laughed with genuine, unbridled amusement. The strong lines of his throat vibrated with laughter and his teeth gleamed white as the spray that beat against the ship's sides. "Odds but it didn't, darling girl! Never mind," he said, bending his head now to look at her with a smile that heated her blood like a caress, "I like you better the way you are."

His fingers brushed against the wisps of bright hair that flamed about her face, and this time she didn't move away. "All of you," he murmured, bending closer so that his breath was warm on her cheek. "I like everything I've seen so far. . . . Why the devil do you confine that glorious hair in this contraption?" He tugged at the wire ring that held her hair down, swore and sucked his finger when the end of the wire pricked him.

Hilary laughed at his comical expression. "You look like a small boy who's been caught filching sweets out of the stillroom."

"That's a truer word than you know," Patrick muttered. He wiped his bleeding finger on a kerchief of fine lawn and gave the wire ring a baleful glance. "All right, I'll keep my hands out of the sweets . . . for the moment. Were they kind to you?"

"Who?" For a moment, startled, Hilary couldn't follow the abrupt change of subject. Then she remembered, and her face took on the masklike lack of expression that had been her protection in the Grahamite community. "They gave me a good Christian upbringing," she said.

"Poor child!" Patrick reached out as if to ruffle her hair, then, looking at the wire ring, withdrew his hand.

"Oh, it wasn't that bad," Hilary said. Ebenezer Graham had been stern but just; once he agreed to keep her, she'd never feared that he would abandon her as her mother had done. All she had to do was follow the endless rules, keep up with the endless work, and try to keep her redheaded temper under control. And, of course, there'd been Jephthah to make everything easier for her. As long as he was there to speak for her and make excuses and comfort her when she was lonely, she'd been able to bear the rest. Jephthah . . . Hilary's lips curved into a smile, thinking of how soon they would meet again. How happy he would be to see her!

"Penny for your thoughts. What's the smile for?"

"The dolphins," Hilary lied. The promise of Jephthah waiting for her in America was a secret delight, too precious to be shared with anybody—even with Patrick.

"The dolphins," Patrick said, "have been gone for some time." He heaved a mock sigh. "Well, never mind, never mind! I see how it is. I'm just a passing fancy to Mistress Hilary, another poor soul bowled over by her smile and her wide gray eyes, a wayfarer to be forgotten the next day, thrown away like a worn-out moccasin, tossed aside like the lees of the wine—"

"Oh, stop," Hilary pleaded, giggling helplessly. "You know it's not like that!"

"No," Patrick said, watching her. "I don't know what you think of me, Mistress Hilary."

The deep blue intensity of his gaze caught and held her, demanding an answer more serious than she was ready to give. What were they to each other but two chance met strangers on a ship? Their lives touched for a moment only. When they reached Virginia, Patrick would go to take up his heritage of wealth and power;

she would follow Jephthah into that mysterious country called the Back Woods.

The thought filled her with unexpected desolation. She reached toward Patrick without thinking and touched his cheek lightly. He sucked in his breath as if she had struck him. Blushing, she dropped her hand. Her fingertips tingled as if she had touched something burning hot.

And he was still waiting for her answer.

"I think," she said slowly, "that you are really a good man underneath. You are kind and you go out of your way to help strangers. Anna Polwhys thinks she owes her life to you. She and Jer will never forget what you did for them."

"To hell with Anna Polwhys," said Patrick. "I want to know where I stand with Mistress Hilary." He laid his hand over hers on the rail, and a treacherous quiver of pleasure ran down to the soles of her feet, weakening her and making her want to lean against him.

"Where do you stand with me?" she repeated shakily. Close to my heart, Hilary wanted to cry, and for a moment it seemed as if she actually heard the words vibrating between them. Too close for a stranger—too close for safety.

"Oh, I've much the same opinion as Anna," she said carelessly when she'd regained control over her errant thoughts. "You're a bit spoiled and demanding, of course, but one expects that of the gentry." She lifted his hand and replaced it on the rail beside her, gently but firmly.

"The devil one does," said Patrick, blue eyes darkening.

"But you've a good heart," Hilary added hastily. "I'm sure you'd never do anything to hurt

. . . anyone." But you hurt me just by standing there and looking at me with eyes like the blue horizon, eyes that ask for a piece of my heart that's not mine to give.

She felt relieved and oddly disappointed when Patrick accepted her gentle dismissal. His eyes sparkled in a way that made her feel afraid, but instead of reaching toward her again, he gave a short laugh and swung away for a moment. When his face turned toward her again, she could read nothing in his expression but the casual courtesy of a gentleman making polite conversation. "Well, you've taught me a lesson, mistress. Perhaps I may teach you something in return. Would you like to see a map of Virginia? I brought one to England with me, to show the lords commissioners the situation of my mines, but since they were not interested, I've brought it home again. It's in my cabin."

"Oh, that would be nice!" Hilary exclaimed with more enthusiasm than she felt. What was wrong with her? she wondered. Two days ago she'd have been delighted to see a map of the colony, would have asked at once if the owner could point out the location of Jephthah's settlement. Now she felt rather let down that Patrick was so willing to go back to impersonal subjects. And she didn't really want to talk to him about Jephthah. "Will you bring it up here?"

Patrick shook his head. "No, I don't wish to expose it to wind and salt spray. There's a good table in my cabin where we can unroll it."

"Oh," Hilary said. "I don't know . . ." Alone in a cabin with Patrick? The thought made her feel dizzy and weak and excited all at once. And afraid.

"There are some books you might want to look at, too," Patrick added, watching her under lowered lids. "I've a complete copy of Master Beverley's book on Virginia, which I'd be happy to give you to replace the pamphlet that my friend so carelessly destroyed. And a manual of methods of husbandry in the colonies which you could study to your benefit, as the way we do things in Virginia may not be just what you're used to."

His dry instructive tone relieved Hilary's momentary fears. It was as she'd thought, she told herself: Patrick was really a good man and would never intentionally hurt her. And she wanted another copy of that book. If she refused his invitation, showed that she didn't trust him, he would be hurt and angry. Then he might not give her the book.

"Thank you," she said at last. "I should be grateful for your instruction. It's true, I need to learn more about the ways of the colonies."

"This evening, then," Patrick said. "After dinner."

3

Anthony Hazelrigg was sulking in the cabin when Patrick returned, stepping lightly over the clutter of gun cases and embroidered sword belts and shaving boxes and wig stands that filled the narrow space between the bunks. He glanced at Anthony, lying on his back with arms crossed behind his head and booted feet propped on the wall, and decided not to say anything. In the weeks of the voyage he had learned that his cabinmate was subject to fits of deep depression that vanished as suddenly as they came. Perhaps all English were like that, Patrick thought; damp misty climate probably got into their brains. Anthony would cheer up when he reached Virginia. He'd said he was going out to visit a childless uncle who meant to leave his plantation in the Northern Neck to him; a prospect like that should be a good cure for depression and temper tantrums.

Whistling a frontier dance tune under his

48

breath, Patrick began picking up the objects that cluttered the cabin and shoving them into an open trunk.

"What's made you so devilish cheerful?" Anthony growled.

Patrick smiled. "I think you know."

"Yes. You had better luck than I with the little redhead. I saw you take her aside. I'll wager you didn't get as far as laying a hand on her, though—damned spitfire!"

Patrick smiled again and stroked his chin with one hand. Anthony's eyes widened as he took in the trickle of dried blood on Patrick's forefinger. "Zounds! I'm wrong. You tousled her and she bit you," he hazarded with the beginnings of a return to good humor.

"Not exactly," Patrick corrected him. "I pricked my finger on her damned hairpin."

Anthony sat up, laughed, and slapped his knee. "Same thing! That little rose comes with thorns, my friend. You got no farther under her skirts than I did—admit it."

Patrick's fingers twitched and he became conscious of a strange desire to wrap them into a fist that would make contact with Anthony's pointed chin. He was at a loss to explain his sudden surge of anger. After all, it wasn't as if Anthony were traducing a lady's name. They were both gentlemen, they knew the rules better than that. Women like Hilary were for amusement and not to be taken seriously. Only he didn't like to remember her on her hands and knees before Anthony, staring upward in helpless fury as his boot came down on the pages of her precious book.

And why should he like it? he thought with relieved understanding. He'd seen her first. What the devil did Anthony mean by butting in on his game? It hadn't been Anthony who was soft enough to let the girl drag him down into a stinking hold to calm a hysterically birthing woman. By God, he'd earned a little reward from Hilary, and Anthony could just get out of the way while he took it.

"Well?" Anthony prodded. "Have you? Lifted her skirts?"

"In full view of a hundred steerage passengers?" Patrick laughed, though something about the conversation left a bad taste in his mouth. "No wonder you've no luck with the ladies, Anthony—not a bit of subtlety in your approach. Wait for tonight and ask me again."

"Tonight?" Anthony's brows shot up.

"She's coming to the cabin after dinner," Patrick said, adjusting the curled ends of his traveling wig in the glass that hung above his bunk. "To learn the way we do things in Virginia."

He smiled at the image of Anthony's dropjawed face, reflected over his shoulder in the glass. "And I'll thank you to occupy yourself elsewhere for an hour or two at that time. I'd as soon be private with the lady."

"Lady!" Anthony guffawed and lay back on his bunk. "That's a fine name for a girl coming to your cabin alone. Zounds, for every Virginia trick you show her I'll wager she can teach you three ways they do it in England."

"I . . . think not," said Patrick, biting off the last words between his teeth. "Your servant, sir. I feel a powerful need of some fresh air."

Snatching up his hat, he left the cabin. He didn't understand his own irritation, but he knew that if he lingered for any more discussion of Hilary, he would end by planting a fist in the middle of Anthony's leering face.

Carefully avoiding the area of the deck where the steerage passengers were allowed to congregate, he leaned on the rail just outside his cabin, arms folded, and stared moodily into the cloudy green depths of the sea. The trouble, he thought, was Anthony's damned coarse mind. There was nothing wrong in the little trick he meant to play on Hilary. He wasn't going to force her into anything. He'd make it easy for her to do what she really wanted. As an actress's daughter, she had to know what he wanted; if she didn't want it too, why would she lead him on by coming to his cabin? Yet when Anthony started in about lifting skirts and teaching tricks, he felt as if somebody had rubbed a muddy finger across a shining piece of silver.

Shaking his head to clear away unwelcome thoughts, he stared into the foaming water and slipped into a long dream of Hilary as she could be when he'd taught her to laugh and love— Hilary with her glorious fiery hair loose about shoulders that must be milk-white and smooth as cream, Hilary slipping out of a silk dress as green as the sea and trimmed with lace as soft as the foam on the waves.

In the tiny cabin, Anthony lay back with his arms folded and indulged in a little speculation on his own account, though his thoughts were somewhat more practical and less poetic than

Patrick's. The girl was hardly worth so much trouble, he thought; but he hated to see Patrick get ahead of him, and hated even more to hear Patrick's implications that he lacked finesse. Perhaps, he thought with a foxy smile, there was a way to turn the tables on this damned colonial! It would require very careful timing and a little help, but he thought he could manage it.

The sun was setting when Hilary made her way up to the main deck after the evening meal of salt pork and rice. In the brisk evening air it was too cold to go about barefoot as she did during the day. She was wearing the wooden clogs that Jer Polwhys had carved for her to save her one good pair of shoes, and the noise of the wooden soles on the bare boards of the deck made her feel horribly conspicuous.

She slipped into the wardroom with a sigh of relief that no one had challenged her right to come up here when the rest of the steerage passengers were all in their places in the hold. Patrick wouldn't have thought of that when he invited her up, she excused him in her mind; it would never occur to him that her sort were supposed to keep their distance from the officers and cabin passengers. But the sense of being out of place made her even more nervous than she was already.

The long narrow wardroom, lit by a single hanging lantern, was redolent of the smells of the meal served to officers and passengers. Hilary saw a single chicken leg still lying on the wardroom table and had to fight an urge to pick it up. Just the memory of fresh meat made her mouth water, after the weeks of dried salt peas and rock-hard ship's biscuit that were the re-demptioners' fare.

The strength needed to resist that urge, the determination not to behave like a beggar in front of Patrick, carried her forward to knock on the door of his cabin without more thought. The unlocked door swung open under her hand, and she saw a bewigged figure bent over the corner table, busily writing by the light of a hanging lantern suspended from the wall.

"Come in," he whispered without turning his head. "Close the door behind you."

Why was he whispering? Hilary wondered guiltily if she'd been too noisy, clattering over the bare planks of the deck in her wooden clogs, and this was his way of hinting that she should be quieter. She closed the door as quietly as she could; one warped board stuck against the jamb and she had to ease the door shut very gently to keep from slamming it. While she was con-centrating on the delicate task, the lantern light flickered and went out.

Startled, she spun around and saw a dark shape interpose itself between her and the nar-row porthole. Behind the silhouetted head, the sky still showed pale green with the last light of the day. There were hands on her shoulders, and a body too short to be Patrick's pinned her against the wall.

Anthony's deep, satisfied chuckle only con-firmed what she had already guessed. She stood frozen in disbelief and fear as his mouth came down on hers. The taste of tobacco and brandy was heavy about his lips. She turned her head from side to side, seeking to escape the kiss, but his weight held her in place and he seemed to enjoy her struggles.

"That's a good girl," Anthony murmured when he came up for air. "Nice, friendly little thing—knew y'wouldn't be averse to a little fun. Eh? In the dark—nobody here to tattle on you."

His hand slid inside her neckcloth and closed over the firm globe of her breast. The touch of his fingers, the unwanted intimacy, sickened her. And his free hand still gripped her shoulder, while the bulk of his body pressed against hers. "Let me go," she said in a low voice. "I came to see Patrick—he will be here in a minute."

"Patrick!" Anthony chuckled again. "No, love. We tossed for it, see, and I won first goes. He'll not trouble us till we've had our bit of fun."

Hilary fought back comprehension. "I don't understand," She gave a desperate heave against his body, trying to free herself, but he only laughed and slid one knee between her legs.

"I won the first toss with you," Anthony explained, speaking slowly and patiently. "Patrick agreed to clear out and let me have you alone—then you can sport with him. Or the three of us could have a little fun together, eh?"

Hilary shook her head. "No. Not Patrick. I don't believe you. He wouldn't do that to me!" But even as she spoke, doubt assailed her. How well did she really know Patrick? "Earthen pot and iron kettle," Mother Graham's voice rang in her ears, "that's us and t'gentry. And earthen pot always gets the worst of it—like when y'r fine lady slut of a mother stuck me with raisin' you!"

Even if she screamed, she thought with sick despair, what chance was there that anyone would come to her aid? Who'd care what Patrick and Anthony did with a girl from the steerage, just so they did it in the privacy of their own cabin?

"Oh, I was a fool to come here!" she cried, and Anthony planted a smacking kiss on her neck where he'd dragged the linen cloth away.

"Nay, I'll show you a good time," he promised. "Y'll not find me ungenerous after, if that's what's troubling you. Play your cards right, girl, you could land in Virginia with a nice little store of golden guineas to give you a start in the New World."

His arm clamped about her waist and he half-lifted, half-dragged her toward the bunk. He threw her down with a rough push that knocked the breath out of her; before she could recover, he was on top of her, fumbling with his breeches and pushing his knee between her legs again. She drew breath to scream and his hand covered her mouth, pushing her head back against the edge of the bunk with a force that she thought would snap her neck.

"Nay, I'll have none of your tricks!" he whispered in her ear. "You came here willing, didn't you? And I reckon you'll be willing again, when you've had a feel of what I've got waiting for you." His gusty laugh swamped her in stale tobacco smoke. Nauseated and terrified, she struggled against his hands and heard her skirt rip as he tugged it up about her hips.

* * *

Patrick paced back and forth on the deck, one hand drumming an idle tattoo against the side of his leg as he waited with mounting impatience. He couldn't, he thought with a wry smile, really blame Hilary for deciding at the last minute that she'd rather meet him on deck than come to his cabin. He'd even tipped the boy who brought him the message, thinking that perhaps it was better for both of them this way. He'd been feeling uncommonly low ever since that talk with Anthony; almost as though he meant the girl some harm! Well, this way they'd both be safe from temptation. A little quiet flirtation here on the deck, a few kisses stolen and maybe given back again, and she could land in Virginia as pure as she'd come on ship—however pure that might be.

But, by heaven, it was cold on deck by night, and he could damn well fault her for keeping him waiting all this time! Fine lady or actress's bastard, he thought with a wry smile, they were all alike. She would spend as much time making herself ugly by pinning that glorious hair back as a London lady would spend to make herself beautiful with false ringlets and beauty patches. In either case, what was a poor devil of a lover to do but kick his heels and wait?

A spatter of rain passed over the deck and drummed on the brim of his hat. Clouds darkened the moon; there was a squall coming up. That did it, Patrick thought, jamming his hat down firmly against the tug of the wind. He'd not freeze and drown for the doubtful luxury of two words in the dark with a redheaded trollop who didn't have the sense to profit by her gentleman admirer. Let her stay in the steerage, and welcome to it! He wasn't so hard up for girls that he needed to take this kind of treatment—though it was galling to think how Anthony would laugh when he heard that Hilary had stood him up.

Anthony was laughing already, before ever Patrick reached the cabin. As he sidled through the wardroom he heard the sound clearly through the thin wall. Anthony seemed to be laughing and thrashing about and gasping. Patrick wondered briefly if his cabinmate had drunk himself into a fit. He pushed the door open with an impatient shove that unstuck the warped plank and sent the door banging against the opposite wall.

The cabin was dark; a puddle of pale light from the wardroom lantern jiggled on the floor. As the ship rolled, the light slid up the side of Anthony's bunk and revealed a long, slender, undoubtedly feminine leg. Patrick pursed his lips in a soundless whistle. That explained the thrashing and gasping noises! "My apologies," he said. "Didn't mean to disturb anything."

He had his hand on the door, ready to withdraw and leave Anthony to his pleasure, when the girl's leg shot upward and Anthony yelped in pain. "Please . . . please, Patrick, help me!" gasped a low voice that Patrick knew only too well.

With an inarticulate growl of fury he launched himself upon the bunk where Anthony knelt over his victim. One fist twisted in the smaller man's coat collar, he hauled him from the bunk and threw him to the floor.

"Now, Patrick" Anthony said, sitting up painfully, "don't get excited. Just because your slut from the steerage wanted to sample a real man for a change—"

Patrick's fist crashed into the side of Anthony's face and the sentence ended in a strangled grunt. "Out," he advised.

"My breeches?"

Groping on the bunk, Patrick found the garments and hurled them at his cabinmate. "Put them on outside," he advised tersely. "I might yield to the temptation to rearrange your features if I have to look at 'em any longer."

Anthony limped from the cabin and Patrick slammed the door behind him. He lit the lantern and saw Hilary crouched at the head of Anthony's bunk, arms wrapped around her knees, staring at him with big gray eyes that didn't seem to be properly seeing him.

"It's all right, darling girl," he said in the low, soothing voice he employed to calm frightened animals on the plantation. "It's all right now." She was shivering; he sat down on the bunk beside her, meaning only to put a comforting brotherly arm around her shoulders, but she pressed herself back against the wood paneling at the head of the bunk to avoid his touch.

"It's all right," he repeated, not knowing what else to say. "I won't let him hurt you. Er . . ."

He didn't know quite how to ask the question that was uppermost in his mind. He'd been waiting on the deck for Hilary a plaguey long time.

"No," Hilary said in a low, strained voice. "No, he didn't rape me. You got here in time. Or too early, depending on what the arrangement was."

"Thank God," Patrick exclaimed before the strange tenor of her last sentence struck him. He looked at her cautiously. Perhaps the shock of the experience had turned her brain. No, surely not. She couldn't be that innocent, an actress's brat who'd been dumped on strangers at the age of eight, then somehow found her way to London and an immigrant ship. "Er . . . what exactly do you mean, too early?"

Hilary clasped her arms tightly around her knees and buried her face in her lap. Tendrils of red hair, loosened in the struggle, floated around her bowed head. Patrick put out a hand, unthinking, to caress a lock; she jumped as if she'd been stung by a bee, and he hastily withdrew his hand.

"He told me that you had an agreement. That he was to have me first, and you'd come in afterward."

Her voice was muffled by her coarse thick skirt; it took Patrick a moment to be sure he'd understood the words. When their sense did sink into his head, he felt the blood throbbing in his forehead with a furious rush of energy.

"You thought I'd do that to you?" Unable to sit still, he jumped up off the bunk and went to the table. He leaned down on clenched fists, his arms straight, fighting off the anger that threatened to overwhelm him. "I wonder you'd come to the cabin of such a lecherous rake."

"Patrick, I didn't think that." Hilary raised

her head and put out her hands to him, pleading. He saw now why she'd been huddling so, and caught his breath in wonder at the beauty of shoulders and the white swell of her breasts, exposed down to the top of the low-cut chemise where Anthony had torn her dress clear off her shoulders. "I wouldn't have come, would I, if I thought you meant to use me so? But you weren't here, and Anthony . . . Anthony . . ."

Small white teeth clamped down hard on her lower lip and she shook with the effort to keep from crying. Forgetting his anger, Patrick dropped down on the bunk beside her and gathered her into his arms. This time she didn't fight him, but went trustfully into his embrace. "Darling girl, forgive me. I'm a thousand times worse than the worst brute you've ever known, even to dream of such a thing," Patrick accused himself. "But when I had your message—"

Hilary pushed herself away from him and sat up straight, eyes blazing. "Message? I sent no message."

"Saying you'd not come to the cabin, but I should wait for you on deck—"

Patrick bit off the words in mid-sentence and pounded one fist into his open palm. "Of course! Anthony bribed the lad to say the message came from you. I'm a fool," he said, "a fool and a brute, and you should hate me forever, darling girl."

Hilary's lips trembled in the beginning of a smile. "Of course I don't hate you," she said. "He tricked both of us. It was only . . . oh, Patrick, I was so scared!" she wailed, and launched herself at his shoulder again.

Patrick held her there, patting her back and trying not to think about the effect it was having on him, holding a half-naked girl in his arms and patting the milky skin of her that had never seen the sun. She was calming down now, sobs dying away into hiccups and long deep breaths, but he was getting most devilishly excited. That momentary glimpse of her long slender leg, bare almost to the waist, returned most unchancily to his mind and made it even harder to suppress his lower urges. Was she calm enough yet? He'd no wish to take a frightened girl who would scream rape afterward; his women had always been willing, and Hilary would be as eager as the rest of them, once she relaxed and let him pet her. He shifted uncomfortably to relieve the growing pressure in his loins.

"What's the matter?" Hilary asked.

"My coat," Patrick lied. "I'm afraid the gold braid may catch in your hair. Just a minute, I'll take it off, then we can be more comfortable."

While he shrugged out of the tight velvet coat, Hilary put her hands up and felt the disordered mass of her hair. "Too late," she said, making a face. "I'll have to bind it up again before I go below." She tugged at the wire-ring fastener that had given him so much trouble and it came free in her hand, sending clouds of red-gold hair floating about her face. Patrick groaned and sat down hurriedly on the bunk, bending over in the hope that she wouldn't notice the effect she was having on him.

"What's the matter?" Hilary asked again. "Were you hurt in the fight?"

"Not a bit of it," Patrick said, "and that was no fight, that was just me refraining from giving Anthony the thrashing he so richly deserves. Come here and I'll show you whether I'm hurt or not." He tugged her into his lap before she could resist.

With only the fine linen of his shirt between them, he could feel the soft fullness of her breasts pressing against his arm, the warmth of her skin. A lock of fiery hair floated over his hand, it's touch almost burning him.

"You saved me," Hilary whispered, pressing her lips to the back of his hand. "Patrick, I'm so grateful."

And if the touch of her silky hair was fire brushing across his skin, the touch of her lips was pleasure so intense it was a different agony. Patrick felt his newly awakened conscience slipping away again. If she were as innocent as she looked, he rationalized, how did she know so well just how to drive him mad?

"Are you?" he murmured, shifting his position again and finding no relief. "Stay here and tell me about it."

Hilary laid her cheek against the snowy whiteness of Patrick's fine linen shirt, feeling the strength of the muscular shoulder beneath like a promise of warmth and safety. His arms were tight around her and his breath was warm on her cheek. In the exhaustion that followed her tears, she couldn't think beyond the moment, nor did she want to. It was enough just to be with Patrick.

When his hands brushed through the floating masses of her hair, a tingling sensation began in her head and spread downward. She gave a sleepy murmur of contentment and snuggled closer. "That's nice," she sighed as he lifted her hair and weighed it in one hand, tracing lazy spirals on the nape of her neck with one finger. "Don't stop."

"Darling girl," said Patrick, "I've no intention of stopping." The light touch that thrilled her moved lower, following the low line of her chemise across her back, then passing over the soft curves of her breasts and leaving them shivery and aching for a firmer touch. She pressed herself against his chest, seeking some relief for the new feelings that tormented her, and moaned with frustration when he took her by the shoulders and laid her back against the bunk. His head bent and she knew a moment of panic. *He's going to kiss me. It's wrong to let a man kiss you,* she thought to herself. But, as if he'd read her mind, he bypassed her lips and lowered his head into the snowy valley between her breasts. His lips just touched the taut, aching peak of one breast and she felt like crying with the intensity of sensation that gathered there, tugging, demanding. No one had ever warned her about this, and the sharp sweetness was too much to resist. Her back arched upward, pressing against his mouth, demanding more, and he gave it generously.

Somehow her chemise had slipped down and his lips and tongue were caressing her naked flesh. Hilary shuddered with delight at the gentle tugging of his lips; the flickering motion of his tongue against her throbbing breast was exquisite torment, always making her want more and more, never quite enough. His hand caressed her cheek and she turned to press her lips into his palm. His hands were warm and strong, and as her face was caught between them, all thought of resistance passed.

His mouth came down on hers, and the fierceness of his kiss sucked life and breath and will from her, carrying her away into a dark demanding world where all that mattered was the need to still the raging torment in her blood. She was entirely his now, soft as warmed clay to be molded into whatever shape he liked; the pressure of his body over her was not frightening as Anthony's had been, but a gentle invitation, in response to which she raised one knee to make space for him. He released her face and one hand tugged gently at her coarse brown skirts, drawing them up toward her hips.

Just as Anthony had done.

"No!"

The strangled cry broke from Hilary's lips before she finished the thought. With all her strength she pushed Patrick away from her, knowing only that she had to break his touch, break the sensual spell he was weaving.

"What the devil . . . ?" Patrick's arms tightened around her hips, holding her close to him, and the shame of it was that her body flamed in response to the embrace even while she knew she must stop him. She twisted and scratched and bucked madly, knowing nothing but the imperative need to get free, until she was once again crouched at the head of the bunk and Patrick stood before her, blood trickling from his hand where she had scratched him.

"*Now* what's the matter?" he inquired in tones more exasperated than loverlike. "Here I thought we were getting along so well."

"You're just as bad as Anthony!" Hilary panted. "Oh, Patrick, I thought I could trust you." She didn't cry; the tears would come later, when she was alone. Now anger kept her head high. Never taking her eyes from Patrick, she swung her feet to the deck and sidled slowly along the partition that divided this cabin from the next, holding the tattered remnants of her dress up with one hand.

"Hilary, wait!" Patrick extended one hand and she flinched back. There was no way she could pass out of the cabin without touching him; he stood blocking the narrow space between the bunks.

"Let me pass," she ordered him, with no idea of what would happen if he didn't obey her order. She knew that if he touched her again he wouldn't need much force to make her surrender. Even now, in the midst of her anguish, her own body betrayed her, urging her to join with the enemy. Her breasts ached for his kisses and the drumming blood in her veins cried out for release. She shut her eyes and tried to conjure up the picture of Jephthah that had so often consoled her and given her strength throughout the voyage. It wouldn't come clear. All she could see was Patrick's smiling face, dark eyes glinting with mischief, lips coming closer and closer to her own.

"Hilary, you must listen to me," pleaded the real Patrick and she opened her eyes to see a face that had little enough of mischief or fun in it. "I can see you got the wrong impression, but believe me, I'm not like Anthony. He only wanted to use you for his own pleasure, and maybe to score a point off me."

"Fine games you play," said Hilary, "with women as counters! Let me pass."

"I wouldn't do that to you," Patrick insisted, and the shadowy blue depths of his eyes added their own plea to his words. "Hilary, darling girl, I wanted to take care of you—I thought you understood that. I don't know what you think you're going to in America, but I can tell you it's a hard life, being an indentured servant. Little more than a slave you'll be, scrubbing and hoeing and running at someone else's beck. I can give you a good house with a garden, servants of your own, laces and satins to replace that homespun rag. Even if you don't like me," he said, head bowed, looking up at her through lashes as dark and sooty as a black cat's fur, "won't you give it some thought? You might grow to like me better, in time."

Hilary hadn't been able to cry in her anger, but now she felt tears come unbidden to her eyes. How kind and generous Patrick was. Surely she had misjudged him! She felt a fleeting instant of regret, sharp and cold as a sliver of ice driven through her, that she could not marry him. She couldn't tell him she liked him better than any man she'd ever met. And she couldn't leave dear Jephthah, who had done so much for her. He would think that Patrick's wealth had bought her.

"Oh, Patrick," she said through the mist of tears, "I'm sorry indeed that I didn't tell you earlier. I can't marry you, Patrick. I'm promised—"

Patrick's head came up sharply, and Hilary read in his expression that she'd made a terrible mistake, though she couldn't guess what it was.

"Marriage?" he said on a high note of surprise, and Hilary knew just what her mistake had been.

"You meant me to be your whore!"

"I wanted to offer you my protection, yes," Patrick said. "Is that so terrible? Think, darling girl, we could be happy together."

If she'd thought she was angry before, it was nothing to the fire that blazed through her now, warming her so that she no longer felt the chill night air raising goose pimples on her bare shoulders, until the long snakes of her red hair seemed to writhe and crackle about her head. Words tangled on her tongue, leaving her speechless as he advanced with a confident smile.

' He must think that he had only to lay hands on her and kiss her into compliance. And the shaming truth was that it might work. Hilary put out both hands and pushed with all her might. The sudden movement took him by surprise and he sat down heavily on the bunk, falling backward. His head cracked against the low beam with a satisfying thud.

"*That's* what I think of your offer," Hilary said. She gathered the trailing rags of her dress and the remains of her dignity about her and marched past Patrick while he sat dazed and rubbing his head with one hand.

Outside the cabin, she had to edge past the wardroom table again. As she reached the door and felt the welcome fresh salty air cooling her face, she heard steps behind her.

"Hilary, wait," Patrick pleaded in a low voice. "You don't understand."

"Oh, yes, I do!" Hilary picked up a coil of rope and threw it at his ankles, entangling his feet long enough for her to race to the forward hatch.

"I'd treat you fairly," Patrick insisted as he untangled the rope from his ankles. She tugged at the hatch and managed to open it just as he freed himself. It was tricky getting down the ladder with one hand holding up her dress, and he was kneeling at the open hatch before she was quite down to the orlop.

"I'd recognize any children we might have."

Hilary dropped the last foot to the orlop deck and felt her way along the narrow passage to the steerage hatch. Patrick was close behind her—she could hear his steps on the ladder.

"If we parted, I'd dower you to make a good marriage."

The steerage hatch was still open. Hilary scrambled down the ladder, blessing the darkness that kept her fellow passengers from seeing her state of disarray. She let her dress fall down about her waist while she groped for the rope that would pull the hatch closed from below.

"Think it over," Patrick called from the heights of the orlop deck. "You'll not get a better offer in Virginia!"

Hilary's fingers closed around the thick greasy rope. She gave it a vicious tug and heard the hatch come down with a crash that startled half the steerage awake. The last sound she heard was a yelp of pain and surprise from Patrick.

She hoped the hatch had broken all ten of his fingers.

～4～

Patrick's quick reflexes saved his hands from being bruised by the fall of the hatch cover, but his pride had taken a severe battering. Hands in his pockets, he attempted an insouciant stroll back along the orlop deck and up to his cabin, whistling as he went. The pose of calmness was abruptly lost when he entered the wardroom and saw Anthony leaning against the table with his arms folded. A vulpine grin accentuated the sharpness of his features and the light of the swaying wardroom lantern threw his pointed face into strong relief.

"So she turned you down too! So much for gentler courtship." He rubbed the side of his face gently. "I ought to repay you for the slap she gave me, but it looks as if the vixen paid you back for both of us."

Patrick stared uncomprehendingly until Anthony took him by the shoulder and pushed him into their cabin. In the glass on the wall he saw that his face was marked by three long scratches where Hilary had struck out at him in her panic.

A cold anger possessed him. What the devil did she mean, he thought, by making such a piece of stage tragedy over a perfectly sensible offer? It was her right to refuse him, though she was a fool to give up the chance of a soft life just to slave for some frontiersman; but she'd no call to make him look like a booby, scratching his face as if he were a rapist, making him chase after her through the ship with his offer.

Without speaking, Patrick wiped the oozing blood away from the scratches and endured Anthony's heavy-handed teasing.

"Forget it," he said tersely when he'd had enough. "We've both lost. There's no sense chasing an unwilling wench when there's plenty of willing ones on board."

"Aye, but most of 'em need a good dousing in salt water before I'd use 'em," Anthony complained. "That red-haired vixen of yours is fresh and sweet as a clove pink."

"And," Patrick reminded him, "she's got a temper like a snapdragon. To hell with wenches! Let's tap the cask of claret in the wardroom and have a game of renegado before we go to bed."

Patrick found it harder than usual to concentrate on the cards. Between him and the pips there kept arising the vision of a pale face framed in billowing clouds of fiery hair. Sometimes the wide gray eyes were like shards of ice as he'd last seen them, sometimes they were fixed on him with a beseeching expression that made him want to kiss all their troubles away. He forced himself to concentrate on the cards, playing with a cold fury that gave him three quick victories in a row while he downed glass after glass of claret to drown the picture of Hilary's face.

"Damn all women!" Anthony tossed his purse across the table to Patrick. "Let's have 'nother round."

But the claret cask was unaccountably empty.

"Ne'mind," Anthony mumbled. He shuffled the cards and peered at them in the uncertain light. "Damn, but this deck's marked! Look here, y'can see the pips on the backs of the cards!"

Patrick took the cards from Anthony and gave them his full, if bleary-eyed, concentration. "I think," he said at last, "y're looking at the front."

Anthony gave an owlish nod. " 'Splains why t'other side was so plaguey hard to read."

Patrick threw the cards down so that they fanned out across the tabletop. The queen of hearts teetered on the edge of the table and then fluttered to the deck, giving Patrick a flashing glimpse of red hair and gray eyes swathed in royal robes.

"Damn girl's haunting me," he muttered.

"Y'll have to lay the ghost." Anthony sniggered. "I say, that's good. Get it? Lay the ghost by layin' the girl. Only she'll not let you near her again."

"Sure she will." Patrick swept the rest of the cards off the table. "Wait an' see."

"Lay y'r money on it?" Anthony challenged. "Give me a chance to win back that purse. Lucky in cards, un—hic!—lucky in love."

Patrick threw Anthony's purse down on the

table. His own followed it. "Wager you another seventy guineas," he said, mouthing the words with exaggerated caution, "I have her eating out of my hand before the ship docks."

Anthony guffawed. "She's more like to bite y'r fingers! Y're on. But you'll not get two civil words out of her."

"I have a plan," Patrick lied. At the moment all he was possessed of was a raging headache and a determination to make Hilary see that no girl snapped her fingers at him with impunity. Somehow, he didn't know how, he meant to woo her back upon speaking terms with him; then he flattered himself it was only a matter of time before she was hanging on his sleeve, waiting for a renewal of his offer. Which, he vowed, she could wait for until approximately two weeks after hell froze over. He wasn't so desperate or so foolish as to set up a girl with that kind of temper for his mistress.

In the morning, the headache was added to by a mouth furred like the inside of a cat's litter box. Patrick cursed women, the swell of the sea, and Anthony's teasing with equal ferocity.

"How about the plan?" Anthony badgered him while he was attempting the difficult task of shaving himself in heavy seas with a hand that trembled more than it ought.

"Wait awhile," Patrick said with sweet reasonableness. "You don't expect me to seduce her when the ship's rolling like this, do you? Poor lass is probably puking her guts up like the rest of the poor devils in steerage. The atmosphere's not conducive to romance. Wait until it's calmer."

By which time, he devoutly hoped, he would have come up with a plan to woo her back to him.

By midafternoon both the heaving seas and Patrick's quivering stomach had calmed somewhat. Selecting a lace-trimmed monogrammed kerchief from the litter in the top shelf of his trunk, he straightened the sleeves of his velvet coat, flicked an imaginary speck of dust off his breeches, and announced to Anthony that he thought he might take a stroll through the hold.

"Take more than a scrap of lace to win her round." Anthony grinned. "If that's your best plan, you might as well pay up now."

Patrick's brows shot up and he regarded Anthony with innocent surprise. "Oh, I'd not insult the lady with a gift at this stage of our acquaintance. This kerchief is for . . . er . . . another lady entirely."

"Pull the other one, it's got bells on," Anthony muttered as his cabinmate sallied out to try his luck again.

Patrick had in fact been speaking the literal truth, as Anthony would have learned if he'd followed him down to the hold where the steerage passengers were packed in. He strolled the narrow passage between three-foot partitions with a nod here and a smile there for the passengers, perfectly conscious of the stir his visit was causing but determined to appear perfectly at ease. As he approached the area where the women and the families with small children lay, he saw a flash of red hair and heard a disdainful sniff as Hilary turned her back on him and flounced toward her bunk. When he stooped to avoid a low beam and entered the partitioned area that Hilary shared with the Polwhys family, she sniffed again and turned to face the partition, affecting to be mightily busy with a piece of coarse sewing.

It was a pity, Patrick thought, that she wouldn't look at him to see his surprised expression. "Why, Mistress Hilary," he said, allowing the surprise to creep into his voice, "there are other people in this . . . er, cabin, you know. May a man not visit his friends without your permission? I came to see Mistress Polwhys." He allowed himself a moment to appreciate the view of the flush creeping up her white neck before he made his most elegant bow toward the bunk where Anna Polwhys lay with her baby girl.

"Servant, Mistress Polwhys," he said. "I thought I'd just do myself the honor of dropping by to see how our baby was doing."

Anna looked at him blankly and Patrick flashed an ingratiating smile as he unfurled the lace handkerchief and handed it to her.

The words might have been incomprehensible to Anna, but Patrick's smile spoke to her in a universal language. She gave him a shy smile in return and reached wondering fingers to touch the scrap of fine lawn with its deep fringe of Alençon point lace. Patrick noted with satisfaction that Hilary glanced over her shoulder, doubtless impelled by curiosity.

"A small christening gift," he explained, "as I hoped you might consider me in the capacity of . . . er, a sort of honorary godparent?"

Anna's smile grew a little strained around the edges as Patrick continued to talk.

"She can't understand what you're saying," Hilary snapped. "She doesn't speak English."

"Perhaps," Patrick suggested, "you'd be so kind as to translate for us."

Anna Polwhys turned her thin white face toward Hilary's corner and added a few lilting words that Patrick guessed were the same request, in Cornish. Hilary shrugged her shoulders and turned to face them, giving Patrick a mighty scowl as she did so. Bending toward Anna, she murmured in the same tongue. Anna's jaw dropped and she pointed at Patrick, asking a question.

"She's sorry," Hilary announced, "but they're Catholic, and no one outside the faith can stand sponsor for their children."

"Sure, and I'm a good Catholic meself," said Patrick with an exaggeration of the brogue his father had never quite lost, "and me father one of the king's own cavaliers who came to the New World to escape the persecutions of that ranter Cromwell."

Hilary looked surprised. "But, Patrick—" she began to say.

Patrick raised one finger. "Now, now, Mistress Hilary, I didn't come below to annoy you with my conversation. You'll be so kind as to tell the lady that I'm as good a Catholic as she is and would be honored to sponsor the youngling when we reach Virginia."

Reluctantly Hilary obeyed Patrick's request. The hypocrisy of it! she thought scornfully. It was bad enough that he used Anna's baby as a pretext to bother her when she never wanted to see him again. But on top of that, to call himself a good Christian. when he was really a liar and would-be seducer!

"Not knowing your true character," she announced at the end of a brief colloquy with Anna, "she says she'd be proud to have you sponsor the child."

"Now, why do I feel that's not quite a literal translation?" Patrick asked the air. He had the satisfaction of seeing the blush creep up Hilary's neck and over her face.

"Would there be anything else, gracious sir?" she asked with an exaggeratedly deep curtsy. "Or may I be permitted to retire to my humble tasks now?"

"Er . . . yes, I mean, don't go, I have something else to say to Mistress Polwhys," Patrick stammered, his mind racing to come up with some excuse to keep Hilary in conversation a moment longer.

Hilary folded her hands before her and sighed with exaggerated patience.

"Please tell Mistress Polwhys," he said, "that I'm heartily sorry if I have misjudged or offended anyone on board this ship."

"The word," Hilary said, "is 'insulted.' The misjudgment was mine—in thinking you to be a man of honor."

"No," Patrick insisted with a smile quirking the corners of his lips, "I cannot accept your apology, Mistress Hilary."

"I didn't mean—" Hilary started to say.

Patrick waved his hand. "No matter. The error," he said with a gracious inclination of his head, "was entirely mine. I can't conceive what could have made me think you were . . . not entirely averse . . . to my advances. I should never have leapt to that conclusion just because you generously allowed me to remove your—"

"Oh, stop!" Hilary implored him, her face turning as red as her hair.

"And kiss you on the—"

Hilary placed her hand over his lips before he could burst out with a revelation that would embarrass her before any English-speaking passengers who might be eavesdropping. Patrick seized the opportunity to press a kiss on the small work-roughened palm. Then he courteously lifted her hand, keeping hold of the slender fingers that fluttered in his palm. She was staring at the floor; he would have to make her raise those glorious gray eyes with their border of thick dark lashes.

"But I haven't finished apologizing," he insisted. "I meant to explain exactly how I came by this terrible misconception."

"That won't be necessary."

"And to give you my word of honor that you'll not be troubled again by my ungentlemanly advances."

"Oh." Hilary looked up and Patrick caught his breath, wondering if he could indeed withstand the invitation of those wide, dark-fringed eyes and parted lips. At that moment he longed for nothing more than to sweep her into his arms and repeat all the offers he'd made the previous night, and more: a house, a carriage of her own, anything she wished, just so she would be his.

All his self-control was required to keep a courteous distance. "I give you my word."

"That's good," Hilary said, her voice trailing off uncertainly. She sounded just the faintest bit disappointed.

Patrick bowed again and released her hand before she could protest his continued hold. "I promise that my behavior from this time forth shall be impeccable in every respect." Unless, of course, she grew bored with impeccable behavior—in which case he would be happy to oblige the lady. "Pray tell me that you accept my heartfelt apology. You do," he asked with just the right shade of anxiety, "understand just how the misunderstanding came about? Otherwise I could explain further."

Hilary's enchanting mouth curved upward in the beginnings of a smile. "I would really prefer that you did not. I see now that it was as much my fault as yours, and I'm sorry if I misled you, Patrick."

Excellent, Patrick thought, mentally congratulating himself on his quick wit and ready words. He had the girl halfway ready to take the blame for her own near-seduction. Ah, there was never a man like a Lyle for luck with ladies and cards! It only remained to show his triumph where Anthony could acknowledge it.

"Then you'll take a turn about the deck with me?"

Hilary's eyes dropped and she retreated a pace. "Well . . . I don't know . . ."

"You don't forgive me, then." Patrick heaved a sigh. "Or trust me. Well, it's no more than I deserve, the vile dog that I am, and me only wishing the chance to show you that I could behave like a gentleman." Bowing very low, he looked upward to gauge the effect of his self-abasement. It seemed to be working; she looked flustered and unhappy.

Her lips parted, but before she could speak, Anna Polwhys called from her bunk, saying something that sounded like an urgent question. Hilary knelt by her side and Patrick rose somewhat unsteadily as the ship heeled over on a new tack, cursing the interruption.

Hilary and Anna talked for several minutes, both of them looking at him; Anna kept pointing one thin hand upward while Hilary shook her head. Patrick felt distinctly uncomfortable but he was determined not to withdraw until he'd made one last attempt at winning Hilary's favor.

Just as his resolution was sinking under the repeated glances at him and the liquid trill of incomprehensible syllables, Hilary rose and came toward him. "Anna thinks I need fresh air," she announced ungraciously. "She wants me to ask if you'd escort me on deck; she's afraid I'll be insulted by some of the crew if I go alone." Her arched brows showed all too clearly the irony with which she relayed Anna's statement.

Patrick smiled broadly. "Well, now. It would hardly do for me to refuse a lady's request, would it?"

He crooked his arm for Hilary, prepared to lead her up on deck and demonstrate the triumph of his charm in full view of Anthony. But as he waited for her to rest her fingers on his sleeve, he happened to glance at the white-faced woman whose concern had won him this favor, and an unfamiliar feeling took hold of his heart. "On second thought," he said, giving way to an impulse he did not entirely understand, "this hold is no place for a woman to recover from her lying-in. I'm sure Mistress Polwhys could do with the fresh air too. If you'll help me, I believe we can get her on deck."

Without waiting for Hilary to translate, he bent over Anna's bunk and scooped her, the baby, and the trailing blankets all up in one untidy bundle. Anna squeaked in alarm and clutched his arm, but as Hilary hastened to explain, she relaxed and favored Patrick with a dazzling smile of gratitude.

He came near enough to regretting his impulsive gesture a dozen times on the unsteady journey from hold to top deck. Anna was thin and small-boned, but a woman and a baby were no light weight to manage with one arm while climbing a narrow ladder from deck to deck.

At the first ladder he persuaded Anna to let Hilary hold the baby while she put both arms about his neck to steady herself, but even so he was distinctly out of breath when they reached the orlop deck, and his knees were quivering with strain before they were on the top deck. That was what came of soft living in England and aboard ship, he thought ruefully. He needed a Virginia plantation to run and a good Virginia horse under him to give him the exercise he was accustomed to.

"I knew you were a kind man at heart," Hilary said when the sunlight broke over Anna's tired face and the baby crowed with delight.

"Not a bit of it," Patrick said, smiling down

at her and restraining the urge to pant for breath. "It's all a dastardly plot to win your innocence, d'you see? Pose as a man who loves children and dogs and ailing women, and when you're thoroughly fooled, I pounce and sweep the innocent country maid off to a life of debauchery amid silk dresses and lace collars and good wine and rich pastries . . ."

Hilary laughed with delight and Patrick's smile grew broader. If she chose to take his words as foolery, so much the better. Meanwhile, perhaps his hints of the delights of debauchery might grow on her.

Besides, it was true enough that he'd brought Mistress Polwhys on deck only to win Hilary over. Wasn't it? He certainly couldn't think of any other reason. And now that she was up here, his first concern was to dispose of her while he enjoyed a little chat with Hilary.

Patrick looked about the deck and found a sheltered corner where a convalescent woman could be propped up amid pillows and blankets. A request of the cabin boy brought the requisite articles out from his—or somebody's— cabin, and a few minutes' work saw Anna Polwhys comfortably ensconced with pillows to soften the hard boards of the deck, and a blanket around her to protect her and the baby from the cutting edge of the salt breeze.

"Now," Patrick said, firmly placing Hilary's hand on his arm, "let's talk."

"What about?" she asked.

Patrick was momentarily speechless. What did she *think* a gentleman of his rank wanted to talk to a pretty girl about, the rise in tobacco duties? But he'd promised to be on his best behavior.

"Yourself," he suggested. "You never did explain to me how you came to leave the Grahamites and take up with this group of Cornishmen."

Hilary's face clouded. It was evidently an unhappy memory. Perhaps, he thought hopefully, she had gotten into a wee bit of trouble in that strict religious community. He could just imagine the sort of trouble a girl with slim white legs and hair like the flames of hell could get up to. Didn't they say that all redheaded women had lascivious natures?

"The enclosures," she said as if that explained everything.

"The what?" Perhaps he hadn't heard aright.

"There's a fashion in England for taking up the common land and enclosing it to raise beasts where men used to live," Hilary explained, patient sarcasm fairly dripping from her voice. "No doubt it would have escaped your notice, not being a topic much in vogue in court circles. Lord Mellors got a writ of partition to take up the fields the Grahamites had been farming, and put our people out on the roads to beg, though they'd been good tenants for three generations. Ebenezer Graham, who had taken me in, died of a fever the week after we were evicted, and Mother Graham followed him. The rest of the community mostly went into service. I was so fortunate as to be offered a position in Lord Mellors' own household." The sarcastic note was back, and Patrick decided not to bother asking why she hadn't accepted the position.

"You said something about a betrothed in

America," he prompted. That didn't jibe with the rest of the girl's story—maybe the story of being promised already had been an invention of desperation, to keep him from pursuing her.

Hilary's gray eyes widened and shone like the sun breaking through clouds. "Jephthah." She said the awkward name almost reverently. "Ebenezer's oldest son. He was always kind to me, even when . . . Well, it doesn't matter now." She flushed and bit her full lower lip, looking away for a moment; Patrick's quick mind filled in the pause with his own ideas of the torment a sensitive orphan child could suffer in such a strict, disapproving community, and he mentally damned the Grahamites and all their kin.

Kin. Wait a minute. That name was familiar. "You're never promised to Ranting . . . I mean, to *Jephthah Graham*?" he asked unbelievingly. Good God, she couldn't be serious! Patrick knew the Dissenting preacher called Ranting Jephthah; a gaunt, homely man who looked to be in his early fifties, he had established a small community in the disputed backwoods territory between Carolina and Virginia, tithing to the church of neither state and roaming both of them in search of converts.

Patrick's own vast acreage in Virginia was at the southern fringe of the settled area, and from time to time Ranting Jephthah stopped there for a meal and a night's rest. The staff had standing instructions to feed the man well but to invent some good story as to why Patrick couldn't join him at dinner; the man was a crashing bore, totally insensitive to the feelings of others and totally committed to his own queer-headed version of God's word.

A vision of Ranting Jephthah rose before Patrick now: a lean figure dressed in ill-fitting homespun, with deep lines graven in his cheeks and the roll of damnation's thunder in his deep voice. Even to think of him in the same breath as this fresh-faced girl beside him was an obscenity. "Jephthah Graham is your betrothed?" he repeated. Surely he had mistaken her.

Hilary nodded, breaking into a smile that made Patrick realize he'd been all wrong about her eyes looking like the sun breaking through clouds; the real light was in her smile. "You know him? Oh, tell me how he does in Virginia! You see, I haven't seen him since he left for America five years ago. And I was only twelve then. Oh, won't he be surprised to see how I've grown up!"

He will indeed, Patrick thought sourly. "But you surely can't have engaged yourself to him when you were twelve? Hilary, no one could consider such a promise binding. He can't hold you to it."

Hilary drew herself up to her full height of almost five feet, four inches, trying to look down her nose at Patrick. "I want him to hold me to it," she said, and then spoiled the effect by giggling. "No, of course I'm not traveling to America just because he promised to come back and get me when I was grown up! But there are such things as letters, you know," she said with a return to her former attempt at dignity.

"Jephthah wrote to his parents every few months, and it was settled that I was to come to him when I was eighteen. And I wrote to him whenever I could get paper and ink. So he knows my feelings have not changed. I am only going a year earlier than we planned, that is all. When . . . when the Grahams died I was not sure what to do, but I did not wish to take service with Lord Mellors. And there I met a very kind man who explained to me how I could go to America even though I did not have the passage money. So I signed the papers of indenture and came aboard," she said with a sunny smile, "and isn't it a lucky chance that all these good Cornish folk are on the same ship, and we can all look after each other and take care of one another! And, of course, a few of the other sort," she finished with a dark glance at Bet, who was spending the sunny hours in an attempt to beguile one of the seamen who worked on mending the storm-torn rigging.

"Er . . . quite so." Patrick had no particular wish to discuss the slatternly Bet. With her dark red snake-locks falling down all over her provocatively skimpy chemise, she presented a picture whose earthy appeal he could well understand. But somehow he didn't think Hilary would be able to offer Bet the same understanding. Besides, there were a few points that Hilary's story hadn't made quite clear.

"Hilary, my dear," he said, "you do understand that those papers you signed mean that the captain can sell you for a servant if you can't pay your passage money in America? You could be bound for years and years to slave at the beck and call of a total stranger." Unless, of course, some kind soul paid her passage money.

In which case she might well be grateful to the kind soul, mightn't she?

"Yes, I understand," Hilary said, "but that won't happen. You see, I sent a letter to Jephthah by a ship that left three weeks before ours, the *Rose and Thorn.* So he knows to meet me and to bring the passage money with him. I thought of everything," she said with modest pride.

She certainly had. Except for one detail. "About Jephthah," Patrick began, cautious, aware that he was treading on sacred ground. "Er . . . how well do you remember him?"

"I think about him every night and every morning," Hilary said. "I shall never forget how kind he was to me when I was scared and crying for my mother, and Ebenezer wanted to whip me for being so ungrateful as to cry, and Jephthah stopped him."

If he had, it was the one time to Patrick's knowledge that Ranting Jephthah had tempered justice with mercy. His mobile lips twisted with distaste as he remembered the girl who'd come to the plantation one night, begging for succor after Jephthah turned her out into the woods for brazen harlotry—translated, meaning she'd got herself pregnant by one of the male Grahamites and hadn't been willing to tell who the father was.

"People change," he hinted.

"Not Jephthah," Hilary said with calm certainty. "He is a rock."

"You never said a truer word," Patrick snapped, his short supply of tact exhausted. "A piece of granite has more charity and human compassion than this saint you're bent on wedding.

Wait till you see him, I'll wager you sing a different tune. He's an old bigot who's getting a sweet young virgin to warm his bed. Oh, yes, I'll just bet he's there to meet you at the pier, money in one hand and marriage license in another, and before you know it you'll be trapped into a marriage you'll regret all your life, just because you didn't have the sense to take a mere human being instead of a saint!"

Hilary's right hand flashed out and caught him across the cheek with a stinging blow. "How dare you!" she cried. Her face was quite white except for two poppies that flared in her cheeks, and her gray eyes were cold as the Arctic snowcaps. "You tell lies about Jephthah when he's not here to defend himself!"

"Love, I'll be more than happy to repeat them in his presence," said Patrick, ruefully caressing his stinging face. "But I won't need to. When you see . . . Ahh, no you don't!" He caught her hand as she raised it to strike him again, imprisoning the slender wrist in an effortless grasp. She twisted and clawed at him with her left hand; he captured that too and bore both hands together down to her sides. She was forced to stand before him, his arms pressing her wrists down and imprisoning her body, and the heat of her filled his own body with warmth that all but made him forget the urgency of what he had to explain to her.

"Hilary, the Jephthah you remember isn't there anymore. You're not going to a kindly elder brother. He's become a bitter old man."

"Old?" Hilary smiled. "Oh, Patrick, there's some mistake. Jephthah is only thirty-five."

"Well, he looks fifty," Patrick snapped. "Anyway, thirty-five is too old for a girl of seventeen." With a twinge of conscience he reflected that he himself was almost thirty. But he wasn't proposing to tie her to him for life. Only for pleasure.

"If his hard life in the wilderness has aged him," Hilary said, "that is all the more reason why he needs me. And I'll thank you not to try to make trouble between us. Will you please to release me, sir?"

Patrick's hands dropped away from her wrists and he watched her back away with a sinking feeling of unreality. Damn the girl! With her eyes raised to heaven and her mind on higher things, she was likely to walk straight into a mire she'd never get free of. And it would serve her right—except that it would be such a damned waste.

"All right, don't believe me," he told her. "You'll see for yourself next week when we dock. And if you change your mind then . . . well, my offer's still open. You can choose between us."

"As I recall," Hilary said, her nose tilted up so high she was about to fall over backward, "there's a slight difference. Your . . . offer is not one that any decent woman would wish to take up."

"Decency," said Patrick, almost under his breath, "can be a damned bore."

Hilary's slap caught him by surprise, reddening the other side of his face to match the marks of her fingers on the right side.

"Termagant!"

He started for her with intent to teach the brat a lesson, but she dodged lithely away from him and ran across the deck to the shelter of the hatchway. After the first start of surprise, Patrick remained where he was, moodily caressing his stinging cheek and watching as her red head flashed down into the darkness of the lower decks. He'd made a fool of himself once too often with that little girl; let her wait and see what sort of man she'd promised herself to; then she'd sing a different tune.

He was not unduly surprised when a pointed shadow like a fox's face under a tricorn hat signaled Anthony's presence beside him.

"Don't say it," Patrick sighed. He tossed a leather purse toward Anthony without looking. "You've won your winnings back. Damn all women!"

~ 5 ~

Hilary stumbled below with her face burning as if she, not Patrick, had been slapped. Her hands were cold, except for the tingling in the left palm where she'd struck at Patrick, and her head was buzzing as if the creaking of the ship's timbers had crept into her brain. Oh, what a fool she'd been to trust Patrick's pretense of friendship! How could he be so cruel as to lie and call Jephthah a bitter old man? She didn't understand. If only she could think clearly! The swaying of the ship mimicked her shifting thoughts, and she felt as if her head were full of a thick liquid that rolled like the waves outside.

The image made Hilary dizzy. Holding onto the deck beams overhead for balance, she felt her way forward through the densely packed hold. She knew people were looking at her and speculating, but she couldn't bring herself to nod and smile and greet her particular friends among the passengers as she usually did. Her eyes were dry and burning; it would be a relief to cry. If she could get to the cabin of bunks behind a three-foot partition that she shared with the Polwhys family, she could cast herself facedown on the bunk, pull the blanket over her head, and try to forget every word she and Patrick had ever exchanged.

She made it to the bunk. That part wasn't so hard. It was the forgetting, she thought wearily, that would be hard. Patrick was a liar and untrustworthy and not worth her thinking on; but her traitorous brain insisted on replaying every word of every conversation they'd had, over and over, until she could have screamed. And not just words. His hands and lips on her body in the little cabin above—the sweet intoxication of his touch—how could anything be so wonderful, yet so false? How could he share that sweetness with her, and then propose to make her his whore?

Hilary tossed on the bunk, tangling the blankets about her aching limbs and drifting in and out of a miserable, feverish series of waking dreams in which Patrick apologized and asked her to marry him. Yet how could she trust his apologies again? And even if she were such a fool as to trust him, she couldn't marry him. Jephthah was waiting for her, though in her dreams Jephthah's kind, weary face turned into the withered lineaments of a bitter old man, and she screamed until she awoke and found Bet by her side, forcing her down on the bunk and tucking the blankets around her.

At first she thought it was a continuation of

the vivid dream. "No, not you," she whispered.
"I don't want to be like you."

Bet winced and set her jaw more firmly.
"Righty, love. You be as pure and virtuous as
you want, but if you don't eat some of this here
gruel, you'll be a pure and virtuous little corpse
afore we get to America." She held a pannikin
of lukewarm, cloudy gray stuff in front of Hilary and tilted it toward her mouth.

The smell of fat pork and peas nauseated
Hilary, but it also woke her up enough to make
her realize it was no dream. She tried a stumbling apology to Bet, but the older woman shook
her head and tried to spoon the gruel into her
mouth.

"I've heard harder words before, dearie," she
said. "Now, be a good girl and take some food."

"Where's Anna?" Hilary whispered.

"Moved to another partition," Bet told her.
"Her and Jer and the three little 'uns. You
wouldn't want them to take the fever, would
you?"

The next few days passed for Hilary in a
feverish blur. Bet was always by her side, coaxing her to take another bite of nauseating gruel,
wiping her face with a damp cloth, cheering her
up with fantastic stories about America. Hilary
did not really believe that there was a savage
king behind the mountains who sat on a throne
of gold decorated by bright feathers, but in the
lassitude that came between attacks of fever she
was content to lie still and let Bet spin the tales
she'd picked up on the London streets.

When she grew stronger, she began to worry
that Bet would take the fever from nursing her.

"Not me, ducks!" Bet laughed and winked. "I'm a Whitechapel girl. That's a tough district— you gotta be mean to grow up. I reckon I'm too mean for the fever to risk itself on me."

And in fact, it wasn't Bet who came down with the fever next. It was the muscular little cockney she'd been sharing a bunk with since her failure to attract more profitable customers above decks. Bet moved Dickie Baynes into the bunk abandoned by Jer Polwhys and nursed him and Hilary together, praying that the contagion wouldn't sweep through the rest of the steerage passengers. For once, however, fortune favored them. The storm that battered the ship had driven it on the right course, and they docked at Yorktown a week early.

"Fresh food," Anthony exulted as he tossed his things into a trunk. "Something to stand on that doesn't sway back and forth. A horse to ride, and a choice of pretty girls." He rose, hat in hand, and shouted for a man to carry his trunk ashore. "Aren't you coming?" he asked Patrick.

"In a moment." Patrick was staring out the porthole with a bemused look on his face. Anthony peered over his shoulder but could see nothing but another ship riding at anchor in the bay. "Isn't that ship the *Rose and Thorn*?"

Anthony squinted. "Could be. You've better eyes than I have if you can read a name at this distance."

"Recognized the figurehead," Patrick explained. "She used to carry m'father's tobacco. Maybe still does, for aught I know. But it looks as if she's just come in."

Anthony glanced at the waiting sloops receiving cargo from the *Rose and Thorn* and agreed that, yes, a ship that was unloading rather than loading probably had indeed just arrived, and what was so interesting about that fact?

"See you later," Patrick said, cramming his hat on his head and making for the cabin door with unseemly haste. "I've just thought of a message I've got to deliver. No, I guess I won't be seeing you later. You're here to look over your uncle's lands in the Northern Neck, aren't you? I go the other way. Good-bye. Been a nice voyage. Glad to know you. P'raps we'll meet again sometime. Your servant." With a sketchy bow he was gone, leaving Anthony with his mouth hanging ajar like any slack-witted lackey.

He made his way out of the cabin and to the wardroom door. Patrick was already climbing down the ladder that led to the orlop deck. He must be going to the hold.

"She won't talk to you," he called after his cabinmate's retreating figure. "You're wasting your time."

Patrick heard the words but paid no heed. He had already reckoned up the chances on being snubbed again and figured that he would be able to get enough words out to get Hilary's attention before she ran away from him. And this was something she had to hear. If the *Rose and Thorn* had arrived so recently that she was only now unloading her cargo, there was no possibility that Hilary's letter could have reached Jephthah. Nobody would come to buy her out; she'd be sold to the first purchaser as an indentured servant.

Unless, of course, some generous young man just happened to pay her way. In which case—Patrick grinned—she just might be grateful to said young man. *Very* grateful.

And, he soothed a suddenly prickly conscience, it was a favor of sorts he was doing the girl. Once she saw Jephthah, she'd be even more grateful at being saved from marriage to that dour ranting self-anointed parson. She'd be much happier with him in the long run.

The one thing he hadn't counted on was the excitement of the steerage passengers. The women were twittering like a flock of magpies while the men clustered around the ladder, waiting for permission to go up and severely impeding his progress. How many people were there in the hold? Three hundred, the captain had said. Nonsense, there were at least twice that many standing around the ladder, and none of them were Hilary.

"Where's Hilary?" he demanded of the first man he met. "I need to see her at once."

The man stared blankly and said something in Cornish.

"Hilary," Patrick repeated loudly, too distraught to seek out someone who spoke English. Anyway, these people would get the idea if he talked loudly and slowly. "I. Want. To. See. Hilary."

His clear, carrying voice penetrated the babble of the hold and reached Hilary where she lay on her bunk, too dizzy to join the other passengers. She raised herself painfully on one elbow and stared toward the knot of men surrounding the ladder, trying to make out Pat-

rick's dark head and blue eyes in the center of
the crowd. She wanted to see him more than
anything in the world, and she hated herself for
it. How could she be thinking of that vile seducer when dear Jephthah was waiting for her?
She would *not* let him fill her brain and heart
this way. "Tell him to go away," she begged
Bet.

Bet relayed the message to Jer Polwhys, who
passed it on to his wife's Cornish friends. They
hissed and shooed at Patrick as he tried to get
through the crowd. He stopped, looking uncertainly around him, and Bet climbed on the post
supporting one of the partitions. "Go away!"
she called. "She won't see you!"

As Patrick stared blankly, she was inspired to
waggle her hips at him, and leaned forward to
give him a provocative view of the full, firm
breasts inadequately covered by her skimpy chemise. "But I could show you a good time, Cap'n!"

At Patrick's undisguised look of horror a roar
of laughter went up from the Cornish men and
women crowding around him. They might not
have understood the words, but the byplay was
perfectly clear to them. Patrick's face turned
dark red and he retreated without another word.

"You shouldn't have let that woman tease
him," Anna Polwhys murmured to her husband. "He's a good man."

Jer put his arm around his wife to support
her. This was her first day on her feet and he
was afraid the excitement of landing might be
too much for her. "Good for you. No good for
the little redhead."

Bet, looking at the bunk where Hilary lay

with her face under the blanket and her slim body shaking with sobs, would have agreed with that assessment. "It's all right, lovey," she murmured, stroking Hilary's shoulder. "It's all right. He's gone now. He won't trouble you no more."

She understood exactly why that thought made Hilary cry even more passionately. Let her have her cry, she thought. She'll be the better for it. But Lord, if she breaks so easy, what's to become of her here?

The same question troubled Patrick as he strode across the deck to his cabin, but he set his chin and told himself firmly it was none of his business. She'd made that perfectly clear, damn her!

And yet he knew that he couldn't just abandon Hilary to her fate, even though it would serve her right to worry when she found out that Jephthah was nowhere near the ship.

Patrick came to a full stop on the deck, stroking his chin and smiling at the empty air as he thought of a way to save Hilary from her own folly and at the same time pay her back for snubbing him. The only catch was that he'd need an accomplice . . . and Anthony had already disembarked.

Patrick's eyes narrowed and he stared in surprise at the tubby figure of a middle-aged man who was clambering aboard the ship, one hand clutching at the rope ladder and the other balancing his oversize bob-wig as it slipped from side to side with the swinging of the ladder.

"Master Patrick! Thank God I've found you!"

"For once," Patrick said as his agent hurried across the deck, "the feeling is mutual. I've got a job for you here, Carruthers."

"Here? Nonsense!" Carruthers gave a final pat to his bob-wig and pushed a pair of wire-rimmed spectacles up on a pudgy nose that looked as if it had been modeled from a blob of red Virginia clay. "We've to ride to Williamsburg, Master Patrick. The governor is waiting to see you."

"We've got business here first," Patrick corrected irritably, "and I wish to God you'd learn to call me Mr. Lyle instead of Master Patrick. It doesn't sound right for my man of business to be addressing me as if I were still in the nursery."

"I remember you when you were in the nursery," said Carruthers, as though that settled everything, "and if I called you Mr. Lyle, how would we ever tell you apart from your father?"

Patrick's black brows met over his nose in a scowl that should have made Carruthers fear for his life.

"Now, enough nattering," Carruthers said. "We've just time to get to Williamsburg before the close of business. There's a fast horse waiting for you."

Patrick folded his arms. "Not until you tell me what this is about."

Carruthers glanced pointedly at the seamen bustling about them. "I'd really rather not go into it here, Master Patrick. It's a financial matter of some delicacy."

Patrick thought rapidly. He knew that none of the steerage passengers would be allowed off the ship until they had either paid their passage or been sold for the costs of the voyage. Hilary had no money, Jephthah wasn't going to show up to ransom her, and it would take the captain a day or two to advertise his cargo and collect some interested buyers. There seemed no harn in disembarking long enough to find out what was biting Carruthers under his wig. Besides, the instructions he wanted to give his agent would better be given ashore, where there was no danger that anyone on the ship would hear them.

To his chagrin, Carruthers remained equally uncommunicative while they were being rowed ashore and walking to the inn where a manservant waited with their horses. "Not here, Master Patrick, not here," was all he would say whenever Patrick interrogated him.

"How about here?" Patrick asked when they were standing outside the stableyard of the inn. He nodded at the tall, heavyset young man who held their horses. Thomas Ryan was an indentured servant in the last year of his term, counting the days until he was free to take up his headright of land and marry the girl from the kitchens he'd been courting. "You can trust Thomas, surely."

Thomas grinned and touched his forehead at this mark of attention.

"I'd really prefer to discuss it on the road to Williamsburg, Master Patrick," Carruthers said. "We can't waste time."

Patrick sighed and accepted the inevitable. "All right. But Thomas stays here. I've an errand I want him to do for me." It occurred to Patrick that it might in some ways be even better to employ the taciturn Thomas rather than Carruthers, for the tubby little estate agent would probably have slipped up and mentioned his name at some point. Thomas Ryan had been working in Patrick's stables for four years and Patrick had never heard him string three words together at one time. Yes, the hulking, taciturn Thomas would serve excellently.

"I want you to buy me a girl," Patrick began, drawing Thomas to one side. "A girl who came in on this ship."

Thomas nodded. "Yes, master. Any particular one?"

"Of course a particular one, you dolt!" Patrick scowled and Thomas cringed appropriately. "She's about five feet, four inches tall, slender, white skin, long red hair, gray eyes like pearly clouds when dawn is breaking, a sweet little kissable mouth . . ."

He became aware that he was rhapsodizing rather than describing. ". . . and a tongue on her like the horned viper's venom," he finished. "Think you'll know her?"

Thomas nodded again. "That's not all," Patrick cautioned. "I don't want her to know I'm buying her. So you'd better pick up a dozen others at the same time—good sturdy field hands. We can always use a few more strong backs. And don't mention my name! Understand?"

He felt in his pocket and found only two guineas. Of course—that cursed bet with Anthony. "Carruthers, I need money."

"We'll discuss that on the road," said his agent.

"Didn't you bring any . . . Oh, to hell with it." Tearing a scrap of paper off the edge of one of Carruthers' documents, Patrick scrawled out a blank tobacco draft and signed his name. He thrust the paper into Thomas' hand, wrapped around the two guineas. "Fill this in with the amount it takes to purchase them, and give it to the captain. But make sure the girl doesn't know I'm involved in it. If she asks, just tell her she's going upcountry to work in the fields."

"But, master, you never work women in the fields," Thomas protested.

Patrick clutched his wig and yanked at the neatly curled sides. "I know that, you booby! *Just tell her that,* all right?"

"Master Patrick, we really must go." Carruthers tugged at his sleeve. "I'm afraid it will be too late to meet with the governor if we don't hurry. And about this girl, Master Patrick, I really don't think it is wise—"

"When I want you to advise me on my love life," Patrick snapped, "I'll tell you! And *stop calling me Master Patrick*! I'm a grown man! I demand to be treated like one!"

"Your maturity and self-control are indeed evident," said Carruthers dryly. He mounted his horse with an agility surprising in one whose form so closely resembled a sphere and waited patiently for Patrick to join him.

Thomas stood and scratched his head in some bemusement as Patrick and Carruthers rode off on the Williamsburg road. Master Patrick surely must be in a powerful swivet about something, the way he barked out all those confusing instructions and then took off. Come to think of

it, Mr. Carruthers had been in a swivet about
something too, all the way here, though he
hadn't told Thomas what it was.

All very confusing! Thomas lowered his head
between massive shoulders and scratched with
renewed energy. Let's see, he was to get a
girl—no, several girls, but one of them had to
have red hair. Well, he reckoned he'd be able to
pick her out okay when the time came. Any girl
who got Master Patrick that excited had to be
something special. But then, he was supposed
to be getting her for field work, and Master
Patrick never put women in the tobacco fields.
It didn't make no sense, that it didn't.

Thomas clinked Patrick's two guineas in his
hand thoughtfully. The tobacco draft would pay
for the redemptioners; no harm in spending a
little of Master Patrick's money on a bowl of
rack-punch while he waited for the ship's captain to get the redemptioners lined up ready for
sale.

Near midday the hatch cover was thrown
back and a shaft of dim light came from the
orlop deck down into the hold. "On deck, and
look lively!" a seaman ordered the steerage passengers. "Captain wants you all cleaned up some
before the sale."

The men and women nearest the ladder were
nearly crushed in the press of eager bodies seeking to get up on deck for their first glimpse of
the new land. Hilary, supported by Bet, was
one of the last to go up the ladder. Her knees
trembled with the weakness left by the fever,
but she was determined to make the ascent.

Perhaps she would be able to see Jephthah waiting on shore. Once she saw him, surely she would be able to remember how much she loved him, and this interlude with Patrick would be no more than a fever-dream in her memory.

Once on deck, she made for the rail nearest shore and strained her eyes eagerly. All she could see was a mass of green trees, like a forest growing out of the water, and a huddle of low buildings near the water's edge. They were too far from shore for her to make out individual people.

Disappointed, she turned her eyes the other way, and saw a large ship riding at anchor some distance from them. The carved figurehead, in the shape of a woman whose draped garments were blown back by the wind, roused a nagging sense of familiarity in her. Frowning slightly, she studied the figurehead for several minutes, while around her the other passengers chattered and pointed at the town. Then her eyes dropped to read the name painted below the figurehead, and she felt a shock, as though the sea had come up to smack her in the face.

"The *Rose and Thorn*," she murmured with a sense of disbelief. How could this be? The ship bearing her letter to Jephthah had left three full weeks before this one. Hilary had counted the days, eking out her last few shillings to live in London as long as she could so that Jephthah should have ample time to receive her letter and make plans to meet her.

She reached out beseechingly and stopped a sailor who was yelling at the steerage passengers to line up on deck so that they could be counted.

"Please . . . please, tell me, how long has that ship been here?" she asked, pointing over the water at the proud outline of the *Rose and Thorn*.

The sailor stopped his haranguing of the passengers, pushed his knitted cap back on his head, and rubbed a stubbly chin. "Well, missy, I don't rightly know. She got in ahead of us, that's all I know for certain."

Hilary felt weak with relief. She was even able to release her hold on the rail and move to her place in line with the other men and women.

As the pushing, chattering crowd gradually formed into some semblance of order, the captain came out of his quarters and marched around the deck, looking over the shabby men and women whose sale as servants was to repay him for the cost of transporting them over the Atlantic.

"A sorry lot," he observed to his first mate. "Stunted little men and sickly, pale-faced women. Why the devil did I let you talk me into taking a load of Cornish miners? They'll be no use here. The colonists need farm hands. I'll never move this lot."

"Aye, sir. They're not all Cornish, sir."

"No," the captain agreed sourly, "we filled in the corners with the sweepings of London slums. Miners, whores, and pickpockets! I'll lose my shirt on this kind of cargo."

The mate chewed his quid of tobacco and spat expertly into the scruppers without paying overmuch heed to the captain's complaint. The old man always threw a fit at the end of a voyage, predicting doom, disaster, and debtors' prison for them all. In a couple of days, when the passengers had been cleaned up and the first buyers were here, he'd cheer up again.

The sailor whom Hilary had questioned hurried back along the rail, urging the passengers to stand up a little straighter and for God's sake smile when the captain looked at them! He noticed that the pretty redhead who'd been interested in the *Rose and Thorn* was right at the end of one line. Perhaps she'd like to hear the extra gossip he'd picked up on his circuit of the deck.

"Psst! Missy!" he whispered. The redhead looked at him with wide, dark-fringed gray eyes and he felt already repaid for his effort in questioning the other crew members. "I heard a little more about the ship you're interested in," he whispered. "She was held up at Gravesend nigh on a month, waiting for a good wind. Only got in the day before us. So if you've got a friend on board, you'll be able to meet up with 'im easy enough. If not"—he winked—"well, I'd kinda like to be y'r friend."

The pale girl with the fiery hair stared at him for a moment, lips parting as though she were trying to speak. Then her eyes rolled up and she sagged to the floor in a dead faint.

The sailor pulled off his knit cap and knelt over her, fanning her face. "Well, hell, missy," he muttered, "I ain't that ugly. You could of just told me to go to hell, you didn't need to pass out."

"Let her alone!" Bet crouched over Hilary, gathering her into her arms protectively.

"What the devil is going on here?" a voice roared above them.

Bet looked up past pointed leather shoes, striped knit stockings, and dark cloth breeches into the scowling face of the captain. "Nothing, sir," she said with the slum-dweller's instinctive desire to minimize contacts with authority. "Me friend's just still a little weak with the fever, that's—"

"No, she isn't!" the captain snapped. "There's no fever aboard this ship. Think up some other reason."

"I didn't do it," the sailor whined, backing away and twisting his cap in both hands.

"Take her into my cabin," the captain ordered. "Get her on her feet again. You!" He pointed at Bet. "Any other sick below?"

Bet thought quickly. If the sick passengers were to get special treatment, her Dickie might as well get his share. "One, sir," she admitted. "Me man, Dickie Baynes—'e's—"

"I didn't ask you for his life history," the captain cut her off. He ordered two crewmen to bring the sick man up and put him, too, in the great cabin.

When Hilary regained consciousness she found herself lying on lace-trimmed linen sheets instead of on the hard boards of the deck. The smell of the sheets, unwashed since the beginning of the voyage, did combat with the strong musky scent the captain favored, making her feel sick. Her head felt as if it was full of lint; she couldn't quite remember what had happened to bring her here. "Patrick?"

Then she remembered. Patrick was gone. And

Jephthah wasn't coming. He would not even have received her letter yet.

"You awake now? Good girl." A red-nosed man in a brown scratch wig was peering into her face. She caught the whiff of brandy and guessed that he might be the ship's surgeon, who had been so difficult to find when she really needed him. "We'll have you feeling better in a trice. Drink this."

The small glass he handed her was full of a murky dark mixture that Hilary looked at with some apprehension. "Go on, drink it down," the surgeon urged.

Obediently she raised the glass to her lips and took in the contents in one quick gulp. It burned like fire going down, and started a roiling in her stomach that made the fuzziness in her head of minor concern. But she found that she was able to sit up without support, and after a moment she stood, though somewhat unsteadily.

"My own composition," the surgeon said with pride. "Brandy, salts of wormwood, and—"

"That's all right," Hilary said quickly. "I think I'd rather not know."

The surgeon pouted. "It's a good draft. If you'd taken it when you first felt ill, we'd not have this problem."

"I'm sorry to have troubled you, sir," Hilary said. Some portion of her brain was crying out indignantly that the surgeon had not been around when she fell ill, indeed had been no use at all to any of the steerage passengers. But it was too much trouble to force her slow tongue to express those thoughts. The surgeon's drink had given her strength, but all that brandy on an empty stomach was mounting to her head with powerful effect.

"I'm all right now," she promised, as he still frowned at her. "I'm weak from the fever, that's—"

"Hush! Don't use that word!" The surgeon clapped a hand over her mouth and released her only when she nodded to show her understanding. "Listen, my dear. If there's fever on this ship, we're all in quarantine—understand? And the captain will be very angry. You don't want to make the captain angry, do you?"

Hilary shook her head. She didn't want to make anyone angry, but it just kept happening. Like Patrick. Two tears rose to the corners of her eyes at the thought of Patrick, who'd gone away angry, and whom she'd never see again.

"That's a good girl." The surgeon wiped her eyes with a flourish of his stained linen handkerchief. "You never had the fever. Understand? If you're weak, it's because you were seasick on the way over. But you're all right now."

Hilary nodded obediently. "Seasick," she mumbled. "All right now." Her lips felt thick and tingly, and it was hard to speak.

"All right," the surgeon repeated, but for some reason he was shouting over his shoulder. "You can bring the others in now."

Suddenly the cabin was full of people. Hilary recognized Dickie, standing on wobbly legs and clutching the walls for support, and half a dozen others whom she had hardly spoken to on the voyage, mostly cockneys like Dickie.

The door opened again and the captain entered, talking volubly to a little stooped man whose bright eyes peered out sharply from under a bushy wig. The large brass buttons on his blue coat winked at Hilary like extra eyes. "As you know, Mr. Norris, I prefer to sell my people to local colonists so that I can know they're in good hands, but in view of our long and successful business relationship, I've put aside some of my prime stock for you. How many did you say you wanted?"

"Not over a dozen," said Norris in a deep voice that came oddly from his spindly frame. "I'm just looking to fill the wagon, y'see."

The captain chuckled and rubbed his hands together. "Well, here's eight good sturdy workers, just what you'll be wanting to make your name as a good tradesman in the back country."

"I'll take these," Norris said, pushing his way through the crowd and separating them so that Hilary and Dickie stood to one side. "Not these two. They look puny to me."

The captain shook his head. "Sorry. They go as a lot, or not at all. Anyway, those two will soon pick up. They were seasick on the way over, that's all. You can see the lass looks like a delicate-stomached sort. But she'll soon get the bloom back in her cheeks, and then . . ."

He moved closer to Norris and whispered something in his ear. Norris nodded and rubbed his hands together with a chuckle. "Good point, Captain Lanyard. Not all of my customers are looking for field hands." He chuckled again and eyed Hilary in a way that made her feel uneasy. "All right, four pounds the head."

"Eight."

"Four and a half."

"It's a deal!" the captain roared. He pumped Norris' hand up and down so violently that the little man was almost thrown off balance by the action. "And you're a lucky man. If it wasn't for my long-standing fondness for you, I'd never let you get away with this barefaced highway robbery. Will!" A seaman came to the door. "Get this lot into a shallop while I sign over their indentures to Mr. Norris."

Hilary barely caught the last words as she was being hustled out of the cabin. Something about indentures? She frowned, puzzled. Perhaps she should have explained to the captain that she had to wait for Jephthah. "Wait a minute," she said, hanging back. "I have to tell the captain—"

"Now, dear, the captain knows all about you, and he's doing what's best for you," said the surgeon, taking her arm. "Don't you want to go ashore? I should think you'd be tired of being on the ship. Here, drink this, it'll give you strength."

The neck of a flask clinked against her teeth. Hilary automatically opened her mouth and gasped and choked as a dram of neat brandy flooded her throat. She swallowed desperately and felt the fiery liquor coursing through her limbs, making them thick and unwieldy. Someone was tying her into a sling, she was swaying over the water, and then the shallop at the ship's side came up and hit her and she was sitting between Dickie and a big woman whose name she did not know.

"What's happening?" she asked. "Where are we going?"

She looked up and saw the little man called Norris scrambling down the rope ladder on the ship's side, agile as a trained monkey. The sight struck her as inexplicably funny, and she began to giggle helplessly.

"All happy, are we?" Norris asked as he settled himself in the shallop. "That's good."

He beamed at Hilary and she repeated her question.

"Going?" Norris repeated. "Wherever I can sell you, love. There's a grand demand for servants up in the Northern Neck, and it's my profession to meet the ships and collect gangs of redemptioners to satisfy that need."

Hilary's mouth fell open and she started to scramble out of the shallop, but her arms and legs felt heavy and sluggish and she couldn't quite keep her balance. A tug on her skirt brought her back down to her bench.

"There's no going back, dear," the big woman advised her. "Look."

Already some twenty yards of blue water separated them from the ship.

6

Some hours after noon Thomas Ryan raised an aching head from the rough wooden table in the common room of the inn. His two golden guineas were gone, as were the friends who'd helped him down bowl after bowl of rack-punch, and the last bowl stood empty before him. He peered disconsolately into the depths of the heavy pewter bowl, where a soggy lemon rind and two cinnamon sticks lay in a little puddle of sugary liquid, and tilted the bowl to his lips experimentally. There were just enough drops of sweet, fiery punch to tantalize his palate.

In a sudden panic he patted the pocket of his coat where Patrick's tobacco draft lay and was reassured by the crackling of the paper. At least that was all right, then. Better get on with it— Master Patrick and Carruthers had said something about returning from Williamsburg that night.

He rose on slightly unsteady legs and made

his way outside, screwing up his eyes against the harsh attack of late-summer sunshine. The choppy voyage of the rowboat he hired to take him out to the ship was a further assault on his queasy stomach and aching head, as were the indignant shouts of the boatman when they arrived at the ship and he discovered he would have to wait until Thomas spoke with the captain before he got paid.

"Money to pay the boatman? For a buyer?" The captain's indignant voice reverberated through the great cabin and bounced through a porthole to boom in Thomas' head. "What kind of a beggarly buyer can't even scrape up sixpence to . . . Oh, all right, all right."

A moment later the first mate strode out of the cabin and tossed a coin over the side to the waiting boatman. The sixpence flashed as it turned over and over on the way down, finally landing on the bare planks of the rowboat and bouncing into a corner. The mate and several watching seamen roared with laughter as the boatman scrabbled on hands and knees to recover his pay, cursing them as he did so. Thomas wanted to put his hands over his ears to drown out the raucous laughter that scraped along the delicate fabric of his eardrums like a rusty nail on chalk.

"A redemptioner? Which one?" the captain inquired when Thomas was ushered below.

"Several redemptioners," Thomas said, belatedly remembering his master's instructions. "Maybe half a dozen or so."

"Oh? And what d'you propose to pay me with?—a starveling who couldn't find a coin for the boatman?" The captain's harsh bark of laughter made jagged lines of pain on the inside of Thomas' head.

"My temp'ry financial embarrassments are none of your concern." He patted the pocket where the tobacco draft resided, reassured again by the crackling of paper. "I have a draft on my master's plantation."

The captain extended one hand and Thomas reluctantly gave him the paper. His eyebrows shot up as he noted that the place where the sum of money should be written was still blank. A blank draft! And from that young wastrel who'd bent his ear about silver mines on the voyage over.

"Well, Mr. Ryan." A new warmth infused his tone. "You'll pardon my natural caution; a man in my line of business meets so many scoundrels and cheats. As an experienced businessman yourself, no doubt trusted with many of your master's affairs, you'll understand how it is." He rose from his desk. "Will you wish to be picking out the servants yourself, or will you have a glass of wine with me while I send a man below to bring up some likely hands for inspection? I'm afraid the steerage hold is not all it should be after our long voyage." How much pleasanter, his tone suggested, for Thomas and himself to lounge in the great cabin together—two gentlemen sharing a convivial glass—while the rude business of selecting redemptioners was left to their inferiors.

"Oh, ah, I'd best go and have a look at them myself," Thomas said. "One of 'em has to be red-haired, y'see."

"Oh?" Visions of a quick and easy sale to this country bumpkin vanished, to be replaced by curiosity. There was some mystery here; gentlemen like Patrick Lyle didn't normally send clod-hopping grooms to do their purchases for them, and the mention of a redhead added to the intrigue. "Very well, we'll go below and you can make your own selection."

A single lantern dimly illuminated the cavernous interior of the hold, where the passengers waited patiently to be allowed up on deck again. Thomas paced the narrow aisles, wrinkling his nose against the smell of so many unwashed bodies. There was a plump red-haired slattern in one corner, crying quietly into a chemise that showed her nice full legs every time she pulled up the dirty petticoat to wipe her eyes. Now, there was a woman after Thomas' taste, if she'd only smile. But Master Patrick had said slim, not well-rounded. He sighed and moved on.

At the end of an hour's searching he'd identified a full dozen red-haired women, none of them quite matching the description Master Patrick had given. Besides the buxom doxy he'd first noticed, there were a child of twelve, a young mother with a baby in her arms, a matriarch of forty-five with three missing teeth, three girls with big brown cow-eyes, and five with blue eyes. And the captain was getting noticeably impatient, coughing and making side comments about folk who wasted a poor working-man's time by fingering the goods when they'd no intention of buying.

"I don't know." Thomas mopped his forehead. It was stifling in the hold; he didn't know how these poor folk stood it. They were back at the ladder now, standing close to the crying woman. Her muffled sobs got on his nerves. "You sure that's all? You didn't sell any already, did you?"

"Never a one," said the captain firmly. The redhead's sobs redoubled in force and he scowled at her. Bet glared back in between sobs but dared say nothing. "As God's my witness, Mister Ryan, you're the first customer I've seen this day. And it's a good clean ship, we swill down the hold with boiling vinegar twice a week and give 'em hot food three times a week. They're all in prime condition."

"I'm sure they are," Thomas agreed to be polite. They looked like a scabby, ragged lot to him, but he'd not looked much better himself when he came over some years earlier. Six weeks in the hold of a merchant ship took it out of you. These poor souls would recover fast enough once they got on good solid land.

The captain coughed. "Made up your mind yet?"

"I'll take 'em all," Thomas said recklessly. Hadn't Master Patrick said he could get as many as he needed to conceal his motives? And it was Master Patrick's fault anyway, for not telling him the girl's name before he jumped on a horse and rode pell-mell for the capital.

"I'm afraid that won't be possible," the captain said with regret in his voice.

Thomas blinked. "I thought you said I was the first customer."

"Oh, you are, you are," the captain reassured him. "But some of 'em are in job lots, y'see. Indentured together, and I promised they'd be sold together. I'm a kindly man, Mister Ryan; I couldn't reconcile it with my conscience to break up families for my own profit."

"Which ones," Thomas asked, "are sold as part of a lot?" Maybe he could buy the families too. After all, Master Patrick was rich enough to stand a little extra expense.

The captain put one arm around his shoulders, straining upward to do so. "That's a wee bit complicated to figure out. Come up to my cabin. We'll have a glass together while I go through their papers of indenture and figure it out."

While Thomas Ryan listened to the captain's confusing explanations of which servants had to be sold in which groups, his master was on the road to Williamsburg discovering that he was not quite as rich as he thought.

"So what's this meeting with the governor about," Patrick demanded as soon as they were out of earshot, "and why the devil couldn't it wait a day longer?"

"Governor Spotswood may already have left Williamsburg," Carruthers replied obliquely. "We need to meet with him as soon as possible."

Patrick shrugged. "You couldn't have expected my ship for a week yet; what odds if you waited for me to finish my business there?"

"Business?" Carruthers coughed. "If that's what you want to call it, Master Patrick." He looked over his wire-rimmed glasses at his employer with the mixture of fatherly indulgence and exasperation that never failed to make Patrick feel like screaming. "Really, Master Patrick, aren't there enough girls in Virginia, but you must go to importing them as well? And your poor mother wishing nothing more than to see you happily married and settled down—not," he added more severely, "that your affairs are in any condition to allow it. Unless we found an heiress. There's the Beaufort girl—"

"To hell with the Beaufort girl," Patrick cut his agent off brusquely. "I'm not interested in marriage, Carruthers. There are too many sweet young things in this world for me to tie myself down to one. One at a time, maybe." He smiled to himself, thinking of Hilary's gratitude when she learned that he was the mysterious buyer who'd purchased her, and not some bastard who'd put her to work in the tobacco fields. Yes, Hilary should keep him busy for quite some time. He'd no objection at all to remaining faithful to her as long as their liaison lasted.

"General Stilwell's niece—" Carruthers began.

"Squints, and has a giggle like someone stepped on a chicken. What are you gabbling on about heiresses for, Carruthers?"

The horses trotted on over several hundred yards of white oyster-shell road before Carruthers answered. Patrick sat easily in the saddle, relishing the sensation of being in control of his own movements once again after the long weeks on board ship. Even though the hot August sun was a torment after England's gentle fogs, even though the unused muscles of his thighs protested at this first day back in the saddle, there was nothing quite like riding his own horse down a road in his own homeland. Of course, it would be even better if it were Hilary beside him instead of this pudgy fool Carruthers, and if they were on his plantation instead of the Williamsburg road. He smiled again, thinking of what a delight it would be to show her around his broad acres, a few improved with buildings and cleared fields, most still forest stretching along the banks of the river.

"Marrying an heiress," Carruthers said at last, reluctantly, "would be the best insurance against losing your land. If things don't go well with the governor."

"What!" Patrick sat up straight, giving Carruthers his full attention. "What's this nonsense about losing my land?" That broad tract along the Nottoway was dear to his heart as his father's rich plantation in northern Virginia could never be; something of his own, carved out of the wilderness by his own efforts. "I'll be damned if I give up that patent."

"You may be damned if you don't." Without breaking the easy jog-trot rhythm of his riding, Carruthers produced a sheaf of papers from the inner recesses of his waistcoat. "This new governor is demanding quitrents and treasury rights for the last five years—ever since you took up that extra fifteen thousand acres."

"He can't *do* that!" Patrick's jaw hung open for a moment. "It was clearly understood that all taxes were to be remitted for ten years. To encourage new settlement."

"Don't tell *me*," said Carruthers, "tell Governor Spotswood. And you'd better make it good. He's about to leave town, and I had to pledge my dead mother's honor that you'd meet with him the instant your ship docked, to try to get this settled before he left. You can't keep a governor kicking his heels in Williamsburg, Master Patrick."

"And he can't take my land back," Patrick muttered sulkily. "Anyway, he'd be a fool to try. The silver mines should be ready to start production by now. I didn't get the patents yet, but if Spotswood will look the other way for a few months, I'll have enough silver out of the ground to pay his damned taxes ten times over."

Carruthers cleared his throat and shuffled the papers that he balanced on his saddle horn. "Er . . . the silver mine may not be quite ready, Master Patrick."

"May not be? What the devil are you talking about, man? Either it is or it isn't. And if it isn't ready, what's holding things up? I left Traynor enough money to build a furnace and a water wheel and to buy eighty men to work the ore. What kind of problems has he run into?"

"It might be easier to answer that," Carruthers said, "if we knew where he'd run to."

Patrick's jaw dropped. "He's gone?"

"*With* the money." Carruthers sighed. "Master Patrick, I told you it would be wiser to leave the financial management of the mine in my hands. I never trusted Traynor."

"You never believed in the mines in the first place," Patrick said. "No vision, always making difficulties—"

Carruthers sniffed just loudly enough to remind Patrick that he had been right.

"Well, to the devil with Traynor!" Patrick

slapped the loose end of the reins against his open palm and his horse speeded up in response to the sound. Carruthers kicked his own horse in the side and tried to keep up, puffing with the exertion. "I know," Patrick called over his shoulder to Carruthers. "We'll find a partner. Maybe Spotswood himself—I hear he's interested in promoting local industry. Somebody to finance the initial construction. It'll take a while to get started over, but I'll still be able to pay the taxes out of my share of the profits—and if Spotswood's the partner, he'll not want to bankrupt me by pressing for payment too fast."

Carruthers shook his head until the curls on his bob-wig bounced sideways. He called out something that Patrick couldn't hear as the distance between them widened. "How's that again?" He reined his horse in to a walk and waited until Carruthers came puffing up beside him.

"I said," Carruthers repeated, "that there's no silver. When Traynor decamped, I thought it might be wise to have an independent assay of the ore. Here are the results." He handed the last paper from his stack to Patrick.

"No silver," Patrick muttered, scanning the discouraging assay report. "And they've never seen any other samples from Lyle land? Wait a minute. Traynor sent in three different . . ."

He stopped as the truth broke in on him.

"It seems," Carruthers said gently, "that Traynor forged the initial assay reports."

And it was ten miles to Williamsburg yet. Well, Patrick thought, there was one good thing left in his life. Maybe he couldn't afford her, but he had Hilary. She'd be waiting for him when he got back from Williamsburg.

The thought of Hilary sustained him through a brief and acidulous interview with Governor Spotswood. The governor was eager to escape the sultry August heat of Williamsburg for the cooler air of the Piedmont, where he was building a summer retreat; he made it clear to Patrick that he had granted him an interview only out of consideration for his father.

"I didn't ask for favors," said Patrick, holding a tight rein on his anger, "only for simple justice. It was clearly understood that land taken up along the Nottoway was to be free of all taxes for the first ten years."

"The object of that agreement," countered Spotswood, "was to get land cleared and settled along our southern frontier, as a buffer against the Tuscaroras and other raiding Indian tribes." He dropped Carruthers' sheaf of papers on his desk and stood up, a tall, full-fleshed man whose level dark eyes challenged Patrick to defend his position. Though he was only a few years older than Patrick, his long periwig, fleshy face, and gold-embroidered waistcoat gave him an air of solidity and authority in contrast to the younger man who faced him defiantly.

"I've noticed the raiding Indians," Patrick said dryly. "They take their own taxes from my outbuildings. You can't leave an iron nail or a brass cook-pot unwatched for ten minutes but one of them sneaks out of the forest and collars it."

"My sympathy." Spotswood's full-featured face, red with the heat and the constriction of

his tight coat, showed no sign of any but per-
functory sympathy. "That doesn't alter the fact
that the remission of taxes was intended to open
the land for settlement, not to concentrate large
tracts in the hands of individual landowners.
Your twenty-thousand-acre holding is in direct
contravention of the spirit of the act, Mr. Lyle,
and I intend to hold you responsible for payment of every penny you owe on it. If you
refuse to pay, I'll have your houses and farm
implements sold at public auction to raise the
money. Is that perfectly clear?"

Patrick gulped and nodded, his mind racing.
There must be some way he could persuade the
governor out of this ridiculous stand. "Sir," he
said at last, "I don't believe such extreme measures will be necessary. You may not be aware
that I have put considerable land under cultiva-
tion in the last two years and have settled a
number of new colonists on outlying tracts."

"You have?" Carruthers exclaimed with a start.
His glasses slid down to the end of his shining
nose and one curl of his bob-wig slowly un-
kinked itself in the stifling humidity of the governor's office. "I mean . . . er, right. Master
Patrick has been most assiduous in developing
his property."

"If you'll give us time, Governor Spotswood,
I believe we can come up with a plan for paying
the taxes out of tobacco revenues over a period
of . . . say, five years?" Patrick offered hopefully.

"Two years."

"Three?"

"Maybe. But I don't have time to listen to the
details now. I'll be touring the southern frontier

in September, marking sites for forts against the Indians and the Carolinians—damned if I know which is the greater menace," Spotswood muttered, mopping his sweating forehead. "I'll be at . . . What did you call that plantation of yours? Moonshadows? Damn silly name. I'll be there the last week in September. You two meet me there, with a plan *in detail* for how you're going to repay these revenues to the crown, and I'll listen. If it's satisfactory, we may accept payment over time. If you can't come up with a plan, my first statement still holds."

Spotswood waved away Carruthers' thanks and explanations with an irritated flap of his hand. "All right, all right. Get going. Remember, young Lyle," he said as they left, "have a plan, and show me those new cleared lands, last week in September. No excuses! I'll see results, or your house and lands get sold at auction. I'll have no aristocratic contempt of the law under my administration."

Patrick breathed a deep and heartfelt sigh of relief as they emerged into the open air. One good thing about the shortness of the interview, he thought—they'd got out while the shops were still open. He still had to prepare for Hilary's arrival at Moonshadows; she was coming with nothing, and he wanted to dress her as befitted her beauty. "Well," he said, "you see, Carruthers, things are never so bad as they seem."

"Right. All you have to do in the next six weeks is plant several thousand acres with tobacco, write up a master financial plan, and think up some way to pay your outstanding debts that the silver mine was going to take care of."

It *was* a rather daunting list of obligations. Tomorrow, Patrick promised himself, he would head straight back for the plantation and institute a regime of hard work and strict economy. But tonight . . . ah, tonight! He rubbed his hands together and started briskly down the broad avenue of Duke of Gloucester Street for Market Square.

"Master Patrick! Master Patrick! Where do you think you're going? The horses are back over here. We have to get back to the plantation at once."

Patrick shook his head with a smile. "No, Carruthers. You have to get back to the plantation and start work on the new financial plan. I have a lady to meet in Yorktown tonight."

"Well . . . but what are you doing now?"

"Isn't it obvious?" Patrick gestured toward the gay array of shop fronts where hanging signs proclaimed the presence of mercers, milliners, cobblers, and all other tradespeople necessary to supply a lady's wants. "I'm going shopping."

Night had fallen before Patrick arrived at the Yorktown Inn to meet Thomas Ryan with his new indentures. He was tired from the long ride on his first day ashore, and his brain buzzed with plans to meet the governor's deadline and get at least a temporary remission on his taxes. And then there was the matter of the nonexistent silver mine. Patrick shook his head as if to rid himself of the buzzing of an insistent fly. All details, trivial details. He wasn't ruined; he wouldn't let that happen. Trivial setbacks could be overcome, and he wasn't a businessman like Carruthers who would let himself get depressed over money matters when ahead of him there were the welcoming lights of Yorktown, an inn from whose open windows wafted the smells of hot punch and smoking tallow candles, and a redheaded girl who should, by now, be damned glad to see him.

The stableyard of the inn seemed to be uncommonly full of people. Patrick couldn't even ride his horse inside. Dismounting, he tossed the reins to a ragged boy who squirmed to the front of the crowd to see the fine gentleman on his horse. He pushed his way through the ragamuffins who filled the yard and entered the inn only to find more tattered skeletons filling the benches, lying on the tables, sitting on the floors. It was with some relief that he slowly discerned the bulky figure of Thomas Ryan, rising through the uncertain firelight and the smoke of the tallow candles like a giant out of legend. Thomas looked even larger than usual as he stepped over and around the scrawny, undersized people on the floor.

"Where is she?" Patrick demanded as soon as Thomas was before him.

The big man moved his shoulders uneasily. "They're over here, master."

"They?"

For the first time Patrick felt a stab of apprehension that something might have gone wrong with his casual plan.

"Didn't know which one you wanted, master. You didn't tell me her name. So I bought all the redheaded women on the ship."

Patrick began to laugh as Thomas steered him to a private chamber in the back of the inn, where a collection of redheads awaited his inspection. "Forgot to mention her name, did I? Damned careless of me. Well, better safe than sorry . . ."

He stopped, jaw hanging, and stared at the women who waited in nervous attitudes around the little room. "Wait a minute. Thomas, this had better be some sort of joke. Where is she?"

Thomas stared helplessly at his master. "She's not one of these?"

Patrick shook his head.

"You sure? Look again, master." Thomas snatched a candle stub from the spike near the door and carried it around the room, holding it to show each woman's face in turn. The first was London Bet; Patrick recognized her teasing smile and the other attributes she'd been so busy to show off on board ship. She stuck out her chest and gave him a saucy grin, though her cheeks were streaked with tears; the young mother with her three babies flinched away from the light; two of the young girls clung to each other, crying. The middle-aged harridan with the head of copper curls complained loudly that she was an honest woman, she was, and she hadn't come all the way to Virginia to be some lordling's plaything, and if that young debauchee laid one finger on her, she'd have the law on him, she would—

"Hush, grandma," Patrick snapped. "Nobody's laying a finger on you. Nobody would want to." He turned back to Thomas. "You were the first customer, weren't you?"

"Yes, master." Thomas gave several vigorous nods. His longish fair hair flopped forward over his forehead and bounced with each nod. "That is, I waited awhile, like you told me. Not to seem eager, like. But the cap'n assured me I was first buyer."

Then there was only one way Hilary could have got off the ship. Jephthah must have showed up after all to pay her fare. It probably hadn't been the *Rose and Thorn* carrying Hilary's letter after all, but some other ship like the *Richard Thompson*. The *Ride and Tie*. Damn women, they never got anything straight.

"You're sure that's all?" he asked Thomas again with sinking hopes.

"Well . . ." Thomas scratched his head vigorously. "You can look at the ones in the common room and stableyard too, but none of them is redheaded. Or those that are, they ain't females," he corrected himself with painstaking exactitude.

"In the stable?" Patrick shut the door to the little chamber behind him and leaned on it. The old harridan was still screeching in there. "What have that rabble outside to do with me?"

Thomas launched on a long and complicated explanation about how this redhead had to be sold with the rest of the folk from her village, and that one couldn't be separated from her large family, and . . . "Well," he finished, "what it boils down to, master, I 'ad to buy the entire shipload to be sure of getting all the redheads."

Patrick felt a powerful urge to sit down. He

closed his eyes for a moment. "I suppose you filled in my tobacco draft and had the sale registered."

"Yes, master." Thomas nodded eagerly. "It's all legal, right and tight."

"Somehow," Patrick sighed, "I felt sure it was."

"Got 'em at bargain rates, too," Thomas went on. "Three hundred redemptioners, and only seven pounds a head."

Patrick tried not to multiply the sum out. He didn't want to know just how much more in debt he was.

"Wonderful," he summed up. "I have five years' back taxes to pay, a two-thousand-pound tobacco draft in the hands of that rascally ship's captain, three hundred servants that I don't know what to do with, two trunkloads of women's frills and furbelows being delivered to the plantation by Carruthers, and Ranting Jephthah got my girl." That last thought was the one that hurt most. If only Hilary had waited for him . . . but she hadn't known he was coming back for her. Why did he have to play such clever games?

Patrick stopped his self-recriminating thoughts quickly. After all, he reminded himself, she had refused to speak to him that morning. What made him think she would have waited for him? Let her go with her backwoods preacher, and be damned to them both. Patrick's face creased in lines of pain as he realized that Hilary was lost to him forever. "Damn all women!" he burst out under his breath. He would just have to forget her, that was all. He didn't have *time* to think about her. He had a plantation to save.

"Sir?"

Patrick looked at Thomas' worried face, the broad forehead wrinkled by unaccustomed care and the blue eyes filled with vague concern. "Never mind, Thomas." He reached up to clap his pet giant on the shoulder. "It's not your fault. I've been a damned overconfident fool in every possible area." He looked at the ragged mob that filled the common room, all those faces turned hopefully toward him, and began to laugh. "Who knows, maybe it'll all work out for the best. I've just remembered, Governor Spotswood wanted more people settled on my land. Three hundred new settlers ought to put him in the right frame of mind to hear my petition."

❦ 7 ❦

Hilary trudged along a muddy road, resting one hand on the empty wagon beside her for support and hoping that Norris would not catch her leaning on it. At the beginning of the journey north, when she'd been so ill, Norris had let her ride in the wagon; but now that she was better, he made her get out and walk up the hills with the other redemptioners to save his horses. Even though there were only two of them left unsold, he wouldn't allow any extra weight to drag on the undernourished horses that he nursed along from one ordinary to the next on a handful of hay and the memory of oats.

One of the stack of preprinted handbills that Norris carried with him fluttered over the side of the wagon and lay faceup in a mud puddle. "Choice, well-disposed servants for sale," the handbill read, "Available for viewing to all interested buyers."

Hilary had cringed with shame on the first day, when Norris inspected her and wrote her description on his papers of sale. She'd tried to explain to him that there was no need to put her up for sale at a public inn; if he would only wait for Jephthah, he would surely pay for her indentures. But Norris only chuckled and said that goods fairly bought went to the highest bidder, and he wagered someone would bid high enough for a pretty girl like her, once she recovered her health.

Under the red-lettered heading was a blank space where Norris wrote in descriptions of his current stock-in-trade. At the beginning of the journey the space had been filled with glowing descriptions of "Skilled Craftsmen, Strong Farm Hands, and Cleanly Women Servants with Experience in Dairy Work and Spinning." Now, three weeks later, he was down to two entries: a "Good Worker" and a "Handsome Girl."

The stunted little cockney, Dickie, had found no favor with the planters who crowded around Norris' wagon at each inn to feel the muscles and check the teeth of his redemptioners. And Hilary had been a dead charge on him all this time. The shock of being sold had brought back her fever, and for two weeks she had lain ill in the bottom of the wagon, her head and bones aching as they jounced along the rough country tracks, too sick to know or care where she was being taken. When she recovered enough to sit up, she was too thin and pale to appeal to buyers.

She suspected that by now Norris regretted not having waited for Jephthah to buy her. For the last week, as Hilary recovered her strength, his behavior to her had alternated between blows and curses whenever he remembered how he had been cheated, and kindly urgings to eat more whenever he remembered how beautiful she had once been and what a good price she could bring him once she filled out a little.

For the last couple of days he'd been hovering around her at each stop, pinching her cheeks and urging her to smile, while Hilary feigned more weakness than she felt. She shrank from the idea of being exposed for sale in the smoky common room of some ordinary or the dirty stableyard outside, where any chance comer could slip a hand under her skirt or fondle her breasts on the pretext of examining "the merchandise." She'd seen the other women suffer such fondling, even having their jaws forced open so that their teeth could be examined. They might as well be put up for sale in a stockyard with the rest of the cattle.

Thank goodness, tonight they would arrive at wherever they were going too late for Norris to announce a sale! He'd warned her that morning that he was through coddling sickly servants; he wanted to get her and Dickie off his hands as soon as possible so that he could head back to the coast with his cash and pick up a new load of redemptioners. But they'd taken a wrong turn somewhere in the forest, and by the time Norris figured out which faint set of cart tracks was the "main road," night was falling. They'd be lucky to arrive at the ordinary before dark.

Hilary suspected that Dickie had helped to confuse Norris. He'd certainly expended a lot of energy running back and forth, nosing out different tracks and triumphantly announcing the discovery of a new "road" every few minutes. Now, as she glanced upward where the afternoon sun filtered through rows of trees, he gave her a conspiratorial wink. "Why'ncha ride awhile?" he whispered. "I'll walk up ahead and keep old Norris too busy to look back."

Hilary smiled and shook her head. Last time one of the redemptioners had tried that trick, Norris had knocked him sprawling off the wagon with a blow of his cane that broke the man's arm. Then he'd grumbled about the reduced price he'd get for him. She didn't dare imagine what he'd do to Dickie and her if they started playing games with him; he was angry enough already about being delayed on the road.

As they trudged on up the endless hill, the sun dipped out of sight and a flock of birds rose like a black cloud from the marshes to the right of the road. Clouds of stinging insects hummed around their faces, greedily darting in on every square inch of exposed skin. Hot though it was, Hilary pulled the hood of her woolen cloak well down over her head and hunched herself up to expose as little as possible to the midges. From the corner of her eye she could see that Dickie had taken off his shirt and wrapped it around his head, apparently preferring to be stung on the chest and shoulders rather than on the hands.

The yellow windows of the ordinary, glowing in the dim blue-gray air of evening, were a welcome sight. Hilary almost forgot her weariness and her fear of the sale in the anticipation of hot food and a place to lie down.

A lanky, skeletal figure clothed in shirt and breeches three sizes too small for him ambled to the door as Norris pulled the wagon up and shouted for an ostler. "Inn's closed f'the night," he announced, scratching vigorously between his shoulder blades as he spoke. "Death in t'old woman's family. No food."

"Beds?"

A thumb jerked forward, pointing to the stables. "Y'can rest warm enough in t'hay. She told me as not to let no one in."

Norris cursed and fulminated about the folly of turning away paying customers, but all his objections were met with "Told me not to let no one in, she did." Finally Norris gave up and shouted at Dickie to unhitch the horses.

In a vain attempt to retrieve his dignity, Norris piled a stack of sweet-smelling hay into the wagon and made himself a bed there, hanging his clothes over the side and wrapping himself in the one smelly horse blanket. Dickie philosophically nestled into the remaining hay and advised Hilary to do likewise. "Best t'sleep when y'r hungry, love," he told her. "It's better than lying awake listening to your belly complain."

Hilary made herself a nest in the hay and curled up under her cloak. She'd thought she was tired enough to fall asleep standing up, but aching muscles and fears about the sale tomorrow kept her awake. She was lying on her back, counting stars through the holes in the roof, when a scratching at the door awoke her.

"Missy! Hey, missy!"

It was the stableboy who'd turned them away, with something wrapped in a napkin. "Missus won't let me have anyone in when she's away, 'cause she's afeard of thieves," he apologized. "Says I'm too simple to tell an honest man from a thief. Told me not to let no one in, she did. But she didn't say as I couldn't come out!" He laughed under his breath and jigged up and down gleefully. "An' she left me a cold pie for supper. Here!"

He thrust the bundle at Hilary. As soon as she'd taken it he was gone again, creeping across the yard and sidling into the clapboard tavern as though he thought "Missus" would rise up out of the night and beat him for bending her orders this far.

Hilary slithered back to her nest in the hay and shook Dickie's elbow. When he woke, she broke the pork pie in two and pressed his piece into his hand. For a few moments they both munched greedily, eager to enjoy the unexpected meal before Norris woke up and demanded his share.

Dickie finished first, cramming the pie into his wide mouth in three monstrous bites that Hilary feared would choke him. He sighed and patted his shirtfront. "You're a good girl, love," he whispered. "Sorry I can't take you with me."

Hilary dropped the last piece of the pie and sat up, suddenly very wide-awake. "Are you running away? Where? How?" She'd thought of it herself. Not, she told herself, that she meant to cheat Norris; no, when she reached Jephthah she'd see to it that he was paid back. Hateful little man though he was.

"Hush, ducks." Dickie patted Hilary's arm awkwardly. "Wouldn't work for two of us.

They'd be onto us too fast, see. Besides, you'll
be all right. Pretty girl like you, they'll put you
to housework, you'll live like a lady. Probably
wind up married to your master. But me, see, I
got to get back to Yorktown and find Bet."

"You do?" Hilary's eyes widened in the darkness. She hadn't thought there was so much
fondness between Bet and the little cockney.
Certainly Bet had been free enough to offer her
favors elsewhere, she thought, remembering certain scenes on shipboard from which she had
learned to avert her eyes.

Dickie shrugged. "She's all right, old Bet," he
mumbled, sounding slightly embarrassed. "Took
care of me through the fever, didn't she? An'
. . . well, I miss her, and that's a fact."

"But, Dickie," Hilary reminded him, "we've
been gone nearly three weeks now. She'll have
been sold off the ship."

"Then I'll find out where she's gone," he
said, "and get her back. They got records, you
know."

"They do?"

Dickie nodded. "Heard the captain talkin'
about it one day. When y'r sold, they has to
write it down in a big book in the Coun . . .
Con . . . well, somewhere. All I got to do is get
away from Norris, get back to Yorktown, find
that book, get somebody to read me where Bet's
gone, go there, and get her back."

It sounded like a staggering project to Hilary.
No wonder he didn't want to be saddled with
her as well! It seemed unlikely that the little
cockney would get more than a league before
he was picked up and brought back in disgrace,

but she couldn't argue against so much devotion. Besides, his information about the records of sale gave her new hope.

"What about when Norris sells people?" she whispered. "Is that recorded too?"

"I dunno," Dickie confessed.

"It must be," Hilary said firmly. "That's why he's always writing in that black notebook of his. Maybe when he gets back, they copy it all into that big book of records. And maybe, if someone wanted to find me, he could look in there and come after me and buy my indentures . . ."

She lay back in the hay, feeling a wonderful warmth and contentment seeping through her tired limbs. Much of her despair had risen from the thought that she was cut off from . . . well, from anybody who might want to know what would become of her.

She fell asleep murmuring Jephthah's name, but her dreams were populated by a dark-browed rogue with dancing blue eyes, who kissed and caressed and teased her and told her all the sweet things she'd never quite believed when he said them in person.

"Hilary, I couldn't do without you," he told her, crushing her in a passionate embrace. "I tried to forget you, but it was no use. Will you—"

His sword hilt was digging painfully into her side, and somebody's shouting drowned out his next words. But she knew what they had to be.

"Yes, Patrick," she whispered, lips raised for his kiss. "Of course I'll marry you."

"Who the hell is Patrick?" an angry voice inquired. "It's Dickie I want to find, the lying little swine." The prodding in her ribs intensified. Hilary gasped and rolled over, away from the pointed leather shoe that was attacking her. She looked up to see Norris, his face empurpled with fury, standing over her and drawing his foot back to deliver a vicious kick. For some reason he was dressed in Dickie's ragged shirt and patched leather breeches, though he had his own shoes on.

Sun flooded through the open stable door behind him, partially blinding her. She got to her knees and dodged the kick, holding her hands up to protect her face. A massive woman in a calico print apron and several leagues of brown petticoats rolled through the door and laid one large pink hand on Norris' shoulder.

"Now, now, dearie, don't take on so," she said coaxingly. "If'n your story's true, we'll have all right and straight soon as the justice comes. All I need is my money back, and you can go."

"To hell with your money," Norris cursed. "I've got to go after him now, woman! He's getting away at this very moment."

"Naah, he be long gone," put in the lanky stable lad, peeking over his mistress's shoulder. "Left at dawn, he did."

Norris cursed some more. As he argued with the woman who kept the tavern, Hilary slowly figured out the situation. It seemed Dickie had arisen at dawn, dressed himself in Norris' fine new blue plush coat and buckskin trousers, and tiptoed out to make a deal with the innkeeper. He'd represented himself as the master of two redemptioners, claiming that he was in a hurry to sell them so he could get back to the coast. He'd sold two servants, one horse, and the wagon to Mistress Johnson for sixteen pounds, a ham, and a saddle so that he could ride the other horse away.

"And here you'll stay and work," Mistress Johnson said cheerfully, "for I've too much invested in you to put up with these tantrums. Mind you, Dickie, Mr. Norris warned me you'd try to pull this trick, but once is enough—y'understand?"

"I'm not Dickie!" Norris bellowed.

"Man about forty, squat stature, bowlegged, sly countenance," Mistress Johnson read out Dickie's description from the papers of indenture. She looked Norris up and down and nodded. "I'd've said 'villainous countenance,' myself, but we'll not quarrel over a phrase. Now, I've sent for the county justice, and he'll hear your case, and then I expect you to shut up and get to work. In fact, you can start now. Water the horses. As for you, m'dear"—she turned to Hilary—"I've need of another serving girl in the tavern. And this morning there's a joint to turn and two fine plump partridges to be stuffed and roasted. Unless you're the Queen of England incognito?"

Hilary smiled. She had a feeling she was going to like Mistress Johnson. And this ordinary was as good a place as any to be working until Patrick . . . that is, until Jephthah found her. She followed Mistress Johnson into the tavern. A stout middle-aged man with an old-fashioned periwig flowing down about his shoulders was standing in the middle of the room, tapping one foot impatiently.

"Justice Hazelrigg!" Mistress Johnson spread her skirts in a curtsy. "I didn't expect you so soon."

Hazelrigg? For some reason the name filled Hilary with foreboding. After the blaze of morning light outside, she was half-blinded in the shadowy common room. She peered at the justice, trying to make out his features, and behind him another man moved—short and wiry, overdressed in a laced coat and ruffled neckcloth, with sly foxy features.

"My nephew," Justice Hazelrigg said. "Anthony. About this unruly bondsman, Mistress Johnson—"

"If this is the problem servant," Anthony Hazelrigg interrupted, "I think we can take care of the little matter." He grinned at Hilary over his uncle's shoulder. "I've a fancy to buy her myself. We'll pay double whatever you gave the runaway."

Patrick, back at his plantation on the Nottoway, could not forget Hilary. Wherever he turned, there was something to remind him of her. He walked over to the farm hands' barracks to see how his new colonists were getting on, and there was Anna Polwhys, smiling shyly and asking her husband to tell Patrick how grateful they were that he'd bought them all together so that the families weren't broken up. He returned to the great house and found that Carruthers had returned from Williamsburg with the trunks of feminine frills Patrick had bought, ivory fans and a green satin ball gown to set off the beauty of a red-haired slip of a girl with skin whiter than the Mechlin lace ruffles on the gown. Even the sight of the great house reminded Patrick of his visions of Hilary gracing his hall and his table and the four-poster bed upstairs where he fell into an exhausted sleep each night to dream of hair like flame and eyes like summer thunderclouds.

It wasn't, he thought wryly, as if he didn't have enough to do. He'd come home determined to turn over a new leaf, to work and develop his lands and prove to Spotswood that he should be given a remission on those taxes that would cripple the plantation. No more dreams of silver mines! From now on it was to be cleared land, girdled trees standing in a green sea of tobacco plants, houses for the new families he'd brought back, and every possible sign of a productive working plantation to replace the miles of forested land he'd taken up.

With only a month's grace he couldn't hope to make much change in the plantation. It was mostly forest, with only a few cleared acres on which he grew food for the plantation and tobacco to pay for the things that had to be bought. But he could demonstrate his serious intentions by clearing more acres in preparation for the spring planting. While his few experienced field hands harvested the growing tobacco and hung it in high-raftered barns to dry, Patrick took an ax in his own hands and set out to show his new settlers how he wanted the forest cleared for planting.

It was an uphill task.

"No, no, not that way!" he said a dozen times a day. "You'll cut your foot off. Swing it like this, nice and easy, with a two-handed grip. See?"

The Cornishman looked at him with blank incomprehension. Patrick sighed, spat on his hands, took the ax, and decapitated a sapling in one neat stroke.

"Sorry, sir." Jer Polwhys came up and apologized for his friend. "He does not have the English . . . and we are miners, not farmers."

Patrick winced at this reminder of his folly. "Well, you're farmers now—or will be, as soon as I teach you which end of a hoe to take up. There's no mining here."

Jer looked through the trees toward the half-built furnace by the riverbank, with lumps of rock piled beside it where Traynor had abandoned the "silver ore" and the work as soon as Patrick left for England.

"Forget that," Patrick said. "There's no silver. I've had the ore assayed—by an honest man this time." He clapped Jer Polwhys on the back, smiling to make up for his initial harsh response. "We'll have to make our fortunes the slow way, my friend. Now, let's get these trees barked and out of the way."

Then he was off again, explaining to a bewildered Londoner who was patiently chipping away at a monster oak that there was no need to cut the larger trees down. "Girdle them," he explained, taking the fellow's ax and expertly slicing the bark off the tree in a ring near the base. "They'll die of their own accord before time for spring planting."

The Londoner shook his head. "Naah, guv'-nor, you're fooling! I read about farming once," he said proudly. "In a book. You have to plow the land. Can't plow through roots, can you? Trees have to go."

Patrick reached for his wig and yanked at a double handful of hair. Pain shot through his scalp and he remembered too late that he had discarded the wig along with his coat and waist-coat when he arrived to show these city fellows how to work. He slowly disentangled his hands from his own hair. Then he sighed and ex-plained slowly and patiently that tobacco plants weren't raised by dropping seed into a plowed furrow. They were transplanted individually from the raised starter beds, set out amid the roots of the dead trees, and cultivated with a hoe.

"Sounds like a lot o' work," the Londoner said glumly.

Patrick nodded and went off to supervise the building of the new long barracks in which the new colonists were to be housed. At present half of them were sleeping in canvas tents, and the other half on the floor of the existing bar-racks; that would have to be changed before the snow came.

And at the end of the day, as he'd been doing for the last week, he staggered back to the great house with aching muscles and blis-tered hands. He sat in his office by candlelight and worked on his memorandum to Governor Spotswood about the finances of the plantation and his plan for paying the taxes in installments.

Evening brought a welcome relief from the steamy heat of August, a breath of cool air rising from the river, and a gentle blue haze replacing the glare of the afternoon sun. Patrick's steps slowed as he approached the house, and he took a deep breath of the humid, sweet-scented air, hardly caring about the malarial vapors that the night air carried as he gazed with the pride of ownership on his house and outbuildings. The two-story house with its matching wings of four rooms each, curving out as if to embrace the pillared portico in the center, stood tall and proud against the dark green of the forest.

Each time that Patrick came up the drive, he paused to enjoy the contrast between civilization and wilderness. Before him was a white-washed portico supported on slender Grecian columns, with green-painted shutters thrown open on either side to show candles flickering in the windows. The house would not have been out of place in Williamsburg—or even, Patrick thought with pride, in London. But behind it, instead of city streets, one saw the mysterious deep shadows of the forest that stretched for uncounted miles westward; and far in the distance, like blue smoke floating above the trees, were the mountains that only a handful of fur traders had crossed.

And on this particular night, Patrick recognized with surprise and some displeasure, there was something else in front of his house. A bony, swaybacked black horse grazed on the close-cropped green grass of the lawn, occasionally raising its head to sample a spray of leaves from the young trees that guarded either side of the portico.

Quickening his steps, he wrenched the horse's head away from a particularly succulent cluster of maple leaves. "Hawkins! Why hasn't this horse been stabled? What kind of hospitality do you think we offer, that a guest's horse has to eat my new-planted saplings instead of oats?"

A tall black-clad figure emerged from the shadows of the hall. "Do not blame your servant," Jephthah Graham said in a deep, even voice. "He has been occupied with hearing the goodly words of truth since my arrival. I am disappointed, though hardly surprised, to find how you neglect the religious education of your servants. 'I will make them hear my words, that they may learn to fear me all the days that they shall live upon the earth.' Deuteronomy Four: Ten."

While Jephthah droned on, Hawkins scurried around him and took the reins of the horse from Patrick's hands, babbling apologies. He was a small, balding man whom Patrick had purchased with his first lot of field hands nearly five years earlier. Showing an unexpected talent for making the then new plantation house into a comfortable retreat, he had become the head of the house servants and had stayed on since earning his freedom to work for wages.

"Master Patrick, I couldn't get away from him, the gentleman were that urgent," he apologized in an undertone. "Walks in and starts inquisitioning me do I know my Bible, sir, and wouldn't stop for nothing, and I didn't want to offend the gentleman, sir."

Patrick nodded. He had been exposed to Jephthah's techniques before and couldn't really blame Hawkins for having been backed into a corner. "See that the horse is stabled. And . . . what will we feed him?" Patrick had been so busy that he'd discouraged the cook from preparing regular meals, preferring to munch on a piece of bread or some cold meat each night while he worked over his papers.

"Don't worry, sir," Hawkins whispered conspiratorally. "I'll see to dinner while you talk to him."

"I rather fancy," Patrick said, "you mean *listen* to him." Hawkins handed the horse over to a stable lad and scurried around the house in the direction of the kitchens. Patrick braced himself to be civil to the man who had taken Hilary from him.

". . . the baptism of infants, meaning immersion and not mere sprinkling as the heretical rites of your so-called Church of England—"

" 'Evening, Jephthah," Patrick broke in. He had learned from previous experience that there was no point in standing politely and waiting for the preacher to run out of words. It never happened. "To what do I owe the honor of this visit?"

As he spoke, he led the way into the dining room that opened off the right side of the hall, where a single candle burned in the window. Patrick took the candle and lighted a spray of tapers over the mantel, shedding a warm glow over the room. In the new light he studied Jephthah, trying to see in him what Hilary evidently saw.

It was no use. Jephthah looked the same to him this time as always: a lanky man whose long, lantern-jawed face and lined features expressed the deepest melancholy and dissatisfaction with this world. His dark hair, liberally streaked with gray, was brushed back over the collar of a rusty black jacket from which bony wrists protruded. As usual, he looked as if he hadn't eaten in a fortnight, and there were inkstains along his callused index fingers and on the cuffs of his threadbare shirt.

Patrick felt an involuntary shiver of revulsion at the thought of this man taking Hilary into his bed, caressing her with those coarse red hands, and doubtless quoting his own sermons to her as he took his pleasure from her body. He wondered if she was happy now with the bargain she'd made, but found such a thought unbearable. He turned his back and pretended to busy himself with lighting another spray of candles. "You'll stay for dinner, of course?"

Tonight he felt as if it would choke him to share a meal with this man who had the right to take Hilary into his bed whenever he wished. But he felt a tortured, self-punishing longing to hear Jephthah speak of her. Was she well? Was she—though it seemed impossible—happy in her new life?

"I thank you," Jephthah said, "I would be glad of the meal, but I cannot stay the night this time—that is, I am called to other duties."

Eager to get back to the arms of his sweet new wife, Patrick thought. He deliberately conjured up the image in his mind, like a man compulsively pressing on a sore tooth.

"Though I see you have brought in new servants who are doubtless in sore need of godly

words of comfort," Jephthah added. "It goes
sadly against my conscience to leave these wandering lambs without the comfort of such poor
words as I can speak—"

"They're Cornish," Patrick interrupted, "and
they don't speak English, so I'm afraid your
words of comfort would go to waste. Besides,
they're good Catholics—like me."

A procession of servants bearing covered
dishes entered the dining room. Patrick sniffed
appreciatively. Ham from the smokehouse, pork
sausages grilled over the fire with sprigs of rose-
mary and thyme wreathed around them, a hot
bubbling stew of squash and beans; Hawkins
had done well, for a man required to produce a
dinner out of thin air. He reminded himself to
raise Hawkins' wages, and then remembered
that unless Governor Spotswood remitted his
taxes, Hawkins would soon be looking for a
new place—and so would he.

Jephthah sat down without waiting for an
invitation and speared his fork into one of the
sizzling sausages. Cramming the spicy meat into
his mouth, he didn't notice the hot fat oozing
from the skin where it had burst over the fire.
"You'll join me?" he inquired indistinctly through
a mouthful of meat and bread, wiping the grease
from his lips onto an equally greasy shirt cuff.

Patrick shook his head. "I've already eaten,"
he lied. He watched Jephthah polish off the
sausage in three bites and move on to a slice of
sugar-cured ham. Normally Patrick rather liked
to feed Jephthah, always cherishing the hope
that one more roast turkey or bowl of pudding
would fill out the cadaverous hollows in his

cheeks and inspire the man to a normal human sigh of contentment. But tonight his curiosity was burning him up.

"In a hurry to get back home, are you?" he asked, fiddling with an edge of the linen table-cloth and staring at the wall behind Jephthah's head. "I hear you've some new members in the Community of Saints."

Jephthah choked on the last bite of ham and bent over the table, wheezing and spluttering. Forgetting his revulsion for the man, Patrick dashed around the table and pounded him on the back. "Easy, man, easy!" He ladled hot rack-punch into a glass and held it to Jephthah's mouth. "Wash it down with this."

Jephthah swallowed the punch in one gulp and breathed heavily. "We have lost more than we have gained. They are tempted away by the sinful pleasures of the coast towns. But I spoke at Martin's Ford three Sundays gone and there were four lost souls there who found the path to light through the words which God gave me grace to say. Brands from the burning! Praise the Lord, but we have lost many good workers from the Community of Saints this year, and we are ill-prepared for the winter. It will be a sore strain on our resources to feed and shelter these new souls, with winter approaching. We must trust in the goodness of the Lord . . ."

Patrick was counting backward in his mind. Three Sundays ago? That would have been the week before his ship arrived in Yorktown. "But since then—you've had more since then?" he demanded. "What of the girl in Yorktown?"

Jephthah looked surprised. "Hilary Pembroke?"

Patrick discovered that he didn't even like to hear Jephthah use her name. "Yes."

"I am even now going to fetch the child," Jephthah informed him, bringing a crumpled and water-stained piece of paper from his pocket. He held the letter with one hand while slurping up soup from the pewter spoon in his other hand. "I fear she has acted with a precipitancy and lack of decorum sorely to be regretted in one raised from childhood in the Community of Saints, but there is, of course, her mother's bad blood to overcome . . ."

"Wait a minute. Let me get this straight." Patrick sat down rather heavily and poured himself a generous glass of punch. "You've not married her?"

Jephthah gave him an incurious glance between two spoonfuls of soup. "Not yet. I told you that my journey to Yorktown is of some urgency. I gather from this letter that the child is utterly without resources."

Amazing, how smooth and sweet the punch was, going down his parched throat. Patrick poured himself another glass and plunged his fork into a slice of pink sugar-cured ham.

"Do you know," he said, "I find that I am hungry after all. Tell me more about this Hilary." He had the distinct impression that birds were singing in the trees just outside the window, and the candles on the mantel seemed to be sparkling more cheerfully. Even Jephthah's lean, lined countenance was not so unpleasant to look upon as it had been a moment ago.

Over the rest of the dinner, Patrick patiently disentangled Jephthah's rambling discourse and gathered that Hilary's letter had come to him by a circuitous but remarkably efficient route. The *Rose and Thorn*, waiting outside Gravesend for a favorable wind, had passed her mailbag to a faster and better-built ship whose captain was willing to set out in any weather. That ship had docked at Charles Town in South Carolina, where a fur trader named Kendall O'Leary had taken the letter and conveyed it to Jephthah in the course of one of his trips to sell brass kettles and iron hatchets to the Tuscarora Indians.

"A worse heathen than the Indians," Jephthah remarked of O'Leary, and for once Patrick agreed with his assessment. The last time Kendall O'Leary's trading caravan had passed the Lyle plantation, three good axes and the large iron dye caldron had taken legs and walked off into the woods with him.

"So you just got the letter?" Patrick prodded.

Jephthah shook his head and explained that Hilary's letter had arrived just before the Sunday on which he was to preach at Martin's Ford. That engagement took precedence over her needs, especially as he didn't know exactly when her ship would dock; and since then he'd been busy helping the newly saved souls to settle in and seeing that they didn't backslide. Only now did he feel free to go to Yorktown to meet her.

Patrick's mind was racing while Jephthah talked. If Jephthah hadn't paid Hilary's passage, how had she gotten off the ship without Thomas seeing her? Had she sweet-talked the captain into letting her go free, or—he groaned internally at the thought—had she, in her des-

peration, offered him some other kind of payment for her passage? That thought was unbearable. There must be some other explanation. Somehow Thomas must have slipped up;
there must have been some redemptioners sold
before he got to the ship, and Hilary among
them. All he had to do was go back to Yorktown,
examine the records of the court, and find out
who had bought her indentures.

Preferably without Jephthah looking over his
shoulder.

"Why, man, your glass is empty," Patrick
said with a well-simulated start of surprise.
"You'll drink to the salvation of souls with me?"

"I do not take alcohol," Jephthah said sternly.
He tilted the glass in his hand and the last
drops of a hot punch mixed with equal propor-
tions of brandy, lemon juice, water, and sugar
trickled down his throat.

"Another glass of this innocent punch, then,"
Patrick proposed. "It was a recipe of my mother's," he added with perfect truth, "and the
fruit juices are good for warding off a sore throat,
which would be a bad ailment for a preacher. I
thought your voice sounded rather rough. You'd
best take a little more. To the new souls in the
Community!" And might Hilary never be among
them.

Jephthah acceded to the toast, and Patrick
followed it up in rapid succession with toasts to
the establishment of God's kingdom on earth,
to the success of the Community of Saints, the
power of the Gospel, and whatever else he could
think of. Finally, to his great relief, Jephthah
slumped forward into the remains of the soup,

arms flung out on the table, snoring heartily. Patrick held onto the wall and made his way outside, somewhat unsteadily.

Perhaps the night air would clear his head. He staggered down the hall and out onto the portico, where he wrapped one arm around a pillar and waited for the stars to stop whirling around. His head ached like the devil and his legs were not obeying his commands. After the long day of work, followed by the evening's hard drinking, he longed for bed. Only thing was, he thought muzzily, he longed for Hilary even more.

"Put 'em together," he mumbled. "Best solution all around."

"Sir?"

Patrick glanced down in some annoyance to see Hawkins bobbing up and down at his elbow.

"Stop weaving around like that, man," he said irritably.

Hawkins wavered and split into two distinct heads and shoulders, joined at the waist. "Sir," the heads said in unison. "Hadn't you better go to bed?"

Patrick shook his head. "Saddle . . . my horse," he ordered. "Going to . . ." He snapped his fingers several times, trying to remember the name. "Place on the river where the big ships come in."

"Sir," the Hawkinses said, "you're not sober enough to ride."

Patrick found that by screwing his left eye almost shut and concentrating very hard, he could make the two Hawkinses coalesce into one worried, balding face. But was it worth the effort? He shrugged.

"Will be sober," he announced. Letting go of the pillar, he launched himself across the lawn in the general direction of the river.

A moment later he was sliding down the bank with no clear recollection of having pushed his way through the intervening shrubbery. At the bottom of the muddy slide the cold river water smacked him in the face while the current dragged at his legs.

There were cries for help from the house. "Help! Master's gone and drowned hisself!"

Cold sober, Patrick stood knee-deep and muddy in the swirling river current and laughed. "Saddle my horse, damn you," he called up to Hawkins. "I have to go to Yorktown."

8

The clerk of the county office at Yorktown was obliging enough in letting Patrick leaf through the records of indenture that were kept for every servant sold off a ship in the harbor, but in his impatience Patrick flipped past the crabbed entry twice before he found the record of Hilary's sale to Jonathan Norris.

"No fixed address!" he exploded after he had deciphered the rest of the entry. "How the devil am I to find him, then?"

The clerk smiled and winked and suggested that he might be able to help in that endeavor—with proper encouragement. A half-crown bought the information that Norris was a soul-driver, and for another shilling the clerk recollected that he'd said something about taking his latest wagonload of servants up toward the Northern Neck. Patrick thanked him for the information and set off again, hoping that Jephthah wouldn't catch up with him too soon.

After all that punch, there was a good chance the man would remain dead drunk for a day or more.

Jephthah awoke with a pounding ache in the back of his head and a sensation of sticky wetness on his face. Somewhat dully he wondered if he had been tomahawked and was even now lying in a pool of his own blood. Somebody was whispering behind him . . . perhaps debating whether to finish him off. Jephthah closed his eyes and recommended his soul to his Maker. What better way to end a life dedicated to the saving of souls than with the crown of martyrdom?

"D'you think we oughta carry him up to a bed?"

That didn't sound like Indians. Jephthah slowly opened one eye, then the other. The light from the open window stabbed him with a fresh lance of pain. Slowly he recognized the paneled walls and polished mahogany table. Patrick Lyle's dining room. With a groan of pain he sat up, dimly recollecting the events of the night before. What had been in that punch? Not the simple fruit juices the man Lyle had given him to believe, that was certain. It was like Lyle to think it a fine jest to make a man of God drunk.

No, Jephthah corrected himself. He must not cast the blame where it did not belong. If he had been thinking of his mission instead of being wiled away by sinful luxury and gluttonous pleasures, he would have noticed what was in the punch. That was what came of straying from the path of righteousness. Strictly speaking, he should not have been going to Yorktown at all; there was God's work to be done at the Community of Saints, which should take precedence over the needs of one foolish little girl who had been in trouble ever since the day she arrived at his father's house.

He blamed himself for going to get Hilary, blamed himself again for getting drunk, and staggered out of the house without a word to the anxious servants. The right thing, he thought, was to forget about little Hilary and go back to the Community, where he was needed. Had he told the girl to come to Virginia? He had not. One would have thought that after all these years she would have outgrown her childish notions about marrying him when she grew up. She should face the consequences of her own actions. If she really wanted to join the Community, she would find her own way there. And if she didn't, he would be infinitely more comfortable and better off. The last thing he needed was a troublemaking redhead stirring up dissension among the Saints.

But when he was mounted, Jephthah felt an uncomfortable twinge of conscience. The girl had been left in his father's charge. Now that Ebenezer Graham was dead, it was his own duty to take up the responsibility for Hilary. At least at the Community he could watch over her and see that she was kept from a life of sin. Left to her own devices at Yorktown, would she not follow in her mother's footsteps? Everyone knew that redheaded women were lascivious by nature. It was his plain duty to bring the girl to the New Community of Saints, where her soul could be preserved by a life of prayer and self-denial.

Sighing with the new burden he was taking on, Jephthah turned his horse's head toward Yorktown. The one crumb of comfort available to him was that in acting so resolutely against his own inclinations, he must surely be treading in the paths of righteousness.

It did not occur to him that Patrick Lyle might be treading the same path, a little ahead of him.

"Jonathan Norris? Oh, dearie me!"

The fat woman called Mistress Johnson chuckled and rocked back and forth in her chair, wiping the tears of laughter from her eyes with the corner of a gleaming white starched apron. "Such a time as that poor old toad had, him with his spindly shanks sticking out of his own servant's breeches, and me thinking he was lying his head off. But it all came right in the end."

Stifling her laughter as best she might, she told Patrick the story of how Dickie had fooled both her and Norris to make his escape with one of Norris' horses and a purse full of money, leaving such a tangle behind him as took a full day of her time and the justice's to straighten out.

"Never," she said, going off into reminiscent giggles, "never will I forget the face of that man when I read the description on Dickie's papers of indenture and told him it fitted him to a T—bow legs, sly face, and all! An' me never guessing he was a gentleman born, not that you coulda guessed it from the language he was using."

"Never mind Norris," Patrick said with restrained desperation. "What of the girl?" The people through whom he'd traced Norris' movements had mentioned the red-haired slip of a girl who was so thin and feverish, and his worry for Hilary increased with each day he spent on the chase after her.

"Oh, she's not with me anymore," the fat woman told him.

"Dead?" Patrick felt the blood draining from his face, leaving the world queerly outlined in sharp, bright shapes of black and white.

"Oh, no, dearie me," Mistress Johnson chuckled. "The justice bought her off me an' Norris both, so glad was he to have her. Paid me back what I'd given Dickie by mistake, and then paid Norris for her again, so all came right in the end. But oh, Lord, never if I live till a hundred years will I forget that poor man's face when he found out he'd been sold!" She went off into a paroxysm of tearful giggles, clutching a stomach that vibrated like a tansy pudding.

Patrick pressed a coin into her hand and got directions to the justice's house. As he left, he couldn't help glancing over his shoulder, though reason dictated that Jephthah could hardly have caught up with him yet. With any luck, the man would give up as soon as he discovered that he'd missed Hilary's ship in Yorktown.

"What do you mean, the *King's Grace* isn't here?" Jephthah stared at the white-sailed ships in harbor and squinted to con the names painted

on their sides. Hilary had distinctly said that
she was coming to Yorktown, hadn't she?

"Discharged the last of her cargo and sailed
yesterday," the potboy from the tavern con-
firmed. He swelled out his chest, enjoying the
opportunity to impress this country bumpkin
with his knowledge of the port. "But if you're
looking for one of the redemptioners, I can tell
you where to find records of the sale—for a
consideration." He crooked one hand invitingly
and winked at the tall stranger in black.

"Lead me there," Jephthah promised, "and
you shall be richly rewarded."

Five minutes later, Jephthah was poring over
the same ledger that Patrick had studied the
day before, while the potboy looked in disgust
at the tract on infant baptism that Jephthah had
pressed into his hand as a reward.

"The Northern Neck." Jephthah groaned at the
thought of pressing his bony horse all that weary
distance, and groaned again to think that he
might have to suffer the extravagance of buying
an extra bucket of oats to give the beast strength
for the journey. But it was an obligation. Who
knew what kind of trouble Hilary might have
gotten herself into by now? She was always a
wayward, disobedient child; he had no faith in
her ability to settle down as a good servant,
obeying her master's wishes as she ought.

"Master Anthony, *no!*" Hilary slapped Anthony Hazelrigg's hand away and bent over the
table she was supposed to be dusting. She
rubbed the dustcloth back and forth over the
polished surface, head bent, praying that she

would hear the welcome sound of Anthony's retreating footsteps. Ever since she had come to serve in his uncle's house, he had given her no peace with his fondlings and touslings and impudent suggestions. As much as possible she tried to avoid being caught alone with him, but this morning when she'd been sent to dust the library he had entered behind her with an alacrity that made her suspect he had planned the situation.

"You'll grind the grime into the face of that table, the way you're rubbing so hard," Anthony pointed out. He came up behind her and leaned his hands on the table on each side of her. "Let me instruct you." His foxy, grinning face peered around her shoulder and his chin nestled into the curve between neck and shoulder.

"Let me *go*, Master Anthony," Hilary threatened, "or I'll scream!"

Anthony chuckled knowingly. "Scream away, m'dear. I've given good orders no one's to come near this wing of the house till I say so."

Hilary kicked backward and felt the edge of her wood-soled shoe hit something with a satisfying clunk. Anthony yelped and jumped back as Hilary wriggled around to the other side of the table. If she hadn't been so afraid, the sight of Anthony hopping up and down on one leg and nursing his bruised shin would have been richly comical.

"All right, Mistress Hilary," Anthony threatened, "if you want it rough, I've no aversion to doing it that way!"

Hilary ran for the library door, but even as

she flung it open his hand came down over hers. For a moment she thought she could get through, but as Anthony exerted his superior strength, the door slowly began to swing shut again. Her arm ached with the tension of resisting his push, and still it was not enough.

"Hilary!" The peevish cry came floating down the broad stairs and through the open door. "Hi-la-reee! La, I don't know what's become of that provoking girl!"

Anthony's hand dropped away from the doorknob as his aunt appeared at the landing, a vision of lace-ruffled dishabille, her scanty graying blond locks hanging about her face. "Hilary!" she called again. "It's time to do my hair!"

Hilary bared her teeth at Anthony and slipped through the library door. As a parting gesture of defiance she shook out her dustrag in his face and left him sneezing.

To Hilary, the wearisome task of standing behind Sophia Hazelrigg in her chintz-ruffled dressing room and arranging her hair was a blessed relief from evading Anthony. At least he didn't yet have the impudence to pursue her into his aunt's dressing room—and if he did, she thought with a gurgle of laughter, Sophia would crack him across the knuckles with her fan for disturbing the delicate work in process.

"La, girl, I don't know what you're laughing about!" Sophia complained. "You are making me look positively hagged this morning! Can't you get the rolls even, like this picture in the *Ladies' Magazine*?" She pointed to a drawing of a blooming young lass in her teens, whose masses of rich strawberry-blond hair were piled artfully on either side of an oval face dominated by large dark blue eyes. "She has just my coloring," said Sophia, patting her own faded tresses and affixing a patch at the corner of one watery gray eye.

Hilary nodded without speaking and bent to the task of combing out and rearranging the offending roll, trying to give an appearance of bulk to the fine, limp hair. Perhaps if she twisted it a little more to the side . . .

"You're pulling my scalp out!" Sophia complained. Crack! went her ivory fan over Hilary's knuckles. "Now, do try to pay a little more attention to your work, dear child," she said with a simper at her own reflection in the mirror.

Hilary suppressed a sigh. Now that she thought about it, perhaps Anthony wasn't so bad. At least she could hit him back.

Even Sophia Hazelrigg professed admiration for the final result, achieved over an hour later with the help of curling tongs, false hair, and strategically placed knots of blue silk ribbon.

"La, child, you do have neat hands," she said, turning this way and that to admire her reflection in the mirror. "Where did you learn to dress a head so finely?"

"I used to help my mother," Hilary replied. "She was on the stage."

Crack! Hilary's knuckles reddened under another blow from the fan. "Odious brat!" Sophia screeched. "How dare you liken me to a whore of a strolling player! Likely you're a whore too— Lord knows what filthy diseases you've brought into my house!"

Hilary clenched her hands on the back of the chair. She'd hated her laughing, selfish mother enough on her own account, but never, even in her thoughts, had she used such language for her. Being an actress didn't make her mother—or herself—the equal of sluts like that cockney Bet. Enough, she thought from a distant corner behind the rage that consumed her, was enough. She would take no more abuse from the members of this spoiled, selfish family.

"If you say one more word about my mother," she said, spitting the words out one by one, "I'll take your hair down and never, never work on it again."

Sophia's hands flew up to protect the towering concoction. "You'd not dare!" she squeaked in a voice made high and trembling by fear. "And here I was going to take you to Williamsburg with us this winter, to dress my head for all the balls . . . and I was going to give you my own good petticoat of pink tiffany with only two spots on the hem—"

A bellow from downstairs interrupted Sophia's frantic cataloging of all the favors she had intended for her new maidservant. "Pembroke!"

Hilary blanched. That was Justice Hazelrigg, and he sounded angry. Had Anthony been complaining to him? She thought briefly of bruised shins and a face full of dust this morning, his wig thrown into the rose garden last week, a bucket of sudsy water spilled over gleaming new shoes. There was plenty of evidence of what she'd done to Anthony, and not a mark on her to testify to all the furtive gropings and attempted kisses she'd been subjected to.

"Pembroke!"

Hilary curtsied with shaking knees. "By your leave, Mistress Hazelrigg?"

She hurried down the broad curving stairway, heart pounding. Justice Hazelrigg was standing in the downstairs hall, thumbs hooked into the pockets of his new blue broadcloth waistcoat, one foot tapping impatiently on the floor.

"Into the library, Pembroke," he ordered before her feet had touched the last step on the staircase.

Hilary hesitated. "Sir, if it's about Master Anthony, I can explain—"

"What the devil does Anthony have to do with your betrothed?" Justice Hazelrigg broke in. "The gentleman's waiting in the library for you. And I must say, Pembroke, if you'd told me you had a lover who'd ride halfway across Virginia to buy you back, I'd have left you at the inn and never bothered with the transfer of indentures. Not seemly for a gentleman to be buying and selling servants in a sennight. Makes me look like a damned tradesman!"

Hilary hardly took in the last of Justice Hazelrigg's speech. All her attention was focused on the closed library doors. Behind those carved oaken panels was Jephthah, the man she'd loved since childhood, the man she'd come across an ocean to marry. He'd come for her as she always knew he would. She ought to be happy. But suddenly she was terribly afraid to walk across the hall and push the oaken door open. Her hands felt cold. She couldn't even remember what Jephthah looked like. What if she didn't recognize him? No, that was stupid. There wouldn't be anybody else in the room.

"Well, girl?" Justice Hazelrigg barked. "What are you waiting for? I thought you'd appreciate the luxury of a private interview before he took you away. We've already transferred your indentures."

Hilary forced her stiff legs into another curtsy. "Yes, sir," she said. "Thank you, sir." With a heart like lead, she walked slowly across the hall and turned the handle of the library door. Once she went in there, once she was with Jephthah, the long journey would be over. And when next she saw Patrick—if ever she did—it would be as a married woman, safe from his advances.

Which was as it should be, and what she wanted.

And once she saw Jephthah, she'd be able to remember how much she loved him, and it would be all right again.

Hilary thrust open the door with a determined push and marched into the room with a smile on her face, ready to greet her betrothed as he deserved. In the middle of the room she stopped and looked around in bewilderment. There seemed to be nobody here.

A lithe, dark-haired figure in a dusty coat that matched the deep rose color of the library curtains slowly uncoiled itself from the window seat and came forward, hands outstretched. Dark eyes sparkled with a sapphire glint under slanting black brows.

"Patrick," Hilary breathed. She blinked in surprise. The dimly lit library, with its thick curtains drawn to keep sunlight away from Justice Hazelrigg's precious books, seemed to be full of exploding iridescent bubbles that danced around her. There was a singing in her blood that almost deafened her; she felt like laughing and dancing and at the same time her legs were so weak they would hardly hold her up.

"I thought Jephthah—"

"I took the liberty of a slight exaggeration," Patrick said, "to procure a private interview with you." He stepped forward quickly and caught her around the waist as she swayed toward the table. "Hilary? You've been ill?"

"Not anymore." But she wondered if her fever might not be returning. The warm strength of Patrick's hands supporting her sent intoxicating shivers through her, making it hard to think or speak. "I'm all right now," she insisted.

"And you always will be." As he spoke, he pressed kisses on her neck, her cheek, her forehead. "I'm going to take care of you, Hilary, I'm never going to let you go. It was all a mistake. I wasn't going to let you be sold, but you wouldn't speak to me and I thought—"

"I was ill then," Hilary interrupted him. All this time she'd ached with the knowledge that he thought she'd refused even to say good-bye to him. "I didn't know until later—"

"Thomas was supposed to get you off the ship," Patrick interrupted in his turn. "Damn fool! I'll kill him when we get back to my lands. Slowly. If you knew what I've been through these last three weeks, thinking you were married to Jephthah."

Jephthah.

The name was like icy water dashed over her, killing the intoxication of Patrick's nearness and leaving her coldly sober. Slowly, painfully, Hilary withdrew from Patrick's arms. She leaned against the table for support. "I'm promised to Jephthah."

Patrick's eyes flashed with dark blue sparks. "You're made for me. Did Jephthah come for you at the ship? Did he trace you halfway across Virginia to get you back? No, he had your letter in time, but he was too busy saving souls to come and get you when you needed him."

"You've spoken with him?"

Slowly, as if unwilling, Patrick nodded. "Is that all you care about?"

No, but it was what she ought to care about, if she were a decent woman. Hilary tried to breathe through the ache in her midsection. "Patrick. I can't go with you. I'm promised to Jephthah."

"I asked," Patrick said, soft and dangerous, "what you cared about, not what childish promises you might have made." He stepped toward her, hands light on her shoulders, holding her with no force at all, and this time she was entirely unable to break away from him or even to look away from the sapphire eyes that searched her face.

Hilary tried to recapture her sense of belonging to Jephthah, but all she could see or know was Patrick. Jephthah was a distant memory of her childhood, a stern yet protecting presence; Patrick was here and holding her warm and alive in his arms, and when next he kissed her she'd have no resistance left at all. She looked up at him, helpless and knowing all the useless love she felt must be written on her face.

"Jephthah . . ." She breathed the name out on a despairing sigh, ready to admit that it was no longer the magic incantation that kept her safe.

Patrick's face hardened into lines that aged him before her eyes, and his hands dropped away from her shoulders. "My God," he said, almost inaudibly. "You care that much for him."

It was a statement, not a question, and his turning away gave Hilary time to compose her face. If Patrick had not guessed that all the light in her eyes was for him, she would never tell him. She would not betray Jephthah. She would not be a light woman like her mother, deserting the one person who loved and needed her for a man who offered nothing but pleasure.

"I love him," she said, and her voice sounded thin and reedy in her own ears, entirely unconvincing. "I will wait for him."

Patrick swung around on his heel, catching her by surprise. "Then I'll take you to him."

"Patrick!" A lump caught in Hilary's throat. "You'd do that for me?"

His eyes shifted away from her. "I'm going that way anyway," he mumbled. "My lands lie to the south, near the boundary where the New Community of Saints has settled. And in any case," he finished on a firmer note, "I've no intention of leaving you here with people who abuse you."

Before she knew what he was about, he caught up her left hand and his lips brushed the red marks on the back where Sophia's fan had struck her. The feather-light caress sent a secret thrill of forbidden pleasure tingling guiltily through Hilary's hand and arm. It was wrong, surely it was wrong to feel so when a man barely touched you! I'm a light woman after all, she thought giddily, like my mother. The Grahamites were right to keep me out of temptation. Jephthah . . .

Patrick turned her hand over and pressed his lips against the blue vein that marked the smooth whiteness of her inner arm. Dark curls tumbled from the tie at the nape of his neck and spilled over her arm, clinging, twining themselves around her.

The library door crashed open and Hilary jumped back with a guilty start. Patrick rose from his bow in a smooth, fluid motion that left him facing Anthony Hazelrigg with no outward sign of embarrassment.

"Thought I'd find you here," Anthony said with a jaunty wave of his hand. "When m'uncle said a gent named Lyle had called for Hilary. Everybody likes to . . . talk . . . with Hilary in the library, don't we, love? Or haven't you told him about our little encounters? He might not be in the market for slightly soiled goods."

Patrick slowly shook the ruffles of lace back from his wrists. Moving very deliberately, he stepped between Hilary and Anthony. "She's told me nothing," he said. "She doesn't have to. Nothing you could do would soil her." He reached past Anthony to close the library door with a soft but definite click of the lock. "It could only incline me to take an extra payment out of your hide." One hand darted forward and seized Anthony's collar, holding him up on tiptoes while Patrick closed the other fist and blew softly on his knuckles. Anthony's sharp, pointed chin dropped.

"There's n-nothing to t-tell," he stammered. "Odds, man! Would I lie to you over a serving wench? If she's worth that much to you, take her and welcome." His eyes rolled toward Hilary. "Tell him I never touched you," he pleaded.

Patrick glanced toward Hilary as if to ask for confirmation. "Did he annoy you in any way?"

"N-nothing to signify," Hilary stammered.

"That means he did." Patrick raised Anthony to the level of his own face. "Stand up straight, man, I don't like hitting a little fellow."

"Patrick, please, can't we just go quietly?" Hilary begged.

Patrick released Anthony's collar, and his heels hit the wooden floor with a thud. "All right, darling girl, if that's what you want."

He dusted his hands ostentatiously and took Hilary by the arm. "I've an extra horse outside for you. Oh, I never thought . . ." His face took on an absurd expression of exaggerated anxiety. "Can you ride?"

Hilary nodded.

"What a relief," Patrick said solemnly. "Here I was afraid I'd have to carry you back all the way to my plantation in my two arms."

"I'll wager it won't take you long to have her there," Anthony drawled from the corner into which he had retreated, "a sweet little piece like that one, and warm and willing into the bargain—"

Whatever else he'd meant to say was cut off by a gasp of terror as Patrick seized him by the

collar. "On second thought," Patrick said pleas-
antly, "I couldn't think of leaving without paying
you as well as your uncle for Hilary's indentures." His left hand darted forward and sank
into the pit of Anthony's stomach, leaving him
bent over gasping and wheezing. "With interest," Patrick added almost tenderly, bringing
up his right hand into the pointed jaw that
Anthony stuck out so invitingly. Staggering back,
Anthony slid down into the corner, his legs
outspread and his head lolling. Patrick stepped
carefully over Anthony's legs and bowed to Hilary. "I believe that concludes our business here,
Mistress Hilary. Shall we go?"

9

The house was a graceful curve of whitewashed boards and green shutters against the darker green of the forest and the hazy blue of the mountains in the distance. As she reined in her weary horse in the drive, Hilary felt an inexplicable sense of homecoming.

She tried to reason herself out of her immediate love for the plantation, reminding herself that this was only one more stop on the long road south that led to Jephthah and the New Community of Saints. It was the last stop— Patrick's plantation. She wouldn't be staying here; it was a mistake to delight in the graceful lines of slender white pillars springing upward to support the roofed portico, the sparkling windows with their many panes of real glass, the smooth stretch of neatly scythed grass sloping down to the river.

"Like it?"

There was undisguised pride in Patrick's voice

as he waved one hand toward the house. Hilary guessed that he'd planned the approach carefully, along a curving tree-lined carriage drive that opened out at the last minute to give this prospect of the house and the forest behind it. As he watched, undisguisedly anxious for her reaction, he looked young and absurdly vulnerable. She felt an aching desire to reach over and take his hand.

"It's . . . beautiful," she said at last, knowing how lame the words sounded. Patrick's face lit up as though she'd paid him a polished compliment.

"You like the way the columns on the portico slant just a little outward? Gives a sense of proportion. And the gabling over the end windows carries out the line, don't you think?"

Hilary was certain of something else about this elegant house in the wilderness. "You designed it yourself," she said, almost accusing. "Didn't you?"

Patrick ducked his head with a shy grin. "I did that. Not entirely the useless gentleman, hmm?" He dismounted and reached up to swing Hilary off her horse. The firm clasp of his hands around her waist filled her with the same dismaying intoxication that his every touch caused. She sucked in her breath and stared off at the horizon while he lifted her gently down.

"Not entirely useless," she said with an effort at composure. "I'm reserving judgment about the gentleman part." She lifted the arm that was casually snaking about her waist and dropped it back at Patrick's side.

"Ah well," he said with one dark brow raised,

"it's only gentlemanly to show appreciation of a lady's charms, don't you think? And we've a custom of welcoming visitors here in Virginia." Before she could move to fend him off, he'd caught her face between his hands, planted an impudent kiss on her lips, and released her so quickly that she'd no time to protest.

"You're very warm to a one-night guest, Mr. Lyle," she said. "Perhaps it's as well I shall be going on tomorrow." To meet Jephthah. But for some reason she didn't want to say that. What was the need? They both knew where she was going, anyway.

Patrick looked away and fussed with the bridle of his horse for a moment. "Yes . . . well, I need to talk to you about that, Hilary. Ah, Thomas!"

A large young man with dull blue-gray eyes under a tousled shock of light brown hair came around the building and put out his hand for the horses' reins. "Glad to see you, Thomas. Everything all right in the stables? . . . Good, good. I want you to give Halfbreed some extra oats tonight, all right? He's had a long hard journey." Patrick stroked the brown gelding's nose and went on interminably giving instructions to Thomas. Hilary waited patiently, wondering what had come over Patrick. Anybody would think he suddenly didn't want to talk to her, the way he was going on and on about the business of the stables. And he was keeping his back to her, too, rudely, as if he didn't even want to look her in the eye.

Finally he ran out of instructions for Thomas. The tall young man bobbed an awkward bow,

collected the horses' reins, and led them along
the winding drive toward the stables. Patrick
turned back to Hilary, all smiles now, and offered her his arm. "You must be tired. Pardon
me for keeping you waiting. Will you come
inside now? There's a chamber upstairs set aside
for your use."

Hilary planted her feet solidly in the springy
green turf of the lawn. "About tomorrow." Patrick had avoided talking about Jephthah all
through the long days of their journey southward, and to her shame she'd cooperated. It
was so much pleasanter to ride along the narrow roads and let Patrick tell her about Virginia.

The first night she'd been a little nervous,
stopping at an inn with him; but he'd kissed
her hand and let her retire alone to a room
where she sank into a wide feather bed thicker
than her body. The next night they'd stayed
with some of Patrick's friends named Rosier,
who'd welcomed them and got up an impromptu
dance for the night without ever asking how
Patrick Lyle happened to be escorting her south.
And now they were at Moonshadows already,
and Patrick hadn't used one word amiss to make
her worry about his intentions.

It seemed he was bent on wiping out the bad
impression he'd made on board ship. And indeed, Hilary had to admit to herself, he'd done
so. She couldn't have asked for a pleasanter
companion or a happier journey. Only one thing
could have roused a quarrel between them. She
knew he didn't like Jephthah, and she had no
intention of listening to any more vicious gossip
about him. So it had seemed simpler not to talk

or think about the end of the journey. Until now. "About tomorrow," she said again.

"Er. Yes." Patrick's glance slid sideways. "Hilary, wouldn't you like to rest here for a few days? It's been a long journey and you must be tired."

She was. All through this next-to-last day she'd been dreaming of a tub with warm scented water—something told her those luxuries wouldn't be lacking in Patrick's house—for a chance to wash and mend her worn, faded dress, for a soft feather mattress to envelop her aching body. But Patrick's evasiveness alarmed her. It was time, Hilary considered, to get some things clear between them. Because she hadn't spoken of Jephthah for the three days of the journey, did he think she'd forgotten him? She blushed to think how nearly that was true. It was much too easy to look at Patrick, and laugh with Patrick, and forget that there was a man in the back country whom she'd loved since childhood.

"You said you would take me to Jephthah."

"So I will," Patrick promised. He put one hand up and rubbed the back of his head in an unconscious gesture that revealed his own weariness. "The thing is, Hilary, I'm not just exactly sure that Jephthah's at the Community just now. He was leaving when I last saw him. For . . . a journey of some duration."

Hilary raised her brows at this halting statement. Patrick's eyes were darting from side to side like fish in a barrel, never once holding her with that steady blue gaze she found so difficult to escape. If betting weren't sinful, she would have wagered all her worldly goods that he was lying. "How convenient of him. You don't want to take me to him, so you suddenly decide that he's traveling. Why didn't this come up before we reached your house?"

"And what would you have done if I'd told you at the first?" Patrick retorted. "Stayed with Anthony? You trust him more than me?"

"I could have found work at the inn!" Hilary's cheeks were burning and she felt her hair escaping from the tight knot in which she'd bound it, the individual strands curling around her face. "You lied to me. You said you were taking me to Jephthah, not luring me into your . . . your den of iniquity!"

She flung out one hand at the house, whose gracious, welcoming curved lines now seemed like arms outspread to trap her.

Patrick threw his head back and burst into hearty laughter. Hilary stared at the strong column of his throat, vibrating with merriment, and heard the ridiculous overstatement of her last words for herself. Of course Patrick's house wasn't a den of iniquity. What had possessed her to make such a statement? All the same, something was wrong here, and she wanted to know what it was before she succumbed to the temptation of feather beds and cans of hot water and . . .

With a conscious effort, Hilary wrenched her mind away from images of luxury. She tapped her foot on the soft green turf and waited for Patrick to get over his laughing fit.

"Hawkins!" Patrick shouted when he'd caught his breath. "Hawkins!"

A balding, pudgy little man in a tight waistcoat of striped osnaburg scurried out of the house.

"Hawkins, is Preacher Graham back yet?" Patrick demanded without preamble.

Hawkins' high, shiny forehead wrinkled. "Why, no, Master Patrick, at least I've not seen or heard of him since he dined here that last time, and you know he always stops by here for a meal on his way back. In a powerful hurry he was, too, riding off to—"

"That'll do, Hawkins," Patrick cut him off sharply. "I didn't ask you to give me the reverend gentleman's full itinerary." He made a bow in front of Hilary. "Satisfied, mistress? Your true love is journeying about the colony in search of souls to save, as is his wont. Since my plantation lies just off the only decent road into the back country, he will pass here on his return. By staying with me you assure yourself of being reunited with him sooner than if you insisted on continuing this wearisome journey."

There was an underlying tone of sarcasm in his words that did not escape Hilary, but she began to think she might have deserved his teasing.

"I was foolish?" she hazarded.

Rising, Patrick offered his arm once again. "Mistress Hilary, I would never call a lady foolish." He spoke gravely, but there was a twinkle in the depths of his eyes that only added to her embarrassment. "Let us say rather . . . that your natural and reasonable suspicions of my unworthy self are, for once, unjustified. Will it please you to accompany me into my den of iniquity?"

Hilary's face felt as red as her glowing hair. "Please," she begged. "I never meant that."

"The words," said Patrick with a grand flourish of his feathered hat, "are as if they had never been spoken."

Hilary placed the tips of her fingers on his forearm and sailed into the great house with her head as high as any fine lady's.

There was nothing in Patrick's manner that night to cause Hilary the least uneasiness. He did not even show her to her room himself. After a brief whispered colloquy, Hawkins escorted her upstairs. They passed through a hall cluttered with fencing rapiers and hand-tooled leather saddles and specimens of rocks, and into a pretty bedchamber hung with flowered chintz and furnished with everything a lady could desire.

Hilary exclaimed involuntarily over the delicate beauty of frilled bed hangings and curtains in palest shades of green and delphinium blue. A dressing table of black walnut, the corners and hinges bound with silver, stood against the far wall between two casement windows. Carved ivory trinkets were scattered across the gleaming surface—a comb, an ivory-backed mirror, a fan whose delicate lace tracery reminded Hilary of Sophia Hazelrigg's favorite weapon. A scarf of sea-green silk, its hem edged with silver lace, trailed from a half-open drawer; she glanced toward the tall wardrobe and saw a matching pool of green silk—a negligee or Indian gown, she guessed—half-folded over one of the shelves.

"There must be some mistake," she said, frowning in confusion. "Someone is using this room." Why had Patrick never mentioned a woman living with him? Well, she thought, what sort of a woman lives with an unmarried young man and lets him dress her in sea-foam silk gowns? A woman like my mother, she answered herself, biting her lip at the reminder. Yet it wasn't a thought of her mother that sent a stab of pain through her heart. It was something to do with Patrick—something she shied away from examining too closely. It was nothing to her if he chose to live with a dozen women, she told herself fiercely.

Hawkins coughed and drew a tinderbox from his pocket. "No mistake. This is the room he told me to show you to."

"But, these things . . ." Hilary gestured in bewilderment.

"I understand," Hawkins said stiffly, "the master purchased these things for a young lady he was very fond of. Thought she would be coming here to live with him."

"Oh!" Hilary's vision of a coarse, blowsy woman with light skirts and lighter morals vanished, to be replaced by the image of a sweet young girl wearing Patrick's ring on her finger. The daughter of another Virginia planter, no doubt. She felt rather sad at the thought, and told herself she ought to be glad that Patrick, who was really a good man under his cynical airs, wasn't mixed up with loose women. "I didn't know he was engaged to be married. Are you sure she won't mind my using her things?" Hilary herself minded fiercely, but she couldn't say why.

"No, mistress. I understand something went wrong with his plans."

"She's not coming?"

Hawkins' slight bow was entirely neutral; Hilary took it for agreement. "There is no one but yourself to use the things in this room, mistress. I'm sure the master would be pleased if you would make yourself at home. If you'll excuse me . . ."

Tall candles of a pale green color stood in silver holders on either side of the dressing table. Moving past her, Hawkins lit the candles and Hilary sniffed the air appreciatively. The subtle herbal scent was much nicer than the odor of burning fat released by rushes dipped in tallow, the only lights she had known in the Community of Saints. "My mother had wax candles, I think," she said, half to herself, "dozens of wax candles burning in her dressing room. But they didn't smell as sweet as these."

"No, they wouldn't," Hawkins agreed. "These are made from bayberry, mistress. A local plant. You'd not have anything like it in England." He straightened, the last candle lit, and went to the door. "Elspeth will be up with your hot water directly, mistress."

A moment later a tap on the door heralded the entrance of a black-haired, red-cheeked young woman dressed in a good plain gown of blue linen with a flowered dimity shawl pinned crosswise over her shoulders. Behind her, two girls sidled into the room carrying leather buckets of hot water that slopped over onto the floor when they moved.

"Elspeth Hawkins, at your service, mistress," the young woman introduced herself.

"How do you do?" Hilary felt distinctly uncomfortable at the way everyone was treating her as a guest when she was only a bondservant like them, but she couldn't find a way to stop it. Besides, she rationalized, it was only for a day or two, until Jephthah came to buy her freedom. It wasn't as if she were really Patrick's bound girl. "I'm Hilary Pembroke. And you must be Mr. Hawkins' daughter," she hazarded.

"Wife," Elspeth corrected her, dimpling, "and thanks for the compliment, though I don't know what Hawkins would say! I take care of the house, mistress, but Master Patrick asked me especially to wait on you while you're here, being that there's not time to train these country-bred lasses of ours to wait on a lady. . . . Not on the floor, you silly gowks," she snapped at the girls with their water buckets. "Pour what you've not spilled already into the hip bath! D'you think the young mistress wants to bathe in a puddle on the floor? That's better. Now, clear out, she don't want a lot of people gawking at her while she refreshes herself after the journey!"

Elspeth shooed the girls out with brisk gestures, like a farm wife herding geese across the green, and Hilary seized the chance to drop her tattered dress and kneel in the hip bath while Elspeth's back was turned. She remembered that her mother had made nothing of being naked in the presence of her abigail and hairdresser, but life in the Community of Saints had taught Hilary more modest ways. It would be hard to readjust to the customs of the gentry, even if it were for only a short time.

It must be fatigue that brought tears to her eyes. Hilary bent her head and scrubbed vigorously. While she was crouched in the oval tub, trying to submerge as much as possible of her body without sloshing too much water onto the wide oak floor with its golden finish, Elspeth whisked her old brown dress away and laid out in its stead a shimmering froth of lavender lustring, with pleated elbow-length sleeves that fell open to reveal a contrasting lining of white silk. Hilary dried herself thoroughly when she rose from the bath, afraid of splashing a drop of water on the silk dress. It was much too fine for her. Of course, she remembered, Patrick had bought it for his fiancée, not for a poor indentured girl whom he was charitably helping.

She stroked the lustrous fabric with one longing finger, fearing lest her hands, roughened from salt water on shipboard and scrubbing brushes at the Hazelriggs', should catch and mar the perfect smoothness of the lustring silk. It was the most beautiful thing she had seen since her mother left her at the Grahamite community, and her heart yearned after that beauty. But she couldn't quite bring herself to go down and meet Patrick over dinner in a dress he had chosen for his fiancée.

"I can't wear this," she said with regret.

"Why not? You're wearing the underthings, aren't you?" Elspeth lifted the full white petticoat with a saucy smile, frothing out the knit lace that gathered and weighted it down around the hem. "Be a pity to be so fine underneath and nothing but that old rag on top. Besides, I'll wager 'twill fit as though it was made for you." She stifled a giggle and turned away, but not quickly enough to hide the merriment dancing in her eyes.

"I don't see what's so funny," Hilary said, and tried a woman's reason to persuade Elspeth to bring back her old dress. "That lavender will clash abominably with my hair."

Elspeth only shook her head and giggled between the fingers she held over her mouth. "Wager it don't," she got out between giggles. "Got a good eye for colors, Master Patrick has."

"A lot you know about it," Hilary said with resignation. "Master Patrick didn't pick this dress out for me, but for the woman he was going to marry, and I don't think he's going to like me sailing down to dinner in his fiancée's clothes, even if he did let me use her room."

In the end Elspeth was right. The lavender lustring fitted as if it had been made for her. And though Hilary felt some qualms about the length of white shoulder and curve of white bosom exposed by the dress's scoop neckline, she had to admit that the shimmer of the silk and the coppery gleam of her smooth-brushed hair worked together instead of clashing. She turned this way and that before the mirror, delighting in the discovery that she had as neat a waist and as pretty a shoulder as any fine London lady prinking her way to the theater.

Only when Elspeth held up a branch of green bayberry candles in a silver candelabrum, the better to light her reflection, did Hilary momentarily think a ghost passed through the room—a

laughing ghost with a tumble of red curls, trailing the scent of musk and half a dozen admirers
behind her. Suddenly chilled, she turned away
from the mirror. "I'm ready," she said, and
marched through the cluttered hall and down
the stairs with a flat-footed lack of grace that
did nothing to improve the effect of lavender
silk whispering about her ankles.

If Patrick found any fault either with her appearance or with the manner of her entrance,
he did not show it. Throughout what he de-
scribed as a simple dinner of two or three plain
dishes he was the perfect host, helping her to a
spoonful of ragout of hare, inviting her to take
a little mushroom sauce on her roast chicken,
calling back the quivering green mound of the
tansy pudding in time for her to take a second
helping.

"You need to eat more," he said. "You're too
thin. Have Elspeth take that dress in tomorrow.
The others, too."

Hilary glanced guiltily at the loose waistline
of her dress, where she'd refused to let Elspeth
pin it to fit for fear that pinholes would mar the
perfection of the delicate silk. "Then they might
not fit her," she pointed out.

"*Her?*" Patrick arched one brow, his face perfectly blank. Hilary had to admire the perfect
control of his expression. That was one thing
you had to say for gentry, she thought, they
knew how not to show their feelings. It was
just like that night of the storm when everybody else babbled their prayers, save Patrick
and Anthony, who cracked jokes and made bets
on their chances of survival. And now look at

him! He might have forgotten that he ever had a fiancée.

"The girl you bought these for," she said, painfully aware of her gaucheness in bringing up the subject. "I mean, she might come back . . ." Somehow, though she knew it was rude, she couldn't keep from talking about this other girl. She wanted to know about her. Was she pretty? Was she a great lady? And—strangest question of all—why had she jilted Patrick? A frightful thought rushed through her mind, flooding her face with the scarlet of embarrassment. "She didn't die?"

Patrick smiled. "Die? No. She prefers another fellow to me."

"I don't see why," Hilary blurted out, then clapped one hand over her mouth too late. Decidedly she had had too much wine.

Patrick's smile broadened. "I must confess that I share your good opinion of me. Well, it's not final yet; she may come back. Will you drink to that hope?"

"Of course," said Hilary politely. She raised her glass and took a token sip of wine. The gesture seemed to please Patrick inordinately; his smile took on an added brilliance and his eyes danced with deep blue lights.

"You bring me luck, Mistress Hilary. With your good wishes added to my own heart's desire, I feel certain that my lady will come to me in her own good time."

He must love her very much, Hilary thought, if a simple gesture like drinking to her return could bring blue sparks to his eyes and such a smile to his lips. She rose quickly and ungracefully, scraping the legs of her chair on the uneven wide oak floorboards. "I'm tired," she said. "If you'll excuse me now . . ."

"Of course. You'll wish to rest after this long ride." Patrick rose also and bowed. "I wish you pleasant rest and sweet dreams of your love, Mistress Hilary, as I shall dream of mine."

He did not follow her, but sank back into his seat at the dining table with the glass wine decanter in one hand. She glanced back once and saw him sitting with a glass of dark red wine raised in one hand, apparently lost in contemplation of the blood-hued flames that danced through the wine where a candle's rays fell upon the glass.

Elspeth was waiting upstairs to help her out of the lavender lustring dress and into the shimmering pool of sea-green silk that she'd glimpsed earlier. This time Hilary was too tired and sad to protest. She dismissed the girl and almost immediately fell into a deep, troubled sleep in which confusing dreams kept her tossing on the edge of wakefulness all night.

Waking late to a flood of sunlight, Hilary was glad Elspeth was not hovering over her. She selected the plainest of the dresses in the chest, a brown calico bodice and petticoat printed with a gay little design of golden flowers and red apples. And having done that much of her own volition, she could not resist the temptation of a neat little pair of brown shoes in leather softer than any gloves.

Downstairs, the house was quiet except for the soft humming of Elspeth dusting in the dining room and Hawkins setting out clean serving dishes on the sideboard. "The master?" He looked surprised at her question. "Long gone, mistress. I believe he said something about working in the new fields they're clearing south of the river. If you'd like to visit him, I'll have Thomas saddle your horse and show you the way."

Hilary winced at the mention of riding and barely restrained herself from rubbing the sore spots left from the last three days' exercise. "Thank you, no," she said. "Perhaps I could help you and Elspeth around the house?"

Hawkins looked shocked. "That wouldn't be suitable for a lady, mistress."

"Maybe not, but I'm not a lady," Hilary said. "I'm a bound servant and I need to start earning my keep." There was no telling how long it would be before Jephthah came back to buy her indentures from Patrick, and in the meantime she would feel more comfortable if she weren't forced into a false position. Besides, work might keep her from the thoughts that had disturbed her sleep and carried over into an aching head this morning.

At her insistence, Hawkins reluctantly allowed her to start polishing one of the heavy chased-silver bowls that ornamented the sideboard, but he was clearly relieved when Elspeth suggested that Mistress Hilary might be more help to the plantation in another way.

"It's them new bondservants that Master Patrick brought back from Yorktown," she said. "There's only two or three of them speaks any English at all, and none of the women. And when I try to show them how to set things up proper in the barracks, they stand around me jabbering in that foreign tongue and I can't make out a word of it. But if you came from that same ship, Mistress Hilary, maybe you'd know how to talk to them."

Hilary was surprised and delighted to learn that most of her old shipmates were on Patrick's plantation. She hurried down to the large barracks where they were housed in cramped conditions not much better than on shipboard, and threw herself into Anna Polwhys' arms. Laughing and crying and talking at the same time, they caught up on the news of the last few weeks while Anna's baby waved its arms and gurgled and tugged at Hilary's hair.

"She's a beautiful baby," Hilary said. "What did you name her?"

"Pa-tri-cia." Anna sounded out the foreign syllables carefully. "For Master Patrick. Oh, Hilary, he is a good man indeed! He bought all of us together, so that we didn't have to be separated. The work is hard, yes, and we live like pigs here." She glanced around the crowded barracks, where every inch of floor space was covered with straw ticks and the redemptioners' bundles, giving an eloquent sniff. "But Jer says that Master Patrick says we are to have two new long houses like this one—I don't remember what he calls it. Before the winter. And next year, the men can build cabins for their families if they want to, and he gives building tools and nails."

Anna had to go to the kitchens then, to help in preparing the midday meal of soup and bread for all the field workers, and Hilary followed her with the baby Patricia in her arms. A stout woman with pink cheeks and gray hair above a starched linen apron greeted the Cornishwomen with a volley of signs and shouts. Here Hilary was at last able to feel that she was of some use, in translating the cook's brusque orders to the willing but confused women. The bustle and noise made her feel dizzy, but she managed to remain on her feet and keep rocking Patricia while the other women hurried around the great fireplace with its three iron caldrons hung from hooks, pulled flat yellowish cakes of bread out of the bake oven on wooden peels, set up trestle tables outside, and ladled soup into bowls.

The rush of activity was barely over when the men trooped in from the fields. They were hot and sweaty and most of them had blisters on their hands from the unaccustomed work, but they seemed cheerful enough. And there was nothing wrong with their appetites! Mountains of the round yellow loaves disappeared from the tables as fast as the women could carry them there. The meal was almost over before Hilary, squeezed between Anna and Jer Polwhys, broke off a corner of one of the loaves and tasted it for herself. The bread was coarse and sweetish, and it crumbled in her hand like cake.

"They call it Indian bread," Jer put in between bites. "Tastes kind of funny, but it's good and filling. And we get all we want!" He grinned and patted his stomach appreciatively.

The meal over, the men relaxed for a few minutes before going back for the afternoon's work. Some wandered off to smoke, others talked with their wives.

Jer Polwhys took an oddly shaped dark piece of rock out of his pocket. "Went up the river a piece on our morning break," he told Anna. "There's a furnace half-built, and piles of ore. I wonder why the master isn't doing anything more with it? Thought maybe he bought us to work a mine, I did, but all he wants is trees girdled and land cleared." He stretched luxuriously and rubbed his aching back with one hand while Anna examined the rock.

"The silver mines?" Hilary nodded. Patrick had told her of his disappointment while they were riding back from Justice Hazelrigg's. "He told me about that. He had the ore assayed. There's no silver after all. It was a great disappointment to him."

"Silver!" Jer leaned forward and peered at Hilary as if he thought she might be joking. "No, there's no silver there."

"I should think not, indeed," said Anna, passing the rock back to her husband. "What was the land like where you found it?"

Jer and two or three of the other miners plunged into a technical discussion that meant nothing to Hilary. She sat playing with the baby until a banging on the big kitchen triangle announced that it was time for the men to get back to work.

"I suppose I should go back to the great house," she said, rising and handing Patricia back to Anna. "I don't know yet exactly what Patrick wants me to do while I'm here."

"I don't know either," said Anna, serenely

rocking the baby, "but he is a good man. You will come to no harm with him."

Remembering Patrick's lecherous behavior on board ship, Hilary was tempted to contest that statement. But she had to admit that he'd done nothing to alarm her since he found her at Justice Hazelrigg's house. Perhaps, she thought hopefully, the shock of losing his fiancée had reformed him. Not that it made any difference to her, of course. She was going on to live with Jephthah, who was a good man in every way and in no need of reforming.

"Hilary," Jer said as she left, "if you talk to the master, will you tell him that he should not have left that furnace half-built as it is? When winter comes, the frost will get into the mortar and crack it wide open. He should finish the job. And some of us would be better employed at a furnace than with an ax for girdling trees." He rubbed his blistered hands and picked up his ax with a wince.

Hilary promised to bring up the subject of the abandoned furnace if she could, but she did not have very high hopes that Patrick would listen to her.

Patrick did not come back to the great house until dusk was falling. Hilary had spent the afternoon in the library, enjoying the guilty pleasure of dipping into half a dozen books—more than she'd ever seen at one time before—while feeling that she really ought to be doing something more useful. The trouble was that she didn't know exactly what her position here was. Patrick had bought her indentures from the Hazelriggs, but he was treating her more like a guest—like the lady her birth entitled her to be, rather than the working girl life had made of her. Hilary could not be entirely comfortable with such luxury. It raised uneasy reminders of her tempestuous early life, dining off crusts and water one week and champagne and roast swan the next, depending on whether Mama had a new part or a new admirer or some new jewels to pawn.

Hilary reminded herself that this life of luxury would vanish as quickly as the last one had. In a few days Jephthah would come for her and she would be with him, building their home in the wilderness, finding her happiness in a life of hard work and prayer and contemplation.

It all suddenly sounded remarkably unappealing, compared with the immediate prospect of curling up on a cushioned window seat with the volumes she'd taken from the library shelves. Hilary plunged into a translation of Ovid, with guilty glances at the volume of Bray's sermons that she was neglecting for this more enticing fare. The stories of ancient lovers held her entranced and she leafed through the book of translations without noticing the time. The stories in the *Metamorphoses* were succeeded by a translation of a book she'd never heard of, called *The Art of Love*. Hilary's eyes widened as she read Ovid's advice to a young man seeking to win a mistress. She blushed at certain passages, but read on, unable to put the book down.

What if Patrick had taken these suggestions, instead of arrogantly announcing that he intended to make her his mistress? Would she have been able to resist him then? Perfumed love letters, meaningful glances, subtle accidental-seeming caresses . . . Her fevered imagination created vivid images that kept her reading with parted lips and pounding pulse.

As the light from the windows dimmed, Hawkins glided into the room and silently lit the candles in the wall stands. Hilary noticed only after he had gone that the quality of light had changed; she was too absorbed in a passage that she could not quite understand, something about the ways to enhance pleasure by delaying it. The words made no sense to Hilary, but the images of sunlight sparkling on dancing waves, of lovers rocked in a boat carried on the seas of pleasure, kept her enthralled. The warm glow of candlelight was a poor substitute for daylight. She brought her nose closer to the page and continued reading.

A brown hand waved between her eyes and the fine print, bringing her out of her trance with a jolt. Hilary looked up and saw Patrick standing before her. His dark hair was pulled straight back and tied with a ribbon; his face glowed with the effects of the sun, and the full sleeves of his fine lawn shirt stuck to his body with sweat.

"You look as if you'd just come in from the fields!" Hilary exclaimed.

"I have," Patrick said. "Somebody has to show those new hands how to do things. And there's a lot to be done before winter."

He twitched the book out of her hands and his brows went up. "*The Art of Love?* My, my,

Mistress Hilary. Is that a book for an innocent
young girl to be reading?"

"I don't know," Hilary lied, trying in vain to
control her blushes. "I've just started it. Why
don't you give it back and I'll tell you when I'm
done?"

Patrick grinned and tossed the book back into
her lap. "All right. Maybe Ovid can soften your
hard heart where I've failed. Shall I sit by you
and explain the difficult passages? There are
things an innocent young girl wouldn't understand. Or perhaps you understand them well
enough already . . . ?"

Such teasing byplay had kept her perpetu-
ally off balance on the ship, but now Hilary simply folded her hands together and sat up straight
on the window seat. "On second thought," she
said, "it is getting too dark to read."

"That it is." Patrick moved closer, and she
began to feel how narrow and tight a space the
window seat was. His presence was inescap-
able; standing directly before her, hands on his
lean hips, his shirt half-open to expose a tanned
chest that rose and fell with his even breathing,
he dominated her thoughts and her vision. She
found it hard to control her own breathing; the
room seemed too close and hot, and the words
she had just read about the delights of love
burned in her memory.

"If you will excuse me, I should change before dinner," she said, and jumped up.

It was an unwise move. It brought her in
even closer proximity to Patrick, who neither
stepped back nor moved aside. With each breath
she took, the small frill at the neckline of her

gown brushed against his white shirt, and her eyes were magnetically drawn to the tanned V of dark skin sprinkled with crisp black hairs.

Since he hadn't touched her on the journey here, she had forgotten to be on her guard. Now she remembered, all too clearly, the sweet intoxication of his embraces on the ship, and her own weakness. She'd broken away from him once, but would she have the same strength again? She trembled with fear and desire, unable to bear the tension of their closeness. If he put his arms around her now, she would be lost, drawn down into that dangerous thrill of pleasure that his touch provoked, her aching breasts crushed against his chest, his hands firm on her back and legs, his kisses fluttering over the red curls that escaped from her tight modest knot . . .

Still he neither reached out for her nor stepped aside, and with each moment her breath fluttered in her throat and the warm closeness of his body disturbed her more. She would have to brush against him to get out of the alcove, and that would be as disastrous as if he swept her into his arms; one touch, Hilary thought, and she would go up like dry timber struck by lightning. "Please," she murmured. "Let me . . . go . . . upstairs." The words dragged out one by one, heavy and slow as molasses, having nothing to do with the darting flames of temptation that were so quick within her.

"Is that what you really want?" Patrick's low laugh sent prickles along her backbone. "Or do you want me to relieve you of a little of that troublesome innocence . . . Mistress Hilary?"

The gibe released her drugged senses. Without thinking, Hilary swung her hand forward and hit him in the face. He made no move to ward off the blow, though it was strong enough to jar his head backward. "I think you forget," she said, "that I am only waiting here for my betrothed."

Sweeping past him with a disdainful sniff, she made for the stairs, buoyed up by the force of her anger. How dared he, she raged silently, how *dared* he treat her as if she wanted him as much as he desired her!

He let her go without a word, though the back of her neck prickled with a premonition that he was about to call her back—worse, that his hand would fasten on her arm and he would haul her back to demand his own form of payment for that blow. At the door she glanced back and saw him still standing where she had struck him, one hand slowly caressing the dusky red marks of her fingers against his tanned cheek.

Upstairs, safe in the privacy of the green-and-delphinium-blue chamber, she dropped into a low basketwork chair before the dressing table. The oval mirror in its carved dark frame showed her a white face that seemed to float out of the darkness between two tall unlit candles. Her gray eyes glittered with excitement or anger, bright patches burned on her cheeks, and her coppery hair spilled loose about her face in seductive loops and swaths of gleaming silk. The low neckline of her brown calico dress exposed white shoulders and the tops of breasts as sweetly curved as any play actress's treasures.

"Look what he's made of you," she told herself, "and in only a day's time at that. Jephthah, you'd better get here before I succumb to temptation entirely and become a loose woman like my mother."

Which did not explain why, a little later, she swept down to dinner in a dress of jade-green satin whose petticoat looped up to reveal foaming frills of hand-worked French lace, with her hair brushed loose and smoothed into lustrous copper ringlets that glowed like fire against the deep jewel green of the dress and the whiteness of her bared shoulders.

～ 10 ～

Patrick had to conceal his smile of triumph at Hilary's tempestuous exit. In his experience, a woman's final surrender was often preceded by a show of anger. True, he'd feared to affright her by moving too fast. But the effort of pretending that he'd no interest save to deliver her safely to Ranting Jephthah was fast becoming too much for him. And when she stood before him looking so sweet, lips parted and cheeks flushed from the spicy stories she'd been reading—well, what the devil else did the girl expect? Why did she think he'd been at so much trouble to find her and bring her to his plantation? Pure brotherly love for the preacher?

Ever since finding her at the Hazelrigg house, pinched and abused and frightened, Patrick had vowed to himself that he would take his courtship slow this time. He'd no wish to frighten her away. She needed time to recover her strength; time, too, to experience the life he could give her on his plantation and to compare it with the backwoods cabin she was going to.

Time to forget the preacher for a real man of flesh and blood who was longing for her kisses.

And while he waited, he'd told himself, he would treat her like a sister, until she herself tired of the playacting and demanded the kisses that her lips must be burning for. He knew what she felt toward him, he could read it in her lowered eyes, her trembling when he was near, the way her voice quavered out of control. All that he needed now was for her to admit it herself, to get over this foolish prudery and let him make her happy as he knew he could.

The only obstacle facing him was not knowing when Jephthah might be back. Sooner than convenient, he was sure. Patrick wanted weeks for his courtship of Hilary, and he had only days to make certain of her.

Fortunately, she seemed to possess remarkable powers of recuperation. The flushed virago who'd given him such a hearty box on the ear was a far cry from the thin, pale girl he'd scooped out of Anthony Hazelrigg's lecherous hands. Patrick fingered his burning cheek and smiled as Hilary swept out of the room. She felt it, the pull of the senses between them—she'd not be able to resist much longer. Soon, perhaps tonight, she'd be in his arms, warm and sweet and yielding as he'd always imagined her.

And then? Patrick scowled and shouted at Hawkins to have his own bath prepared. He wasn't accustomed to measuring out the consequences of his actions like some pinchpenny

old maid. Take what you want and pay for it—
that was a gentleman's way. What he wanted
was Hilary, and he was ready to pay for the
privilege, settling an allowance upon her, pro-
viding for their children, dowering her when
they parted. A virtuous girl—and whatever
Hilary's past, she certainly put on airs of virtue
now—couldn't be had like one of the lightskirts
in Williamsburg, for the price of a meal or a
jeweled bauble according to her standing. He
was ready to do the gentlemanly thing.

Standing in the narrow hip bath, sloshing
soapsuds and tepid water over the broad oak
planks, he scowled and scrubbed himself vigorously. The thought of parting, of dowering Hilary so that she could find some hearty farmer to
make an honest woman of her, held no appeal
for him. But that was, after all, the inevitable
end of such affairs. Patrick had never had any
trouble parting from his temporary loves with a
smile and a purse of guineas, and there was no
reason why this one should be different.

Of course, he'd never before moved a mistress into his home. Those fine chambers in the
upper story had been built to house his wife
and children, come the day when he was well-
established enough to wed. Moving Hilary in
there would . . . well, make it difficult, when
the time came, to move her out.

Still half-damp from the bath, Patrick thrust
his head into a clean shirt with a fresh-starched
cambric frill around the collar. What the devil
was the matter with him, that he was brooding
over the end of an affair before it had fairly
begun? Succumbing to sober old age before his

time? Anybody would think he was proposing to marry the girl, not to share delight with her for a season until they inevitably tired of one another.

Patrick gave a tight, thin-lipped smile and selected a pair of dark buckskin breeches from his wardrobe. A Lyle from Lyle Hundred, the master of Moonshadows, did not marry an actress's brat. Nor could she reasonably expect it. She would just have to choose: virtuous poverty and an early old age in the backwoods with Ranting Jephthah, or love and delight with sinful Patrick Lyle.

"Cheer up!" he admonished himself. When you put it that way, there could really be no doubt what the girl would choose. Whistling a gay jig tune under his breath, he shrugged into a tight-fitting blue velvet coat with silver buttons and silver braid on the reversed cuffs. He pulled his dark hair back into a queue, contemplated the tie-wig sitting on its stand, and shook his head. More dignity in a wig, but it led to problems toward the end of an evening. His first love, a lush little piece who carried ale in a tavern not far from his father's lands on the Rappahannock, had confided to him that gents always looked funny when they were taking off their breeches, but downright ridiculous when they were removing their wigs and setting them aside with meticulous care.

"Breeches," Patrick confided to the bright-eyed reflection in his shaving mirror, "are unavoidable. But we'll do without the wig, in the interests of simplicity later in the evening."

At his first sight of Hilary in the jade-green

silk, he knew he had made the right decision.
She was ready for him—no question of it: why
else would she have come downstairs in a dress
calculated to drive any healthy male mad? He
could think of nothing but the desire to slip it
just two inches farther off her shoulders and let
those white curves rise free from the green sea
that barely covered them. He'd seen that dress
in the shop at Williamsburg and had ordered it
altered to fit Hilary's slender frame on the spot,
set afire by the thought of her creamy skin and
glowing hair set off by undulating waves of
cool green silk. Now, as she entered the dining
room, her white flesh glowing with its own life
in the candlelight as it rose from the jewel-
toned frame of silk, he caught his breath with
delight at the picture that he'd brought to life.

"Mistress Hilary." He made an elegant bow
and was rewarded, as he rose, by the sight of
her sinking into a curtsy that gave him a new
and entrancing perspective of the shadowy cleft
between her breasts. As she rose, he took her
hand and drew her into the dining room, seat-
ing her beside him instead of across the table
where she'd sat the previous night.

Hilary looked up in alarm as he indicated the
chair beside his, and Patrick reminded himself
to go slowly. By the end of this evening she'd
be in his arms, soft and pliant and begging to
be taken; no need to spoil things by snatching
at her like a greedy child after sweetmeats.

"I thought this would be more companion-
able than shouting at each other over the cen-
terpiece," he said with a smile, "but if you are

afraid even to sit on the same side of the table with me, we can dine more formally."

"I'm not afraid of you," Hilary said, slipping into her chair with a rustle of silks and a defiant tilt of her chin. "Should I be?"

Patrick caressed his bruised cheek with a smile. "Faith, and if I should offend you, you know how to repay the offense, mistress. Never have I felt such a mighty blow from such a delicate little hand!"

He was pleased to observe that Hilary blushed and looked down at her plate. "I . . . I'm sorry," she said almost inaudibly. "It was . . . you said nothing to—"

"It is of no matter." Patrick brushed her stammered apologies aside and lifted the cover of one of the silver dishes. "Ah, a ragout of veal. May I offer you a taste of this dish, mistress?"

He contrived to brush her hand while serving the ragout, but as he pretended not to notice the "accidental" touches, she could hardly take open offense.

"And you'll take a glass of wine with me." His tone brooked no discussion. Hilary barely sipped at the red wine, but Patrick was satisfied for the moment with that much cooperation. "It seems there are more candles in the room to-night, but I believe 'tis only the glow of your hair that deceives me." He ventured to lift one of the heavy, shining ringlets that flowed over her white shoulders.

Hilary flushed and moved her head to get away from his hand. "I went to visit my friends from the ship today," she announced.

"Yes?" Patrick dropped his hand.

"You were kind," she said in a grudging tone, "to buy them all together so that the families would not be separated. Anna asked me to tell you how grateful they are."

Eager though Patrick was to appear well in Hilary's eyes, it stuck in his craw to take credit for an accident that had happened while he was trying to entrap her. "Er . . . well, it's not an act of pure charity," he said, clearing his throat uncomfortably. "I need more hands if I'm to develop these acres that I've taken up." Especially if he was to make a good show of developing them before Governor Spotswood's visit at the end of the month. But he didn't want to confess his financial troubles to Hilary either. The point in bringing her here was to show her what he could give her, not to lay his problems on her head.

"Well," Hilary said, "I think you are kind anyway, particularly since most of them were miners in Cornwall, not farmers. Jer Polwhys said some of them might be better employed in finishing the mining furnace than in clearing fields."

Patrick felt his face darkening with a rush of blood. Was he never to be allowed to forget his folly in the matter of the silver mines? "No work on the furnace! If I set anybody to it, it'll be to tear the damned thing down, that I may forget it ever existed."

"But he seemed to think—" Hilary began.

"Forget it," Patrick advised her, "and tell your miner friends to forget it too. The assayer reports there's no silver in my ore. I don't suppose Jer Polwhys wants to contradict a scientific report, does he?"

Hilary shook her head. "No, he said there was no silver in the land and he couldn't think what had led you to think so. But he thought—"

"Spare me what he thought." Patrick picked up his knife and stabbed into a slice of smoked ham. "I'm through with such folly as silver mines and all that truck. There's no shortcut to riches in this land—they come through work, clearing fields and planting tobacco. I've learned my lesson and your Cornish friends will have to learn the same."

It took him a while to recover his equilibrium, but watching Hilary's hair glowing in the candlelight and the gleam of her white shoulders rising out of the sea-foam border of her dress did much to calm him. How beautifully she graced his table! How much more beautifully she would grace his bed! Patrick congratulated himself on his wisdom in taking his courtship slow this time. Truly he'd learned a lesson over the matter of the silver mines. One mustn't rush into anything. When he'd grabbed at Hilary on the ship, hasty as a lovesick boy, she had naturally repulsed him. Now that he was taking his time, letting her see the life that could be hers if she stayed with him, arousing her senses slowly and subtly, see how much better things were going!

Over the dinner he discoursed easily and fluently on a number of impersonal topics, quite pleased with Hilary's fluttering lashes and scarcely audible murmurs of response. He kept up a light barrage of casual touches on arm or shoulder or hand; she trembled but did not move away. Patrick hoped that his continued low-key assault on her senses was having half the effect on her that it was on himself. If so, he was surprised she didn't throw herself into his arms over the remains of the ragout and the shivering remnants of the Quaking Pudding. He himself was having to clench one hand and drive his fingernails into his palm to remind himself not to grab her and ravish her right there among the dinner dishes.

But then, straight Turkey-work chairs, a mahogany table, and some silver platters covered with congealing sauces and crumbs hardly made the best possible atmosphere for seduction. "Shall we sit in the library for a while?" he suggested. "There's a harpsichord in there, sadly out of tune I fear, but perhaps you might make shift to give me a song for after-dinner amusement."

"I don't play the harpsichord," Hilary said. The few sips of wine she'd taken during dinner were enough to relax her; she laughed at Patrick's momentary surprise. Of course, all the young ladies he'd known were accomplished in the harpsichord and needlework and watercolors. "Really, Patrick! You know how I grew up. Did you think Ebenezer Graham gave me lessons in music in between hoeing the potatoes and feeding the pigs?"

She stood up and her foot caught in one of the flounces of lace with a sharp tearing sound. "Oh, no!" Hilary gasped. She knelt and felt for the damage with anxious hands. How could she ever replace such a fine piece of hand-worked lace? A single one of the flounces with which this petticoat was trimmed cost as much as her indentures. "I think I can mend it," she announced with relief. But the small incident had sobered her. She stood, more carefully this time, and looked at Patrick with grave gray eyes. "You see," she said, "I'm a masquerader. I don't belong in this fine house, pretending to be a lady and wearing your fiancée's clothes. And you know that. Why are we playing this game?"

Why indeed? thought Patrick. But it was not time for the game to end, not while she was in so serious a mood. "I don't know what you mean," he said. "I offered you shelter for a few days while you wait to decide what you will do next."

"You mean," Hilary corrected him, "while I wait for Jephthah."

Patrick ground his teeth. Always Jephthah! By God, he was beginning to wish this black-coated ghost who haunted him would show up. Perhaps when Hilary saw the man she'd promised herself to, she would begin to understand what a mistake she'd made. As it was, how could he hope to compete with a ghost?

"As you wish," he said. "Just remember, that's not your only alternative." Before she could interrupt or argue, he took her hand and pulled her across the hall into the library. "Come on. Sit down. I've a fancy for some music after dinner, and if you don't play, I shall."

There were distinct possibilities in sitting down beside a pretty girl on a music-bench, putting one arm around her to turn the pages of the music, and using the other hand to correct her

fingering. Patrick had exploited those possibilities often enough. But Hilary spoiled everything by marching across to the window seat
and plunking herself down amid the books she'd
collected there that afternoon. Patrick suppressed
a curse as he looked at her, sitting so primly
in that outrageously low-cut gown. Bastions
of books, serpentines of sermons, moats of
memoirs—was ever a fortress so well defended?
Suppressing a sigh, he sat down at the harpsichord, flicked the lace of his shirt frills back
from his wrists, and launched into a melting
song of love:

> I attempt from love's sickness to fly in
> vain,
>   Since I am my self my own fever and
> pain . . .

He glanced sidewise at Hilary between verses.
By the end of the song he was pleased to see
that her prim upright posture had relaxed somewhat, while her flushed cheeks and dreamy
eyes showed that the music was working its
spell on her.

> For love has more pow'r and less mercy
> than Fate,
>   To make us seek ruin . . .

A long tinkling shower of notes with the right
hand, and his voice raised to repeat the last
phrase with all the throbbing tenderness it
deserved:

To make us seek ruin, and love those that
hate.

As the last bright notes died away, he lifted
his fingers from the keys and sat waiting for her
response.

Hilary giggled.

For a moment Patrick couldn't believe what
he was hearing. But it was a definite giggle.
No, more of a snicker.

"You find my singing funny?" he inquired.

"No," Hilary said, "the song." She looked up
at him, all wide-eyed innocence. "Well, it doesn't
make any sense, does it? When people really
love each other, they don't sing about fever and
pain and hatred."

"No?" Patrick dropped the lid of the harpsichord with a crash, stalked over to the window
seat, and swept a dusty armload of books to the
floor. He sat down on the square dent that
Bray's Sermons had left in the cushion and rested
one arm casually behind Hilary. "Instruct me in
love, then," he said silkily, "since you know so
much about it."

Hilary flushed and would have jumped up,
but Patrick's free hand clamped down on her
arm and held her to the seat. "Go on," he said,
still in the same silky, dangerous low voice. His
finger traced the swelling outline of her breasts
above the jade-green silk ruffle that dipped so
dangerously low in front. "You know how to
drive a man mad, and how to slap his face and
run away when it gets too hot for you. Am I to
believe that's all you know?"

Hilary found it difficult to breathe. She dared

not look down at the finger that was tracing such tantalizing lines of desire on her flesh; but when she stared straight ahead, she looked into a mirror that faithfully reflected Patrick's dark head bowed above her own shoulders. His arm behind her came closer, holding her around the waist so that she could not move without a struggle.

"Please let me go," she said, and heard her own whisper as something weak and unavailing against the dark power that Patrick asserted. "This isn't right, Patrick."

"Nothing was ever more right," Patrick contradicted her. "Hilary, my love, my darling girl, you know we're made for each other. Why do you keep fighting it? If you didn't want me to do this, why did you wear such a lovely, tempting, revealing scrap of silk to dinner?" One hand slid boldly under the border of jade-green silk and closed over her breast with a firm, irresistible touch that set her senses whirling. He moved his fingers back and forth slowly and she felt her nipple stiffening against his palm as though it had a life of its own. His other hand was on her waist, moving lower now to caress the smooth curve of hip and thigh, and her body was taking fire and defying all her attempts at control.

"No . . . no, it's wrong," she murmured, weakly moving her head without escaping the kisses that choked off her words and made her lips throb almost painfully. Why was it wrong? Hard to remember, when his hands were awakening new and dazzling vistas of delight within her body, flooding her with pleasure too intense to bear. "Jephthah . . ." Jephthah was far away, a distant faceless figure out of her past; a symbol to which she'd clung all these years. What did Jephthah have to do with the living, breathing warmth that was Patrick holding her close as she longed to be held? "You have a fiancée."

Patrick's low laugh sent shivers through her body even as she responded against her will to the hand that had somehow found its way under her skirts, gliding up and down her leg with long tantalizing caresses. "No, I don't."

"She might come back," Hilary insisted through the sensual maze that confused her thoughts. "Remember, we drank to that."

"Hilary, there's no fiancée," Patrick insisted, and the urgency of his words broke through her dazed brain. "There never was anybody but you, darling girl. Why do you think these dresses fit you so well? I bought them in Williamsburg for you. I was coming back to the ship to get you, my love. I never meant to leave you, even for a day. Thomas was supposed to buy your freedom from the captain."

It was too much for Hilary to take in all at once. She fastened on the one fact that seemed of most importance. "No fiancée."

Patrick nodded. His arms were around her now, and she was lying against his shoulder while he looked down at her with that intense blue gaze that she never could resist. "Hilary, how *could* there be anybody else for me?" he whispered. "From the moment I saw you on the ship, I've not been able to think of anyone but you, my love, my only dear delight. Hilary, darling girl, don't torture me any longer. Admit it, this is where you belong."

In Patrick's arms. Yes, this was where she'd wanted to be all along, and all her rages against him were only ways of fighting the inevitable end. She understood that now.

Hilary raised her hand to his face, trembling, feeling the slight roughness of his clean-shaven jaw and the firm pressure of his lips and the crisp curls at the back of his neck as if she were exploring a new and wonderful world. "Patrick . . ." she murmured.

It was all she could say. Apparently it was enough. In any event, she'd no chance to say another word, for in the next breath he was devouring her, his mouth fastening greedily on hers, hands boldly exploring where the layers of silk and lace fell away from her body as if by magic under his touch. Hilary's breath came raggedly as new and unfamiliar sensations coursed through her body. No, not unfamiliar. That time on the ship . . . in Patrick's cabin . . .

She'd slapped him and run away from him then. "But this is different," she said aloud, thinking to herself that he'd spoken words of love before.

"Different from whom?" The ruffles of silk around her bodice slipped away with a quiet rustle of surrender, and Hilary felt a new bolt of pleasure stabbing through her as Patrick's mouth fastened over the rose-tipped peak that his hand had caressed into throbbing awareness. Drowning in that sea of delight, she could not speak or move, except to throw her arms around Patrick's neck and hold him closer to her. Nothing could be more wonderful than this, the warm tug of his lips and flickering circles of his tongue teasing her uncontrollably.

"Hilary, my love, my darling girl." His arms were under her, wonderfully strong and safe, and she was floating in midair in a rustling green cloud of silk. She caught sight of them in the mirror across the room as he stood up with her in his arms. There was that strange girl with the wanton face again, her eyes large and shining, her coppery hair falling in gleaming swirls over the breasts that her loosened bodice framed. And Patrick's dark face above hers, looking down at her with all the love and tenderness his eyes had shown only in her dreams. Hilary sighed with pure happiness and pressed her face into Patrick's shoulder, ready to let him carry her anywhere, do anything with her.

The creak of the library door opening made her look up in surprise. How had Patrick opened the door, when both his hands were holding her?

The lean black-clad man who stood in the open doorway was a figure from her nightmares, Ebenezer Graham risen from the dead to smite her for wickedness.

"I see you had better success than I in the search for my promised bride."

The face was Ebenezer's, but the voice was Jephthah's, deep and full and resonant. Hilary clutched Patrick tighter and buried her face against his body, willing the vision to go away. Burning tears of shame forced their way through the eyes that she kept squeezed tightly shut. This could not be happening, not now, not when she and Patrick had just discovered each other!

Patrick's arms slowly released her and she slid to the floor on shaking legs. Head bowed, she fumbled with her bodice, trying to draw the crumpled silk ruffles up into some semblance of decency. Her face burned with shame and she could tell from the corner of her eye that Patrick was standing between her and Jephthah, as though to shield her.

"It seems it did not take you long to seduce her," Jephthah went on inexorably.

Cheeks flaming, Hilary forced herself to stand beside Patrick and face her accuser. "Jephthah?"

The grim dark man nodded. Now that Hilary looked more carefully, she could trace the lineaments of the young man she remembered under the weather-beaten, lined face before her. He was too thin, as always, and he looked very tired. And unutterably sad. A wave of remorse rushed through Hilary. While she'd been enjoying herself in shameful luxury, Jephthah had been wearing himself out in the Lord's work, only to find out that she was betraying him in the arms of a man who stood for everything he despised!

"Jephthah, he didn't seduce me," she said hurriedly, before her courage could fail her. "That is, it's not what it looks like . . . I mean, nothing happened. Yet," her incurable honesty forced her to add.

Jephthah gave a weary nod. "Hilary, your definition of 'nothing' and the Lord's are poles apart. Do not seek to excuse your sin with unworthy prevarication." He sighed. "I had hoped to find you in Yorktown, but I see you could not wait for me there."

Hilary felt a flash of anger. How dared Jephthah talk as though she'd just walked out of Yorktown into Patrick's arms? Didn't he understand that she'd had no choice? That when he didn't arrive to pay her passage, she'd been sold as a servant?

"Although," Jephthah added with another sigh, "I can hardly blame you for succumbing to the wiles of a practiced seducer. It is in your blood. 'For her mother hath played the harlot, she that conceived them hath done shamefully.' Hosea Two: Five. If I had heeded—"

His speech was cut off by Patrick's fist crashing into his jaw. Jephthah swayed like a tall tree in a storm but did not fall, nor did he raise a hand to return Patrick's blow.

"Speak of Hilary like that again," Patrick threatened, "and I'll take you apart in small pieces and feed you to my hogs!"

"Threats do not deter me from speaking the truth as I find it," Jephthah replied, somewhat indistinctly, as his jaw was swelling. "I see a wanton—"

Patrick sprang forward again, but Hilary got both hands on his arm and held him back in time to weaken the force of his blow. "Patrick, no!" she cried. "He's right. I forgot everything. It's all my fault." She couldn't bear the look of pain in Jephthah's eyes. What a way to repay the only man who'd been kind to her in the Grahamite community—to let him find her in Patrick's arms, flushed and disheveled and wan-

ton! She deserved everything he said of her,
and more.

When Patrick relaxed, she let go of him and
went to Jephthah. "Jephthah, can you forgive
me?"

"It is not for me, who am another weak and
sinful being, to forgive you, but for the Lord,"
said Jephthah. His hand caressed her tumbled
curls and for a moment Hilary felt as safe as
when she was a little girl and Jephthah had
interceded with his father to spare her another
whipping. "Pray to him to save you before it is
too late. 'Repent, and turn away your faces
from all your abominations.' Ezekiel Fourteen:
Six."

"I do repent," Hilary pleaded. If even Jephthah
cast her off, she would know she was wicked
beyond the hope of salvation.

A guttering candle flared up in a sudden blaze
of light, sending deep exaggerated shadows over
Jephthah's lined face and making him look like
the replica of Ebenezer Graham reproaching a
sinner. "Pack your things," Jephthah said a-
bruptly. Hilary felt like weeping with relief. So
he didn't reject her! "We will leave for the New
Community tonight. I will not stay longer in
this house."

Leaving tonight! The words struck Hilary like
a blow. In her embarrassment at having Jephthah
see her like this, she had forgotten that his
arrival meant her parting from Patrick.

"You may leave, if you will," said Patrick.
"Hilary stays." He held out his hand to her.

With all her heart she longed to go to him.
But had she not betrayed Jephthah enough al-

ready? "I'm sorry, Patrick," she said. "Jephthah is right. I . . ." She swallowed hard over the lump in her throat. This was worse than she had ever imagined it could be. "I came to America to marry him." She looked up at Jephthah's patient, tired face. His father would have struck her across the room for daring to speak when the men were deciding her fate. He waited to hear from her unworthy lips whether she still cared for him. How could she disappoint him now? "If you really think it is best, Jephthah, let us go now." The most she hoped for was that he would agree it was too late to ride away tonight. It was already dark. Surely they could delay their departure until morning, giving her a chance to say farewell to Patrick in private?

"I think you don't understand me," Patrick said with a half-smile. "I have not given you permission to leave, Hilary."

"Permission!" Hilary stared at him in shock. "You don't own me."

Patrick raised one eyebrow. His eyes glinted with the deep blue of polished lapis. "No?"

The word was enough to remind her of the papers of indenture that he had taken from Justice Hazelrigg's house. "But I thought . . ." she stammered, torn between anger at being treated like property and shameful relief at the excuse not to go with Jephthah. "You promised . . . I thought . . . you said you wanted me to wait here until Jephthah came, and then . . ." Her voice trailed off helplessly as she tried to remember exactly what it was Patrick had said.

"And then?" he prompted.

"You would release me from my indentures so that I could go with him."

"Release?"

From the blandly inquiring expression on his face Hilary thought he'd never heard the word before. Her knees sagged in relief as she began to understand that, protest as she might, Patrick was simply not going to let her go. At the same time she felt ashamed of her own relief. She ought to go to Jephthah, for he was a *good* man, he'd protected her in England and he'd waited for her here in Virginia and he wanted her to lead a decent life—and, she tardily remembered, in all those sweet love words of Patrick's this evening, there'd been not one word of marriage.

"Liar!" she blazed up at him. "Seducer! It's all your fault. Why couldn't you let me alone—I won't stay with you!"

"Oh, yes, you will," Patrick corrected her. His imperturbable smile made her want to crack something heavy over his head. Flailing behind her, she grasped one of the silver candlesticks and hurled it at him. He ducked out of the way, caught the candlestick in the same motion, and set it upright on a library shelf. A volume of sermons followed, then a calf-bound book with Greek lettering on the spine. He caught both items with the dexterity of a juggler, laughing in a way that infuriated her even more.

"I'll *kill* you," she gasped, and went for a heavy pewter vase that would surely have done the trick, had not Patrick reached her in two strides and caught her arms. His laughter died away and he held her tightly before him, searching her face with that intent blue gaze that made her feel naked and helpless.

"Hilary, trust me a little longer," he pleaded. "It's for your own good—"

"My good? Ha!" Hilary twisted her head around to look at Jephthah. He had withdrawn into the shadows near the door of the library. He must be disgusted by this entire scene. "Jephthah, you have to take me away with you. Don't you see what will happen if you don't?" It was as near as she could come to voicing the fear and longing that possessed her when Patrick held her close.

"I see what will happen if I do," Jephthah's deep sonorous voice offered. "It is not seemly for a man of God to take unto wife a contentious woman. It is best if you remain here and serve out your years of bondage, Hilary. When you have come to mature years, perhaps you will be ready to accept the discipline of the Community."

"Years?"

Patrick grinned over her head at Jephthah. "You're a wise man, preacher. Leave the spitfire with someone who can tame her, eh?"

Jephthah sighed and wiped his forehead with the back of one hand. "The girl was always impetuous, and a sore trial in our house," he said to Patrick. "But I must admit I am partly to blame, for often I interceded to spare her just punishment. 'Foolishness is bound in the heart of a child, but the rod of correction shall drive it far from him.' Proverbs Twenty-Two: Fifteen. If my father had beaten her as often as he wished, perhaps she'd have learned to curb that vicious temper by now."

"Jephthah, you can't leave me here!" Hilary cried in desperation. "Don't you see? He doesn't want me for a servant—he wants me in his bed!"

"I've never raped a woman yet," Patrick said softly.

Jephthah's deep, burning eyes fell on Hilary again. "If you have faith and are strong in the Lord, you will surmount this trial. 'When thou walkest through the fire, thou shalt not be burned; neither shall the flame kindle upon thee.' Isaiah Forty-three: Two. Now go and put some decent clothes on, Hilary. When I say good-bye to you I want to remember you looking like a girl who is fit to join the Community of Saints, not like a brazen harlot."

To Patrick's astonishment, Hilary bowed her head and left the library meekly, without a word of protest.

He was even more astonished when she returned a few minutes later dressed in her simple brown calico day dress, with a cambric neckcloth covering her bosom. The rebellious red curls were braided into tight coils around her head and she kept her eyes lowered while Jephthah gave her a formal blessing. Looking at the dark shadows under her eyes and the pallor of her cheeks, Patrick felt more than ever sure that he was doing the right thing in keeping her. If Jephthah could wreak that much havoc in one visit, transforming his redheaded spitfire into this chastened wench, what might he not do to her spirit once he got her alone in the wilderness!

Unaccustomed feelings of tenderness and pro-
tectiveness stirred in his breast. Hilary was so
young and fragile to be tugged this way and
that between the two of them! Look at her now,
doubtless scourging herself with Jephthah's
words about wanton women and the taint of
her mother's blood, when any fool could see it
had been his doing from start to finish!

The tender feelings vanished in a flash when
Hilary put up her lips for a farewell kiss to
Jephthah. Patrick could not bear the thought of
Jephthah touching her. He stepped between
them, pulling Hilary away, and missed the look
of relief in Jephthah's eyes. "Enough farewells,"
he said. "Preacher Graham has a long way to
ride tonight." He gave Jephthah a curt nod of
dismissal over Hilary's head and held her fast
by his side as the black-coated figure vanished
into the night.

"But where will he sleep?" Hilary protested.
"It's no fit time to start on a journey."

Did the girl not remember that he would have
dragged her as well as himself out on this night
ride, had not Patrick intervened? No, all her
thoughts were on the preacher—curse his black
coat and black heart! "There are cabins between
here and the Community," Patrick told her.
"From my land south it's never been settled
who owns the territory, Virginia or Carolina,
and all the runaway servants and shiftless back-
woodsmen in the colony squat there to hoe out
a patch of corn and build a lean-to. He'll find
shelter enough."

Hilary nodded and gave up her protests, but
she looked so white and forlorn as Jephthah

rode off that Patrick felt another twinge at his heart. The trouble with her, he thought, was that she'd never learned to have fun. A girl of seventeen should be dancing and flirting, not acting out morality plays with some fanatical preacher who didn't even want her.

"Cheer up, dear girl," he said. "It won't be so terrible staying in my house a little longer. I promise not to be a hard taskmaster."

She flinched and looked away from him. "I know what sort of tasks you want me to do," she said tonelessly. "And I'll never comply."

Patrick grinned. What she needed, he thought, was to be surprised, distracted, and kept off balance. It never worked to seduce a woman when she was protesting her virtue; one had to give them a little time to save face. "That's a pity," he said. "I was counting on your help to entertain my guests at the end of tobacco harvest. It's my turn to give the party this year," he improvised wildly. "The planters take it in turns, you see. But I have so much work to do that I was counting on you to organize the party and act as my hostess. If not . . ." He sighed. "I fear I'll just have to default."

Hilary raised clouded gray eyes to his face. "You mean it? You have real work for me to do?"

"I do indeed," Patrick promised. "This is a working plantation, Mistress Hilary! D'you think I buy girls just so they can loll about the library all day reading naughty books and looking decorative? Off to bed with you, now. You'll need your rest, because starting tomorrow I mean to keep you too busy for any more temper tantrums."

Hilary's eyes brightened and Patrick congratulated himself on finding the perfect distraction for her. He sent her up to bed with no more than a chaste kiss on the brow, somewhat surprised at his own forbearance but more than rapaid by seeing the color and animation return to her face.

When he called Carruthers into the library to inform him of the need to send out messengers inviting his neighbors to a party, he encountered somewhat sturdier opposition.

"Master Patrick, this extravagance will be the ruin of you!" Carruthers protested.

Patrick shrugged. "Either I'm already ruined or I'm not. Either way, I'll keep Hilary happy as long as I keep her at all."

"I thought you wanted to make a good showing when Governor Spotswood comes," Carruthers tried. "Convince him that you're a serious planter, that you've given up all that nonsense about silver mines and settled down to bringing in settlers and working the land."

"I have given up all that nonsense about silver mines," Patrick snapped.

"Only to throw more money away pursuing this girl." Carruthers pushed his glasses down and regarded Patrick sternly over the tops of their wire rims. "What kind of impression d'you think it'll make on Governor Spotswood when he finds out you've squandered all next season's tobacco crop to pay for clothes and parties?"

"Ah, but he won't find out," said Patrick with a winning smile, putting his arm around the other man's shoulders. "You'd not peach on me to the governor, would you, Carruthers?

It's but to sit up late a few more nights, making some additions to the financial plan."

Carruthers shrugged and turned away, mumbling something about the folly of young men who threw away good money after bad for a casual love affair.

"Not a casual love affair," Patrick corrected him.

"What else would you call it? You'll not pretend you mean to take her to wife? And what would your father say if you brought home a common bound girl to be the next Mistress Lyle?"

It was the same question Patrick had been asking himself, but coming from Carruthers, it made him feel cheap. What sort of man dithered around about his father's or society's opinions when he found his love? Let the old man cast him off if he would, him with his noble line of cavaliers and his titled Irish relatives.

"My father," Patrick said with the silky-smooth intonation that signaled danger to those who knew him best, "has nothing to do with the matter. Just as he has nothing to do with anything else on this plantation. I love the girl—by God, I do!" he repeated with some surprise, only realizing the truth of his words when he heard them. Of course, that was why he wanted to protect Hilary, to keep her from all sadness or harm; that was why he wanted to kill when he thought of the preacher handling her, why he'd been so reluctant to consider the end of their affair.

"I love her," he repeated, a shade overloud, "and I'm going to marry her." His fist crashed down on the table, setting the silver candela-

brum rocking crazily and splashing a brown
splotch of homemade ink from the crystal
inkwell.

"Yes, by God, that's it. I'll marry her, and
Ranting Jephthah can whistle for his bride!" He
laughed exultantly and clasped Carruthers by
his rounded shoulders. "It's the devil of a clever
fellow I am, Carruthers. With any luck, the
party will be a wedding too, but we'll not give
my guests forewarning of that; I've no wish to
suffer a frontier shivaree. Take tomorrow to
write out the invitations. We can work on the
financial plan some other time. Now I'm for
bed. I've a plantation to clear and a bride to
win."

Carruthers watched his young master's jaunty
departure with a worried frown. Aye, you'll
have to be the devil of a clever fellow indeed,
he thought, if you mean to win your father over
to this match. And in this mood, young Master
Patrick was likely to announce his engagement
at the party, before they knew how the governor would rule on the taxes, before they knew
how much he was likely to need his father's
help to save Moonshadows. If only he could
postpone this foolish party! Still, an order was
an order, and Master Patrick would be justified
in sending him packing if he didn't write out
the invitations as specified. And there'd be no
sleep for him that night, concerned as he was
over the young master's folly; he might as well
get to the task.

Carruthers blotted up the puddle of brownish
ink, seated himself at the library table, and began scratching out invitations to a party at Pat-

rick Lyle's plantation. After he'd written out
several bidding letters and folded the sheets
into envelopes, a smile crept over his worried
face. Master Patrick had ordered him to write
out the invitations, yes, but he hadn't specified
where they were to go. A hint addressed to the
right quarters might bring somebody down here
who could talk some sense into the lad. Carruthers added a postscript of his own to the
just-finished letter, folded the sheet, and addressed it to Patrick Lyle Senior, of Lyle Hundred on the Rappahannock.

~11~

Hilary woke the next morning with an undefined sense of guilt. For a moment, as she snuggled into her luxuriously soft feather bed, she couldn't figure out where she was or what was wrong about it. Then, with an unbidden rush of memory, the scene in the library came back to her in blistering detail. With a little whimper of shame she burrowed beneath the covers, reliving the moment when Jephthah had walked into the library to find her shameless and half-naked in Patrick's arms. How hurt he must have been! No wonder he'd been cold to her.

But that wasn't the worst of it. Hilary's cheeks burned as she recalled that she had actually enjoyed having Patrick put his hands on her. Even now, remembering the warm tug of his lips on her breast, she could feel her nipples standing up and aching for more kisses, while a deceitful warmth throbbed downward through her body. She couldn't blame Patrick for seducing her. No, she'd wanted him to do all those things to her, and more too—just what, she was not exactly sure, but she thought she had been about to find out when the door opened.

Head under the pillow, Hilary submitted her conscience to a ruthless self-examination and came to the conclusion that more than half her anger the night before had been, not because Patrick started to seduce her, but because he hadn't finished.

"Jephthah would have been right to cast me off," she moaned into her pillow. "I'm a wicked, wanton female, just like my mother, and nobody can trust me." But Jephthah did trust her—even with the evidence of her shameless behavior right before his eyes! Why else would he have left her here with Patrick while he prepared their home? He wanted to give her a chance to redeem herself, that was why! He had said as much last night. If she were really good enough to be his wife, she would prove it by resisting the temptation of Patrick's presence and keeping herself pure until he returned.

Full of reforming virtue, Hilary jumped out of bed and combed out her long red braids with vigorous strokes that pulled at her scalp and brought tears to her eyes. Damping the rebellious curls with water from her ewer, she dressed her hair in neat tight braids that wound primly around her head, and selected a modest dove-gray dress from the riches in the wardrobe.

A last glance in the mirror left her doubtful about the success of this reformed image. The morning sun streaked across her braids and turned the prim ring of plaits into a blazing coronet of fire over her brow; the dove-gray cambric was so soft that it molded perfectly across the firm lines of her breasts and hinted at the smooth curve of hips and thighs under her petticoats. Well, Hilary thought, there were limits to what a girl could do about her appearance, and at least she was trying to look dull and virtuous.

Halfway down the stairs she stopped. Dull and virtuous. She'd never coupled the two words before Patrick's irruption into her life. Patrick was a bad influence, Hilary thought, and she was going to work very hard and not let him corrupt her thinking anymore in the two weeks while she waited for Jephthah's return.

The hard-work part of the resolution worked perfectly. Hilary discovered that there was rather more than she'd ever imagined to planning a party in the backwoods of Virginia. "We'll need to set up extra beds in the upstairs hall," Hawkins told her, explaining that travel was so difficult in Virginia and people lived so far apart that most of them came the night before the party and stayed until the day after.

"The downstairs hall, of course, will be cleared for dancing," Elspeth added with a disgusted glance at the clutter of masculine gear, broken-down chairs, and scarred tables with which Patrick had littered the long room.

"You'll need to give me the menus now, so I can send to Williamsburg for spices and special flavorings," the cook put in.

All of them knew perfectly well how to entertain the neighborhood gentry and could have done their tasks without Hilary's lifting a finger; but they also knew that the young master wanted Miss Hilary kept too busy to think for a few days. And they knew exactly how to accomplish that, too.

"Roast suckling pig! Cattail fluff to stuff extra mattresses! Where do we put Master Patrick's second-best fencing foils? It's too late in the season for flowers—how shall we decorate the hall?" Toward the end of that first exhausting day, Hilary plopped down on a leather-covered sofa that had yet to be moved out of the downstairs hall and fired off another volley of questions at Patrick. At sight of his bemused face she giggled.

"That's only a sample of what I've been getting all day," she warned him. "You're wise to stay out in the fields, where you're safe. Hawkins and Elspeth are determined to turn the house upside down to make this the grandest party ever given on the Nottoway."

"They seem to have made a fair start already," said Patrick, perching gingerly on the arm of the sofa. "Er . . . you haven't seen the trunk with the brass studs in the lid, by any chance?" He indicated an empty corner where the trunk had once stood.

Hilary frowned, trying to remember. "I think it's in the library . . . No, that was the carved oak chest. Maybe we put that trunk in the dining room. No, I think it was carried out to one of the outbuildings. I hope there wasn't anything in it that you need urgently?"

"Only my good hand-painted cards and the

ivory dice," said Patrick with resignation. "Never mind, I suppose they'll turn up later."

Hilary regarded him severely. "You shouldn't be gambling."

Patrick raised his hands palm-upward with a smile. "Now, who said there'd be any money wagered? A contest of wits, Mistress Hilary, a test of skill, a little harmless amusement for the hardworking planters. Surely even Ebenezer Graham himself, God rest his canting soul, couldn't object to that."

"Painted cards are the devil's picture gallery." Hilary repeated the familiar words uncertainly. Somehow what had seemed obvious and clear when she lived in the Community now seemed . . . well, a little excessive.

"Ah, well," Patrick sighed, "I suppose the dancing will be enough to entertain my guests. Now, don't tell me." He raised one hand, the long powerful fingers spread out as if to ward off her objections. "Dancing's sinful too—right? Though I seem to recall you enjoyed that evening at the Rosiers' well enough."

Hilary blushed, remembering how her foot had tapped to the lively music and how she'd let Patrick and the youngest Rosier boy take turns in pulling her through the moves of the lively country dances. Already, on the journey from the Hazelrigg house to Patrick's plantation, her moral fiber had been weakening—she could see that now. No wonder she'd been such easy prey to Patrick's seductive moves. But it was all going to be different now. That resolve stiffened her spine and kept her head

high in the face of Patrick's mocking, questioning smile.

"I was wrong to dance then," she told him.
"I'll not do it again."

Patrick shook his head in bemusement. "What's
come over you today, sweet Mistress Hilary?
Here I thought we were making some progress
toward turning you into a normal girl who knew
how to laugh and have fun, and now I've got
Mistress Propriety back on my hands."

"If you mean that I've come to my senses,"
Hilary snapped, nettled by his casual denigra-
tion of the standards she'd been raised to respect, "you're absolutely right, and high time
too! It shouldn't have taken Jephthah's visit to
show me the error of my ways. I may have to
serve out my time here, but I'll certainly not
countenance gambling and dancing and drinking at any party for which I'm the hostess!
What if Jephthah came back then and found me
dancing?"

"Or laughing?" Patrick inquired silkily. The
dark flush on his high cheekbones and the blue
glitter deep in his eyes were the only outward
signs that he was losing his temper, but they
were enough to make Hilary shrink as he rose
and stalked toward her. "Or enjoying yourself
like a normal human being? No fear, mistress!
I'm tired of trying to thaw that splinter of ice
you have in place of a heart. I was going to give
you time to come round of your own accord,
but if you won't give me even an inch, then I'll
have to show you again what you really want!"

She backed away, knowing that when he put
his hands on her she would be lost. What had

Jephthah said? Be strong in the faith, and the fire shall not burn you. But the flames were leaping in her already, from the closeness of Patrick's lithe masculine body and the sweet memory of his caresses. "I can't do it," she moaned. The call of her mother's blood was too strong within her, the sensual laughing impulse that would drag her down in the end.

"Never fear, darling girl," Patrick said with a dangerous glinting smile that belied the sweet reason of his words, "I'll do all that needs to be done. And it won't be as terrible as all that."

No. It would be sweet, and fiery, and wonderful, and when it was over she would be a bad woman like her mother, and Jephthah would never, never forgive her or understand how she could betray him so.

"You'll do *nothing*." Hilary folded her arms and glowered at Patrick. "I'm not having it. You take me to Jephthah now, or I'll . . . I'll . . ." She faltered, envisioning the miles of dark untrodden forest and swamp that stretched southward from here.

"Yes? And just what will you do if I don't agree to your ultimatum, mistress?"

But Patrick himself had said that there were cabins scattered through the back country, places where Jephthah could shelter on his way to the Community. Where he could ride, she could follow on foot. "I'll leave by myself! I don't need your help to find the Community. I don't need you for anything at all, Patrick Lyle, and I'll thank you to let me go my own way from here on."

It was impossible to face the blaze of anger

that lit his eyes. She turned away to gather up a random handful of the junk that was still scattered around the hall, the scraps of harness and tools and fowling pieces and broken fire irons and God knows what that Patrick had littered the hall with over the course of the years. His hand on her arm stopped her as she rose with her hands full of leather harness pieces from whose ends the broken buckles jingled merrily.

"You may not need my help," he said, "but you do need my permission before you go anywhere, mistress. Or have you forgotten that I hold your indentures?"

"I won't stay with you." Hilary clasped the unwieldy load of straps and buckles to her chest like a shield and glared up at him.

"Oh yes you will," Patrick said softly. "You're my bound servant, Hilary Pembroke, and you'll stay exactly where I put you and do exactly what I tell you."

In your bed, for instance. The thought flashed through Hilary's brain with such intensity that she could hardly believe she hadn't spoken it aloud. She knew that was what this whole fight was about.

"No!" She took a step backward, away from the flash of blue deep in his eyes, the hands that reached for her body. "I don't belong to you, Patrick Lyle, and I'll not stay with you, so there!" He followed her slow retreat, and in a panic she swung out at him with both her hands full of the heavy leather harness. One of the straps swung up and the buckle caught him on the chin.

"Spitfire!" A trickle of red showed on his face

where the buckle had landed. He caught her wrists and turned them easily until her fingers opened and the harness landed on the floor in a jingling tangle of straps and buckles. "Someone should have lessoned you long ago."

His fingers were still closed on her wrists, holding her so close to him that the tips of her breasts brushed against his loose white shirt and she could feel the heat of his body. In a moment he would put one hand behind her head and bend his own head to kiss her—she could read the intention in his eyes—and once his lips found hers, she would be weak and pliant in his arms as always. Words were her only defense now.

"You see," she panted, still struggling weakly to get away from him, "you're just like all the rest of them. Anthony Hazelrigg . . . Norris the soul seller—you want just one thing, don't you, and if you can't get it by fair words, you'll use force. I suppose if I try to go to Jephthah, you'll placard me a runaway? That's a cheap way to keep a woman, Patrick Lyle, but I should have known better than to expect fair dealing from the gentry. Why don't you just put an iron ring around my neck so everybody will know I'm your slave? It would make the relationship so much clearer, don't you think?"

Patrick heard her out without moving a muscle, either to clasp her or release her. His face paled beneath the tan as she went on lashing him with angry words, and his tightly compressed lips went almost white. Exhausted and out of breath, Hilary stared up at him, fearing she knew not what from this strange pale man whose dark eyes glittered with sapphire sparks.

He pushed her backward onto the sofa with one hand and crouched over her before she could recover herself. Hilary kicked out at emptiness as he dodged away from her feet. "See how you like . . . having it clarified!" he panted.

One hand ground her shoulder into the sofa and his knee pinned her thrashing legs down in a welter of gray cambric skirts and lacy white petticoats. He held her down with his whole body, the lean muscular thighs pressing against her legs, the rapid rise and fall of his chest crushing her breasts.

For a moment, Hilary was afraid, but then, as suddenly as he had cornered her, Patrick lessened his grip.

"Calm down, Hilary," he said, rising and releasing her.

He grinned as if the brief tussle had entirely restored his good humor. Well, why not? He'd won, hadn't he?

He started toward the stairs. "Now, if you'll excuse me, I'd like to wash and change clothes before dinner."

Still struck by Patrick's violent reaction and her own feelings of helplessness, Hilary decided she too had better change before dinner.

Wearing a clean gown for dinner, Hilary marched downstairs.

The separate building that housed the kitchen was a bustle of activity as the women cleared up after the field hands' meal. In the cool blue light of early evening the banked hearth fires shone warm and friendly on the white arms of girls with their sleeves rolled up to scrub the cooking pots, on copper milk pans, and on the dull red gleam of unbound hair falling down into one laughing woman's face.

"Tie your hair back, you slut," the cook was raging as Hilary slipped into the kitchen. "D'you want to float those lousy red hairs of yours in the master's dinner?"

Hilary recognized London Bet's defiant laugh and blessed the distraction as the cook lumbered toward Bet with one meaty hand upraised.

"Lord love you, mistress, but you do look in a fine state. Why, only a few moments ago I thought I saw you racing upstairs looking like you'd set the house on fire."

Suppressed snickers behind her told Hilary that the story of her tussle with Patrick had already reached the kitchen. She stalked out without looking back.

Footsteps pattered behind her, and a strong musky scent enveloped her nostrils as a hand clasped hers. "Best apologize to him, duckie," Bet breathed in her ear. "They do say Patrick is a hard man to deal with when his temper is roused—and he's in the right, you know."

"He is not." Hilary jerked her hand free of Bet's and plodded on without looking at her. Bet darted in front of her and planted herself on the path, arms akimbo, forcing Hilary to look up at her.

"Oh no? I suppose your indentures don't have the same terms as everybody else's? You're bound to him for four years or until he says different, duckie, and if you've any sense you'll do as he tells you. I don't see what you're complaining about. Don't you live soft in the great house, with dresses of silks and satins like any fine lady? Don't you think you owe him something for all you're taking?''

"I don't want to live like a fine lady," Hilary protested. "I want . . . I need . . . oh, you don't understand! Let me pass!" She tried to go around Bet, but the other woman darted to the side and blocked her way again.

"That I don't," Bet agreed. "You telling me you'd really rather have the preacher than Patrick? Honey, I've seen 'em both, and take it from one who's sampled the market"—she winked—"your Patrick's a proper man and one as any sensible lass would be glad to have in her bed."

"Sensible in your terms, no doubt," Hilary retorted. "I happen to have somewhat different standards."

Bet grinned. "Oh, aye, I know that, ducks. You just watch that your 'different standards' don't leave you out in the cold. There's plenty as would be glad to take what you're passing up." She patted Hilary on the shoulder. "Now, I'm a fool to be ruinin' my own chances with the master, for I know as long as you're around he'll never look at an old slattern like me." She preened and thrust out her ample bosom, unconsciously contradicting her own words. "But I hate to see a girl throwing away a good chance like this. Listen, play your cards right, he might even marry you."

"How condescending of him," Hilary said, opening her gray eyes wide. "I fear I might be overwhelmed by the great honor. Now, if you please, I have to get back." She pushed past Bet and marched back to the great house.

Dinner was an uncomfortable meal. Every bite Hilary took seemed harder than the last to swallow, and every sip of wine was made bitter by the amused glances Patrick kept giving her. He behaved as if she were not there at all, keeping up an easy flow of conversation with Carruthers about estate trivialities while Hilary glowered across the table at them.

She made it through dinner and retired to her room, pretending not to hear his muttered comments about girls who preferred sulking to accepting their situation. But once alone in the delphinium chamber, she realized that sleep would be next to impossible.

She waited at her dressing table until light steps coming upstairs, two at a time, signaled his approach. Then she opened the door a crack and called to him in an undertone.

He was swaying a little and smiling foolishly, as though he and Carruthers had been sitting too long over the wine; but when he heard her voice he straightened, bowed, and tried to restrain the smile twitching at the corners of his lips. "At your service, mistress. What is your desire?"

"I promise not to run away."

"Do you now!" Patrick came toward her, hands outstretched, and she felt a primitive thrill of terror. She backed away into the safety of her room, and he followed her. The tall bayberry candles twinkling on the dressing table woke sparks of merriment in the blue depths of his eyes.

"Now, now," he chided her, "how can I free you if you won't stand still?"

"Free me! To go?" Hilary felt an unpleasant jolt at the pit of her stomach. So he didn't really want to keep her here. It was just a game he'd been playing, and she'd pushed him too far with her wild accusations. In an uncomfortable moment of self-realization she acknowledged that she'd felt quite safe in ranting and raving and threatening to run away—safe that Patrick wouldn't let her do any such thing.

Patrick raised Hilary's hand to his lips and held it there for a long time. She felt her pulses responding to the gentle pressure of the prolonged kiss; she tried to draw away, but he wouldn't let her. "You'll stay with me," he murmured into her fingers.

"Yes . . . no . . . as long as I have to . . ." Confused, Hilary tried again to free herself. But somehow his hands had slid up toward her elbows now, drawing her so close against him that she could smell the spicy herbal scent of his breath and feel the movement of his chest. "You've been chewing mint," she identified the aroma.

"Don't change the subject." His hands were behind her shoulders now, and she had to raise her head to look at him. That was a mistake, for he was looking at her exactly as a man gazes on a woman he loves, tender and desirous at once, the look she'd dreamed of night after night. His gaze was making her dizzy, and there was no place to hide. "You'll stay . . . as long as you want to."

"It's the same thing." Hilary found it hard to move her lips. They felt swollen and sensitive, tingling with expectation of what was surely to come: the heat of his mouth on hers, the raw strength of his embrace sweeping her away. She shut her eyes and tried desperately to think of Jephthah.

"Is it?" Patrick's voice was low and tender and amused. "We'll see if we can't make something more of it, shall we?"

She looked at him then, her lashes fluttering, and saw his face coming nearer with the slow inevitability of the dreams that tormented her nightly. "No! That's all there is!" She twisted in his grasp, trying to turn her head away and knowing herself foredoomed to failure. Gently, inexorably, his hands forced her backward step by step until she felt the soft edge of the feather mattress against her hips. Then his lips descended, not on her mouth, but brushing flickering, tantalizing kisses all over her neck and shoulders and cheeks. The sweet agony of his touch robbed Hilary of strength and sense together. She felt her legs trembling, unable to support her any longer, and did not protest when he lifted her onto the bed.

"Give up, spitfire," he whispered in her ear. "You're mine and you know it. How many more ways do you want me to prove it?" He caressed her through the apricot silk and she felt her body outlined in fire where he touched her.

"Please . . ." Hilary tried to whisper through

a mouth suddenly dry, but no sound came. They were locked together in a moment of still- ness. Hilary stared at the lips so perilously close to her face, at midnight-blue eyes shaded by the black locks that had fallen forward over his forehead, and knew herself the prisoner of some- thing other than force. It was her own desire that held her there, helpless under the weight and pulsing warmth of his body, while one hand moved slowly across her shoulder and cupped her breast and left her trembling with a weakness like floodwater rushing over the fen- lands in spring. He rubbed the nipple back and forth, stimulating a new and sharper desire that stabbed through her and left her open to his will.

What was the use of fighting? He was so much stronger than she in every way. He knew what he wanted, had been sure from the very first, and she was always torn two ways. Be- tween Patrick and Jephthah, temptation and righ- teousness. She was too weak to fight any longer. There was nothing for her but Patrick, leaning triumphant over her now, his hands hot on the unprotected skin left bare by her disarranged skirts. Her head fell back against the soft feather bed and she waited in a trance of longing for his mouth to cover hers, for him to begin drink- ing the delights he had won from her.

"Please . . ." she whispered again, and he gave a soft exultant laugh that made her fully conscious of the depths of her defeat. His fin- gers were playing tunes on the white skin of her thighs, her body was flowering and cresting under him, the whole scene might have been arranged by him to show her how little worth all her protestations of virtue had.

"No."

The word came from some reserve of strength she had not known she possessed. But Patrick ignored her, and she was shamefully glad of it. He had slipped to his knees now, kneeling on the floor and pushing the white foam of her petticoats aside with slow reverent hands. Hilary knew that she should push him away now that he was no longer holding her down, but he had laid his lips where his fingers stroked before, and she cried out in surprise at the intensity of the new sensation.

"Patrick," she repeated, trancelike, reaching to push his head away and hypnotized by the crisp wealth of his black hair springing under her palm. "Patrick." All that she was seemed to be centered there, pulsating under his mouth, while he lapped at her sweetness and the vibrations of delight spread out from that center in an endless series of rippling circles. The strength and sweetness together swelled to new heights, until all she was aware of was the aching need that only more of Patrick's touch could satisfy. She arched against his lips, moaning deep in her throat, and his tongue thrust forward to pierce the last veil between her and that molten white-hot pleasure that had been hovering just out of reach.

In the aftermath of that bolt of passion she knew nothing but the trembling in her limbs and the sighing of her own breath. Patrick was over her again, lips warm on her cheek, hands holding her close, and she came back slowly from that little death to the warm safety of his embrace.

"Hilary, my love, my darling girl." He reared above her now, fumbling with his breeches, and a primitive stab of terror raised Hilary from her sensual dream.

"No! Let me go!" Striking out blindly, she twisted away from him, and this time he didn't reach to take her back, but knelt with his hands dangling by his sides and a wounded look on his face.

"Hilary?"

"I don't want you to . . . I told you I wouldn't . . ." she panted. "Patrick, you know I'm betrothed to Jephthah. And you're just amusing yourself with me. Please don't play games with my life!" *Or my heart.* But that was already his. Thank God he didn't know it, or she'd never get away from him. Her only chance was to conceal the extent of her weakness.

Patrick's smile, thin-lipped and dangerous, hurt her eyes. "Indeed? Seems to me you just played a fine little game with me, mistress. Tussle and moan and let me pleasure you, but when I want to love you the way a man loves a woman, then suddenly I get Mistress Propriety back again. You weren't so prim and proper when I had your petticoats up around your ears and my head between your—"

"Stop," Hilary all but shrieked, covering her ears, "stop, stop! I didn't know what you were going to do . . . I couldn't stop you . . ."

Patrick's hands rested very lightly on hers. Obeying the gentle pressure, she let her hands fall, looked up at him, flinching in anticipation of the cold anger she'd seen in his eyes before. But now he only looked tired and sad. "No? It seems to me," he said gently, "you stopped me fast enough when you really wanted to."

"I didn't know," Hilary repeated, squeezing her eyelids shut against the hot gush of tears that threatened to overwhelm her. "Please, Patrick, try to understand. You do this sort of thing all the time. I don't. How was I supposed to know what you were going to do?" The tears would no longer be denied; they were hot and stinging in her eyes, cold salty trails over her cheeks. She waited in an agony of suspense for Patrick to walk out the door or to lash her with more angry words, and she didn't know which she feared more.

Instead, a hand gently wiped away the cold trails of tears on her face. "You really didn't know, did you." It was a statement, not a question, and his voice was gentle. "I'm sorry, Hilary. I thought you were playing the same game I was. I thought—"

"You thought," Hilary finished for him, "that I was like my mother. An actress's brat! A redheaded, lascivious woman!" Her mouth twisted in pain. "Oh, I've heard the taunts often enough. Don't you see, Patrick, that's what I would have become, if it weren't for Jephthah. Ebenezer Graham didn't want to take me in, but he spoke up for me. If not, what would I have done when Mama abandoned me, but go on the streets? He saved me from that. I owe him—"

"You owe him your gratitude," Patrick interrupted her. "Not your body."

Head high, Hilary faced him and ignored the tears that still found their way down her burning face. "I owe him everything. And I will go pure to him."

Patrick's hand jerked and Hilary started back, knowing fear for a moment. His shoulders sagged and he turned away, releasing her. "Oh, don't be afraid of me," he said in low, tired tones. "I'll never hurt you, my darling girl. Not knowingly. I seem to have done enough harm," he said, "in my stupidity and ignorance. Wanting you so much, I convinced myself that you cared for me too, and would be willing to come to me."

He believed she didn't care for him? The thought squeezed Hilary's heart painfully. "Patrick, it's not—" she began.

"It's all right." He walked to the door and opened it. "If it interests you," he said, his back to her, "I've never forced a woman yet, and I don't mean to start now. You're safe enough in my house, Hilary . . . as safe as you want to be, that is. You don't need to run away to preserve your virtue." He turned and looked directly at her, and his direct blue gaze stabbed through her. "Do you believe that? God knows, I've given you small reason to do so, but I need to hear it from you. I'd never forgive myself if you ran off into the forest and got hurt trying to get away from me."

"I believe you," Hilary whispered. "I won't . . . run away."

Patrick's smile was a thin, strained shadow of his former merriment. "And I won't force my attentions on you. Do you think we can be friends on that basis, if we can't be lovers?"

"Friends." It was an empty, cold word beside the blazing desire that had flamed up between them. But it was all they could have. Hilary nodded, new tears filling her eyes, and she did not even see when Patrick left the room.

～⑤ 12 ⑥～

Patrick was true to his word. In the days that followed he kept scrupulously out of Hilary's way. He left the house before dawn to oversee the work in the fields, dined outside with the men who were clearing the new land and putting up shelters for their families, and returned to the great house at night only to vanish into his office with some mumbled excuse about paperwork. He didn't even sleep upstairs, though Hilary did not know this until the morning when she woke early and went into the office for pen and paper with which to write out menus for the party. She found Patrick sleeping on the leather sofa that had been banished from the downstairs hall to this cramped little room.

In sleep, without the lively play of expression that animated his face during the day, his features looked worn and tired. There were new lines across his forehead, and he stirred and mumbled restlessly in his sleep. He looked ten years older than the laughing young man who had helped her one stormy night at sea and pursued her relentlessly ever since.

She tiptoed backward out of the office as quietly as she could, but the hem of her full skirt dragged a crumpled scrap of paper along the floor and made a rustling sound that brought him instantly alert. "Carruthers! Did you indite the list of my debts? We must give the governor a full accounting. I'll not have him say I held aught back . . ."

His voice trailed off and he knuckled his eyes, blinking at Hilary where she stood frozen with one hand on the door handle. "Oh. It's you." He twisted his head and took in the cool morning light that shone in the one small window, the blackened wick in the lamp on the wall and the pool of candle wax overflowing onto the table. "I must have fallen asleep over my work. Forgive me, I didn't mean to be startling you."

"It's I should be asking for forgiveness," said Hilary. Fallen asleep over his work indeed! The woven counterpane and the goose-feather pillow piled on the couch told a different story. How long had he been sleeping down here to avoid her? Ever since that night when they quarreled and she threatened to run away to avoid his attentions? He looked so tired and worried Hilary knew he must not be sleeping well. Impulsively she moved forward to brush the tangled black hair away from his forehead. "Oh, Patrick, I'm sorry. Is it so hard for you?"

His head jerked violently away from her touch. "Oh, spare me the brow-smoothing and pillowplumping," he said. "Haven't you anything better to do than hover like a blasted nurse?"

Hilary put the back of one hand to her mouth and pressed it hard against her teeth. "I'm sorry," she repeated, her eyes filling with tears, not knowing what else to say.

Patrick looked up and forced a smile. "No, I am. I didn't need to snap at you," he said more gently. "I'm tired and overstrained, but it's not your fault, Hilary, my love."

"But you're sleeping down here because . . ."

"Because I have the devil of a lot of paperwork to get through before the governor comes," Patrick finished the sentence. "Oh, I see. You thought it was because I couldn't trust myself near your maidenly charms? Darling girl, when you're a little older you'll learn that there are many things a man may lose sleep over besides the love of a woman. You're much prettier than a bill of lading for last season's tobacco or an estimate of next year's crops, but until I'm clear with Governor Spotswood," he said with a wry smile, "those little things have more fascination for me than any woman, be she ever so fair."

He rose, bowed as gracefully as though he had not been surprised in shirt and breeches with his hair flying loose in dark elf locks, and opened the door for her. She noticed that he managed to show her out without brushing against her hand, or touching the loose strands of her hair about her face, or making any of the other seductive gestures that had so tormented her before the night of the quarrel.

Once outside the office, Hilary forgot completely about pens, paper, and menus of party dishes, and set about finding someone who could tell her what was troubling Patrick.

Carruthers, when she ran him to earth tallying the bundles of dried leaves in one of the tobacco barns, was professionally uncommunicative. "Master Patrick has been paying more attention to his estate recently," he said when she pressed him. "It's very commendable in a young man, and not beforetime. A planter has much to occupy him, Mistress Hilary. I really couldn't say which of the many estate questions he was thinking on last night."

"Something about debts," Hilary said, "and the governor coming to visit."

Carruthers coughed. "Very likely. Now, if you'll excuse me, mistress, I have my work to do, as no doubt you have yours."

It was an unmistakable dismissal, polite and final as a door silently closing in her face. Hilary left Carruthers in the barn and stood looking around the cluster of outbuildings that surrounded the great house. Smithy, kitchen, and dairy all hummed with activity, and in the week that she'd been on the plantation she'd already grown familiar with the work and with the people who worked in the various buildings. But she felt sure that any of them would meet her inquiries with the same bland unrevealing face that Carruthers had shown her. Whatever the young master wanted, Hilary thought, he would have—be it a girl or silence on the subject of his debts.

"Psst! Hilary!"

The sibilant whisper broke in on her thoughts. Startled, Hilary looked at the side of the barn

from which the whisper had come, and saw a
flash of tangled dark red locks and a smudged
petticoat disappearing around the corner.

"Bet?" She followed the whisper and found
Bet leaning against the back of the barn, posing
with her usual blend of insolence and seduc-
tiveness. In the few weeks since she'd been on
Patrick's plantation, Hilary noticed, Bet had managed to transform the decent osnaburg bodice
and wool skirt given her by the estate manager
into a costume more fitted for a London back
alley than for a backwoods plantation. The skirt
was hiked up on one side to reveal a flash of
once-white petticoat with a torn lace frill, the
neckline of the bodice had been lowered with
artful snips and stitches, and a grimy red sash
six inches wide passed around Bet's midriff to
pull in the bodice and emphasize the generous
curves of her breasts. A mobcap was perched
on her head in token obedience to the cook's
orders, but most of her wild red mane tumbled
about her shoulders, setting up a screeching
disharmony with the crimson of the sash.

"Heard you asking Carruthers about what's
troubling Master Patrick," Bet said. With a grin
and a wink she pointed out a knothole in the
back of the barn, just about ear level. "I hear
most things that's going on around here," she
added unnecessarily.

"I'm sure you do," said Hilary with an involuntary frown of distaste.

"That's right." Bet tossed her tangled hair
out of the way with a flip of one shoulder that
set her unbound breasts bouncing. "Look down

your long nose at me, Mistress Propriety, and don't hear what I know!"

Hilary's curiosity drove her unwilling feet a step closer to Bet. "What?"

"Wouldn't you like to know?" Bet teased, retreating a few paces as Hilary advanced.

"Yes," Hilary said. "I would. Please, Bet! I'm worried about Patrick, and . . ."—she tried a shot at random—"I think you care for him a little, yourself."

Bet's face darkened under the layer of kitchen soot that gave her skin such a dusky tinge. "Mayhap I do," she mumbled, looking at the ground, "and mayhap I don't. He's a fine, well-set-up man, your Patrick."

"Not *my* Patrick."

"No?" The familiar impudent gleam came to Bet's eyes. "Not anybody else's, though. I had a try for him myself," she admitted without shame, "but he can't see anybody else but you. Why don't you take the poor man or leave him alone, Hilary, and not leave him dangling on the hook?"

"It's not like that. You wouldn't understand." Hilary crossed her arms protectively over her breast as if the gesture could defend her against Bet's words.

"I understand more than you think," Bet said, darkly mysterious.

"Well, understand this," Hilary flared up at her, "I can't leave the plantation unless Patrick consents or Jephthah comes to get me. And neither is likely to happen before spring. So whose fault is it if he's unhappy? All he has to do is let me go to Jephthah."

"So it's his fault now!" Bet sneered. "Because he's got more sense than to let you go traipsing off in the back country to a man who doesn't want or welcome you? Because he's trying to protect you from finding out what sort of man your precious Jephthah is?"

"No!" Hilary shook her head violently. "It's not true, you've got it all wrong, Jephthah has forgiven me—he will forgive me . . . he needs me. He's waited for me all these years, waited in his lonely life for me to grow up and come to him. Would he have done that if he didn't care for me?" When Jephthah was in America, and she in England, Hilary had knelt by her bed and thought of him in her prayers every lonely night. The promise of coming to him when she was old enough had been the thread to which she clung when Ebenezer beat her and Mother Graham showed her hatred, when the Saints were turned out of their village to beg by the roads, when she was lost in London, when the ship seemed likely to sink. Wrapping her arms around herself, Hilary repeated, "No, no, no," over and over again to drown out Bet's false words.

A kindly arm around her shoulders provided warmth and support. Stumbling, eyes blinded by tears, Hilary let Bet lead her to a fallen log at the edge of the woods behind the barn. "Sit," Bet urged, giving her little shoves. "Aw, duckie, I didn't mean to upset you. We won't talk about Jephthah, then—though I've heard tales . . ." She stopped and compressed her lips firmly over whatever she'd meant to say next. "Listen, luv, I just wanted to help. I know you don't think much of me, but I kind of took a liking to you on the ship, and I hate to see you making a mess of your life here when you got such a good chance."

Against her will, Hilary remembered Bet's hands sponging her down when she burned with fever on the ship, Bet patiently coaxing her to take in just one more spoonful of watery porridge. "I'm sorry, Bet," she said. "I . . . I owe you a lot. I've never told you how grateful I am to you for helping me when I was sick. But this is different."

"Yes. This time it's Patrick Lyle who's sick, and you're too proud to help him."

"It's nothing to do with me," Hilary protested. "He said so himself. He's worried about his debts."

Bet gave a snort of disgust. "Debts! Tchah! Oh, aye, I know all about that. Thomas in the stables heard Carruthers talking to him about it when he came back from Williamsburg. Owes back taxes on this land, see, and doesn't have the money to pay up. But the king's coming here in person to let your Patrick explain why he shouldn't have to pay just yet."

"You mean the governor?"

"King, gov'nor, what's the difference?" Bet shrugged. "The gentry'll settle their own affairs without help from us. And your Patrick *is* gentry. Thomas says his old dad owns thousands and thousands of acres up on the Rappahannock. Has a seat in the Parliament, too."

"House of Burgesses?"

"Whatever. Quit interrupting. Point is, a man like your Patrick, with a dad in the Parliament

and a friend of King Spotswood, he's not going
to lose sleep worrying over a little matter of
back taxes. You know better than that. That's
why I told you—so you wouldn't keep using
that as an excuse." Bet poked Hilary in the
chest with one grubby finger. "It's Hilary Pembroke as put them dark shadows under his eyes.
You think I'm blind? You think because I work
in the kitchen, I don't know what goes on in
the hall? That man's hurting bad for love of
you, and all you can do about it is look down
your pretty little nose and wring your soft white
hands and say, 'Oh, dearie me, I'm sure it's
nothing to do with me.' " Bet's mincing tones
were a vicious parody of Hilary's soft voice.

Hilary crouched motionless on the log, struck
to the heart by Bet's words, unable to respond.
She heard the rustling of the other woman's
skirts as she got up and marched back toward
the outbuildings.

Patrick hurting for love of her? She didn't
want to believe it. He'd denied it himself, said
what worried him was estate matters. But Bet's
words rang too true to deny. Land and money
troubles among the gentry weren't the same
thing as for their sort of people. Poor folk could
be turned out of their cottages on a landlord's
whim, but the great landowners settled everything with influence and promises. As for debts,
she remembered well enough from her mother's stories of various protectors that the gentry
thought nothing of running up outrageous debts
with poor tradespeople and leaving them un-
paid for years. It didn't seem credible that such
problems had worried Patrick to the point that

he was losing weight, unable to sleep, afraid even to touch her hand.

"Wait! Oh, Bet, please wait!" Jumping up, she hurried after Bet and caught up with her between the tobacco barn and the kitchen.

"I don't know what to do," she confessed. "I . . . I think I love him."

"Think?" Bet snorted. "La-di-dah! Can't you even make up your own mind about that? Oh Gawd, I'm sorry, love." She put her arm around Hilary's waist and offered the hem of her skirt to wipe the tears away from her eyes.

"I promised Jephthah . . ." Hilary whispered.

Bet nodded. "Promised to one man, and in love with another. Well, don't take on so, love! It's not the end of the world." Her own eyes misted over. "I spoke too harsh to you. The fact is," she admitted, "I been angry at you because you've got your Patrick here, and I'm lonely."

This time Hilary didn't dispute the implication that Patrick was somehow "hers."

"Lonely?" she asked, looking over Bet's provocative figure with the beginnings of a smile. "What about Thomas-in-the-stables?"

Bet shrugged. "Oh, he's all right," she agreed, "but . . . don't laugh at me . . . I kinda miss Dickie. Got attached to him on the ship, the way he always had a smile or would crack a joke, even when he was sickest. You'll scarce credit it," she confided, "but when he got sold off with your gang, I cried for a whole day, I really did!"

Hilary began to feel better. Her own life might be in a miserable tangle that could never be solved, but perhaps she could do something for

Bet's. Perhaps, she thought, she had misjudged Bet. She might not be a loose woman, not really, not if she had the right man.

"Bet, there's something I didn't tell you about the time when I was with the soul seller . . ." she began, drawing Bet over to the side of the kitchen in case the cook should look out and see them gossiping when Bet was wanted for work.

Quickly she sketched in the tale of her last day with Jonathan Norris. Bet laughed till the tears came over the tale of how Dickie had fooled the soul seller and slipped away with a new suit of clothes and a bag of money to start life with; then she cried over the idea that Dickie remembered her and meant to come seeking her, and Hilary found herself crying too—she wasn't exactly sure why.

"But it's been near three weeks since then," Bet said at last, drying her eyes with the hem of her skirt. "He'd 'a been here by now if he meant it."

"He may still be looking for you," Hilary insisted. "Remember, we'd no idea where you'd been sold. He'd have to go to Yorktown and check the records, then come up the Nottoway. And he wouldn't be able to travel easily, being a runaway."

Bet nodded, but Hilary could tell that her words hadn't really convinced her. "Thanks, love," she said, patting Hilary's hand. "It's something to look forward to, isn't it? Now I better get back to work, and you go find that man of yours and set matters straight between you. He's too good to throw away, though if you

insist"—she winked—"do me a favor and throw
'im this way, all right?"

That sent Hilary back toward the great house
with a laugh on her lips, but before she reached
the back door her feet dragged in the grass and
she was frowning again. All very well for Bet to
give her easy, laughing advice. She had no con-
cept of the yawning chasm that divided right
from wrong. Nor did she have any idea of what
it was like to deal with a man like Patrick,
black-browed and short-tempered and absolutely
frightening when he had his temper up. What
did Bet expect her to *do* about Patrick, anyway—
march in and announce that she had just decided to give herself to him for the good of his
health?

"Yes, I can just see myself doing that!" Hilary
muttered. "Besides, I haven't decided any such
thing." The mere thought of yielding entirely to
Patrick's tempestuous passion, going down into
that sensual darkness, frankly terrified her. "Besides, it's wrong," she recalled with a sense of
relief. No, the only way out of this was for
Patrick to send her on her way to Jephthah.
Hilary put out of her mind Bet's hints that
Jephthah might not be so eager to see her. It
was the only solution for the two of them, she
thought, meaning Patrick and herself. And she
would just have to go and tell him so, and in
words that would brook no denial.

Chin high and back straight, she marched
through the clean-swept downstairs hall and
threw open the door of Patrick's office. "Ah, Mistress Hilary, I'm glad you're here," said Elspeth,
turning from Patrick's desk with a dustcloth in one

hand. "Cook tells me we've only enough brandy for three gallons of punch, and none at all for the Flaming Pudding. I'm sending a man over the river to ask Colonel Quincy for the loan of a couple of ankers of brandy. Is there anything else we need?"

"Don't send anybody," Hilary snapped. "We'll have no alcoholic punch at this party." She left the study to search for Patrick elsewhere, while Elspeth stared after her mopping her forehead absently with the dustcloth. No punch! Who'd ever heard of such a thing? Mistress Hilary must be thinking of something else, she decided, with a sly smile at the thought of what most likely preoccupied the girl. Best send Thomas to the colonel's, and no need to bother Mistress Hilary about the matter at all. As if she'd see young Master Patrick give a party without brandy punch and claret and shrub and everything proper!

Hilary's newfound determination died a slow death over the course of the next few days, as Patrick managed to keep himself so thoroughly out of her way that she couldn't even manage a showdown with him. The only time he was in the great house at all was for a couple of hours after dinner each night, and he spent that time closeted with Carruthers. He wasn't even sleeping in the office anymore, as she discovered when in desperation she tiptoed down early one morning intending to barge in on him asleep, if necessary, to get this matter resolved.

"Damn the man," Hilary muttered on the morning before the party, when she was helping Elspeth to pin up the lengths of flowered cotton that she'd found in the plantation store-house and decided to use as a backdrop for the decorations of autumn leaves and berries. Stand-ing on a high stool with a basket of pins in one hand, she took lengths of cloth as Elspeth handed them up and pinned them over a long rod that the estate carpenter had obligingly hung from the ceiling near the wall.

"Languishing indeed!" Hilary gave the last fold a vicious jerk to make it hang evenly with the rest. Bet had cornered her just that morning in the storehouse to ask whether she'd talked with Patrick yet, and she didn't seem to think his unavailability was any excuse. To hear Bet tell it, Patrick spent his days and nights pacing in remote corners of the plantation, visibly suf-fering so that she was hard put to it not to comfort the poor lad herself. "Languishing for love of me indeed! I don't believe a word of it. And if it's true, what does he expect me to do about it, unless he bothers to languish in front of me?"

"How's that again?" Elspeth inquired. "I can't understand you when you've got your mouth full of pins. And don't jerk at that curtain so, mistress, you'll have it down on us an' all."

"It's nearly down already," said an amused voice behind them. Hilary felt her stomach give a lurch as if she'd just stepped onto a stair that wasn't there. Her right hand loosened and let go of the basket of pins; she made a frantic grab for it and felt herself overbalancing on the high stool.

"Hilary, darling girl," the voice continued as she swayed back and forth, "don't ever hire out as a seamstress. Your hems are all ragged and— Ouf!"

Hilary knew an instant of vengeful satisfaction as they went scrambling to the floor together. If she had to fall, she couldn't have wished better than to knock the breath out of Patrick while she was doing so.

His arms had tightened about her automatically when she lost her balance and fell toward him, but before they hit the floor he'd released her again. He was up again with the quickness of a cat, shaking himself free of her touch as if it would poison him, while Elspeth's cry of surprise still echoed through the hall. Hilary sat up, rubbing her elbow where it had come into contact with the hard oak boards, and all her satisfaction vanished as she looked at Patrick's stricken face.

"Master Patrick, are you all right?" Elspeth gabbled, plunging toward him with her arms still full of cotton cloth. "You look—"

Patrick cut her off with an irritable shake of his head. "I'm . . . perfectly . . . all right, Elspeth," he said, with a pause between words as if he suffered the same shortness of breath that afflicted Hilary whenever they touched. "Look to Mistress Hilary."

"I'm fine too," Hilary said, scrambling to her feet. Her midriff still ached with the force of the fall, and there was a white sunburst of pain radiating out from the point of her elbow. But overriding those minor matters was the memory of Patrick's arms about her, locked tight for that one instant as though he would never let her go. And now he was backing away and staring at her as if she were a poisonous serpent.

Elspeth looked back and forth between the two of them and drew her own conclusions. "Did you come to help us, Master Patrick?" she said. "Indeed, and I'm grateful for it, but the best help you can be is to take this girl away from the house for the day and get her rested. She's been working her fingers to the bone getting ready for the party, exhausting herself with never a word of thanks from you. Look at her," Elspeth lied cheerfully, "so weak and tired she can't even stand up on a stool without help!"

It was Patrick who looked frighteningly tired, but Elspeth knew well enough he'd never rest on her orders. But he might do so for Hilary's sake. She stepped up her brisk no-nonsense tone. "D'you want your guests to think you starve folk on this plantation? For pity's sake, Master Patrick, take her out on the river for the rest of the day, and see if you can't bring her back here looking like a young girl about to go to her first party. I'll have Cook put up a basket of food for the two of you, so there'll be no need to come back for anything."

Elspeth overrode Hilary's faint protests with a firm hand. "You've done more than your share to get this fine fellow's house in shape for a party, mistress. There's naught left that me and a couple of the girls can't manage. What we need is to have you ready to act as a hostess, not fainting at Master Patrick's feet."

Before she knew what was happening, Hilary found herself lying on cushions in a small sloop of Patrick's, a basket of food and wine at her feet, while Patrick raised the sail and loosed the boat from the wharf. A gentle breeze carried

them upriver along the boundary of the plantation, giving Hilary a view of new-cleared fields,
acres of trees girdled and dying to make room
for the next year's planting, long barracks hastily thrown together with unbarked logs to house
the Cornish families.

"What's that?" she asked, pointing at a small
flat-topped pyramid of stone that stood in a
clearing upriver from the last of the barracks.

Patrick scowled over the water in the direction of her pointing hand. "The furnace for the
famous silver mines." He squinted, shaded his
hand, and let go of the tiller. "I'll be damned.
Carruthers told me that Traynor had scarpered
off with the money as soon as I left for England, but I could have sworn the building of
the furnace wasn't so far advanced when I left.
I'll say that for the man, he worked like a demon as long as I was here."

A vagrant breeze and an eddy of river current
spun the boat halfway around and made it wal-
low so that water slopped over the low sides.
With a squeak of alarm Hilary grabbed at the
tiller and waggled it this way and that, to no
avail. The loose sheets from the sail flapped
about her head, and the boat gave another
clumsy heave in the water.

"Give me that." Patrick sprang to the tiller.
"Haul on that sheet—now the other, steady,
that's the way." It took a few minutes of hard
work to get the boat righted and pointed upriver
again, and Hilary blessed the distraction. If she'd
realized what the stone pyramid was, she'd never
have said anything to remind Patrick of his
ill-fated mining venture.

All his attention now was bent on the tricky currents and shoals ahead of them, where sand-banks and tree roots menaced the boat on either side, while the current in the center was so fast that the sloop could make little headway. Hilary watched his face, dark, intent, alive with the exhilaration of pitting his wits against the river's force. Her heart ached with love and desire. If only she had the power to make him look like that more often! But when he was looking at her, his face was tense and his movements guarded. He seemed happiest when he forgot all about her, as now when the river claimed his attention.

With expert hands he steered the sloop into a shallow backwater shaded by an overhanging willow tree. They came to rest, rocking gently against the long grasses that grew out from the bank, and Patrick glanced once at Hilary and then looked away, compressing his lips as though he were in pain.

This couldn't go on. Hilary took a deep breath. "Patrick? . . . I need to talk to you about . . ."

Now that she finally had the opportunity, she knew a quiver of uncertainty. What if Patrick were merely tired from overwork? What if he were genuinely worried about those back taxes, and preparations for the governor's visit, and a host of other matters that had nothing to do with her? How he would laugh at her for being so silly as to think that one red-haired bound girl could upset his equilibrium. To be sure, he would admit with that easy smile, he'd tried for a tumble with her, as he would with any pretty lass; but she'd refused him, he'd no intention of forcing her, and there was an end to the matter.

"Yes?" Patrick looked up as silence stretched out between them. Hilary caught the flash of dark blue in his eyes; then he was looking past her as if the eddies of the river currents held some deep fascination for him.

If he would look at her directly, then she would know. But he wouldn't even do that. Hilary reached forward and touched him on the hand.

Only the tips of her fingers brushed across the tanned skin on the back of his hand, but he jumped as if he had been burned, and hastily withdrew his hand. "I . . . What did you . . . want to talk to me about?" His voice was uneven, and he was still staring over her shoulder at the streaks of light and shadow on the water, where deep strong currents troubled the surface of the river.

Hilary was almost sure now. But she still couldn't quite believe it. "You're not very friendly to me these days," she said softly, kneeling toward him on the cushions he'd piled for her in the bottom of the sloop. When she moved closer, the boat rocked under her, and she put her hand on his arm as if to steady herself. There was no place for him to retreat now; he was trapped between her and the side of the sloop.

"Hilary, don't do that," he said. His tongue went out to moisten dry lips. "You don't know . . . You're such an innocent . . . Oh, God help me, will you get away before I hurt you?" His hands were shaking. "Hilary, it is hard enough for me being in the same house with you. How much control do you think a man has?"

The question frightened her. But the wounded look on his face was more than she could bear, and the sweetness of touching him and being close to him intoxicated her senses and drove away coherent thought.

"Patrick," she said, trying out the name on lips that ached to touch his cheek. "Patrick, my love . . ."

That was as far as she got. His arms were about her, tight with no hope of escape, and she didn't want to get away. She held tightly to him, longing for a closeness that would go beyond clothing and flesh and bones, and she kissed his cheek and then his lips, and then the swift strong currents were sweeping her away and she went down into them without a struggle.

Somehow the barriers of cambric and osnaburg and linen and broadcloth that separated them were gone, and her senses reeled with the simultaneous assault of sun warm on secret white skin, cool air of the river breezes, Patrick's strong living warmth close to her and encompassing her and taking her last shred of reason with the kisses that rained down over every place that his hands bared to the light.

"Hilary . . ."

Patrick's weight over her eased away and she opened her eyes to see him kneeling over her. "Hilary," he said slowly, "if you don't mean it this time, you'd better tell me so now. For, my darling girl, I don't think I can stop myself."

All she wanted in the world was to take that look of pain from Patrick's face and to feel him close to her. Hilary knew that, certainly and finally, even while the thought frightened her. After this there would be no going back. She'd be a rich man's mistress, not Jephthah's wife. Hilary shut that thought back into the secret recesses of her mind and raised her arms to draw Patrick back to her. His face blotted out the sun dancing through autumn leaves overhead and became all her world.

Still he hovered over her, his face only inches away, and her lips actually hurt from wanting him to come that last distance and kiss her into forgetfulness. If this was what he had been feeling all these days . . . But then he kissed her at last and she lost all thought.

With that first voluntary kiss, the firm pressure of his mouth on hers, and the bursting shock of joy that accompanied it, there was already no going back. This had nothing to do with the sort of love she felt for Jephthah. It was something stronger and sweeter, a swirling current of desire that was carrying her inexorably away from whoever she used to be. Patrick's hands moved on her body and Hilary felt new threads of pleasure tugging at her senses, her breasts hardening beneath his fingers, thighs welcoming the intrusion of his muscular knees, as though everywhere he touched he made something new and strange out of her.

At the first pressure of his hardening manhood between her thighs she stiffened involuntarily, anticipating the pain she'd heard of. Patrick paused there, and she could sense the effort it cost him by the ragged edges of his breathing and his fingers clutching her shoulders so tightly that it hurt her.

"Hilary, my darling girl, do you know what you're doing?"

Given what trouble her ignorance had already made between them, that had to be the stupidest question in the world. Hilary's fears dissolved in an involuntary gurgle of laughter. "No, but I thought you did."

"Not anymore," Patrick said under his breath. "You turn my world upside down."

She clasped him fiercely to her as he drove into her, wanting him more than she feared the pain, and after all that it was no more than a pinprick against the sweet fulfillment of having him inside her, filling and possessing her as she'd never imagined. His hands tightened again on her shoulders and the driving urgency of his need took over as he plunged deeply again and again, in a staccato rhythm that was like unceasing shocks of pleasure and pain together dancing along the taut lines of her nerves. There was nothing for her now but Patrick, his tanned chest over her, the sprinkling of crisp dark hair that arrowed down toward his stomach, his arms holding her close inside their own little world of rocking boat and sparkling water and the straining to be closer than was physically possible.

He gave a great shuddering sigh and his body relaxed atop her. Hilary felt a moment of disappointment. If that was all there was . . . But when he laid his head on her breast and she saw the lines of pain and worry magically smoothed away, it didn't matter anymore. She put her arms about him and held him close to her, wanting this moment of peace to go on forever.

Too soon, he stirred. The long dark lashes flickered and he looked up at her with those incredible blue-black eyes that held her heart prisoner. "Well, darling girl, I did warn you I might not just be fully in control of myself. But I'll make it up to you now."

"Make what up?" Hilary asked in bewilderment. He couldn't make her pure again and fit for Jephthah, and what else was wrong to be made up? She started to sit up, suddenly wanting to cover herself.

"Lie down." Patrick's open hands, the callused palms and the long sensitive fingers, didn't so much push her back onto the cushions as persuade her there, gliding over her body and awakening her desire again with his expert touch. "I'll show you . . . Take your hair down."

"Why?"

"Because it's beautiful. Because I want to see it loose and free. Because I want to wrap my hands in it." Patrick plucked out the long pins that held her braids around her head and tossed them overboard. Hilary gave a shriek of dismay and snatched unavailingly at the long wires, glinting bright in the sunlight, already sinking out of her reach into the clear water of the river.

"Idiot," she pretended to scold, "now how will I look decent when we go back?"

"I don't want you looking decent." Patrick combed out the freed braids with his fingers until her hair crackled like autumn fire around her shoulders. "I want you most gloriously, indecently beautiful forever and ever." He twisted his fingers in the lustrous coppery waves. "If you could spin silk out of fire, it would look like this. And your skin is like silk and moon-beams." He kissed her hair, lifted it out of the way, and kissed each breast until the nipples stood up taut and throbbing and Hilary closed her eyes with a sigh of pleasure. His hands traced curves of delight over her body, paths that his lips followed with warm insistent touches that made her shiver with delight. Her arms and legs fell back, deliciously limp and relaxed. She had no idea what to expect and found that she didn't care.

"Nobody ever told me . . ." she murmured.

"Told you what, darling girl?" His lips brushed the tight fuzz of red curls between her thighs and Hilary caught her breath at the unexpected sharp dart of pleasure that the kiss brought to her.

"That people do this sort of thing afterward," she finished the thought when she could speak again. A fingernail ran lightly down the inside of her thigh, the merest hint of sharpness as counterpoint to the gentle pressure of hands and lips, and she moaned and opened to his hands.

"Not afterward," Patrick corrected her. His voice vibrated from his throat into her stomach, setting her midriff quivering with a new de-light. "Before."

Her eyes flew open in surprise. "But—"

"Well, darling girl," he said in tones of sweet reason, "I may have been unable to control my desires the first time, but did you think me such a brute as to leave you unsatisfied en-tirely? This time," he whispered into her ear as he slid gently into her, "this time is yours."

And this time he lay still within her for un-counted breaths until she moved against him, setting up a gentle rocking of the boat that set the rhythm for what was to follow: sweet and slow and subtle, a matter of long slow move-ments and caresses that tantalized her imagina-tion, while the pressure built up slowly inside her until she thought she could bear it no longer. She pushed herself against him, holding him with arms and legs, wanting it to be over some-how, anyhow, and he held her firmly and en-forced stillness until with one swift stroke he pushed her over the brink and the world ex-ploded for her in a shattering rainbow dazzle. She cried out incoherently and gripped him close, shaken by the tremors of the explosion, while dizzying shards of light and color danced be-fore her eyelids. And when she came back to herself and her limbs relaxed, he was still there, smiling at her and kissing her and starting to move again.

"No more, Patrick," she pleaded. "I can't bear it."

"Darling girl, you were made for it." With gentle insistence he brought her once again to the peak of arousal, and this time he was with her in the moment when the world tilted side-ways and slid out from under her. She went down into the whirlpool with his arms about her and the sound of his sigh of completion in her ears.

In the quiet aftermath, the boat still rocking against the ripples of the river, they lay in the bottom of the boat with cushions and limbs entangled every which way, and Hilary kissed

Patrick's face wherever she could reach. He stretched as lazily as a cat in the sun and reached for a piece of clothing to drape over them both.

"I believe I did tell you once," he said with lazy satisfaction, "that I'd never had any complaints afterward."

"I can understand that," Hilary said. "You're a very generous man to care so much for my pleasure. I could tell it wasn't much fun for you the second time."

"You could *what*?" Patrick gasped in surprise before the impish smile on her face warned him. "Oh, you wretched brat. I do believe you're hinting for me to prove my love a third time. Watch out, you just might get your wish."

Hilary wriggled free of his amorous hands, giggling, and took the dress away to cover herself. "Not unless you want me to faint from hunger," she announced. "I'm starving."

"Now that you mention it," Patrick said with a look of surprise, "so am I. What's in the hamper?"

❦ 13 ❧

They passed a lazy afternoon moored beneath the cypress tree, half-dressed, eating and talking and kissing.

"The human frame is abominably designed," Patrick complained when Hilary chided him for talking with his mouth full. "I have to kiss you, and I want to tell you all about my wonderful self and make you appreciate what a fine fellow you're going to marry, and I need to eat to keep up my strength so I can kiss you and tell you. Why can't I do all three at once?"

"Marry!" Hilary jumped and set the boat to rocking wildly.

"Well, yes." Patrick regarded her with bland surprise over a hunk of fresh bread with ham stuffed in the middle of it. "What did you think I intended?"

"I thought I was going to be a rich man's mistress," Hilary said, "and lead a life of luxurious decadence." She'd meant the words as a

278

joke, but in the middle of the sentence she thought of her mother, and the last words came out sounding unaccountably sad and lonely.

Patrick put a firm, comforting arm around her shoulders. "I may have had some notions that way once," he admitted, "but that was before I knew what a treasure I had in you. I'll not let you have any excuse at all to get away from me, darling girl. We'll have the preacher here as soon as is decent."

"I never dreamed I'd hear Patrick Lyle talking about decency and morality." Hilary felt so happy whenever she looked up into Patrick's loving face, she could almost put her betrayal of Jephthah out of her mind.

"And I never thought I'd see you lying on silk cushions, looking deliciously wanton with your hair tumbling over your shoulders and a glass of wine in your hand. What else is there to do," Patrick said with a grin, "but for me to become a decent, sober family man? It's self-defense pure and simple. One of us has to be practical and sensible about this thing."

"Wait." Hilary sat up and halfheartedly pushed his hand away from her breast. She shaded her eyes and made a show of scanning the woods on either side of the river.

"See something?" Patrick was instantly alert, kneeling beside her and reaching into a compartment at the bow of the sloop for a musket.

Hilary shook her head. "No, but I wish I did. I was only looking for witnesses," she teased, "to hear Patrick Lyle talking about becoming a sober family man, practical and sensible. It's a moment that should be recorded in history."

"Disrespectful brat!" Patrick snatched her ankles out from under her and tumbled her back
onto the cushions in a flurry of white lace petticoats. "I'll give you practical and sensible!"

Giggling weakly, Hilary made a pretense of
fending off his attack with soft hands, and then
she pretended no more.

The shadows were long on the river when
Patrick finally, reluctantly unmoored the sloop
and cast off for the short journey back downstream to the plantation. "I'm a bad host," he
confessed. "The first guests will be arriving by
now."

"Oh, my goodness!" Hilary tried to braid her
hair as they were whisked downstream by the
swift current. Elspeth had warned her that for a
big party like this, with guests coming from far
away, many people arrived the night before
and stayed until the day after. How could she
have forgotten all about the party? She faced
into the wind and pulled the loose hair back
from her face and neck. The evening breeze,
crisp with autumn's coolness and lightly scented
with pine and dry leaves and wood smoke,
brushed against her face and blew the coppery
tendrils free as fast as she captured them.

"Give up," Patrick urged. "Your hair is too
beautiful to confine, love." He helped his wishes
along with a mischievous tug at the one braid
that she had fairly started.

"And what will your guests think at seeing
you come back from the woods with a blowsy
girl with her hair about her ears and her dress
fastened all awry?" Hilary tugged at her bodice

and smoothed it down over her crumpled skirts, trying frantically to groom herself into some semblance of decency before they reached the plantation landing.

"Oh, I expect they'll figure it out," said Patrick with a smug grin. One long arm reached out and encircled her waist, pulling her down beside him at the tiller. "I like going downstream," he said. "No need to bother with sails, the current carries us right along. Leaving my hands free for pleasanter things."

"Not now!" Hilary pushed weakly at a hand that crept under her bodice. Patrick's long fingers brushed across her breast and reawakened the memory of desire. "Patrick, *please*." They were nearly at the landing; the stone pyramid of the furnace flashed by, grayish-white against the dark brown and green of the forest, and then the white circles of girdled trees gleamed against the dark, and she could see the first of the new long barracks that had been thrown up for the Cornish settlers.

"Please stop?" Patrick asked with a grin. "Or please go on?"

Hilary sucked in her breath as his thumb and forefinger closed lightly over the nipple that his touch had already awakened to aching hard desire. A delicious weakness flooded through her body and she relaxed against him, lips raised and parted for his kiss, as the boat sped downstream past barracks and stables and the cluster of little buildings surrounding the great house.

He needed both hands to bring the sloop in neatly to the landing, and Hilary felt cold under her bodice when he withdrew his hand. She strained her eyes through the gathering dusk, seeing unfamiliar figures standing around the lawn that sloped from house to landing, and burning blushes succeeded the momentary chill.

"A fine welcome for your good friends!" A thick-set, ruddy-faced man with an old-fashioned long periwig came down to the landing to catch the rope that Patrick tossed ashore. "Here we've ridden all day, and where should the master of the house be when we arrive, but gallivanting up the river on a private picnic. I see you're working as hard as ever, Paddy Lyle," he teased with a roguish wink at Hilary. "Always plowing new fields, so to speak."

Hilary blessed the gathering dusk that concealed her fiery face. Perhaps she could just slide over the side of the boat and quietly disappear into the river. Too late. Patrick was handing her ashore, and there were two elegantly dressed women coming forward to greet her.

"Spare my blushes, General," Patrick said with a grin that indicated he was not in the least embarrassed by his friend's speculations. "Hilary, may I present General Stilwell, his good lady, and Catherine Stilwell, his niece. Ladies, Hilary Pembroke, my bride-to-be."

"Charmed, I'm sure," the general's lady breathed while her eyes raked over Hilary's disheveled appearance, her hair loose, her feet bare, and the plain calico dress she'd put on this morning for housework crumpled and stained from the half-day on the river. Both the Stilwell ladies were pictures of elegance by contrast, their high-piled hair and full-skirted dresses showing no sign of the hard day's travel they

had just put in. Mistress Stilwell dropped a
curtsy fully an inch and a quarter deep and
extended the tips of her fingers in Hilary's general direction.

Hilary took a deep breath and caught her
stained calico skirt between two fingers. Bowing her head to the ladies, she put one leg
behind her, bent the other knee, and executed a
sweeping curtsy as low and as graceful as any
her mother had ever performed at the close of a
play. "Your servant, madam," she said in perfectly enunciated tones of freezing disdain.

Catherine Stilwell's piercing giggle rang out
as Hilary straightened her legs. She skipped
forward, narrowly avoiding tripping on her long
skirts, and took Hilary's arm. "Are you angry?
Don't be, *please*," she wheedled.

Hilary couldn't resist Catherine's engaging grin
and obvious friendliness. The flashing grin
brightened a plain face and lent a momentary
charm to her snub nose and freckled cheeks.
Hilary smiled back tentatively, and Catherine
gave a firm nod as though she'd just decided
something important.

While Patrick stood at the landing making
easy conversation with the elder Stilwells, Catherine drew Hilary up the gentle slope of the
lawn toward the house. "I wasn't laughing at
you," she confided as soon as they were away
from the landing, "but you should have seen
Aunt Stilwell's face just now! She'd got hold of
some garbled story about Patrick being involved
with one of his own bondservants, and all the
way over here she was on at me to show my
breeding and put you in your place! I could

have *died* when you swept that *queenly* curtsy. All my life I've been longing to see someone give Aunt Stilwell a dose of her own medicine."

"Yes, but . . ." Hilary made a vain attempt to break in on Catherine's gossipy chatter. "Catherine, I really am a bondservant."

"Nonsense," Catherine said with that flashing gamine grin, "you're twice the lady Aunt Stilwell ever could be—anybody can see that! Oh, and everybody except Aunt calls me Cat. Don't you think it fits?" She opened her green eyes wide and gave a three-cornered grin that exaggerated her pointed chin, and Hilary was forced to laugh.

"Now, don't you want to change your dress? I must tell you, Nan Rosier and I have commandeered your bedchamber for a dressing room, and we are both positively green with envy, my dear, over all those delicious dresses! But he should give you some jewels to go with them."

Catherine surveyed Hilary's red hair and creamy skin with a professional eye. "Pearls," she said with that short decisive nod. "Tell him to give you a string of pearls for a wedding present. Now, come along, you want to be looking your best for your first occasion as hostess of Patrick's plantation. Besides, Nan's brought along those two deliciously wicked brothers of hers, and you know they'll tease you into some romp or other if they catch you with your hair down. Race you to the house!" But instead of racing, she caught Hilary's hand and dragged her along at a breathless pace.

Nan Rosier was still dressing when Hilary

and Catherine stumbled into the bedroom, laughing and breathless. Her curly golden hair spilled down over her shoulders, framing a jolly face with red cheeks and bright blue eyes. She jumped up in her shift and petticoat and ran to embrace Hilary. "How lovely to see you again! I thought you'd be long gone to that backwoods settlement by now. Wasn't Patrick escorting you to the New Community of Saints?"

"She's not going anywhere," Catherine put in, perching on the bed and swinging her long legs with unladylike abandon. "She's going to stay here and marry Patrick. And she's just put Aunt Stilwell marvelously in her place, so I knew at once she was the right sort. *And* I'm going to paint her portrait as a wedding present."

Hilary was left speechless by this floodtide of information, but she saw that Nan Rosier took it all in stride. "Oh yes, our Cat's a famous painter, didn't you know?" she said with a warm smile.

"Going to be, anyway," Catherine said calmly, "as soon as I get control of my inheritance and can travel to study abroad. All I need is a nice biddable man who'll marry me for my money and not complain about anything I do. Until then—heigh-ho! As Patrick's taken, I suppose I shall have to make do with amateurish sketching and a few flirtations with your brother, Nan." She rolled her eyes with a languishing look that struck Hilary as irresistibly comic.

"Which brother?" Nan asked. "Tom or Harry?"

"Both, of course." Catherine jumped off the high bed and spun Hilary around in front of the mirror until her red hair stood out crackling. "I shall paint you in rose-pink," she announced. "No, don't look like that. I know you think you can't wear pink, but you haven't the benefit of an artist's eye for colors."

"What she means," said Nan Rosier, presenting her back to be laced up, "is that she'll paint your hair green, so it won't clash with the pink!" Giggling, she dodged Catherine's pretended blow and hid behind Hilary.

By the time the three of them were ready to go downstairs, Hilary was laughing easily with the other two and had quite forgotten her momentary shyness at the landing. Patrick's friends were nice people, she thought with a glow of pleasure as Catherine Stilwell slipped an arm around her waist and chattered her down the stairs. How could she have forgotten the pleasant evening they'd spent with the Rosiers on their way down to Moonshadows? His friends would accept her, the house was shining and clean, the kitchen was stacked high with pies and puddings and meat marinating in vinegar for the feast tomorrow. The skirts of her lavender lustring dress shimmered about her ankles, a single long coppery ringlet hung down from the high pile of curls that Nan had helped her arrange, the candles were all lit, and Patrick was waiting for her at the bottom of the stairs with a glow brighter than candles in the depths of his blue-black eyes.

She was perfectly happy, Hilary told herself—or would be, once she could rid herself of the nagging memory of Jephthah. She would write to him. Tomorrow. Or the next day. He would understand—he would have to understand. Her love for him had been a child's adoration, not the woman's mature love that filled her heart to overflowing whenever Patrick looked at her or his hand brushed hers.

The two tall Rosier boys flanked Patrick at the foot of the stairs, their fair hair brushed back and pomaded to glossy slickness. "Servant, Mistress Hilary! You'll be my partner in the first jig," said Tom Rosier.

"Not fair, she danced with you all evening when they stayed with us," Harry Rosier protested.

"Gentlemen! Gentlemen!" Patrick's dark brows arched and he spread his hands in a peacemaking gesture. "You forget that it's my promised bride you are wrangling over. Besides, who said there'd be any dancing tonight? The party's tomorrow."

Tom and Harry Rosier exchanged knowing grins as Patrick took Hilary's arm and escorted her into the dining room. What, bring three Virginia families together and nobody dance? Unheard of!

Elspeth had tactfully hinted Hilary into a selection of cold dishes that could be served informally to whatever guests chose to take advantage of Patrick's hospitality for the night before the party, leaving the cook free to concentrate on the problem of feeding fifty guests on the morrow. Hilary was grateful now for the suggestion, as even the Stilwells and the three Rosier children with their parents made too many to be served comfortably at table, not to mention that Carruthers had put on his best and tightest coat of blue broadcloth and joined them for the occasion. After all the guests had piled their platters high with the selection of cold meats and puddings laid out for their delectation, Patrick gathered them around the table for a toast to his coming wedding; then they scattered to find seats wherever they might. Patrick remained at the table with the two older couples, while the Rosier children and Cat Stilwell perched on the stairs in the hall and called occasional comments through the open doors of the dining room.

As hostess, Hilary had waited to the last to serve herself. She glanced around uncertainly, suspecting that politeness demanded she sit at the table with General Stilwell and his lady, but longing to join the younger people on the stairs outside.

"Perhaps you'd care to join me in the library?" Carruthers murmured, touching her arm lightly. "I've been hoping for an opportunity to speak with you."

Feeling some trepidation, Hilary swallowed and nodded her agreement. She had always felt that Carruthers resented her presence on the plantation, though she didn't know why. He had looked distinctly upset when Patrick proposed his toast. Perhaps he was afraid that as mistress of Moonshadows she would give him orders and interfere with his work as Patrick's estate agent. This would be a good time to assure him that she had no intentions of putting herself forward in such a way.

Carruthers led the way into the library with his slow, heavy tread and waited at the door for Hilary to seat herself. He closed the door carefully and Hilary knew a moment of fearful anticipation.

"I have yet to congratulate you on your forthcoming nuptials," Carruthers said. His full jowls hung down on either side of his face in such doleful lines that he looked more like a funeral mourner than a potential wedding guest.

"Er . . . thank you," Hilary said, feeling more than ever unsure of herself.

"You are a very brave young lady," Carruthers went on. "Not many girls who find themselves in your circumstances, penniless in a new land, would affiance themselves to a young man who is about to lose everything."

Hilary's hand flew to her throat to still the fluttering pulse there. "What!"

"Ah, I see he has not told you of his precarious financial situation," said Carruthers. He nodded, and his ponderous jowls sagged even farther downward. "Very reprehensible." There was a strange gleam in his eyes, a reflection of the light from the single candle burning on the table between them.

"If you mean the small matter of his back taxes and Governor Spotswood's visit," Hilary said, striving for an appearance of calm, "I know all about that. It will soon be settled."

"Small matter!" Carruthers' harsh bark of laughter grated on her nerves. "Is that what he called it? Rash, is young Master Patrick—rash and criminally optimistic."

Hilary rose and gathered the sweeping folds of lavender silk in one hand. She made a minimal curtsy to Carruthers. "I did not come here to listen to you miscall your master. Your servant, sir."

"He'll be a broken man within the year," Carruthers called out as she turned to go, "if you persist in this marriage."

Hilary paused with one hand on the latch. A cold whisper of premonition ran down her back. She knew without a doubt that if she stayed to hear Carruthers out, she would regret it.

But if she didn't stay?

With lagging steps she retraced her way to the library table. "Explain yourself."

Carruthers nodded and rocked back and forth in his chair. "Ah, that's caught your attention, has it? A young fellow with a crushing load of debts, disowned by his father, and with nothing but his own two hands to make his way in the world—not quite as good a catch as Patrick Lyle of Moonshadows, is he? You might even," he said with an insinuating smile, "you might even do better to marry the preacher. At least his humble cabin is his own."

Hilary closed her eyes briefly against the murderous rage that shook her. Her fingers curved involuntarily with the desire to pick up the heavy silver candlestick and beat Carruthers over the head with it. "Never mind my plans," she said between two shaking breaths of anger. "Tell me what trouble Patrick is in, and how I can help."

"Disappear," said Carruthers succinctly. "Don't marry him. Refuse this marriage that will drag him down to your level." In short, crisp, undeniable sentences he spelled out Patrick's position. The back taxes owing the colony, the very slim chance that Governor Spotswood would remit the taxes, the fact that even if he gave Patrick time to pay, the plantation would be weighed down by years of payments on these and the other debts Patrick had amassed. "Silver mines! Silk gowns for his light-o'-love! Buying the indentures of three hundred colonists off the *King's Grace* in the hope of getting you with them—ah, you hadn't heard that story, had you, now?"

"You've made your point," Hilary said. She felt tired and old. How had the carefree celebration of this evening turned into this nightmare, where she sat across a table from Carruthers, fighting for her place in Patrick's life? "But the debts already exist. I don't see how marriage to me will hurt him any worse."

"Without you slung around his neck like a millstone," Carruthers said, "he might yet have ways to win clear. He could marry well. There's General Stilwell's niece. She's got a tidy little sum coming to her on her marriage, and the general has influence in Williamsburg. He might be able to secure remission of the taxes as a wedding present to Patrick."

Hilary tried to swallow past the dryness in her throat. "I don't think," she said, trying to keep her voice steady, "that Patrick wants to marry Cat Stilwell. He knew her before he ever met me."

Carruthers shrugged. "He wants to keep Moonshadows. You've seen how he loves this plantation. Freckles and a piercing giggle are a small price to pay, against seeing your home and possessions sold by inch of candle. And even if he didn't take that sensible way out," he went on, shaking his head regretfully at the folly of young men who insisted on marrying for love, "there's his father. Patrick Lyle Senior. A Lyle of Lyle Hundred, with a seat in the Burgesses, he'd not see his only son sold up for lack of a word in the governor's ear, perhaps a small loan to tide him over his cash difficulties . . ."

Carruthers spread his hands with a smile. "These things are easy enough to arrange. But not," he said very softly, "if Patrick flouts his father's wishes by marrying a girl of no family, an actress's brat of dubious background."

Every word struck Hilary like a slap across the face. There was nothing that she could dispute. What a fool she'd been, to dream of marrying such a one as Patrick! He'd understood their relative positions well enough on the ship, when he offered to set her up as his mistress.

The candle flickered in a vagrant draft from the windows, casting long wavering shadows over the room and exaggerating Carruthers' droopy face into the mask of a heavy-jowled demon. Hilary's thoughts fluttered like birds in a net, beating from one memory to another: Patrick's pride in this plantation that he'd built out of the wilderness, his face when he confessed that he'd designed the house himself. She thought of the way he'd spoken of his family then, and how he'd avoided speaking of them at all today. No doubt he knew well enough that his father would never countenance such a marriage. Why, then, had he offered for her? Guilt, upon discovering he'd taken her virginity? A sense of duty?

Hilary's smile was bleak. She knew all about the sense of duty. And she couldn't allow Patrick to make such a sacrifice.

"I will not marry him," she said tonelessly at last.

Carruthers beamed. "Good girl! I knew you'd see reason. After all, if he's to be impoverished by his marriage, what is there in it for you?"

Everything, Hilary's heart cried silently. Just Patrick himself. What more could she ever want? But not at the cost of taking everything he loved from him, plantation and friends and family.

She knew too well what such marriages cost all concerned. Her parents had made a runaway match for love, so they said, but what it meant to Hilary was a father she'd never known and a mother who dumped her on the Community of Saints as soon as she grew old enough to be an encumbrance. She'd not condemn a child of theirs to such a fate.

A child . . . One hand fluttered to her bosom. "I may have his child."

"Then," Carruthers said, "you'd best marry the preacher as soon as may be."

No. Jephthah would perhaps forgive her this transgression too. But she couldn't go to him. Not after Patrick. Dear God, how could she leave Patrick? Easier to leave her right hand behind.

"I won't marry him," she repeated, "but . . . maybe I could stay?" Once he'd offered to set her up as his mistress, and she'd deemed herself insulted by the offer. Now Hilary watched herself with a growing sense of unreality, pleading with this tubby little man for the chance to have what she'd spurned before. "I could stay in a little house somewhere on the estate . . . we could meet sometimes . . . not very often . . ."

Carruthers shook his head. "No, my dear, I'm afraid that won't do. Young Master Patrick is very stubborn when he has his heart set on something—as you," he added gently, "know to your cost. Do you really believe he'd accept your refusal, if you stayed on the plantation? No, you must leave, and let him think it's your free choice. It's the only way to make him forget you."

"I promised Patrick not to run away." Hilary felt like a drowning woman clutching at vines that broke in her hands while the inexorable current swept her down. "I gave him my word of honor."

"A woman's honor!" Carruthers' laugh was dry and scratchy. "Come, come, my dear. We know better than that, don't we?"

Once Hilary would have struck him for that tone. Now, numbed from the blows that had fallen on her, she let it pass. After all, she supposed, he was right in a way. How could she lie with Patrick in the morning and talk of her honor in the evening? She was ruined. She had ruined herself. The least she could do was not to drag Patrick down with her.

Carruthers was nattering on and on, busily producing plans for her departure. After this party, he would engage to find some business to keep Master Patrick away for a few days. Then he would supply her with a horse and a man to take her safe to the New Community of Saints.

"Will that be agreeable?"

Hilary barely heard his words. They seemed to be coming from a great distance.

"All right. I'll get you a second horse, or a pack mule, and you can take the gowns and frivolities Master Patrick bought for you in Williamsburg."

Hilary would have felt like laughing if she could have remembered what laughter felt like. The little man thought she was holding out for a bribe.

"No," she said as he waited for her answer. "You don't have to do that. I don't suppose I'll have much use for silk gowns in the back country." And she couldn't bear to take the constant reminders of Patrick with her. But Carruthers wasn't entitled to see that much of her heartbreak. She pinched her lips together, trying to hold in the anguish she felt until she could be alone with it.

Carruthers was watching her face with those gleaming little eyes that missed nothing. "If you leave," he suggested, "I make no doubt the estate could provide a sufficient dowry to sweeten the marriage with the preacher."

"No!" Hilary rose, knocking over the chair with her skirts in her haste to be away. "No, I'll take nothing from the estate."

"As you wish." Carruthers shook his head as Hilary almost ran out of the room.

The hall was bright with candles. Tom Rosier had brought out his fiddle and was scraping away at a lively jigtime tune while Harry tried to persuade his sister or Cat Stilwell to dance with him.

"Nay, Harry, I'm too tired from the long ride," Nan said.

"And I," Catherine laughed from her seat on the stairs.

"Then here's a girl without that excuse!" Harry caught Hilary by one hand as she ran past. "Mistress Hilary, you'll dance with me, and show that lazy sister of mine what a lively pair of heels can do! Play up, Tom!"

Hilary tugged her hand free of Harry's large sweaty palm. "I'm . . . tired," she said. "Tomorrow?"

Harry Rosier grinned down at her and blocked her escape to the stairs with one large arm. His blue eyes sparkled in the candlelight and his hair gleamed like polished brass. His boyish smile was proof of a charm that seldom met with resistance from the girls he knew in Virginia. "But what will we *do* if none of you girls want to dance?" he demanded plaintively. "Mistress Hilary, this is no way to be a good hostess for Patrick."

Patrick's hostess, his wife, mistress of Moonshadows. No, she would never be any of those things, and she'd been a fool catching at the moon to dream of them, a worse fool than Patrick with his dream of silver mines. Hilary felt tears spring to her eyes and knew that in a moment she would disgrace herself before them all.

Help came from an unexpected quarter.

"Give over, Harry, can't you see the poor girl's out on her feet?" Cat Stilwell gave Harry an unceremonious shove in the back and drew Hilary past him to the stairs, one arm about her waist. "Tired! I should say she is, and all the work of getting this great house cleaned and ready for a party. You men think nobody works but yourselves. Let me tell you, it's no light task to be mistress of a place like Moonshadows. You dance with your sister, and I'll be down in a minute to teach you a game that's more fun than flirting with another man's betrothed."

As Hilary and Cat went up the broad curving stairs, Tom Rosier's jig tune started over behind them, and she heard Nan's laughing protest as Harry pulled her to her feet.

Once they were upstairs, Cat gave Hilary a broad wink and released her. "I know what it's all about," she said.

"You do? But how . . . ?" Hilary put one hand to her aching head. Did everybody in the world know about Patrick's debts? Was she the last silly girl to understand what was common knowledge elsewhere?

Cat nodded. "And I don't blame you. I wouldn't want to waste my evening dancing with Tom and Harry either, not when I'd just got engaged. You want to sneak off and be with Patrick, don't you? I'll wager he grows 'tired' in a few minutes too, and leaves the Rosiers to talk to Uncle and Aunt Stilwell by themselves. Shall I tell him you're waiting upstairs?"

"No! No, don't do that." Hilary couldn't face Patrick now. She needed time to be alone, to think over Carruthers' revelations and decide what she was going to do. No, that was already decided. But she still needed time alone—time to cry, time to compose her face and her heart.

Cat winked again. "Ah, planning to meet him somewhere else, are you? Good thinking. Patrick Lyle's not a man to let into your bedchamber until you've got his ring on your finger. I don't know how long I'd hold out myself," she sighed, "if he gave me one serious look out of those dark eyes. But he's never seen me as anything but a sister, and now I guess he never will." She kissed Hilary. "Not that I hold it against you. To prove which, I'm going downstairs to force my poor aching bones through a dance or two, just to keep Tom and Harry busy while you slip off with your sweetheart."

At last Hilary was alone in the green-and-blue bedchamber with its dark polished wood and its delicately pretty hangings. She fumbled in the dark for the tinderbox, lit the tall green candles on either side of the dressing-table mirror, and stared at a reflection she hardly recognized. The white-faced girl who looked back at her with wild gray eyes sparkling in the candlelight seemed to be a total stranger to her elegant trappings. The glossy pile of copper ringlets, the dress of many whispering folds of lavender silk, were like a costume—an actress's costume, Hilary thought with sudden disgust, nothing real about it at all, only a tawdry pretense at glamour. She had been mad for a little while— quite mad—and now it was over. She had permitted herself to love a man who belonged to a different world, and now she must pay the price.

Her imagination showed another face behind hers in the mirror, a dark young face with eyes like cloudy sapphires and a tender smile that would break her heart all over again, if she let herself think on it.

"Well, Patrick," she said with a dry sob for the tears that now refused to soothe her burning eyes, "it seems Mother Graham was right

after all. Bring an earthen pot next to a silver
tankard, you know which one will crack." But
was that true? What if her departure left Patrick
as aching and empty as she felt right now?
Didn't she at least owe it to him to tell him why
she was leaving, so that he should know it
wasn't because she didn't love him?

No. That way lay easy tears, and kisses, and
the end of her resolution. Hilary knew her own
weakness too well by now. Patrick would take
her in his arms and kiss the tears away and
persuade her that everything would be all right,
and the next thing she knew she would be
married to him. And when he stood beside her
and watched the house and furnishings of
Moonshadows sold off? When his family turned
him off, would he give her that tender smile
then, or would he regret his mistake?

She dared not talk to him at all until she
could meet him with a composed face and play
out the farce of this engagement until the part
was over. And then—when the guests departed—well, then Hilary Pembroke would depart
too, back to her proper station in life, and perhaps Patrick would not mourn her for very long.
There were girls enough ready to comfort him;
Nan Rosier and Cat Stilwell, for starters. No,
he'd be sad for a little while, but then glad to be
relieved of the consequences of his folly.

With fingers made clumsy by haste, she
stripped off the lavender lustring, combed her
hair out, and confined it in two crackling bushy
braids. "There," she told the plain slip of a girl
in the mirror, the girl in a linen shift who stared
solemnly back at her with the brushfire of her

hair confined into decent plaits. "There, that's who you really are, Hilary Pembroke, and don't you forget it again! If Jephthah will take you after all this, you should thank God fasting every day of your life."

Always before, when Hilary had been sad and lonely, she'd called on the memory of Jephthah's kindly love to warm her. Now even that consolation was gone. She knew now what married people did together, and the thought of Jephthah's fumbling embraces in Patrick's place was unbearable pain. She would almost rather that he cast her off when he found out what she'd done.

But she had to give him that choice. Hilary blew out the candles and curled up in the middle of the big feather bed, feeling hopelessly cold and lonely. Somehow, she didn't know how, she would get through the next two days. Then she'd take Carruthers' offer of an escort to the New Community of Saints, and would see for herself how Jephthah was doing. If he would still take her even though she hadn't served out her time as he bade her—if he wanted her at all—well, she owed it to him to stay. And she would try to be a good and faithful wife to him and never let him see how much of her heart remained at Moonshadows.

And if he didn't want her? Hilary stared into blackness and gave a weary shrug of her shoulders. She would meet that problem when it came. One thing her short stay in Virginia had taught her, there was always work for willing hands. At worst she'd be back where she started, a hired servant in somebody else's house.

The tears started then, as she remembered how Patrick had found her and swept her out of Justice Hazelrigg's home like an angry whirlwind. Ever since then, without acknowledging it, she had felt his love strong and comforting around her. Now deep, aching sobs rose from her chest and she buried her head in the pillows to muffle the sounds of her anguish.

Eventually the tears brought their own release. When she had exhausted herself with crying, her head felt stuffy and everything seemed too far away to matter any longer . . . even Patrick.

The light tapping at the door brought her unwilling out of a dreamy state in which nothing seemed quite real. Awareness brought memory and a stab of returning pain. Hilary stuck her head under the pillow and tried not to hear the sound.

"Hilary!" A whisper, the faint creak of the door opening, a step near her bedside. Hilary raised her head, knowing at once, with a sudden incredulous leap of joy, who it was.

"Darling girl," Patrick's voice came to her out of the darkness, "since you didn't come to me, I've come to you."

Without waiting for her reply, he was on the bed, arms enclosing both her and the billows of the understuffed feather pillow that had formed part of her nest. "Darling!" He sneezed, brushed feathers away from his face, reached for her again. Hilary scrambled out of reach.

"You shouldn't be here," she whispered.

"Darling girl, we've already anticipated the wedding," Patrick said aloud in tones of sweet reason. "Don't you trust me?"

"Shh! Somebody will hear you!"

"If you'd come a little closer," Patrick said, "I could be doing something better than talking." He raised his voice. "I'd hate to wake up the Rosiers and the Stilwells with our brangling, but if you don't care for the embarrassment, why should I—?"

Hilary put the palm of her hand over his mouth. He promptly kissed it and his tongue flicked out to print her palm with little shivers of desire. His other hand brushed across a breast in the darkness, and she jumped, startled by the shock of pleasure that his touch brought.

"Sorry," he whispered, sounding not at all penitent. "It's hard to find you in the dark. If you'd move a little closer . . . There, that's better."

Hilary settled into his arms with a sigh of defeat and happiness mingled. After all, she reasoned to herself, how much worse could it be to sin twice with Patrick? She was going to go away as soon as she could, wasn't she? Didn't she owe it to him—and to herself too—to make their last few days together as happy as could be?

Then Patrick lifted the linen shift over her head, and she forgot reason and rationalization together as he explored her body in the darkness. His questing fingers, long and sure and tender, glided over her skin and woke the fires that made her forget everything but her need for him.

"Patrick," she whispered into the muscular swell of his shoulder, feeling the warm taut skin under her lips. She loved even the sound of his name; shaping her lips to it increased the dizzy exultation his caresses made her feel. "Patrick, Patrick . . ."

"My love?"

"Nothing." She wrapped fierce arms around him, holding him close against her, wanting nothing more than this sweetness that made her feel as if she were drunk on honey and happiness.

His soft laughter, muted by caution and darkness, sent shivers of desire down her spine. "Oh, I've something more than *nothing* for you."

Suns blazed behind her closed eyes and she received his inward thrust with a half-choked cry of joy, rising to meet him as surely and inevitably as the tide. Nothing mattered but this happiness that they could share, she told herself over and over, until the pleasure he brought her drove her beyond knowing. Nothing but this moment, no tomorrow, no duty . . . nothing but Patrick.

✧ 14 ✧

During the long night's joyous reaffirmation of their love, Hilary managed to put all else out of her head. Patrick insisted on lighting the candles again, throwing away her shift, unbraiding her red hair, and adoring every white and blushing inch of her with eyes and lips and hands, until she was all aflame for him. There was no world for her beyond the sphere of candlelight enclosing the bed where they lay together, no day to follow this night of love.

But when he fell asleep, head pillowed on her breast and one hand tangled in the coppery loops of her long hair, she lay long awake, watching the shadows that moved across his face as the candle flickered and sputtered, and thinking cold hard thoughts that robbed her of the peace they had found together.

If their loving that day had been a revelation to her, this night had been more: a sensual fever in the blood, a madness that could carry her away past redemption. If this was what her parents had found together, she understood why they'd defied their families and counted the world well lost.

But she knew, too, what Patrick did not—that such mad joy was an evanescent bubble, all too soon broken and leaving plain mud and daylight in place of the iridescent hues of happiness. Her parents' love had broken on poverty and hardship before her birth. And afterward . . . Hilary's teeth clamped down hard on her lower lip.

She had managed, over the years, to push down all memories of her mother into a dark little corner of her mind from which they seldom escaped. Now the ghost was freed. A red-haired, laughing witch, her full white breasts exposed by the low cut of a tallow-stained satin stage gown, her milky complexion enhanced by artfully placed black patches, moved through the room like a vagrant breath of musk-scented breeze. She stooped over Hilary and made as if to embrace her, but the ghostly arms passed through Hilary's real body and left only a chill behind, instead of warm human touch.

Generous, smiling, offering easy warmth and love and laughter—that was how Hilary remembered her mother. But that "love" was as unreal as a ghost's embrace. Because when it stopped being easy, when it was a choice between her daughter and the latest "protector," then she was gone without warning, leaving Hilary to be dumped on the Community of Saints as an unwanted burden.

"I won't be like that," Hilary whispered at the guttering candle.

"Mmm?" Patrick stirred in his sleep and rolled over, leaving his hand open on her breast.

"I can't be like that." But she could, more easily than she'd ever deemed possible. And this was the first step. There was one plain right thing to do, and that was to leave Patrick. Now. Before another night with him weakened her will to the point that she couldn't do it. She would go to Carruthers in the morning and tell him that she had to leave right away. She would think up some story to explain her absence to Patrick; she would convince him she was ill.

Patrick woke with a start and a cry of surprise, opening confused dark eyes with a dazzle of blue in their depths. "Hilary?"

She put her hand over his.

"Good. Dreamed . . . dreamed you were gone." His hand closed over her breast. "Never leave me, Hilary. Promise?"

"Go to sleep," Hilary whispered. "It was only a dream. I'm here, Patrick. I'm here with you."

Her decision swayed, weakening, as his face smoothed out again into the peaceful lines of sleep. *See?* she pleaded with Carruthers in her mind. It's not *all* one-sided. He does need me.

As sleep overtook her, she thought that after all, she had only Carruthers' word for it that Patrick was in so much financial trouble. And Carruthers had never liked her. Perhaps, with all these guests coming tomorrow, she could find out whether his stories were true. Perhaps he was exaggerating to scare her. Perhaps . . .

* * *

"Dear Alexander Spotswood!" Mistress Stilwell gave a peal of brightly artificial laughter. "*Such* a coincidence, his becoming governor here. The general and I knew him years ago, when he was a young ensign in the Earl of Bath's regiment. That was when the dear earl told me how charming my new French styles were . . ."

Hilary nodded and tried to look interested as Mistress Stilwell nattered on about long-past balls and long-dead beaux, set off on a breathless round of social reminiscence by the mention of Governor Spotswood. This had been her first chance all day to ask anyone who might know about Williamsburg politics and the chances that Patrick was in serious trouble. Perhaps, if she were patient, Mistress Stilwell would get back to the point. Eventually.

All morning, guests from neighboring plantations had been arriving by horse or wagon or river sloop, and Patrick had kept Hilary at his side to meet his neighbors and be introduced as his future wife. Most of them were unreservedly friendly, happy for Patrick's sake to welcome his bride and not inclined to ask too many embarrassing questions about her background.

Like the Rosiers and Cat Stilwell, these other neighbors were a far cry from the family-proud Virginia aristocrats Hilary had pictured. Their free-and-easy manners and warm welcomes to her made her begin to doubt Carruthers' stories. It certainly didn't seem that Patrick was courting social ruin by marrying her; perhaps Carruthers had exaggerated the other problems too.

The fall weather was so mild and warm that

they were able to eat at long trestle tables under
the trees near the kitchen. As the press of arriving guests slacked off, Hilary was kept busy
darting from one place to another, making sure
that clean linen cloths were brought out to cover
the rough tables, checking on the progress of
the roast pig that revolved over a pit of coals
behind the kitchen, refusing to taste the brandy
punch that Hawkins was mixing in the dining
room. It seemed that at some time when she'd
been otherwise occupied, Colonel Quincy had
arrived with not one, but two ankers of brandy
strapped to either side of his stout mare. Hawkins was having a fine time preparing the mixture of home-brewed beer, sugar, cinnamon,
and brandy.

Finally the tables were spread with food, the
fifty-odd guests were seated, and Hilary had a
chance to catch her breath. She nibbled on a
chicken wing and a compote of apricots while
the gentlemen and ladies around her carved
generous slices of roast pork with crackling fat
and shouted generous wishes to Patrick for his
new family. It was hard to respond to the bawdy,
good-humored jests with appropriate smiles; Hilary managed by pretending to herself that it
was all true, that she really could stay here and
marry Patrick. As the day wore on, it became
easier and easier to believe that Carruthers had
been exaggerating.

Still, she would feel better if one or two of the
influential planters would assure her that Patrick's back taxes would surely be remitted. And
it was hard to get a word alone with anybody in
this jolly, friendly crowd. Finally the meal was

over and people began to wander off in twos and threes. The men gathered around the second bowl of brandy punch and the women were slipping into the house to unlace their gowns and lie down for a while before the dancing. Hilary intercepted the general's lady and asked her about Governor Spotswood while they were strolling back to the great house. And Mistress Stilwell had so much to say about long-ago social affairs that Hilary was beginning to despair of ever getting any real information out of her.

She was still nattering on about Lord This and the Earl of That! "Did you ever meet . . . ? No, I suppose you wouldn't have had the opportunity, would you, dear? After all"—she smirked, patting the long ringlets of false hair that hung down on either side of a neck liberally painted with white powder—"you would hardly have moved in the same social circles as the dear governor and myself."

"Hardly," agreed Hilary. Her desperate need to find out the truth about Patrick's troubles rendered her temporarily immune to insult. "That's why I am asking you about him. He wouldn't really demand that Patrick pay the back taxes on all this land he's taken up, would he?"

Mistress Stilwell shrugged and fluttered her fan. "Oh, surely not," she said with sugary sweetness. Hilary relaxed and was unprepared for the sting in the next words. "So much depends upon influence in these cases, dear child," the general's lady purred. "Take the general, for instance. Of course he's not been so rash as

Patrick, taking up thousands and thousands of acres that he'd no intention of working. But if he had . . . Well!" Her tinkling laugh rang out again. "Alexander Spotswood would hardly beggar our family, with whom he has so many close ties, because of a shift in government policy."

"I don't see why he'd do that to Patrick either," Hilary insisted with a feeling of standing upon shifting sand.

Mistress Stilwell's laugh was bright. "Not if Patrick's father spoke for him. But then, your Patrick is so independent, isn't he? A young man who marries to disoblige his family must be very sure that he doesn't need their help. Oh, I am sorry, I did not mean to insult you. But I am sure you may make your mind easy about this little matter, Mistress Harmony."

"Hilary." Every sentence was like a swift current washing away some of her footing. She wished Mistress Stilwell would stop talking.

"After all," the general's lady said with a smile that was denied by the hard brightness of her eyes above the fan, "if the outcome of the case had been in the least doubt, I'm sure Patrick wouldn't have bartered his influence for the chance of wedding a pretty face."

"And a pretty face indeed it is!" rumbled a jolly face behind them. Hilary felt an arm around her shoulders, pulling her backward, and before she could recover her balance, she was being given a smacking kiss by a pink-faced man whose bristling mustaches scratched her skin.

"How-de-do, my dear," said this unexpected

apparition when he released her. "I'm Colonel Quincy, one of your neighbors across the river. Patrick told me I could find his young lady by the blaze of burnished copper on her head, and for once he's told no more than the truth. You light up the day, my dear. Dance with me tonight?"

Before Hilary could answer, the colonel had turned his attention to Mistress Stilwell. "So you think there's no problem about Patrick's case, do you, mistress?" Evidently he had heard only the last few words, and had entirely missed Mistress Stilwell's sarcastic intonation. "Glad to hear it . . . glad to hear it. I've been thinking of taking up another tract myself, but we're all waiting to see which way the governor jumps."

"I think you're well advised to wait," said Mistress Stilwell. "In my opinion, that rash young man is likely to lose his house and furnishings over this matter!" She snapped her fan shut with a vicious click that broke one of the delicate ivory ribs, and nodded at Hilary. "I was just telling young Mistress Harriet here—"

Unable to bear a repetition of Mistress Stilwell's gloomy prognostications, Hilary murmured her adieux and escaped into the house. She had hoped to find someone else to ask about the taxes, but after what she'd heard, she lacked courage to approach the men who were gathered around the punch bowl outside.

The hall was bright with the swags of calico and the branches of autumn leaves that they'd pinned up for decorations, and the upstairs rooms resounded with girls' voices, hurrying feet, and laughter. Hilary stood with one hand on the knob at the end of the polished stair rail, trying to compose her countenance and her thoughts before she went up to rejoin her guests. Patrick's guests.

"Aha!" Firm hands imprisoned her waist from behind, and Patrick's cheek rested against hers for a moment while his hands crept upward. "Going upstairs to rest? It's crowded up there," he insinuated. "You'd maybe find more rest in some quiet private spot."

Hilary closed her eyes against the rush of tenderness and desire that weakened her knees and her willpower alike whenever Patrick laid hands on her. After a moment she was able to retort in the light tone she knew he expected. "With you there, precious little rest there'd be in it for either of us!" She turned within the circle of his hands. Smiling lips, sapphire eyes with a tender light in them, black hair glossy as a raven's wing glinting in the sunshine—she cataloged his features against the day when she'd have only memories to live on.

"Why are you staring so?" Patrick inquired, shifting his grip to bring her close against him. "Seen a ghost?"

Only the ghost of her own lonely future. And with him holding her against his chest, where she could feel the warmth of his skin through shirt and broadcloth coat, where the even rise and fall of his breathing troubled her pulses, she was quite unable to think of any flippant reply.

"Let me go. You mustn't . . . People will see," she said, desperately pushing at his chest.

"And they'll see nothing to surprise them," Patrick argued, but he released her anyway. "My little puritan!" He laughed down at her, and she could not bear to see the tender light in his eyes. "There's nothing so shocking about a man kissing his promised wife on the stairs."

"No, but if you stopped with kissing, it would be the first time," Hilary retorted, turning away from him and pretending to fuss with her bodice. The sound of horses on the gravel drive outside, their bridles jangling as if loaded with bells, gave her an excuse to change the subject. "And new guests coming in the door, too! You'd better go and greet them."

Patrick used several short words whose meaning Hilary preferred not to guess at. "Bridle bells! I'll be damned if that isn't that rascal Kendall O'Leary." Frowning, he strode outside to greet the new arrivals. Hilary lingered for a moment in the hall, trying to feel proud of herself for resisting Patrick's lovemaking. All she felt was desolation. Another moment, and she would have thrown herself into his arms, begging him not to let her leave him.

She had better leave before that happened. But how? If she'd been busy all day, Carruthers had been busier; if she couldn't slip away for two minutes to consult with him, how on earth was she going to get clean away from Moonshadows without Patrick's catching her?

Frowning over that problem, and hoping against her better judgment that it would remain impossible to get away, Hilary slowly followed Patrick to the drive in front of the house.

There she found a less-than-friendly reunion in progress.

Patrick's attitude became a little clearer as Hilary peeped out the front door at the new arrivals. In truth, they did seem a shabby pair— even sinister—compared with the gaily dressed planters and cheerful frontiersmen who'd been pouring into Moonshadows all morning.

A string of five bony horses, linked one behind the other by long knotted leather reins, stood with heads down in the drive. A tall, good-looking ruffian with long black mustaches and powerful shoulders bestrode the first little horse, his long legs reaching nearly to the ground. Hilary was well able to appreciate his muscular shoulders and chest from her position just inside the hall, for his upper body was bare except for a gaily striped red-and-white waistcoat whose short hem barely covered the tops of his dirty kerseymere breeches.

The three horses behind him were heavily loaded with bulging packs from which strange odds and ends dangled: a long musket barrel, two shiny copper kettles, a jug stoppered with a twist of rag. The last horse carried a similar burden, but perched atop the bundle was a little man whose blue plush coat and buckskin trousers, slightly too large for his frame, seemed vaguely familiar to Hilary. Where had she seen those large, gleaming gold buttons before, almost as big as saucers? She moved forward, trying to catch a glimpse of the little man's face, and he pulled his black slouch hat farther down over his head.

"O'Leary." Patrick was standing on the portico, arms folded over his laced coat, surveying the new arrivals with lips tight and eyes glittering a hard bright blue.

"The same, Mr. Lyle. Kendall O'Leary, at your service as ever was!" The lead rider threw his arms wide and dismounted with a cheery smile.

"Come peddling?" Patrick inquired. "We've no need of your cheapjack trinkets and gewgaws here, O'Leary."

Kendall O'Leary halted with a hurt look on his face. "Now, is that a welcome fitting for a brave man on his way to trade with the savage Indians of the Carolinas? Sure, and I'm asking no more than a bite of cold cornbread and a wee sup of something to keep the chill away . . . and stabling and fodder for these fine horses as represent the most of my capital investment, for sure my partner and me don't get a wink of sleep most nights for guarding them . . . and maybe the damp end of one of your broken-down corn cribs where the two of us could sleep the night . . ."

"And a sip of brandy punch, and the chance to offend half a dozen of my guests?" But Patrick was beginning to smile. "Oh, all right, O'Leary. You can stay the night. But no sneaking around the toolshed this time. And I'm going to count the chickens when you leave."

O'Leary spread his arms wide and rolled his black eyes toward the sky. "Such suspicion," he mourned, "such tight-fisted narrow-mindedness. Is this fitting behavior for a wealthy Virginia planter, and him with the broad acres uncounted rolling off into the distance, and the land positively dripping with tobacco and Indian corn and silver mines?"

Patrick winced at this mention of the silver mines. "I said you could stay," he said shortly, "not that I'd time to gossip with you. Stable your horses and come by the kitchens; we've done eating, but I'll tell the cook to find something for you."

As Kendall O'Leary led the string of horses toward the stable, Hilary finally remembered where she'd seen those gaudy gilt buttons before. That was the fine new suit of clothes that Dickie Baynes had stolen from Norris the soul seller. Her jaw dropped as she watched the jaunty little figure perched atop the last pack of trade goods. As he passed, Dickie looked past Patrick, and Hilary caught his eye for a moment.

"Dickie?" she mouthed.

He squinted horribly and made pushing-away gestures with one hand. Hilary nodded to show she'd understood. Of course, Dickie wouldn't want to be recognized by anyone who knew of his escape from Norris. Especially not in front of a respectable planter. Not knowing Patrick, he probably thought of "Mr. Lyle" as a pillar of respectability.

"And what are *you* laughing at?" Patrick inquired when he turned back into the house. Then he caught Hilary's eye and began to laugh himself. "All right, all right, I know I sounded like a pompous ass. But if you knew that rascal O'Leary as I do!" He gave a long, doleful whistle and shook his head. "Count the chickens, did I say? You'd best count the hairs on your head when O'Leary has been through."

"I'll take your word for it," said Hilary with a demure curtsy. "I'm sure you're much better qualified than I to recognize a thoroughgoing rascal."

Patrick's mouth fell open and his dark blue eyes widened. "Insolence from my own promised bride! Come here and be taught your place, my girl!" He snatched at Hilary but she evaded him and fled upstairs, laughing, to take shelter behind a phalanx of half-dressed girls who intimidated Patrick into a hasty retreat. To think of Dickie's having the impudence to show up here in the guise of an Indian trader! He must have found out that Bet had been sold to Moonshadows, then teamed up with Kendall O'Leary and persuaded him to swing by here so that he could pursue his plan of stealing her away. Patrick would be angry when he found out that Kendall's target this time was something much larger than a chicken or a cooking-pot . . . but Hilary couldn't bring herself to tell on the unlikely lovers.

Then another thought, less welcome, struck her and she stood quite still among the girls who fluttered around in their white shifts and bright striped petticoats, giggling and gossiping and slowly settling down for their naps before the dancing. Hilary briefly closed her eyes and cursed the day that had brought Dickie Baynes and his partner to Moonshadows. They were going to give her the thing she wanted least in all the world—the opportunity to get away from Patrick.

Hilary felt a cold desolation settling in the pit of her stomach. She lay down on the edge of

her bed, already occupied by Nan Rósier and a
friend of hers, and closed her eyes and pretended to sleep while she thought over her idea
and could find no flaws in it. If Dickie and
Kendall were taking Bet with them into the
back country, they could take her too. She wasn't
exactly sure of the routes taken by the Indian
traders, but Kendall had said something about
going into Carolina, and the New Community
of Saints lay somewhere in that direction. She
could tell them that the price of her silence was
to take her with them as far as Jephthah's
settlement.

After half an hour, the whispers and stirring
among the resting women had died down and
most of them were sleeping peacefully. Hilary
slid off the edge of the bed, fastened up her
bodice and laced the gay green cords of the
stomacher that decorated the front of her dress,
and tiptoed out through a hall full of cots and
resting women, with her shoes in one hand.

She put on her shoes at the back door and cut
a zigzag route through the yard, using outbuildings and trees to screen her passage from
the gentlemen who were still drinking at the
long trestle tables. There were only a few open
spaces where she could be seen, and she streaked
across those at top speed, to arrive at the stables quite out of breath.

There were voices within. Good! O'Leary and
Dickie must still be unloading and feeding their
horses. She wouldn't have to look all over the
plantation for them. Panting slightly from her
last run across the open stableyard, Hilary leaned

against the stable wall and peered through a chink in the rough-cut logs.

The first thing she saw was the tall sturdy figure of Thomas Ryan, standing with his back to her and expostulating with Kendall over the quantity of oats he wanted to give to his five scrawny horses. Behind the two of them, Dickie Baynes stood beside his horse, shifting uneasily from one foot to the other. The wall beside him was as rough and uneven as the one through which she was peering.

Hilary slithered around the corner of the stable and put her lips to another chink between two logs. "Dickie! Dickie Baynes!" she whispered.

Removing her mouth long enough to peer through the crack, she saw Dickie look around with an uneasy expression on his face. "It's Hilary," she whispered, trying to project the words just clearly enough for Dickie to hear them without intruding on Kendall's and Thomas' noisy argument. "Meet me behind the stables if you want to see Bet."

Without waiting to see if he obeyed her, Hilary scurried to the shelter of the trees behind the stable. A moment later Dickie appeared, peering uneasily this way and that through the shadowy forest.

"Psst! Over here." Hilary stuck her head out from behind a tree and motioned Dickie deeper into the shadows.

"Where's Bet?" he demanded as he followed her into the forest.

"I didn't say she was here," Hilary told him. She brushed the dry leaves off a fallen log and sat down, composing her skirts about her. "I said you'd better meet me if you want to see her. Oh yes, she's on Moonshadows," she interrupted Dickie's muffled exclamation. "You came to get her to run away with you, didn't you? Well, I won't make any trouble for you—if you do one little thing for me."

"Anything!" Dickie said at once. "Where's Bet? Garn, don't look like you need much help from the likes of me, though. Ye've fallen on your feet here, haven't you, Hilary? Does me soul good to see you looking so fine. Many's the time I worried about you since I left that night. Sure, sure, just take me to Bet, and any little thing Dickie Baynes can do for you, consider it as good as done."

He was slightly less grandiloquent when Hilary told him what she wanted.

"Take you with us!" Dickie started back and looked nervously over his shoulder. "Naah, you don't want to go with us. Dreadful hard traveling it'll be, through trackless forests and wild mountains, and very likely we'll all lose our hair to them savage Indians." His shiver of fear looked real enough.

"Why did you join a fur trader," Hilary asked, momentarily diverted from her own troubles, "if the life scares you so much?"

Dickie whined that it had sounded better when he met Kendall O'Leary in a Yorktown tavern and the big Irishman expatiated on the joys of the woodsy life. Besides, Kendall had agreed to bring the trading caravan past Moonshadows so that they could get Bet. And now Dickie couldn't quit, because he'd spent all the money he got from "selling" Norris on red cloth and beads and hatchets to fill up his new partner's trade packs.

"Anyway, I'll learn to like it in a while," he declared. "That's what Kendall says. An' Bet, she's tough, she can take it. But you . . ." He looked at Hilary, slender and bright in her dress of grass-green cambric with its tight-laced emerald-green stomacher, and shook his head. "Why'd you want to do such a fool thing, anyway? You're living soft here, and that big oaf in the stables says as the master is even goin' to marry you."

"Things aren't what they seem here," Hilary said. "I can't marry Patrick. I'm promised to Jephthah. Besides . . ." She couldn't explain the tangled skein of reasoning that had brought her here, the fear of ruining Patrick's life, the dark sensual desires he awakened that would make her a bad woman like her mother, the guilty memory of poor Jephthah waiting and working in the backwoods to make a home for them. Instead of trying to explain all this, she simply leaned on her one strong point, threatening to tell Patrick of their plans if they didn't agree to help her.

"Then," she said, "he'll lock up Bet and hand you over to the county justices as a runaway." Actually she didn't believe he would do any such thing. In his present joyful mood he was much more likely to give Bet her freedom and his blessing. But Dickie was afraid of Patrick, as of all the gentry, and he'd just seen Patrick's unfriendliness to Kendall. She saw, rather sadly, that her threats were having the desired effect on him.

"All right," Dickie said at last.

Hilary jumped up. "Can we go now?" If it was settled, she wanted to get the departure over with. It would break her heart to go back and face Patrick, knowing it was the last time. Better to leave him with the memory of their laughing encounter in the hall . . . better to leave him thinking she cared no more than to leave him without a word of farewell.

"No, ducks, can't very well do that," Dickie said with unexpected firmness. "Horses have to rest, we got to rest, and don't you think this Mr. Lyle might notice your absence tonight? No, we'd best stick with Kendall's plan."

He went on to explain that they had timed their arrival to coincide with the party for a very good reason. That night everybody would be dancing and drinking until all hours; the next day they'd not stir from their beds before noon. If Bet—and now, Hilary—slipped away to join them at moonrise, they'd have twelve hours' start before anybody noticed their absence. The only problem Dickie had been worrying over was how to get word of the plan to Bet. And Hilary could solve that. What could be more natural than that she should look in at the kitchen to compliment the cook on the feast she'd served up that afternoon and to check on plans for the lighter evening meal?

"Only where you solve one problem, you make another," Dickie grumbled. "Might be nobody'd trouble to chase after a girl from the kitchens, but this Patrick of yours will raise the country to get his promised wife back."

"No, he won't," Hilary said. "I'll . . . I'll leave a note . . . I'll explain . . . well, anyway, he won't want me back." She would have to make him think that all her love had been an act to lull his suspicions so that she could escape to Jephthah. When he read that letter, he'd be hurt and angry. He certainly wouldn't want her back. She'd be lucky if he ever spoke civilly to her again, not that she expected ever to see him again, so it really didn't matter.

Thinking about how much it didn't matter, Hilary burst into tears. Dickie leaned over her, awkwardly patting her shoulder and imploring her to stop before someone heard them and came to investigate.

"Blimey!" Dickie swore over the muffled sound of Hilary's sobs. "I dunno, that Mr. Patrick Lyle seemed like an all-right sort of fellow, but he must be a right old bastard to make you that unhappy and that desperate to get away from him. What'd he do to you, anyway? No, don't tell me, I don't want to hear about it. Garn, I'm sorry. Here, ducks." A crumpled scrap of linen, none too clean, was thrust into her hand. Hilary wiped her eyes and blew her nose into the limp rag.

"Thanks, Dickie," she said, rising somewhat shakily to her feet. "I'm all right now. And I'd better be getting back before I'm missed."

"Moonrise," Dickie called after her. "Here. Don't forget to tell Bet."

Hilary stopped by the kitchen on her way back to the great house and managed to slip the

news to Bet in a whisper while pretending to
inspect the pudding she was watching over.
Bet's face lighted up with an inner radiance that
almost, but not quite, overcame the external
grime. "Garn," she whispered, folding both
hands over her bosom, " 'e does care, don't
'e?"

"I should think so," Hilary said. "He's risk-
ing capture and imprisonment to get you free.
Try not to look so happy, you'll give yourself
away."

She retraced her way to the great house and
shut herself up in Patrick's office, trying to compose a letter of farewell that should convince
him she was a heartless slut and well out of his
life. After blotting several sheets of paper with
tears and breaking most of the quill pens that
he kept in a cubbyhole over the desk, she settled for a blunt statement that might hurt him
but would surely be convincing.

"Dear Patrick, I have Excaped your Toils to
be with my Promised Husband, Jephthah. I never
Loved you—I was Lyeing so as to Deceive you
into Relacksing your Vegilants over me. This
Decision is Final and IrRevokable, so do not
seek to Persue me, as it will do No Good."

She read it over, frowning and inspecting all
the spelling. Since the days when she'd helped
her mother learn parts for the playhouse, there
had not been many books in Hilary's life; Patrick's library was a treat she'd just begun to
explore. Now she'd never sit in the padded
window seat again, reading and listening for
the sound of his footsteps returning from the
fields . . .

Two large tears dropped on the bottom of the sheet as Hilary folded it up and thrust it behind her laced stomacher. She would have to find some way of slipping it into Patrick's bedchamber tonight before she left. There should be an opportunity for her to slip up there while they were all dancing downstairs.

∽ 15 ∽

"Ladies circle inside, gents to the outside, find your true love when the music stops!"

Fiddler Dan's raucous cracked voice carried easily over the hubbub of laughter and flirtation in the downstairs hall. Hilary found herself holding hands with Nan Rosier on one side of her and the matronly Mistress Upshur on the other. Forty-five if she was a day, discreetly dressed in puce satin with a plume of ostrich feathers ornamenting her graying hair, Mistress Upshur giggled like a girl as the inner circle raced pell-mell through the hall. The rectangular shape of the hall, forty feet by twenty, forced the ladies' "circle" into an elongated oval. Hilary's arms were stretched on the long sides and she had to squeeze between Nan's and Mistress Upshur's shoulders on the short sides of the oval. Around and around they raced as the frenetic pace of the fiddling increased. The ice-blue satin skirts of Hilary's ball gown swished about her ankles, the bodice stuck to her shoulders, and she caught only glimpses of the hall as they were whirled around in a giddy circle.

The hangings of flowered calico, decorated with sprays of autumn leaves, gave the illusion of a dance in the forest by candlelight, just as she'd imagined when she decorated the hall. Behind the laughing faces of the men and boys waiting to catch their partners, Hilary could see the musicians in their corners. Danny McShane, the traveling fiddler who came unbidden to every party in the county, sawed away at one end of the hall. His elbow jigged and his shoulder-length gray locks flapped wildly about his face as he bobbed in time to his own music. At the far end of the hall, Tom Rosier's face shone with drops of sweat as he matched the professional fiddler's tune with runs and flourishes of his own.

When both circles were out of breath, Dan nodded at his young partner and both fiddles stopped in mid-phrase. Hilary turned with the other ladies to see what partner chance had brought her, and looked without overmuch surprise at Patrick's dark face and smiling blue eyes.

"You cheated," she accused. Not that she could tell how anybody could cheat in that romp of a "dance," but it did seem strange that every time they played a game of mixed partners, Patrick wound up at her side: drawing the ace of spades to match her ace of hearts, getting the matching bean out of the sweet cake served halfway through the evening to keep up the dancers' strength, mysteriously in position behind her when the music stopped now.

"Now, Mistress Hilary—Mistress Lyle to be—how could I cheat?" Patrick protested, taking her hands in his for the country dance. But as he spoke, Fiddler Dan winked at him and Hilary guessed.

"You bribed the fiddler!"

Patrick laughed and shrugged, neither confirming nor denying her suspicions, and pulled her into the line of couples forming for the dance. "Watch carefully now, this one's a little different from the last," he instructed her. "Instead of full circle, curtsy, chain across and back, it's half-circle, shepherds hey, and all knock double with your opposite partner. Got it?"

Hilary managed by watching Cat Stilwell, just ahead of her, until the moment when the line dissolved into separate figures weaving a complex path around one another. She turned uncertainly, found herself about to collide with Colonel Quincy, jumped backward, and brought the line to a crashing halt. Patrick's strong hands caught her about the waist and pulled her out of the way of the advancing dancers just in time to prevent a major accident. He drew her into a corner, out of the dance and away from the light.

"If I'd known how much fun it was going to be teaching you to dance," he murmured in her ear, "I'd have started long ago." The other dancers had reformed the line and were going on, tactfully ignoring Patrick and Hilary. His arms were tight about her waist, creasing the flowered blue-and-white paduasoy skirt that billowed out in generous pleats to cover all but the tips of her blue kidskin shoes.

"Patrick!" Hilary removed the hand that had crept upward to caress the line of her low-cut blue silk bodice with its trimming of soft French lace. "We're in public!"

"That can be remedied." His voice was low but strong, thrilling her with the promise of pleasures to come. Hilary felt shivers of desire run through her midriff where his arms were warm about her. She looked down, veiling her eyes, and could see nothing but the long brown hands that had explored her body so thoroughly and knowledgeably last night. Remembrance of the things they had shamelessly done together caused her nipples to stiffen and her cheeks to glow.

"*Please*, Patrick." With an effort she broke free. "You'll shock your guests."

"Our guests," Patrick corrected, "and as for shocked . . ." He directed her gaze around the room. The dance had ended and the exhausted dancers had collapsed against the wall and onto the few chairs left in the hall. Colonel Quincy was bending over Mistress Upshur, fanning her vigorously and making sure to direct the gusts of air down the front of her low-cut puce satin dress where they would do the most good; Cat Stilwell was seated on Harry Rosier's knee while Tom Rosier knelt before her, making play with the project of getting her satin slipper off so as to drink punch from it and slyly tickling her foot to encourage her high-pitched shrieks of protest. Nan Rosier had disappeared from sight, but Hilary could hear her low, amused voice from the dining room, protesting that somebody was a vile rogue who wanted to ruin her and she certainly would not kiss him again . . . and again . . . and . . .

The scene reminded Hilary of something. After a moment it came to her: the green room where her mother and the other ladies of the stage had entertained gallants while changing from stage costume to street dress. A candlelit room smelling of brandy and wine and powder and sweat; women in all stages of dress and undress, laughing and evading groping hands and making witty conversation, while a small red-haired girl watched from her corner unnoticed.

"You're right," she said, compressing her lips. "Nothing would shock these people."

"Don't sound so disapproving, darling girl." Patrick's hand kneaded her shoulder lightly, sending waves of tormenting desire through her body. "It's not often that all the neighbors along the river get together; don't begrudge them their fun if they're a bit wild with it. And the night is young. What would you say to a turn in the gardens?"

Night. Moonrise. Hilary looked at the chiming clock at the far end of the hall. It wanted half an hour to midnight, and the moon would not rise till three A.M. Three more hours of Patrick.

"No," she said, and turned to kiss him on the lips with shameless disregard for whoever might be watching. "No, let's go upstairs."

Hilary's bedchamber, like the other rooms on the second floor, was to be shared by several lady guests that night. Fortunately, the custom was for the men to sleep downstairs, in chairs or on the floor wherever they could find a place. Patrick's chamber was empty.

Hilary gazed curiously about the small room that she had entered only once before, when she slipped in earlier that evening to put her farewell letter in the pocket of Patrick's workaday broadcloth jacket. Then it had been dark, and she'd not dared linger in any case. Now, as Patrick lit the candles, she knew a momentary surprise at the Spartan appearance of the room. A hard narrow bed occupied one corner; the only other furnishings were a washstand and a dark hand-carved chest that stood open against the wall. There were fowling pieces and fencing foils stacked in a corner, and the bed was cluttered with papers and books.

Hilary picked up a handful of papers and looked through them, suddenly shy and afraid to glance at Patrick, who was already stripping off his clothes. There were pamphlets on the tobacco trade, treatises on mining, a sheaf of music for the virginal, and a Latin book whose title meant nothing to Hilary. She remembered her first impression of Patrick as a reckless, pleasure-loving aristocrat. He was all that, certainly, but how much more besides!

"Oh, Patrick . . ." She turned to him and flung her arms about his naked body. "I do love you."

But in a few hours she would be gone, leaving nothing behind but a letter designed to convince him of the opposite. Hilary flushed a fiery red to match her hair. She could have bitten her tongue out.

Fortunately Patrick ascribed another meaning to her sudden confusion.

"Never fear, sweetheart," he said, holding her close and gently stroking her back, "there's nothing here you haven't seen before." With a hint of laughter in his eyes, he pushed her away from him, holding her shoulders so that she couldn't turn away. "Go on, look your fill, as I love to look at you. It's all right, darling girl, between man and wife."

"We're not that." Hilary dropped her eyes, afraid to look at Patrick for the feelings he aroused in her.

"No yet. Is that troubling you? I thought to wait until my parents could be informed, and that means finding a priest to satisfy my father, and that means a trip to Williamsburg . . . which would come more convenient," Patrick admitted with a grin, "after the winter sets in."

"And after your meeting with Governor Spotswood next week."

"Yes." Patrick frowned. "Don't worry about that. It will go all right. . . . Who told you, anyway?"

Hilary shrugged. "I hear things. A word here and there. Is it true you could lose your house if he demands the back taxes?"

Patrick's eyes flickered to the far corner of the room. "No. Of course not! Who's been feeding you such ridiculous stories?"

For such a good gambler, Hilary thought with a fondness that tugged painfully at her heart, Patrick was a terrible liar. He would really be better off when she was gone. She had to keep believing that, or all her resolution would break.

"It doesn't matter." Unshed tears made her whisper husky. "It doesn't matter at all. Just love me, Patrick. Love me tonight!"

Desire concentrated in the pit of her stomach as she gazed through the tears on the ends of her lashes at his long, lithe figure, the tanned chest and the crisp dark hair arrowing down his flat stomach, the long muscles of arms and legs. Her voice broke and she had to swallow before she could go on. "I never knew a man was so beautiful."

Patrick's fingers moved lightly over her gown, unlacing and unhooking with practiced ease. Her breasts ached with longing for his palms as the slippery ice-blue satin slid down about her waist. He freed the high-piled knot of ringlets, and her own hair brushed about her shoulders and tantalized her with the memory of caresses. "Beautiful? If that's what you want to see, my darling, look in the mirror."

His hands were hard on her shoulders as he swung her about before him. Hilary looked with a shock of recognition at the two faces reflected in the glass over the washstand: the man dark and young and intense, the woman with copper hair tumbling over white shoulders. Her eyes were large and glowing, her lips swollen from kisses, the snowy mounds of her breasts rose proudly from the tumble of blue satin that lay in careless folds beneath them like a frame for her beauty.

Wanton. Wicked. Beautiful . . . Hilary closed her eyes and felt Patrick's fingers forcing her chin up. "Look," he insisted. "I want you to know yourself and love yourself as I do. Last night I let you shut your eyes and pretend you weren't there when I lit the candles to enjoy your beauty. Tonight I want all of you, Hilary. Not just your body. Your mind and heart and those big gray eyes that look through a man to his very soul . . . I want you to look at us, Hilary, and know there's nothing wrong or shameful here."

His hand moved down to fumble with the folds of satin about her waist. With an impatient jerk he tore the waistband of the skirt and pushed it down about her hips. Her petticoat went with it, and she'd not worn a shift, fearing to spoil the line of the low-cut, tight bodice. There was nothing now but her own closed eyelids between her and the image in the mirror.

"Look," Patrick said again, his voice low and strong in her ear. He cupped her breast with one hand and she sucked in her breath at the shock of pleasure that stabbed through her at his touch. The other hand slipped lower, smoothing over her thighs, toying with the triangle of red curls between her legs, the palm rotating against her body and awakening the memory of delight. Hilary felt too weak to stand up; she leaned back against Patrick's body and felt his hardness rising against her. That was another sweet torment, an anticipation that sent shuddering pleasure through her body and weakened all the fibers of her muscles.

"Look," Patrick said for a third time, "or . . . I'll stop." His palm lifted and hovered, just brushing the tight triangle of curls. Hilary arched her body to follow it, but he held her back. "If you can do it, you can look at it."

Her lashes fluttered up and for a moment she was dazzled by the reflection of the candle in the mirror. Then her vision cleared and she saw at last what Patrick wanted her to see: the simple beauty of two bodies joined in love, the woman made for the man and the man for the woman. Her flesh glowed with an inner white radiance against the tanned hardness of his muscular chest; her eyes shone with revelation, and behind her she could see the reflection of Patrick's dark sapphire eyes.

"Beautiful," she whispered. "We're beautiful."

"And don't you forget it," said Patrick, while his fingers slipped inside her and began a gentle probing movement that was likely to make her forget everything, even her own name. She put her hands behind her and felt his own desire rising as she caressed the hardening shaft of flesh with fingers that dared anything.

"Hilary, my love, my life." Patrick slipped one arm under her knees, the other about her shoulders, and carried her to the narrow bed, where he knelt over her with such a blaze of desire in his sapphire eyes that she was almost afraid, seeing the power and the intensity that could burn her up like dry leaves in a forest fire. Her unbound hair crackled when he drew his fingers through it, clinging to his hands and her face, and the tremors that began in her scalp raced through her body down to her toes and left her moist and shaking when he finally gathered her into his arms.

"Hilary, Hilary," he murmured, burying his face in the shadowed curve of her neck under the crackling masses of coppery hair. His lips touched there and clung to her skin, tracing a path of warm smooth kisses along her shoulder and down to the blue vein beating so hard in the crook of her elbow. The feathery touches sent quivers of pleasure coursing up through her arm and through her breasts, which ached for his touch.

His head came back up along the path he had traced until his lips closed over her mouth, sending further tremors of sensual desire through her as his tongue flickered between her lips and released a new rush of sweetness. He eased his body over her and she gloried in the lean hard perfection of bone and muscle and warm skin beneath her palms. She slid one hand down the length of him and felt him start with passion as her fingers glided over the firmness of his hip and stroked the crisp dark hairs on his thighs. His mouth took hers with new demanding urgency, pressing kisses upon her until her lips stung while his body pressed into her and turned her to molten gold wherever he touched.

In that blaze of glory there was nothing for her but Patrick, no moment beyond this one in which he possessed her utterly. She held him tightly against her, moving her legs to clasp him with thighs that longed to feel him, and his tongue drew a golden line from the corner of her mouth to the throbbing tip of one breast. The gentle tugging of his lips there sent a piercing dart of desire into the center of her body. She moved against him, wanting to welcome him into her, and moaned with frustration as he still held back.

"Hilary, my precious girl," he whispered. The

vibrations of his throat against her breast intoxicated her beyond understanding the sense of
his words. "We'll have the priest in Williamsburg, but this is the true marriage night for you
and me." He raised himself over her on his
elbows, looking down with a piercing gaze of
such intensity that she felt herself caught and
impaled on the blue dart of his eyes. "You
belong to me," he said softly. One hand tangled in the curls at the back of her neck and
held her fast against the hard bolster. "Once
you denied it, but know this, Hilary Pembroke:
you're mine, not because I bought you, but
because we were made for each other, and not
for a term of years, but forever. You are mine
forever, and God help the man who tries to
take you away from me!"

"No one will take me away from you," Hilary
whispered, raising her arms to bring him back
down to her. She held his face against her cheek
and stared at the ceiling with wide gray eyes
that reflected only emptiness. It was true. No
man was taking her away. She would go of her
own free will, and after he read her letter, he
would never forgive her or look for her. They
had only these last few hours until moonrise.
With sudden fierce passion Hilary tightened her
arms about Patrick, hugging him to her as if she
could bear the imprint of his body against hers
through eternity. "Love me tonight, Patrick,"
she whispered. "Love me as if tonight were all
we had."

Patrick gave a low, throaty laugh. Raising
himself slightly, he ran his fingers over her
breasts, brushing the throbbing nipples lightly

and raising an agony of anticipation in Hilary. "And don't we have a lifetime together? But I'll make this night a lifetime in itself, darling girl."

That was what it would have to be for her. But the cold thought of the future blew away like a wisp of fog under the heat of Patrick's kisses. Bending his head, he sent his tongue circling each nipple in turn, still with that featherlight touch that was almost painful in its restraint. Unconsciously, Hilary arched upward, sending the peak of her breast into his mouth. The warm tugging of lips and the flickering of his tongue excited her until she moaned and rolled her head from side to side, afraid that she could stand no more. His teeth grazed the awakened flesh and sent tiny shocks fluttering through her breast. Then his mouth trailed sweetly tormenting kisses over one breast and up the other, over and over, until she forgot everything but the sweet magic of his lips exciting her to unbearable heights.

"My lovely, lovely girl," Patrick murmured. He ran one hand over the slender whiteness of her body from shoulder to knee, and Hilary shuddered beneath the touch. She reached out to stroke the arrow of dark hair that pointed down from tanned chest to flat stomach, and felt him shaking with desire at the touch of her fingertips.

"Oh God, Hilary," Patrick whispered as her exploring fingers slid farther, circling and stroking him until he moaned with desire. "I need you, my love. I need you now."

She parted her thighs for him and joyously welcomed him into her body, wrapping arms and legs about him and arching to meet his demanding thrusts. Too soon the explosion of light and color came, shaking her body from head to foot and filling her with unendurable sweetness, while Patrick's cries told her that he had found his release at the same time.

They lay quietly, arms and legs entangled, Patrick's head on her breast, her heart pounding as she recovered from an ecstasy so intense that it was almost like dying and being transported into another realm. His hipbones ground into hers and the weight of his muscular frame over her made breathing difficult. Hilary stirred a little, trying to shift him, and her eyes widened as she felt him growing hard inside her.

"I told you," Patrick said, kissing her on the mouth, "that this night would be a lifetime."

This time his movements were slow and sweet and sure, rocking her back and forth on the brink of ecstasy for an eternity, while his arms clasped her tight and he whispered outrageous endearments that set her blushing right down to her toes.

"How can you be embarrassed," he murmured, "when we're doing what I'm merely talking about?" He moved strongly against her and Hilary moaned at the newly heightened sensations that demanded an answering movement from her.

"Please, Patrick!" She arched up against him and he moved away slightly. "You want it? Tell me what you want!"

Hilary's face burned. "You," she whispered. "Only you. Always you."

Patrick relented and came back to her, repeating the slow torturous rhythm that kept her dangling eternally over the abyss, eyes shut and hands clutching at air, until his last movements thrust her over and she fell through chasms blazing with colored fire and cried out and held him to her in the endless spinning vortex of their mutual joy.

She drifted, eyes shut, from the restful aftermath of pleasure into the deeper rest of sleep, and Patrick slept with one arm flung protectively around her and his head pillowed on her shoulder. The sounds of their guests stumbling up the stairs, giggling and gossiping as they composed themselves for sleep, interwove with Hilary's uneasy dreams but could not call her from the deep warm safety of sleep in Patrick's arms.

Some deep-buried alarm woke her in time to see, through the uncurtained window, the first hint of silver light glowing in the horizon. It was moonrise. And time to go.

She slipped away from under Patrick's arm. He shifted restlessly, mumbled something, and reached out for emptiness, his arm still curved to fit the shape of her body. She picked up her skirt and bodice where they lay in a tangled blue-and-silver heap on the floor. The rustle disturbed Patrick and she froze, clutching the dress against her breasts.

"Hilary?" He was awake and sitting up in an instant, eyes wide in the darkness of the room. "Oh, there you are. It's a cold night to have to go outside, isn't it? Come back in and get warm." He lifted the quilt and she slipped under it, letting his assumption that she had been outside to visit the necessary house go unchallenged. She couldn't get away now anyway; she would have to wait until he fell asleep again.

"Mmm." Patrick's hands were everywhere under the quilt, caressing and tantalizing and exciting her. "A cold night and a warm girl. How very hot you must be, darling girl, to warm me so even after you've been out in the cold night air. Feel how warm I'm getting." He took her palm and placed it over him. She felt the throb of his desire strong under her hand and shivered in delicious weakness. Patrick stretched luxuriously, eyes half-closed, almost purring as she moved her fingers gently up and down.

Suddenly he flung the quilt back and she squeaked in surprise as the chill air of the room struck her bare flesh.

"This time, darling girl," he informed her, "you're going to work for it."

Hilary burrowed into the warmth of his shoulder. "I thought we were going back to sleep."

Patrick took her hand and firmly replaced it where he wanted it. "Does this feel like sleep to you? Hmm?"

Ignoring her halfhearted protests, he took her by the hips and pulled her onto her knees astride him, directing her movements until she could slowly lower herself onto him. He groaned with pleasure as he slid into her. "That's it . . . oh, beautiful by moonlight! Why do we ever bother with clothes?" He caressed her body, silvery-white in the moonlight that turned her copper hair to pools of ink spilling across her shoulders, and she sighed and moved over him and felt a warm moist rush of desire as his hands passed lightly over breasts and stomach and flanks to grip her around the hips with fierce urgency.

She hardly needed the urging of his hands to tell her what to do: her body caught the rhythm of desire from him, rocking back and forth in a furious crescendo that brought the curling cloud of her hair snapping with life around her face and shoulders, her fingers digging into his shoulders, her thighs clasping him exultantly. They might have been lovers for the first time, or separated for years, so strong was the uncontrolled passion that tossed them both around like dry leaves in the autumn wind. Naked and shameless in the moonlight, feeling no cold for the deep internal fire that warmed her from within, Hilary gave herself over utterly, wantonly, and completely to the sensual heat in her blood. Nothing now but Patrick, Patrick in her and holding her, and his thighs rough under her, the smell of his skin and his moans of desire and the cries that broke from her own parted lips as he surged under her, bringing their joining to a triumphant conclusion.

"My love," he whispered as she subsided, damp and trembling, into his embrace. "My darling girl, my Hilary, my wife."

And as quickly as that, he was asleep again, while Hilary cast a guilty glance over her shoulder at the moon that had risen over the outbuildings while they were enjoying themselves together.

There was no more time now. She *must* be gone. Patrick's breathing was deep and regular, and his arms had slackened in sleep, leaving her free to slip from his arms. She moved with infinite caution toward the edge of the bed.

"Hilary." She froze where she lay. But it was only a murmur out of his dreams. He rolled over on his stomach without opening his eyes, and threw one arm out across the pillow. His fingers found the curling ends of her hair and closed about one lock.

Hilary tugged gently at the lock of hair, hoping to free herself without disturbing the dream. His fingers only closed the tighter, imprisoning her even more firmly. "Ne'leave me," he mumbled. "Promise . . ."

From the edge of the bed where she lay she could just reach the washstand where Patrick's shaving razor lay, a steel-blue gleam in the moonlight. Hilary reached cautious groping fingers up to the washstand, found the blade, and brought it back to her side. She took it by the handle and slowly, carefully sawed through the imprisoned lock of hair, one strand at a time. It felt as if she were cutting through her own heart, so deep and painful was the ache in her chest.

Finally it was done. Hilary eased silently off the edge of the bed and picked up her clothes. The satin skirt rustled as she stepped into it. As she fastened the bodice, Patrick sighed in his sleep and reached out with his free hand to caress the long ringlet he held so tightly.

Tear splotches made ugly, widening dark circles on the ice-blue silk. Hilary fled the room, tiptoed through a dark hall full of sleeping guests, made her way down the stairs and out of the house without even thinking about the problems of feeling her way quietly through the darkened hall. She felt unreal, like a disembodied spirit, floating silently past the dreamers. Her real self was still there in Patrick's room, cuddled close to his body, holding him tightly. What was left was only a cold, competent shell whose white face, for some reason, was streaked with tears.

She felt both relieved and disappointed when she rounded the stables and saw Kendall O'-Leary's string of horses, packed and ready to go, standing patiently while their long-legged master paced up and down and muttered curses into his mustache.

"Here I am," Hilary said, stepping into the pale pool of moonlight between the stables and the forest. "I'm sorry if I've kept you waiting. I couldn't get away . . . before."

Kendall's frown changed into a smile that alarmed her even more than his anger. "Sure, and I'd never grudge a few minutes of waiting for a lovely lady." His forefinger traced the paths of tears down her cheek. "And it's wise y'are to be coming with me. Kendall O'Leary never did aught to bring tears to the cheeks of a pretty girl."

"Dickie and Bet?" Hilary felt it would be worse than unwise to go off into the forest with only Kendall for escort.

The tall Irishman jerked his head toward the shadowy woods. "Waiting over there. My partner's a bit shy of being seen, you'll understand?"

Hilary saw a movement in the shadows and recognized Dickie's brass-buttoned coat with relief. "All right. I'm ready to go."

As Dickie and Bet came out of the woods, Kendall lifted Hilary and deposited her on the horse just behind his in the string. The pack loads had been redistributed into two bulky saddlebags, one on each side of the high wooden saddle. Hilary's full skirts billowed out over the packs as if she were riding in a hoop skirt.

"The stirrups are maybe a wee bit too long for you." Kendall bent over and made a great play of shortening first one stirrup, then the other, letting his fingers linger around Hilary's ankle as he fitted her foot into the stirrup loop.

"Come on, O'Leary," Dickie urged in a low voice. "We're late already."

Kendall stepped back and gave Hilary a bow and a mocking grin. "Just helping the lovely lady here with the fit of her stirrups." He moved closer and whispered in her ear, "And anytime you want me to help you fit anything else, Kendall O'Leary's your man, my darlin'." He winked and vaulted one-handed into his saddle. As the pack train took off into the forest, Hilary twisted her head to gaze behind her, her throat aching with unshed tears, at her last sight of Moonshadows standing tall and proud on the banks of the river.

Patrick's window was dark.

∾ 16 ∾

The week-long trip to Jephthah's Community of Saints was marked by dissension among the four ill-assorted people who had set out on this journey into the wilderness.

For the first few days Hilary was aware of little but the ache in her heart at the thought that she had left Patrick forever. Her fine dress of blue silk grew stained and crumpled from days of riding and nights of helping Bet gather firewood and cook the evening meal, her skin was burned by the September sun and scratched by the branches that reached out to catch her face on woodland paths, her red hair became a tangled lump twisted up at the back of her head. None of it mattered. Nothing mattered anymore.

Slowly the pain of parting became a bearable sorrow, not any less, but something that she could push aside and not think about for several minutes at a time. She began to notice

other things then: the soreness in her thighs
from hours of riding astride on a clumsy wooden
saddle made for someone twice her size, Kendall O'Leary's rough kindness in helping her on
and off the saddle, the growing tension between Dickie and Bet.

"That feller O'Leary's sweet on you," Bet said
one evening. The two women had been left
alone to fix a meal while Kendall and Dickie
looked after the horses. Hilary took a handful
of cornmeal from a leather bag, mixed it with
water, and formed a flat cake over a stone that
she shoved up into the coals of the cooking fire.
She was aching in every limb from the long
day's riding and longed for nothing more than
to wrap up in her blanket and sleep until it was
time to start again.

"Well?" Bet prodded. "Whatcher goin' to do
about it?" As she spoke, she wielded Dickie's
belt knife with quick deft strokes to skin the
two squirrels that Kendall's long musket had
picked out of the trees as they rode along.
Stewed, they would be a tasty addition to the
flat cakes of Indian meal that formed the staple
of their diet.

"Nothing, I suppose," Hilary said wearily.
"Does it matter?" Did anything matter? Her
world had narrowed to a few essentials: food,
sleep, going to Jephthah. If she let herself think
about anything else, the trail of her thoughts
always led back to Patrick.

"Nothing," she repeated, biting off that thought
before it could get started. "Shall I put the water on?"

"Yes, I'm almost through skinning these

scrawny little beasts. Cor, what wouldn't I give for a decent leg of pork, with apples and potatoes around it, and real bread to sop up the juices!" Bet smacked her lips in memory and dropped the squirrels into the three-legged pot that Hilary stood over the coals. "Well, if you don't do nothing, he'll do something," she warned, reverting to the earlier subject. "He's not a man to court a girl for long without expectin' some kind of payment. Too bad it's not me as he has his eye on—I'd know how to pay him!" She gave a lusty laugh that changed into a squawk of pain as Dickie came up behind her and kicked her sprawling.

"Know how to pay him, would you?" he said, raising his doubled fist. "What about me? Who got you out of Moonshadows?"

"A lot o' thanks I owe ye for that, you little lout!" Bet spat back from her hands and knees. She got up, ostentatiously dusting her hands. "At least at Moonshadows I ate regular and slept soft. When I agreed to come away with you, I didn't know we was going to live in the woods like wild Indians."

"Aw, Bet, it's only for a little while," Dickie coaxed. He put his arm around her waist. "There's fortunes to be made in the Indian trade. Soon I'll be as rich as any planter, and you shall have a good brick house and sit in the parlor with a white apron on like a reg'lar lady."

"Promises," Bet sniffed. "I'd sooner a cabin now than a brick mansion when I'm too old to enjoy it." But she let Dickie lead her off into the woods, and the sound of their wrangling faded to soft murmurs while Hilary sat and stared unheeding into the glowing coals of the fire.

The next day they stopped at a shabby back-woods settlement, two cabins and a lean-to sur-rounded by a clearing where some spindly cornstalks carried ears that were being left to ripen on the stalk. A skinny pig, wild as a woods animal, put its tail up and charged off into the woods with squeals of alarm at their approach. A woman whose calico dress strained at the seams over the bulge of late pregnancy appeared at the open door of one of the cabins.

"It's the trader," she called back into the dark-ness of the cabin.

They spent that night on the floor of Alice Garvey's cabin, after Kendall's gift of a length of blue flowered chintz and his easy flirtatious banter had brought a little sparkle into the tired woman's eyes. Her husband, Ephraim, a·lean man with black hair to his shoulders, dressed in stained buckskins, lifted the heavy cooking ket-tle for her and brought water from the spring and never took his eyes off her. "Our first," he confided in an undertone once when Alice was outside.

The two words were very nearly his sole con-tribution to the conversation. Kendall O'Leary, Bet, and the occupant of the other cabin, a paunchy widower named Leon, kept up a lively flow of banter as Alice cooked. Dickie watched silently from a corner, and Hilary was too tired and heartsick to join in, even if she could have followed the swift flow of naughty puns and quips that Bet and Leon were trading back and forth. Ephraim spoke only once, to hush

Leon when he began talking of the trouble between Tuscaroras and whites farther south. "Not in front of Alice," he said quietly. "Makes her nervous." And his eyes went back to his wife where she bent over the cooking fire.

When they'd first arrived, Hilary had felt sorry for Alice, trapped in this shabby attempt at a settlement with her taciturn husband. But by the end of the evening her pity had changed to envy, as she saw the way Ephraim looked after his wife and anticipated her every need. The quiet devotion that was evident in his every gesture reminded her painfully of Patrick's love and care for her.

Bet too was envious, but in a slightly different way. When Dickie was loading the packs on the horses the next morning, she announced rather defiantly that she wasn't going with them. "I'm tired of living rough," she announced. "Leon's got a nice tight cabin, an' he needs a woman. Besides, he says the Indians in Carolina are fixing to go on the warpath. I ain't traipsing off into the forest just to see me lovely red locks on some savage's trophy belt."

Dickie stormed at Bet, then pleaded with her, but to no avail. She ducked into Leon's cabin and refused to come out, even when the jingling of bridle bells and cracking of Kendall's whip announced the departure of the pack train.

Two days later they reached the New Community of Saints.

"Three houses. No, two cabins and a stable." Hilary dismounted and stared around the forest clearing in disbelief. From Jephthah's letters to

England she had pictured a thriving community, another little village like the Community of Saints in England before they'd been turned off the land. But this was just like Ephraim and Alice's settlement and the other isolated backwoods cabins they had passed: a few low windowless buildings of unbarked logs chinked with mud, a patch of corn, and some pigs rooting in the forest at the clearing's edge.

Then she remembered the love that had made Ephraim and Alice's dwelling a home, and straightened her weary shoulders. Love and kindness could make anyplace a palace. If Jephthah would have her, she would make this a home for them.

Her heart skipped a beat at the sight of his lanky black-clad figure advancing from the farthest cabin. "Hilary! What are you doing here?" The words were not accompanied by the welcoming smile she had been praying for; his eyes were hard and cold. "I thought we agreed that you were to stay with Lyle until I was ready to receive you. Where did you get that dress? It's not decent. Cover yourself."

Hilary flushed but stood her ground. "You didn't tell me I was to stay till spring. Jephthah, I couldn't remain there any longer. Patrick was . . . He wanted . . ." She owed him the truth, but found it impossible to come out with it under Jephthah's cold, disapproving gaze, with Kendall O'Leary and Dickie both listening to her. "He wanted to marry me," she ended. "So I came to you. Jephthah, aren't you . . . aren't you even a little glad to see me?"

"Couldn't? Nonsense!" Jephthah dismissed her

story with a brisk clap of his hands. "If you were strong in the Lord's armor, Hilary, you would have been able to endure much worse tribulations. Now, come inside. You've interrupted our prayer meeting."

Impossible, after that, to tell him the truth about her time with Patrick. Hilary's head dropped and she pulled the tattered remnants of her blue satin bodice about her shoulders, barely hearing Kendall O'Leary behind her making plausible excuses as to why he and Dickie couldn't stay for the prayer meeting.

"Always delighted to hear the good word, Preacher, but we've a good few miles to make before dark. You've heard of the Tuscarora trouble on the border?"

"Idle rumors." Jephthah's deep voice carried total conviction. "We of the Community of Saints have always dealt fairly with the Indians. If you traders did likewise, you'd have nothing to fear."

"Aye, that's as may be," Kendall replied, "but I mean to go no farther toward Carolina than this until these murdering savages calm down. We'll swing west and north and trade with the tribes along the mountains. And if I were you, Preacher, I'd get your people off their knees and set them to building a good stout palisade around this place."

"The Lord will protect us," Jephthah said calmly. "May he do the same for you."

"Aye, but I think I'll help the Lord out by keeping a good charge of powder and shot in my musket," Kendall muttered. He nodded at Jephthah and chucked Hilary under the chin. "Heart up, mavourneen. I'll be back with my pack train in a few weeks, and if you're tired of the settled life by then, you can always have a place in Kendall O'Leary's bedroll." He winked, mounted, and kicked his scrawny horse in the sides.

As Hilary trailed behind Jephthah toward the far cabin with lagging steps, the dying jingle of bridle bells in the distance made her feel more lost and desolate than ever. She was truly committed now, with no way to leave should Jephthah deny her after he heard her story. On the way there she had rested her hopes in the memory of the kindly elder brother that Jephthah had been to her when she was a child. But now, looking again at the harsh lined features of this older Jephthah, she was beginning to acknowledge the truth of Patrick's words. Jephthah had changed—they had both changed—and it was possible she had made a terrible mistake.

The lukewarm greeting of the other Saints did nothing to reassure her. There were only six other people in the community: a tall gaunt Englishwoman named Mary, who followed Jephthah's every motion with her eyes and treated his slightest whim like one of the Ten Commandments; a colonial couple who had been Jephthah's first converts; and a German widower with his two grown children.

At the end of that first interminable prayer meeting, which consisted mainly of Jephthah praying for what seemed like hours while the rest of them knelt, Hilary had been taken aside by the Englishwoman.

"We must cover you decently," Mary said, echoing Jephthah's words as though she had read his mind. She produced a coarse, shape-less homespun gown from the row of garments hanging on pegs at the back of the cabin and slipped it over Hilary's head. The hem came several inches below her feet.

"Is this yours?" Hilary felt more uncomfort-able than ever, to be an object of charity the instant she arrived. "I don't want to take it. I mean, I could make something for myself—"

"You will," Mary agreed, "when you have time. But you can't go around the Community half-naked."

Following Mary's instructions, Hilary wrig-gled out of her blue silk bodice and skirt with-out taking off the enveloping homespun gown. Mary took the garments at arm's length and started to carry them over to the fireplace. "Wait!" Hilary cried. "What are you going to do with my clothes?"

"Burn them, of course," Mary told her.

"There's no need. They're clean . . . well, reasonably clean. Anyway, I can wash them."

"All right," Mary conceded. "The bodice is indecent. It has to go. But the skirt . . ." She measured Hilary with her eyes. "It is too short and shows your ankles. That will never do, but perhaps it can be cut down to fit Grete."

That was the daughter of the German con-vert, a pasty-faced shy girl about Hilary's age but even shorter. Hilary saw the satin skirt go with a slight pang and told herself that was ridiculous, to be sad about something so trivial as a dress. It just showed how thoroughly she had been corrupted in her short time with Pat-rick. But when she saw the remnants of the blue satin bodice turn black and crisp in the flames of the cabin fire, her heart twisted painfully and she had to look away to hide the silly tears in her eyes.

For the rest of the day there was no chance to talk privately to Jephthah, even had she been eager for that meeting. Mary introduced her to the other members of the Community and then took her over to a contraption Hilary had seen and wondered about when she first came in. The stump of an oak tree rose some three feet above the ground. Sticking out of the stump was a tall, thick pole, very smooth for the first foot or so that rose above the stump, but still showing the rough ax cuts above that point, and growing thicker until it terminated in a stubby end with the bark still on it. Beside the stump was a basket of Indian corn.

"This," Mary told her, "is where we grind our corn."

Hilary stared at the contraption in silence. It didn't resemble the tall water-powered mills that dotted the banks of English streams. Where were the grinding stones? And what powered it?

She learned that the hollowed-out stump and the smooth end of the pole were the grinding surfaces, and her own arms were the power source. Mary demonstrated, pouring a handful of corn into the hollow of the stump, then raising the pole and bringing it down like a gigantic pestle into an oversize mortar. Thump, thump, thump, she pounded industriously away until the corn was reduced to fragments. These she shook through a fine mesh sieve into a wooden bowl, returning the coarser fragments to the stump for more pounding.

"It's not such bad work," she said, wiping the sweat from her forehead with the back of one bony hand. "See, the weight of the thick end helps you bring it down good an' hard to split the corn. Takes a long time, though. We spell each other. You start with this lot, and when you've got a bowl full of meal, you bring it to me and I'll set Grete to pounding the next batch."

Hilary learned that it did indeed take a long time to pound enough corn into meal to feed seven—now eight—people, and if the weighted end of the pole helped on the downstroke, it was just so much more weight to lift on the upstroke. Before she'd filled half a bowl with coarse-ground meal, her shoulders were aching and her hands were blistered from the monotonous labor.

After the corn pounding there was fat to be rendered and mixed with lye to form an evil-smelling soft soap, then cabins to be swept with brooms made out of a sapling with one end cut into fuzzy shavings. The frequent visits of the German boy, grinning and speaking to her in his own language and somehow always where she had to push by him, did nothing to enliven the tasks. Hilary was relieved when Mary sent him about his business and showed her the loom in the big cabin. She explained that it was to be threaded with store-bought warp on which the rougher homespun weft could be woven into coarse cloth like that of which Hilary's dress was made.

"We aim to produce everything here ourselves," Mary, who had constituted herself Hilary's chief guide and adviser, told her, "so that we can be entirely independent of the sinful world."

Hilary thought they had made a pretty good start already. She remembered with longing, as though from another world, the peaceful English village where the Grahamites lived at one end and the other villagers at the other. Between the two clusters of cottages there had been a butcher and a baker and a general store where one could buy woven cloth and other things that she'd never before thought of as luxuries. And she'd thought she worked hard then, helping Mother Graham about the house and in the dairy! One day of the New Community of Saints made that old life seem a haven of ease and luxury. As for Moonshadows, she didn't dare even think of it.

The work of the New Community did not cease until nightfall, when Jephthah struck the big iron triangle outside the bigger cabin to call them all to another prayer session. Hilary knelt on aching bones, thankful for the respite from corn mill and loom, and beginning to understand why nobody objected to Jephthah's interminable prayers. She would rather have been lying down, but kneeling and dozing off while he prayed was an acceptable alternative.

Her own name caught her ear and she came awake with a start. Jephthah was telling the Almighty about her arrival in the New Community, with a detailed description of the sinful mode of dress she had been led into at Moonshadows and a prayer that he might be able to guide her footsteps back into the way of grace now that she was under his care. Hilary felt her cheeks burning. Did he have to go into all that right in front of the other Saints? Merciful Lord, what would he do when she confessed to him about Patrick? Would that too be considered a fit matter for public discussion?

But Jephthah's God wasn't merciful.

It was the first time she had allowed herself, even in thought, to criticize Jephthah or anything about him.

The small disloyal thought stayed with her as his extemporaneous prayer rambled on, covering everything from the need for more converts to the need for more seed corn. There were frequent mentions of the disruption to their community caused by the arrival of a new member, and prayers that the men of the community would not be distracted from the paths of righteousness by lusting after her.

Finally he pronounced a long, sonorous "Amen" and Hilary got to her feet with the rest of the Saints. Her numbed legs would scarcely hold her; she caught at one of the pegs that supported a shelf in the wall. The peg came away in her hand and she watched the shelf slowly tilt toward the floor while iron cooking pots and tools clanged and bounced off each other and subsided onto the hard-packed dirt of the floor with a series of dull thuds.

Everybody was staring at her.

"Hilary," Jephthah called. "Would you come forward, please."

Blushing furiously, Hilary approached Jephthah at the front of the room. Ebenezer Graham would have beaten her with a leather strap for a lesser fault, but many times Jephthah had protected her. Now he took her hand, gazing down at her with a kindly smile, and she felt his remote kindness like a shield between her and the accusing eyes of the Saints.

"You have cast yourself upon my protection and I dare not, for your soul's sake, return you to the sinful world," Jephthah told her. "But you cannot be allowed to remain unmarried here, a constant lure to the men. I have decided that we should be married at once." Without waiting for her to speak, he launched into the lengthy prayer written by Ebenezer Graham to solemnize marriages among the Saints.

His large callused hand was firm around hers, but Hilary felt no warmth from his touch. Her cheeks burned and her hands felt icy cold, and she herself felt oddly remote from the words that Jephthah was speaking. She had never thought he would marry her at once, before she'd had a chance to confess to him about Patrick. What could she do now? She lacked the courage to speak out before the disapproving Saints. And in any case, she remembered now, Ebenezer Graham's wedding prayers left no place for the woman to speak her responses. Her silent presence was all that was required; the Saints did not believe a woman should be burdened with such heavy responsibilities as consenting to her own marriage.

Jephthah went on and on, departing now from the words sanctioned by his father to extemporize his own prayers for their godly companionship. The two smoking iron lamps that provided light for the cabin hissed and sputtered as the slender flames encountered impurities in the animal fat they burned. The greasy smell of burning fat made Hilary feel sick. Would Jephthah never stop? She had to be alone with him, she had to confess to him, she had to . . .

A picture of what else would happen when they were alone together stopped her frantic, scurrying thoughts in their tracks. She couldn't. Not with Jephthah. Not after Patrick. It would be obscene, indecent—and there was some ironic humor in that, but she was too frightened to enjoy it.

Hilary's fear was nothing to that which possessed the staff at Moonshadows in the days after Patrick woke and discovered Hilary's departure.

"Master's going to kill somebody one of these days, the black temper he's in," Elspeth confided to Hawkins. "Threw a boot at me when I tried to get him to take a little nourishment, he did."

"If you mean that sour gruel you forced down my throat when I was sick last winter," Hawkins said with a sniff, "I don't blame him. What a gentleman needs is some good brandy and the consolation of another gentleman as can understand how a man feels in these trying circumstances. Let me deal with him."

A moment later Hawkins was retreating down the stairs at top speed, while the other boot flew over his head, followed by the silver tray on which Hawkins had presented the brandy decanter. Elspeth clutched her sides and laughed heartily at Hawkins' discomfiture.

"Well," Hawkins said, determined to make the best of the situation, "he kept the brandy, at least."

"If you think *that's* a good sign," Elspeth retorted, "you don't know as much about gentlemen as you claim to. Now we'll have a foul-tempered drunk on our hands instead of a foul-tempered gent. See how much of an improvement that is!"

It was three days before Patrick finished off the brandy, slept off its effects, and emerged from his chamber looking sober, quiet, and pale. He acceded without question to Carruthers' urging that they spend the entire next week preparing a final draft of the financial plan that they were to show to Governor Spotswood.

"Five days to work," Carruthers emphasized the short time remaining to them. "We can just do it—if you'll concentrate this time, Master Patrick." He looked at the young master over the tops of his glasses with a glance in which sternness warred with unwilling sympathy. Who'd have thought the boy would take it so hard? No matter, Carruthers told himself. He had only done what needed to be done. Since Patrick Lyle Senior hadn't arrived in time to talk some sense into the lad, it had been necessary to take sterner measures.

Patrick made a valiant effort to interest himself in the details of Indian corn and oxen, tobacco and shipping, that had seemed so important a few days ago when he thought he was building a new life for himself and Hilary. Now,

what was the point? He was half-tempted to let
the whole matter slide into oblivion, let the
governor sell Moonshadows, and take off into
the back country with his gun and his buckskins like any other frontiersman. Why labor to
preserve a home that was no home without a
certain redheaded sprite flitting from dairy to
stillroom and back to the great house again?
Only Carruthers' kindly, patient nagging, and
the faint desire not to disappoint the old man,
kept him at the now meaningless task.

"I thought she cared for me," he said in the
middle of an inventory of the plantation's resources for the tobacco trade. "She was so sweet
and loving. But then to go off with nothing but
this heartless letter!"

He crumpled the scrap of paper in his hand.
Carruthers sighed and began adding up again
the projections for the number of wagons that
could be built and placed in service over the
next five years, and the cost of a skilled wheel-
wright to be deducted from the anticipated tobacco profits. He had to admire Mistress Hilary.
She'd kept her end of the bargain, leaving Patrick a letter so blunt and uncompromising that
he believed it without question. And for what?
She'd not taken the bribe he offered—she'd gone
to a life harder than any she and Patrick would
have known, even if Moonshadows had been
sold. Carruthers felt, and ruthlessly quashed, a
faint suspicion that he might have been wrong
about Hilary. Perhaps she loved Patrick more
than his property, after all.

And what of it? He'd still done the right
thing in the long run. The young fool would get

over this infatuation and go on to marry a girl of family to match his own, a girl fitted to be hostess of Moonshadows—and thanks to Carruthers' intervention, he'd still have Moonshadows when that day arrived.

"With the new settlers we can clear as many fields again next year, Master Patrick, doubling our tobacco harvest in the following season. You've forgotten to add that into the projections."

"But why would she leave me a lock of her hair if she didn't care at all? Merely to torture me? I ought to throw it into the fire!" Patrick moodily patted the breast pocket of his coat where the precious lock reposed, carefully tied with a black velvet ribbon and wrapped in black silk.

It was a rough five days for Carruthers. As if he didn't have enough to do with trying to keep the young master on track, there were also outside distractions to fend off. Three separate times a group of those Cornish miners they were trying to turn into decent settlers came up to the great house asking to speak with Patrick. The first two times Carruthers was able to shoo them away, saying that the young master was busy with important affairs. The last time he was out of the room and they made it as far as the office; he came back from a visit to the necessary house to find Patrick throwing them out of the office.

"I don't want to hear about mines," he told them. "Mines are where all my troubles started. I've reformed. I'm not chasing a will-o'-the-wisp anymore. I know there's no silver there except what I've poured into the land in my own folly."

"No, Master Patrick," Jer Polwhys agreed. He had been appointed spokesman for the group. "No silver. But we've been looking at the rocks—"

"Well, go and look at the tobacco fields instead, that's what I bought you for!" Patrick slammed the door with an oath and Carruthers nodded placid approval. Young Master Patrick was getting on the right track at last; even his loss of temper was a good sign, coming as it did in a good cause.

"Do you think, if I'd found silver, maybe she'd have stayed with me?"

Carruthers realized that the cure was not quite complete. "Back to work, Master Patrick," he said briskly. "We were, I believe, projecting the expected revenues from selling your surplus Indian corn to the neighbors. That should provide enough cash to meet the day-to-day operating expenses of the plantation, leaving you free to devote the entire tobacco crop to paying off the back taxes and those other . . . hem . . . debts. In five years you should own Moonshadows free and clear."

The promise didn't cheer Master Patrick as it should have done, but at least he took up his pen again.

Carruthers was less successful with the buckskin-clad trader who rode out of the woods from the south on the eve of their departure for Williamsburg, brandishing his long musket and demanding to see the master immediately.

"Kendall O'Leary! Haven't we seen enough

of you for one season? No, you may *not* come in and speak to Master Patrick. We've serious matters to deal with here," Carruthers said, trying to block the rascal's entrance to the house with his own pudgy body. "Master Patrick will see you upon his return from Williamsburg."

"That'll be too late." The dirty fellow poked his long musket into Carruthers' chest. "Indian trouble on the frontier. The Tuscaroras are up. They've taken Martin's Ford, they've attacked the white settlers along the Neuse, and they're heading toward the Tar River. Me and me partner barely escaped with our goods!"

Kendall's rising voice called Patrick out of the office. He paled beneath his tan at the mention of the Tar River and sprang to the door, pushing Carruthers out of his way.

"The Tar? Did they take the New Community of Saints?"

"Not yet." Kendall spat out a stream of dark juice from the tobacco quid in his mouth, narrowly missing the scrubbed boards of the portico and bespattering one of Patrick's new-planted saplings. "Heading that way, though. If you're still interested in that pretty little redhead, you might want to know, that's where I left her."

In the next few minutes Patrick's listless frame underwent a transformation. He became a young whirlwind, rampaging through the house, sending messengers to Colonel Quincy across the river, ordering one man to load the muskets in the arms room and another to bring out fresh horses to carry Kendall's pack goods. When Kendall protested that he'd no intention of donating his stock in trade as ransom for any white captives, Patrick snarled wordlessly and the tall Irishman backed down without further argument.

"He's right," Dickie Baynes put in. "Me Bet's in the path of the raid. Me share of the goods is worth it to get her back safe."

Patrick clapped the little cockney on the shoulder. "That's a man, Dickie. Tell you what. If we get her back, in payment for your goods I'll give you two a cabin and a bit of land."

"What about *my* half of the goods?" Kendall O'Leary protested.

Patrick gave him a cold glance. "I'll refrain from prosecuting you over the two bondservants you stole."

Carruthers rolled his eyes heavenward and prayed that these two rascally traders would get on with their ransom errand soon, so that he could get Master Patrick back to work. Only when Patrick disappeared for a few moments into his upstairs chamber and came back down dressed in his old hunting buckskins did Carruthers realize that all this activity might be more than a momentary disturbance.

"I don't know when I'll be back, Carruthers," Patrick told him, striding out the back door of the house and toward the stables.

Carruthers hurried to keep up. "But, Master Patrick! The governor will be here today or tomorrow! The financial plan!"

Patrick briefly suggested that the governor do something uncomfortable and anatomically difficult with the financial plan.

Blushing furiously, Carruthers persevered.

"You can't just run off and abandon your responsibilities like this!"

Patrick paused with one foot in the stirrup and looked down at Carruthers. "At the moment," he said, not unkindly, "my greatest responsibility is in a cabin on the Tar River. I hope to reach her in time . . ."

His mouth was set in grim lines that offered no hope for rational argument. Carruthers watched hopelessly as his young master rode off to get himself killed by Indians, leaving the financial plan and the future of Moonshadows to be decided by the doubtful charity of Governor Spotswood.

~ 17 ~

They seemed to come out of nowhere, the shadows of the forest suddenly come to life. One minute Hilary was laboring at the single task she hated most, pounding corn in the hollowed-out tree stump; the next, she was surrounded by half-naked figures yelling and shooting off their muskets at the cabins. Their faces were fearsomely painted with black circles around one eye and red around the other, making them look like figures from a nightmare carnival, and their naked bodies gleamed with grease.

There wasn't time to scream or run. A muscular arm closed about her neck, dragging her backward against someone's body, and another arm clamped her arms close to her waist. Hilary watched speechless in horror as blond Grete ran past, screaming, toward the safety of the big cabin. She had been carrying water and the buckets still hung from the yoke over her shoulders, bounding wildly and splashing their contents over the ground as she ran.

Two yards from the door she tripped over the blue satin skirt that she'd inherited from Hilary, still too long for her. Before she could rise, a painted figure was bending over her. Something gleamed in his hand, something that rose and fell with short chopping strokes. There was a puff of smoke from the door of the cabin and the Indian jerked, then slowly toppled sideways with a surprised expression on his face. As he fell, Grete's long blond hair came away in his hand, leaving something on the ground that had a red glistening globe where the head should be. And the thing was dressed in Hilary's skirt, and it was still screaming.

A musket went off beside Hilary's head. The powder blast scorched her cheek and the noise of the explosion deafened her. She watched the silent pictures of the raid unfold before her. The Indians had got into the far cabin; one of them staggered toward her, waving his arms and balancing Mary's prized copper cook-pot on his head like a helmet. The bleeding thing in blue satin wriggled toward the door of the big cabin. And the door closed, shutting off the Saints who had reached safety from the two young women who were trapped outside.

After a brief exchange of musket shots on both sides, the Indians withdrew to the edge of the clearing, setting fire to the far cabin as they went. Hilary's captor dragged her with them. She was too terrified to make any resistance, but her legs were shaking and she could barely stand; he had to half-carry her to the shelter of the trees.

He dumped her on the ground at the base of a pine tree and bent over her with a knife in his hand. Hilary closed her eyes, waiting to feel the blade slicing into her head. She prayed that the end would be quicker for her than for poor Grete.

"You stay . . . here," a deep, halting voice said. "We do not hurt you."

English! Hilary opened her eyes and blinked in disbelief as she saw only the painted face of her Indian captor. He was using the knife to cut a strip of leather from the edge of his breech-clout. Stepping behind the tree, he yanked her arms backward around the trunk of the tree and bound her wrists together. The bark scratched her skin, and her shoulders ached from the awkward position. It was a wonderful pain, it meant she was alive. She gulped in the delicious fresh air and felt ridiculously grateful for these few breaths that she'd never expected to take. In the midst of her terror and the horror of Grete's mutilation there was that selfish core of wanting to be alive, in spite of everything. Maybe it would be enough to help her through whatever came next.

What came next were hours and hours of waiting. It had been near evening when the Indians attacked and fired the cabin. It burned like a torch through the first part of the night. Instead of setting the other cabins on fire, as Hilary suspected had been the plan, it lit up the small clearing around the big cabin and made it impossible for the Indians to approach without being fired on. They lay on their stomachs in the forest, shooting just often enough to keep the Saints pinned in the cabin, and cracked jokes with one another as they waited for the firelight to die down and give them a chance to rush the settlers. Hilary couldn't understand the jokes, but the laughter was clear enough. So were the admiring caresses they passed over her coppery hair, gleaming in the light of the burning cabin.

After an hour or two Grete stopped screaming, and all Hilary felt was relief that the torment was over for her. Grete might, she realized, be luckier than she herself was. She'd heard stories from the servants at Moonshadows of the tortures reserved for Indian captives. But that was in the future. For now, she would rather be alive, and chance what might come.

Before moonrise the cabin roof fell inward, putting out most of the flames and leaving only a glowing bed of embers. Hilary's captor stopped stroking her hair and joined the others in a brief consultation. There was a rush on the clearing, a babble of screeching voices, a brief volley of shots from the cabin, and then new flames shot up from the four corners of the big cabin.

Hilary heard the cries from within and longed to stop her ears. Then Jephthah's sonorous voice rose over all, leading the Saints in a slowly chanted hymn. She twisted her body around the tree trunk, not caring about the scratches she received in the process, and peered into the clearing. The door of the big cabin was open and the Saints were stumbling outside, coughing and choking. The German farmer and his son Peter held their coats over their mouths and noses, but Jephthah strode through the smoke with his head high, singing as if they were going to a prayer meeting. One of his arms encircled Mary's thin body. She too was singing, her face exalted, her eyes focused far beyond the painted warriors, who seized them as soon as they were clear of the cabin. Hilary peered in vain for a sight of the colonial couple, Will and Jenny. Perhaps they had been shot in the first attack.

Suddenly Peter raised a knife he had been holding under his coat and thrust himself at the nearest Indian. There was a brief tussle. Hilary closed her eyes. When she looked again, Peter and his father were lying on the ground, their limbs twisted in unnatural postures.

The Indians tied Jephthah and Mary and pushed them toward the tree where Hilary sat. Jephthah was limping, but his face was filled with the same unearthly calm that lit Mary's. When he saw Hilary, the calm shattered and his face worked as if he were fighting the urge to cry.

"I thought you were dead," was all he said.

One of the Indians struck him across the face. "No talk!" Hilary's captor ordered from the ground where he was kneeling to cut her bonds.

When she was standing, they fastened all the captives together by a long strip of rawhide about their necks and set off on a path deep into the forest.

Three days later they reached the home village of the warriors who had captured them. Hilary's immediate fears had quieted somewhat on the trail. The Indians made them walk until they were exhausted and their feet were bleeding from broken blisters, but they didn't seem to be intentionally cruel; it was just the pace they set for themselves. They didn't try to make things any harder for their white captives, and they didn't make any concessions to them either. And Tasqui, the tall young Indian who had captured her and who spoke some English, had showed her how to make a poultice of chewed sassafras leaves to put on the musket wound in Jephthah's leg. They were given no time to stop and search for herbs; Hilary learned to watch for the distinctive three-lobed sassafras leaves as they marched, to grab a handful and get back to the path without slowing down the others, and to chew the leaves as she walked along.

At every halt she changed the poultice on Jephthah's leg, and she felt some satisfaction at seeing the wound begin to heal cleanly. She felt considerably less satisfaction at the glances of approval Tasqui gave her. He commented several times that she was a clever woman and learned fast, and once he said that she would make a good woman for someone's lodge.

"I am his woman," Hilary said, pointing at Jephthah.

Tasqui's black eyes, hard and bright as chips of glass, darted between them and he turned away without responding. Hilary felt obscurely uneasy for the rest of the day, but with evening she forgot her vague fears of Tasqui in the much more concrete fears of what would happen to them in the Indian village. Stories of tortures and ritual sacrifice came back to haunt her, and

Jephthah's and Mary's smiling expectation of earning the crown of martyrdom didn't do much to reassure her.

The village was surrounded by a stout palisade of earth and logs, topped with sticks sharpened to murderous spikes. The captives were led in single file through the one narrow opening in this palisade, to face a dancing, screaming crowd of women and children. They pressed close to the white captives, dark faces thrust into theirs, hands poking and pinching at them. A naked boy who might have been seven or eight years old ran up to Hilary and thrust his hand under her skirt. Hilary slapped him without thinking; the boy staggered back and sat down on the ground. A woman dressed only in a blanket tied about her waist grabbed the boy by the arm and hauled him upright, speaking some words in a scolding tone.

Hilary raised her chin and stared over the heads of the mob, trying to make out the arrangement of the village. It consisted of one large circle of huts that seemed to be made of twigs woven together, with grass mats on the roofs that could be let down to cover the window openings. In the center of the circle was a wooden platform, about three feet high and ten feet on a side. They were being slowly pushed toward it by the pressure of the screaming crowd around them. Was that where the Indians tortured their captives? Horrible images flashed through Hilary's mind. She tried to block them out by concentrating fiercely on the small details of the scene: a woman's glossy hair braided with blue feathers, the patterned basket half full of seeds that leaned against the side of a hut, the crook-necked gourd from which a boy drank.

There was a shout from the returning warriors, and the women and children fell silent and backed away. One of the Indians who'd brought them in mounted the platform in the center of the circle of huts and began making a speech, pointing many times to himself and then at the captives who stood huddled together in a tight knot. At the peroration of the speech he held up something that gleamed like gold in the sunlight and ended in a mass of dirty brown clots.

Grete's scalp! Hilary closed her eyes to shut out the hideous sight. Her head was spinning and she swayed where she stood, longing for the merciful oblivion of fainting.

A knuckle dug into her ribs and brought her painfully alert. "Don't faint!" a voice hissed in her ear. It was Mary. Her prim, gaunt figure looked like a scarecrow's tattered shape after the three-day trek through the woods, her hair fell loose from her bun to hang like a witch's graying locks about her face, and one side of her face was swollen where one of their captors had struck her that morning for not moving quickly enough. But her narrow eyes glittered with a determination that infused new strength into Hilary.

"They respect strength, and not showing fear," she went on in an undertone when she had Hilary's attention. "See how they backed off when you slapped that boy down? We have to act calm and like we don't care what they do."

Hilary stole a glance at Jephthah. He was standing immobile, though she knew his leg must still pain him, his arms folded and his long dark hair blowing about his ears as he gazed with a stony countenance on the Indian rejoicings. All right, she decided. If he could act that calm in the face of approaching martyrdom, she wouldn't be the one to shame him. She folded her arms and tried to imitate his expressionless stare.

After the first Indian finished, a second man leapt onto the platform and began speaking. A third followed him. The sun beat down on the captives' heads and thirst plagued them. Hilary cast longing glances at the patch of shade that lengthened beside the nearest hut as the sun moved across the sky.

"I'm sitting down," she said suddenly. Against Mary's protests, she marched the few yards to the shady spot and sat down cross-legged in the dirt. When she had been sitting for a few minutes and none of the Indians had paid any attention, the others moved cautiously into the shady patch.

A few minutes later, as Hilary rested with her head against the woven twigs that were the wall of the hut, a hand tapped her on the shoulder. She looked up and saw Tasqui holding out a basket full of some greasy stuff. Hilary sniffed and recognized cold boiled meat of some sort.

"Oh, thank you, Tasqui," she exclaimed. She passed the basket around the circle. There was barely enough for a bite for each, but the mouthful of meat refreshed them all. Tasqui stood looking down at them for a minute, then turned on his heel and rejoined the group at the center of the village. A moment later a woman scurried out of the crowd, went into one of the huts, and came out again with a much larger flat basket balanced on one hip and a painted gourd in her hand. She brought these over to the captives and offered them with a smile.

"Bread!" exclaimed Mary rapturously. Their food on the trail had consisted only of the dried meat carried by the warriors in their pouches, and precious little of that. Everyone was hungry for bread and they did not dispute her definition of the steamed Indian-corn dumplings that accompanied this platter of cold venison. The gourd proved to contain cold spring water, clear and pure.

The rest of the day passed in uneasy slumber, boredom, and apprehension, as they were left seated by the hut while the speeches and dancing continued. Toward night there was a bonfire, and the Indians danced around it to the accompaniment of a skin drum and some high-pitched, quavering song that sounded more melancholy than celebratory to Hilary. Jephthah forbade them to look at the heathenish rites; they faced the wall of the hut, heads bowed, while he prayed that they might be given strength to endure whatever trials the Lord saw fit to send upon them in this place.

That night they all slept together on grass mats inside one of the larger huts, with their hands and legs bound together with strips of rawhide to discourage any thoughts of escape. Hilary had grown used to sleeping so on the three days of the trip; one woke cramped and stiff, but exhaustion was a powerful narcotic. This night, though, was markedly colder than the last, and she woke every hour or so, shivering and longing for the freedom to draw close to the fire that still burned outside, and whose red glow she could see through the open doorway of the hut.

Suddenly a dark figure rose before her, blotting out the fire—a horrible misshapen form, with the head of a man and great bat wings on either side. Hilary stifled a cry of alarm. Was this it? Were they to be dragged out to sacrifice now? She lay rigid next to Mary, too frightened even to pray.

The figure came closer and threw something toward her. Hilary's breath stopped for a moment as the enveloping folds dropped down over her like the smothering wings of an evil spirit.

Then the strange figure knelt, whispering, "Cold tonight," and tucked the deerskin about her shoulders. It was Tasqui, and the strange outline had been made by his arms holding the blanket of sewn-together deerskins wide before he dropped it over them. Hilary whispered her thanks and snuggled gratefully into the soft skins. Tasqui's hand dropped on her head for a moment and then he retreated noiselessly out of the hut.

With the dawn of the next morning the celebrations were over and the business of the village went on as usual, except that Hilary and Mary were now part of the Indians' daily life. They were herded from spot to spot and given the most monotonous and repetitive of the women's daily tasks to perform.

On that first day Mary was set to watch strips of meat slowly drying in the smoke from a fire of green twigs, while the flat-faced woman who'd brought their food explained with gestures that she must keep turning the meat and must keep the fire at an even level all day.

When Mary understood her task, the Indian woman took Hilary by the arm and led her toward a tall stump that stood to one side of the circle of huts. As they drew nearer, Hilary saw that a long pole with one end smooth and the other end quite thick lay on the ground behind the stump.

"Don't tell me," she said aloud. "I think I can guess." With a shrug of resignation she picked up the pole and dropped it into the hollowed-out stump, smooth end first. "Well? Where's the corn?"

As a few days passed without more excitement, Hilary began to grow used to life as a slave in the Indian village. At least she no longer woke every morning expecting to be burned or have her throat cut. She knew what was waiting for her. Pounding corn!

As the captives settled to their tasks, the Indians gradually relaxed their guard over them. They were no longer tied together at night, and no one was assigned to sleep across the entrance to their hut. They even permitted Jephthah to interrupt the women at their work for his interminable prayer meetings at morning, noon, and sunset. Between pounding corn and prayer meetings, Hilary began to feel that life with the Indians wasn't so different from life in the Community of Saints. In some ways it was better: the monotony was broken by a variety of tasks.

As long as she could keep from thinking of Patrick, it was all right. But that thought, the memory of the love she had lost, was intolerable. She tried to be happy in the belief that her disappearance had saved Moonshadows for him, but every time she let herself remember Patrick and Moonshadows, she was overwhelmed by waves of pain and inconsolable grief that threatened to overwhelm her. She learned to hold the memories at bay by thinking very hard of other things. At night she pretended that she was sleeping in her room at Moonshadows, and during the day she followed her tasks with a fierce concentration that won the unwilling respect of the Indian women. Besides pounding corn, she learned to cook cracked hickory nuts until their milky oil floated to the top of the kettle to be skimmed off and used as seasoning; to bake a kind of bread of cornmeal batter wrapped in dried corn shucks and buried in hot ashes; to grind up dried sassafras leaves into a powder that served as thickening for their hearty venison stews.

"And Weh-dosh is going to teach me to weave those patterned baskets they serve the meat on," she confided to Mary one evening as they settled to rest in their hut. She had gradually learned to communicate with the flat-faced woman who had been their main guide, using a mixture of signs and Indian words that she picked up by repetition.

"Heathens," sniffed Mary. "You should be teaching her godly ways, not learning her pagan customs."

"Well," Hilary said pacifically, "I don't suppose anybody's soul is going to be lost over a basket of colored reeds. Besides, if she tells me to do it, I don't have any choice, do I?''

"Jephthah doesn't do what they tell him."

"I know." Jephthah had steadily refused to cooperate with the Indians in any way. He wandered around the village lecturing the women on their nakedness and the children on their laziness, and whenever the men came back from hunting he preached to them too. It didn't seem to bother him that only a few of the men understood anything he said and that those few found him a source of endless amusement. Tall and uncompromising in the tattered remains of his black suit, he stood like a monument to his faith, refusing to bend a single inch even when the men teased him by whirling their sharp hatchets under his nose.

"His courage is an example to us all," Mary said. "Listen to me, Hilary! We mustn't give in to them! Never! We are white people and our way is the right way and we mustn't forget it, no matter what they do to us!"

Hilary sighed. It was true that Jephthah was very brave, but sometimes she wondered if that was because he hadn't quite grasped the situation. Sometimes she herself was hard put to it to keep from laughing at him; he began to remind her of a stork stalking through a millpond on tall thin legs, darting its head around at every noise and trying to act dignified while it plunged into the mud after frogs.

Mary would have been shocked at Hilary's urge to laugh, but she felt the need to use whatever support she could find for her flagging spirits. Unlike Jephthah, she had fully grasped their situation. They were uncounted miles from home, they'd been warned that any attempt to escape would be severely punished, and Hilary knew that none of them had the woodcraft to get very far from the village without being tracked and brought back. Not a single survivor of the New Community had escaped to bring word of their fate to the outside world. They might be here forever. Under the circumstances, she wasn't entirely sure what there was to demonstrate their vaunted superiority over the Indians. From where she stood it looked as if the Indians had the upper hand in every possible way.

Depressing as it was, there was almost some relief in being so helpless. She had no more decisions to make . . . and no more hope to cling to. Hilary closed her eyes and burrowed under the deerskin coverlet, hoping for the sweet dreams that were her only way of seeing Patrick.

"*Listen*, Hilary!" Mary was shaking her shoulder, not letting her drift away that easily. "You got to pay attention. You're in more danger than the rest of us. I'm too old for them to care about. But you—I see the way that Tasqui looks at you. You're not just another slave to him. You have to stand firm, Hilary! If you go with a red savage, your soul will be lost forever!"

"Tasqui's just being kind," Hilary said. His continued sharp glances and his way of appearing around corners when she thought he was out hunting made her uneasy too. But she'd been trying not to give words to her fear, and she felt almost angry with Mary for making it concrete. She sought for some more reassurance. "Besides, Jephthah says the Indians never rape captives."

"No, but they can have more than one wife," Mary said. "If he takes you into his lodge as a second wife, it's not rape according to their laws. You watch out, Hilary! You been too friendly with them already!"

The very next day Hilary had occasion to remember Mary's warning. Weh-dosh had sent her to the creek that ran just outside the village palisade to gather the reeds that they would scrape and dye for Hilary's first attempt at basketmaking. The tall, slender reeds grew sparsely along the bank and Hilary had to wander some distance before she had cut enough to make even a very small basket.

The autumn air was clear and crisp; the tall pines and cedars that grew down to the very edge of the stream perfumed the air with their resin, and a line of slender maple saplings on the far side of the water blazed with red and orange against the deep intense blue of the sky. Hilary wandered along the stream, cutting reeds and humming to herself and thinking very hard about the pattern of the basket she wanted to make. From the first lonely days in the New Community of Saints she had found that keeping her mind busy was the best way to avoid slipping into thoughts of Patrick and the life that was gone forever. Even if they were ransomed eventually from the Indian village, what difference would it make to her? She would go on pounding corn and praying and living with Jephthah, and Patrick would never . . .

Patrick. Hilary's small white teeth clamped down hard on her lip and she frantically concentrated on the basket pattern, trying to stop the wave of desolation that swept over her. It would be a small round basket with gently sloping sides, mostly in natural colors but with a small diamond pattern of red-dyed reeds . . . and Patrick probably didn't even know she had been captured by Indians, or maybe he thought she was dead . . . no, don't think about that, think about the basket, red reeds, Weh-dosh . . .

"Oh, *damn* the basket!" Hilary flung her bundle of reeds down and sank to the ground beside it, giving vent to the tears she refused to allow herself in the crowded Indian village. It had become almost second nature to her to push those feelings down out of sight, leaving only a calm shell of a girl who could pray with the Saints or work with the Indian women with equal indifference. But now that she let go at last, all the fear and loneliness and sorrow of the last weeks came over her at once, and she moaned and rocked back and forth on the soft carpet of golden-brown pine needles, oblivious of all but her grief.

When the torrent of tears subsided, she felt tired but calm again, as though a giant hand had picked her up and shaken her thoroughly and then replaced her, limp and exhausted, back in the empty remains of her life. The corn to be pounded, prayer meeting, gather the reeds. There was enough of her left to perform such mechanical tasks as those. She bent and gathered up the scattered reeds.

When she stood up again, Tasqui was standing before her.

Hilary clutched the reeds to her bosom and backed away. All Mary's warnings came back to her with renewed force. She felt his eyes raking her slender form as if he could see right through her clumsy homespun dress.

"Wh-what do you want?" she quavered.

Tasqui gave a short nod as if answering some question of his own. He ignored hers. "You work hard. Good. Don't cry. You will be happy here."

Hilary shrugged, raised the bundle of reeds to her shoulder, and backed away, never taking her eyes from Tasqui. He was between her and the path, and she was afraid to try to push past him, and even more afraid to stay here alone with him.

He looked as if he had just come back from hunting. Although the air had the crisp bite of early autumn, he was naked except for a narrow leather breechclout suspended from a belt around his waist. His powerful shoulders and chest rippled with muscles, and his skin gleamed with the bear grease with which the young warriors anointed themselves. His black hair fell in long braids to his shoulders, decorated with beads of shell and copper that dangled from the ends of the braids. The beads sparkled in the clear autumn sunlight and his eyes glowed with an almost hypnotic intensity that held Hilary motionless.

He raised one hand to lift the long red braid that lay over her shoulder. The backs of his fingers just brushed her breast and to her shame

Hilary felt a thrill of response go through her body at the casual touch. It had been nearly three weeks since she left Patrick—three weeks of travel, work, hardship, and loneliness. From the eager response of her body, it might have been three years. She had learned too well what pleasure could follow a man's touch. And Tasqui had been kind to her.

"Don't cry," he repeated. Kneeling, he scooped up a double handful of water from the stream and bathed her face. His fingers were cool and gentle as they moved over her burning cheeks. Hilary closed her eyes and the image of Patrick leapt unbidden into her mind, black brows lifted, dark blue eyes dancing as he smiled out of her memory.

"No!" she gasped. She stepped back again, frantic to get away from Tasqui. One foot sank into the muddy bank of the stream and her other foot slipped. She would have fallen backward into the water if Tasqui hadn't sprung forward and caught her about the waist with one arm. He held her there for three long breaths, suspended backward over the water on his extended arm, as if to underscore his strength and her own helplessness. Then he slowly brought his arm in, making a circle that held her close to his body. His face was inches away from hers, black eyes staring into hers as if he could read all the secrets of her soul.

"You will come to my lodge tonight," he said.

"No," Hilary repeated, closing her eyes against the burning intensity of his gaze. It did no good; she was too sharply aware of the nearly naked male body so close to hers, the power of his muscular arms and the other kind of power implicit in his capture of her. If he had not protected her at the time of the raid, she would have died with Grete; since then, she knew, he had looked on her as his property. That was why Weh-dosh, his wife, had been the one to teach her the women's work. She had been training a second wife to take over the work of the lodge. This was what had been planned for her from the day of the raid.

"Please . . . no," she said more weakly. "I have a husband, Tasqui."

Tasqui released her, but she felt his will still encircling her like a snare around a rabbit. Legs trembling, she stood where he let her go, unable to gather her reeds and go. "The white man? That is a game. He treats you no better than the other, the old woman."

"He is my husband in the eyes of God," Hilary repeated steadily. She hated the words; they were like a barrier between her and even the dream of Patrick. But perhaps this marriage would also stand between her and Tasqui. "What goes on inside the lodge is not for you to question."

Tasqui's smile was slow and sure. "He is an old man. You have agreed to pretend he is your man, but that does not fool me. You will grow tired of being a slave who sleeps alone, when you could be my second wife and have much honor in the tribe. You will come to my lodge, Hi-la-re. You will come of your own will."

His hands passed over her face and arms without quite touching her. He dropped into his own language, murmuring strange guttural syllables that meant nothing to Hilary, although the chanting rhythm stirred her blood. She would have run if she had the power, but the steady gaze of Tasqui's black eyes held her motionless, her legs frozen like sticks of wood, while the slow sensuous passes of his hands continued.

A shout from the direction of the village broke Tasqui's concentration and freed Hilary to move. The Indian stood head-up, listening intently as further shouts and a volley of musket fire succeeded; then he smiled and relaxed subtly. "It is good. Come!" Seizing Hilary's wrist, he set off at an easy run along the path that bordered the stream, dragging her with him.

By the time they reached the village, Hilary was panting and her hair hung in loose wisps about her face, but Tasqui was still breathing easily. He dragged her in through the palisade door and gave her a light shove toward the captives' hut.

Hilary moved slowly toward the hut, holding her aching side with one hand and trying to make out what was going on in the center of the circle, where all the men of the village were gathered about the wooden platform. A strange horse was tethered behind the largest house, the long building where the men sat in council and where travelers were allowed to sleep. It bore an English saddle. Her heart leapt with sudden, unlooked-for hope. Had someone come to ransom them from the Indians? She peered toward the circle and saw, standing amid the half-naked men of the village, a man in the fringed buckskins of the frontiersman, a man with his back to her. As she crept closer, he took off his fur cap and a queue of gleaming black hair slipped down his back.

"Patrick!"

Hilary was not conscious of screaming, nor of pushing her way through the crowd of Indian warriors surrounding him; but she heard her own voice, and then she was in his arms while his blue eyes, dark and concerned, searched her face.

"Hilary! You're all right?" He didn't wait for an answer; his arms were so tight around her that she thought she could not breathe, and he covered her face with kisses that took away what little breath she had left.

"Oh, Patrick, I thought I'd never see you again." Stupid to be crying now, when Patrick was here and everything was all right.

Or was it? Perhaps he was a prisoner like herself. Hilary's eyes widened and she glanced around the circle of men, seeking to read some clue as to Patrick's status in their impassive faces. Only one of the men showed any expression whatsoever. The naked fury in Tasqui's countenance chilled her. She turned back to Patrick, trying to blot out the memory of Tasqui's cold anger. "How did you come here?"

"Looking for you, my love," Patrick said, and she relaxed in the circle of his arms. "I've come to ransom you, my darling runaway, and this time I don't want to hear any nonsense about your not loving me and not wanting to stay with me. I don't care what you want, you're staying where I can keep you safe from now on! Is that understood? I can't afford to keep buying you, my love!" He tried to scowl at her, but a grin of happiness kept breaking through the frown.

"Oh, Patrick." She couldn't stay with him, even if she were free, but for this moment she didn't want to talk about that. Hilary nestled into the curve of his arm, feeling safe despite the circle of unfriendly warriors surrounding them. "But how did you know where to find us?"

Patrick explained that he had heard of the Tuscarora uprising when Kendall O'Leary came to alert the planters along the Nottoway and to call out the militia. They had found the smoking remains of the New Community and the bodies of Grete and her father and brother.

"She was wearing your dress." Patrick's arm tightened about her and his lips thinned to a straight line. "I thought . . ."

It had been Colonel Quincy who had the courage to look at Grete's distorted features and assured him that it was not Hilary who lay there. But then Patrick had been tormented by worse nightmares of what Hilary might be suffering as a captive. While Colonel Quincy took the militia and Kendall's train of packhorses to a village of Tuscaroras who had remained neutral during the uprising, hoping to get their aid in treating with the other Indians, Patrick struck out alone to follow the trail of the warriors who had attacked the New Community.

"I was just showing the chief a letter from Governor Spotswood," he finished with the old devil-may-care light dancing in his eyes. "It says that the governor will attack and wipe out the

Tuscarora nation if any of the white captives are injured. Unfortunately, I don't speak their dialect well enough to translate the letter."

"Show me," said Tasqui. He pushed rudely between Patrick and Hilary and snatched the letter out of Patrick's hand. "I will translate."

"How did you get the letter?" Hilary whispered while Tasqui was involved in his translation.

"Forged it," Patrick whispered back with a wink.

Tasqui's speech was much longer than the brief letter. Hilary suspected he was adding his own commentary and that it was not at all favorable to Patrick's intentions. At any rate, at the end of the reading the chief folded his arms and shook his head, barking out two or three short sentences. Tasqui told them that the men of the village would have to discuss the matter in council that night before they decided what to do. If they gave the captives back at all, they would expect to be compensated with a generous ransom.

"Agreed," said Patrick at once. "We can work out the details later. I have many packs of good things with the militia. We will go in the morning and I will show you the things I have brought."

Tasqui's face fell at the news that Patrick hadn't brought the trade goods with him. Hilary wondered if he'd been recommending that they kill Patrick and keep both ransom goods and captives.

"In the meantime," Patrick added, "I brought this special gift for the man who captured my runaway servant here and kept her safe for me."

He drew a string of glittering glass beads from inside his buckskin shirt. Tasqui's eyes shone and he reached one hand to touch the beads, then reluctantly withdrew his fingers. "You say this woman belongs to you?"

Patrick nodded.

"But she says she belongs to Black Coat." Tasqui gave a sly smile. "How then can a woman belong to two men at once? I say she belongs to me, Tasqui, the greatest warrior of the Tuscarora nation. She has been a good slave and I intend to make her my second wife." His fingers encircled Hilary's wrist and he pulled at her.

"Over my dead body!" The edge of Patrick's hand chopped down on Tasqui's forearm and he released Hilary with a startled grunt. He sprang back a pace and assessed Patrick with measuring, slitted eyes that sparkled like chips of black glass.

"If that is how you want it, white man, I do not object." Tasqui jerked his head and said something that made the men around them move back in a wide circle. "She is my captive, but I will fight you for her."

Patrick nodded. "All right." He pulled his buckskin shirt over his head and tossed it to Hilary. "Hold this for me. And get out of the way!"

The two men faced each other, balancing on the balls of their feet, hands outspread. The muscles of Patrick's shoulders moved slightly as he circled Tasqui, raising and lowering his hands and waiting for a moment of advantage.

His hair was as black as Tasqui's and he was tanned almost as dark as the Indian from laboring in the fields beside his men. Only the dark blue of his eyes and the buckskin pants that he wore instead of a breechclout set him apart from his opponent.

Tasqui moved with a quick twist like a snake striking, and Patrick countered by leaping to one side, slipping easily away from Tasqui's clutching hands. He spun and drove his fist into Tasqui's unprotected side as the Indian recovered from his unsuccessful move. Tasqui grunted and fell back, watching Patrick more warily. He lunged again and caught Patrick's head under his arm. The two of them went down in the dust and for a moment Hilary held her breath, unable to distinguish which had the advantage in the tangle of thrashing limbs. Then Patrick surfaced, hands around Tasqui's neck, and banged his head backward on the hard ground.

At a sharp word from the old chief, two men jumped forward with long poles, which they thrust between the two combatants. "That is enough," the chief announced in English as fluent as Tasqui's. Patrick looked up in surprise and let the men push him back away from Tasqui.

"You speak English too, *ah-kree-eh*, my father?"

"For forty summers," the chief replied with a twinkle in his eye, "I have met the white traders at Catechna. Many of your people have learned to speak our tongue in the trading sessions. Do you think that we are too stupid to learn likewise? I have understood *everything* you have said," he added with a significant glance at the forged letter.

"No, my father," Patrick replied with an embarrassed laugh. "I think you are much cleverer than the stupid white man who underestimated you. Why will you not let me finish the fight?"

"We have not made peace yet," the chief said. "I need my strong young men. I cannot let you break them!"

Tasqui glowered and tried to get at Patrick, but the two guards crossed their poles in front of his chest and held him back. "It was a cheat!" he shouted thickly. "He uses white man's tricks of fighting!"

"Then you will finish with Indian tricks," the chief said with high good humor, "and nobody will be broken." He turned to Patrick. "I see you are strong, white man. Perhaps you are clever also. If so, I will be more inclined to listen to the words you say you bring from the king of your country. You and Tasqui will play the moccasin game. If Tasqui wins, he keeps the woman. If you win, I will permit you to buy her from him."

✑ 18 ✑

At the chief's directions, the three men sat down cross-legged on the wooden platform, while Hilary stood at the edge of the platform between the two guards, one of whom held each of her arms. She could see Mary and Jephthah peering from the distance. She wished she dared call to explain what was happening.

The game itself seemed almost childishly simple. A small stone was hidden under one of four moccasins by one of the players, and the other one had to guess where it was. At first Hilary didn't see how such a trivial game could occupy grown men. But after the first two or three rounds of guesses, she began to understand. When Tasqui had hidden the pebble, he kept up a continuous chanting and swaying, leaning now toward one moccasin, now toward another. Patrick studied the moccasins and made sudden moves toward one or another while watching Tasqui's face closely. When Patrick hid the pebble, the roles were reversed. A single round might take as much as five or ten minutes, and the custom was to play until the heap of tally sticks in front of the chief had all been awarded to one player or another. Then they would count sticks and see who was the winner.

At first Patrick was too quick to guess, and the pile of tally sticks before Tasqui grew alarmingly. The sun crept behind the trees and Hilary shivered with fear of what the coming night would bring. She did not doubt that if Tasqui won, he would claim his prize immediately. And what would Patrick do?

"It's cold," Patrick said. He vaulted one-handed down from the platform, ostentatiously keeping his back turned while Tasqui hid the pebble. "Hilary, give me my shirt."

Their hands joined under the buckskin cloth as she gave it to him. He squeezed her fingers and gave her a quick smile of reassurance. "Don't worry," he whispered. "It's going to be all right from now on. I guarantee it. Trust the luck of the Lyles!"

From then on the tide of the game changed subtly. Patrick's guesses were no more successful than before, but Tasqui's were almost uniformly unsuccessful. Time after time he darted at a moccasin, only to turn it over and find the bare wood of the platform underneath, while Patrick smilingly produced the pebble from under another shoe.

When the last tally stick was placed in front of Patrick, Hilary gave a sigh of relief. His pile was much higher than Tasqui's. The chief raised

his arm and brought it down in a chopping
measure, shouting some words in a high quavering falsetto. Immediately afterward he repeated himself in English, looking at Hilary.
"The white man wins! The woman is his!"

Hilary sagged between her guards as Patrick
leapt off the platform once again and took her
hands in his. He bowed low to the chief, sweeping his hat in a semicircle before him. The polished courtier's gesture somehow did not seem
at all out of place, even though the "king" to
whom he bowed was a half-naked Indian and
the courtier was dressed like a frontiersman.
"With your permission, my father," he said, "I
will take the woman to my lodge now, and we
will talk again in the morning."

Tasqui rose to a crouching position, his handsome face contorted with anger. "You have not
paid the price!"

The chief waved him back down with a sharp
word. Tasqui protested in a lower voice; the
chief bowed his head and they murmured together. Patrick took Hilary by the arm and hurried her away from the platform.

"What are they saying?" she asked.

"Don't know enough Tuscarora to eavesdrop.
The old chief could be telling Tasqui to be a
gentleman about the arrangements, to trust in
my honor to pay for you. Which"—Patrick smiled
down at her—"he can. . . . How many copper
kettles and lengths of red cloth do you think
you are worth, my darling girl?"

They had reached the long meeting lodge,
where Patrick, as a guest of the tribe, was to
sleep. Hilary stooped to follow him in through

the low arch of the door and stood blinking in the dimness of the lodge. Patrick came toward her, arms outstretched, and suddenly she felt shy of him. The blood pounding in her veins at his nearness, the dark interior of the lodge, the days and nights of mourning when she'd thought never to see him again—it was all too much for her. "What about the others?"

Patrick shrugged. "I don't think there will be any trouble about ransoming them too. How long have you been here? Almost a week? I should have waited another week, they'd have paid me to take Jephthah away. Oh, sorry, I forgot . . ."

That Jephthah was her husband. Hilary wanted to forget that too, at least for tonight. This night might be all they had; tomorrow they would be ransomed, and then she would have to go with Jephthah, whether he returned to the ruins of the New Community or started a new settlement somewhere else. She put her fingers on Patrick's lips to hush him. "Not now," she whispered. "We'll talk about it in the morning."

While they stood talking, her eyes had slowly adjusted to the darkness. Now she looked about her and saw that this lodge was much grander than the barren hut where she slept with the other captives. Instead of grass sleeping mats laid directly on the hard ground, there were raised bedsteads of poles driven into the earth, with rawhide strips lashed across to provide a springy base for piles of deerskins. The woven twigs that constituted the walls of the lodge were plastered inside with a mixture of clay and moss; that was why it was so dark, lacking the many little chinks that let both light and cold drafts into the prisoners' hut. A basket of long pine splinters for lights stood by the door, and a row of smooth round stones encircled the central fire pit and kept coals and ashes from spilling out into the rest of the room.

"What a fine lodge!" Hilary exclaimed. Her voice quivered slightly.

She could just see Patrick's smile in the dim light that came from the doorway. "D'you really think so? How your standards have changed, my love." He dropped the grass mat that hung over the doorway, and the darkness swallowed them both. "Come here, then, and help me test this fine bed."

His hands were on her without warning, slow and caressing, and as he removed the tattered homespun dress, she felt no chill as the heavy beat of her own blood warmed her. "That's a terrible dress," he murmured into her ear. "We'll have to get rid of it."

Hilary laughed and sank into his embrace as he pulled her down onto one of the skin-covered couches. "Will you have me go naked through the forest, then? I—"

She caught her breath, speech stopped by the shock of pleasure that was his palm over her breast. His fingertips moved gently over her skin, tracing lines of pleasure like fine gold and silver wires encircling her body and holding her prisoner to his desire.

"I think," he murmured as his hands moved lower, eliciting a low cry of desire from her, "I'll have you go naked always. Practical and decorative at the same time."

Hilary arched against his probing hand, twisting her head at the same time to press kisses upon his cheek. She breathed in deeply of the masculine scent of his body, twining her fingers in his hair and rubbing against him like a cat as the deep insistent caresses continued.

"Prac . . . tical?" Her voice was heavy and languorous, making the simplest word sound like an endearment. She observed the phenomenon almost with detachment through the dark mists that encompassed her senses. He was naked now; she could feel the slight roughness of the hair on his thighs against her own smooth skin. She shivered with anticipation as he gently pressed her back onto the softness of the cured furs. The fur was velvety smooth on her naked back, his lips warm soft velvet on the throbbing tip of her breast.

"Why . . . yes, practical. It's my last resort to stop you from . . . running away from me." His voice was changing too—thick, halting between words, as though he found it hard to speak.

Running away. Hilary made one effort to break through the sensual haze. "Patrick, I . . . we have to talk."

"Tomorrow is for talking." His body pressed against the length of hers, and she felt him rising against her thighs. "Tonight . . ." One hand gently parted her thighs, seeking entrance, while between words his tongue flickered over her breasts and robbed her of coherent thought. "Tonight is for us."

He entered her with an exultant cry of joy and clutched her tightly to him, carrying her with him to heights of passion that left them both breathless in the dark, transformed with something deeper and stronger than pleasure alone. Hilary gladly forgot thought, memory, and duty in the sweet madness of Patrick's love, the demands he made on her more than matched by the eagerness of her body for his. The ways of love that he had taught her and that she had missed so sorely in the past weeks now made their own demands, a sensual current in the blood that swept the last of her reason away and left her floating like a leaf in the wind, until at last she came to rest in the warm circle of Patrick's arms and felt his heart beating strongly against hers.

With a shaky laugh Patrick disengaged himself and went to the doorway, cautiously raising the grass mat. "I need air. . . . You take the breath from a man, my darling girl." Hilary joined him at the doorway, holding her ragged dress around her, and they looked out together at the sleeping village.

It was dark outside now, and late; the council fire had burned down and the Indians had departed to their separate lodges. The moon that had been nearly full when Hilary left Moonshadows was now a sliver that gave no more than a hint of light. The village lay quiet, peacefully dreaming under the stars, and only the gentlest of night breezes rustled the thick branches of pine trees along the stream and released their resinous scent into the cool autumn night.

"You married Jephthah?" Patrick bit out the words without looking at her. His arm was tight and unyielding as a shackle about her waist.

"Yes. We were betrothed . . ."

"A child's promise! You didn't have to keep it!"

"I keep my promises." Hilary wanted to run away, to bury herself among the heaped furs and hide from this inquisition, but Patrick's arm held her prisoner at his side.

"Yet you broke your promise to me." He released her, but only so he could put his hands on her shoulders. What could he see of her face in the dim starlight? His own was only a shadow, but she knew every line so well that she hardly needed light to see the straight black brows, the deep blue eyes with their intense burning gaze, the firm clear lines of nose and chin. "Hilary, I don't believe it, what you said in your letter. I can't believe it. Not when you were so sweet and loving just now. Tell me again," he challenged her, "tell me again that you don't care for me, that it was all a sham."

Hilary's heart contracted painfully. Writing that cruel letter had been so hard! She couldn't face him and repeat the same lie. "I love you," she whispered, putting her arms around his neck. "Patrick, I didn't know what love was until you taught me."

"Then you'll go back with me!"

Hilary thought of the broad acres and the stately house of Moonshadows; the aristocratic couple in northern Virginia whom she had never seen; the governor of Williamsburg on whose favor Patrick's keeping the lands depended. To go with him now would be to wipe out all that she had so painfully accomplished by running away. She shook her head. "You forget. I am Jephthah's wife now."

"I don't forget," said Patrick. His voice quavered with suppressed emotion. "Sleeping or waking, I don't forget for a minute." His hands ground into her shoulders. "To know that I share you with him . . . Tell me, Hilary, what magic is there in the preacher's embraces? Do you compare us afterward? How do I compare with him?"

With every question his fingers tightened until she thought he would crush the bones together. But that pain was as nothing to the one in her heart. "Patrick, I . . . it's not like that," she whispered. "We don't . . ." She stopped and moistened dry lips with the tip of her tongue. "Jephthah is not . . . He hasn't . . . The marriage is not complete."

"Are you trying to tell me that he hasn't touched you? I find that hard to believe." Patrick's hands fell away from her shoulders. His voice was low and incredulous. Hilary felt anger burning under her skin. What right had he to put her through this inquisition?

"Believe what you like," she snapped.

"Oh, I wasn't questioning your veracity." There was a hint of amusement in his voice now. "It's the preacher I don't understand. And you—Hilary, why will you stay in such a shell of a marriage, when you might be with me?"

"It's my duty." Her own voice was a thin, unconvincing thread in the darkness. "Jephthah needs me." Sometimes, in the New Community, she'd doubted that. But she remembered his face when he discovered she had not been killed in the Indian raid. Yes, Jephthah did truly love her, even if he did not show it often. Twice now, once in England and once in Virginia, he'd taken her in at the time of her greatest need. Even if Patrick's title to his land were secure, how could she repay Jephthah's love and kindness by leaving him for a rich man?

"And will *duty* and *need* keep you warm between the sheets? Hilary, you can't waste your life this way. I won't let you."

"You can't stop me."

"No? What if I ransom you and leave the rest of the Saints to their fate? It won't be long before Jephthah annoys the Indians into killing him. And if the only way you'll come to me is as his widow . . ." Patrick left the threat dangling.

Hilary knew she should have been frightened for Jephthah, but she found the threat strangely unconvincing. "You won't do that," she said, and knew that she spoke the truth. "You're an honorable man, Patrick. You'd not leave a man to die just because he's your rival."

"Wouldn't I?" Patrick laughed. "By God, no, I suppose not. But I can remember a time when I might have done worse. If I'm an honorable man, Hilary, it's because you insist on believing in me, and I can't, God knows why, bring myself to let you down. You're changing me." he said in a wondering voice, "and the least you can do, don't you think, is to stick around and see the change bear fruit?"

Hilary rested her head against his bare shoulder. "Please, do we have to argue? We have this night. That will have to be enough."

"Will it, by God!" Patrick's arms tightened about her. "I warn you, Hilary. You may have saddled me with a sense of ethics, but there's nothing dishonorable about fighting for my lady in any way I can. And I'm going to start the fight right here, tonight."

"How?" His hands were sliding under the loose homespun dress now, making her shiver so that it was hard to speak or think.

"By making love to you until you can't see straight. By showing you just exactly what it is you're forgoing in this bloodless parody of a marriage."

"I already know that."

"Do you? Then be prepared for a reminder lesson." His mouth came down on hers, one hand tangled in her hair to hold her head still while he ravished her senses with lips and tongue and teeth. The sweet force of his kiss continued until, robbed of breath and sense, she leaned dizzily against his hard warm body and returned kiss for kiss with equal fervor.

"That," he said when at last they broke apart for a moment, "that was only the appetizer. Now to the main course."

One arm scooped under her knees, the other under her shoulders, and in three steps he dumped her onto the pile of furs that covered their low couch. He lifted the homespun dress over her head, and before she could catch her breath, the length of his body was over her, holding her down among the silky-soft furs.

"I don't want . . ." she breathed, knowing it for a lie. But she was almost afraid. What more could there be than what she'd already experienced?

"No? But you're going to get it anyway." Patrick captured her wrists in the darkness and held them above her head with one hand while the other explored her body. In spite of her anger, Hilary gave an involuntary moan of pleasure as his fingers glided across her, awakening all the secret springs of delight once again.

Much later, Patrick chuckled to himself as one hand lazily caressed Hilary beneath the deerskin covering.

"What's so funny?" she roused herself to ask.

"You might want to watch how thoroughly you reform me. If I were an entirely honorable man, we'd not be here."

"Because of Jephthah?"

"No. I was losing the moccasin game."

The memory of the early part of that game, with Tasqui's smile of triumph as the pile of tally sticks before him grew, made Hilary shiver with remembered fear. "I . . . noticed. But then you learned how to play it."

"I learned how to play immediately," Patrick corrected her. "It just took me a little while to figure out how to cheat." He chuckled again. "That's why I put my shirt on. Did you not wonder why Tasqui's guesses never worked after that? I kept the pebble in my sleeve and waited for him to flip a moccasin over; then I would palm it and drop it under the moccasin *I* turned over. It's a game with many interesting possibilities. . . ."

Hilary fell asleep while he was still turning

over possibilities and musing about teaching the game to some of his white neighbors.

The morning brought an unwelcome reminder that they were not yet free of the Indian village.

"How did you enjoy your night with my woman, white brother?"

Tasqui was standing directly in front of the guest lodge, hands on hips, his deep chest moving slowly in and out with his regular breathing. There was a challenging sparkle in his black eyes.

"My woman," Patrick corrected. He put Hilary behind him with one hand. "I won her from you last night—remember?"

"She is not yours until you pay the ransom," Tasqui replied. "In my generosity I allowed her to share your furs last night. Tonight will be different. A woman who can attract such different types of men as you and Black Coat must surely be something special. I look forward to sampling that specialness while she is still my captive."

"Tonight she will no longer be yours. We will ride to the treaty village today to get my trade goods."

Tasqui shook his head. "No. We wait for my brothers to come back from their raid. Tomorrow we ride. Today I go hunting, and tonight . . ." His dark eyes flickered over Hilary. She tried to make herself small behind Patrick's protective arm. "Tonight the woman comes to my lodge."

Patrick's hand doubled into a fist. Hilary hung on his arm. "No, Patrick!" she whispered urgently. "You mustn't let him provoke you into a fight. It's what he wants!"

Slowly Patrick's arm muscles relaxed and his hand dropped to his side.

"I did not know it was the way of the Tuscarora to dishonor their captives. I was told that the warriors of the Tuscarora nation are too brave to harm women. I see I was mistaken."

The gibe brought a dusky flush to Tasqui's cheekbones, but he did not retreat. "I have seen the ways of the white traders." he rejoined. "I know that a woman who takes one husband but goes to the lodge of another man has no honor among the whites, just as she has none among my people. Last night was a test. If the woman had proved virtuous and stayed with her husband, I would have left her in peace. Since she shares her favors among you white men, I ask only that she give me the same treatment."

"He's not her husband!" Patrick's fists clenched again.

Tasqui laughed contemptuously. "No? She says he is. Settle it among you, you whites. But have the woman ready for me when I return from the hunt tonight." He swaggered off with his waiting friends, giving Patrick no chance to prolong the argument.

It was a strained, tense day that they spent in the Tuscarora village. Nearly all the warriors whom Hilary was used to seeing in the village were gone with Tasqui on the hunting expedition; it had become a village of old women and children. For once the captives were left to themselves, not driven out to share the labor of the women, and this change in the routine only increased their nervousness. The life of the village went on around them, the women grinding corn and stretching hides for tanning and weaving baskets, but when Hilary went to take her turn at the corn mortar, she was shooed away. Mary too was chased away from her regular tasks.

"What do you suppose it means?" Mary asked Jephthah when the captives gathered for their noonday meal of boiled hominy and squash.

He looked at her with cloudy, unfocused eyes, and it was evident that his thoughts were a long way off. "What? Is there something different?"

Mary shook her head helplessly. Jephthah got up, leaving his bowl of hominy half full. "Have we prayed today?"

They had done little else all morning. Only Patrick had refused to take part in the interminable kneeling session, preferring to pace moodily up and down around the palisade. Whenever he approached the opening, an old warrior stepped in front of it and glared at him.

"Then I should preach to the heathen now." Jephthah strode off, limping heavily, and Hilary looked after him with a worried frown. Since they had come to the village, he had refused her ministrations, and she feared that the wound in his leg was not healing as it should.

"Damned few listeners he'll find in this place," Patrick muttered. "The only ones that speak enough English to understand him are Tasqui and the chief, and they've both gone on the hunt."

Hilary shrugged. "I don't think Jephthah feels the need to be understood. The important thing is bearing witness, not what effect it has on others." She'd certainly heard that often enough in her time with the Saints. "What do *you* think it means, that they're not letting us work with the other women today?" she asked Patrick.

He shrugged. "They've as good as agreed to take trade goods in ransom for you. Could be they no longer think of you as their slaves. Or perhaps . . ." He stared off at the opening of the palisade where the one old guard dozed in the sun.

"Perhaps what?"

Patrick seemed to come to himself with a start. "Oh, nothing. They're just making the transition from captives to guests, I reckon. But it might not be a bad idea to leave now, if we got the chance. If nothing else, it'd save me a little trouble, fighting Tasqui again tonight." His lopsided grin tugged at Hilary's heart. "Not, you understand, that I object to fighting for you in every possible way. I hope I made that clear. It just seems it would be a neat and economical solution to leave before the hunters return."

Hilary glanced across the circle of huts. Jephthah was standing at the far side of the circle before the big medicine house that was the only building larger than the guest lodge, haranguing two women and a naked child. He stood with all his weight on his right leg.

"Jephthah's wound is not yet healed," she said. "He could never keep up if we were pursued."

Patrick sent such a black scowl across the circle that Hilary wondered if Jephthah's shoulder blades tingled. "Aye, you would think of that. Well, darling girl, don't worry about to-night. Tasqui's just playing a testing game. We'll work it out when the time comes."

He took her hands and started playing a non-sense game with the fingers, chanting nursery counting-out rhymes and kissing the fingertip on which his count ended. The blend of non-sense and lovemaking distracted Hilary so thor-oughly for a few minutes that she was completely surprised when the shouts and screams began at the far side of the circle.

All the women in the village had converged on the medicine hut. For a moment she could see nothing but screaming women; then Jeph-thah's black-clad figure appeared in their midst. The women pushed him across the open space toward the rest of the captives, slapping at him and herding him with the long poles used by the guards but taking care not to touch him with their hands. All the same, he presented a sorry sight by the time he reached them. His face and hands were bleeding from a dozen small cuts inflicted by the sharp ends of the poles and his coat hung off his back, even more tattered than it had been when they arrived in the village.

The women gave them no time to question him; keeping up their high-pitched rhythmic shrieking, they herded all the captives into the guest lodge. Mary got a smart slap across the rear for running to Jephthah instead of going directly into the lodge.

As soon as they were all inside, the grass flap that covered the doorway was lowered, leaving them in darkness. They could hear shuffling feet going around and around the lodge, accompanied by the rhythmic thump of poles, while in the distance the high wailing chant began again.

Patrick rubbed his head where he had bumped it against one of the roof poles of the lodge and sat down on the nearest couch, drawing Hilary with him. "I knew they wouldn't be able to take your preaching forever," he commented into the darkness, "but I'd surely like to know what you said to get them so annoyed. Especially as I didn't think any of the women spoke English."

"There are more ways of bearing witness than through words. These people can see and learn from good example, as they can be corrupted by bad example." Jephthah's sonorous voice rolled out the words as calmly as if he had been preaching in his own meeting cabin rather than shut into a dark lodge awaiting an unknown fate. Hilary felt her cheeks burning at his words. Earlier he had reproved her harshly for spending the previous night with Patrick. He hadn't seemed jealous, exactly—more worried that she would corrupt the Indians with her wanton ways. He kept referring to them as simple innocent children of nature.

"Er . . . exactly what good example did you give them, Preacher?" Patrick's light, amused voice with its faint tinge of Irish brogue seemed to put everything back into proportion again. Hilary remembered Jephthah's earlier self-righteous preaching and stifled a wholly inappropriate desire to giggle. Simple children of nature indeed! Only Jephthah could have lived in the village all this time and not noticed the way Tasqui, that simple innocent savage, kept looking at her. But then, if he did notice, he'd probably tell Hilary it was her own fault for having red hair and white skin.

Jephthah answered Patrick obliquely. " 'And they brake down the altars of Baalim in his presence, and the images, that were on high above them, he cut down.' II Chronicles 34:7."

"That was the medicine lodge," Hilary said. "Do you suppose they had some sort of idols in there?"

"*Had* seems to be the operative word," Patrick agreed. There was a grim undertone to his voice, and his arm encircled Hilary in an automatic protective gesture.

"I wonder what they do to people who destroy their idols." As soon as she said it, Hilary wished the words back.

Mary's voice unexpectedly broke in on their musings. "Do not be afraid, Hilary. Jephthah did the right thing. I wish I had had the courage to join him. If even one soul is turned from heathenism by his action, our deaths will not be in vain. 'Fear not them which kill the body, but are not able to kill the soul.' Matthew 10.28."

Hilary knew a moment of envy for the faith which sustained Mary to face martyrdom unflinchingly. How was it that she who had lived with the Saints since childhood was so weak and frightened, while Mary, who had only recently been saved, was so strong in her faith? She wished for that inner strength, but at the same time her own spirit cried out rebelliously that she didn't want to die, not yet, not when she was just discovering how wonderful life could be. And even worse was the thought that she had brought Patrick to his death when she was only trying to help him. If she had stayed at Moonshadows, he wouldn't have had to come after her.

They passed the long hours of the afternoon in uncomfortable silence. Patrick held Hilary's hand and whispered encouraging love words into her ear, and Jephthah occasionally emitted another Bible verse. Apart from that, conversation languished and died in their collective fears of the future.

Toward evening, a new sound of triumphant chanting broke in upon the women's wailing.

"They're back." Patrick squeezed Hilary's hand, and a moment later they were almost blinded by the dazzle of light as the grass mat over the door was thrown back. An old woman's crooked finger beckoned them to come out.

~❧ 19 ❧~

The village was more crowded than Hilary had ever seen it. The returning hunters had been joined by a motley crew of warriors who reminded her of her own captors on the night of the raid. One prinked around the circle of huts in a white cape that had once been a woman's petticoat; another fired off a long musket with a gleaming blue-black barrel. Dragged along behind the rejoicing warriors were three captives: a tall man whose long black hair was stuck to his head on one side in a bloody clot, a heavily pregnant woman who plodded with lowered head, and a buxom redhead whose tightly belted shift was about to drop off one shoulder.

"Bet!" Hilary started to run to her friend, but the old woman who'd brought them out of the lodge gave her a shove in the chest that sent her reeling back to Patrick. She turned to him. "It's Ephraim and Alice. They must have raided their settlement after ours. And Bet . . . and

415

. . ." She scanned the group again. No, there were only three white captives. Fat, jolly Leon, the widower, was not with them.

The merriment of the returning warriors was suddenly brought to a halt when one of the old women who'd been watching over the captives hobbled forth and began a long accusing speech, pointing alternately at Jephthah and the medicine lodge. The men scowled at Jephthah and clustered in small groups, talking in low voices. Clearly they considered whatever he had done to be a serious problem for the village.

After some discussion the chief walked over to them. "Your Black Coat is a dangerous man," he said. "He has made the spirits angry with this tribe. He cannot be ransomed now. The rest of you may go if we are offered a fitting price, but he will have to stay to pay the spirits for what he has done."

"Er . . . what form of payment would be acceptable?" Patrick inquired before Jephthah could speak.

The chief's wrinkled face drooped. "I am sorry for you, my friends, that you must see your companion burned. It is our law. He must be the sacrifice, lest a worse evil befall the tribe."

"I am sorry too," Patrick said quietly. "I am most sorry for you, my father, because if you do this thing, evil will certainly befall the tribe. Governor Spotswood might have forgiven the deaths of his people who fell in honorable war, but if you torture this captive, he will certainly bring the white soldiers here until all of your people are dead and the forest grows over the huts and cooking fires of the Tuscarora nation."

The chief sighed. "I have considered this matter. But it is better to offend a man than the spirits. What Black Coat has done will bring doom upon us more surely than all the white soldiers in the world."

"Doom! You bring that upon yourselves!" Jephthah folded his arms and glared down at the diminutive chief, obviously preparing to cite another crushing text. As he opened his mouth, Hilary kicked him in the shin with her heel. He gave a very human squawk and temporarily forgot what he had been going to say, giving Patrick a chance to step between the two men.

"My father, it is not clear to us exactly what he has done," he said with an ingratiating smile. "Perhaps some reparation could be arranged—"

The chief cut him off with a chopping downward gesture of one hand. "Come," he said, and led them across the circle of huts to the medicine lodge.

Inside were two wooden pedestals. On one of them stood a wooden statue about three feet high, painted half red and half white, with a crown of plaited rushes on its head. The statue that should have stood on the other pedestal lay on the ground, split from the head down to the navel. It lay faceup and they could clearly see its ugly. leering face, painted black on one side and red on the other, decorated with long carved fangs.

"This is what he has done," the chief said. "These are the two guardian spirits of the village, whose names I may not speak to you. But know that this one is kindly and benevolent, and this one has an angry heart and punishes evildoers." He gestured toward the fallen statue. "Your Black Coat knocked the angry spirit from his pedestal, and when he fell to the ground he split in two as a sign of his anger against us. If we let Black Coat go free, he will turn his wrath against the village."

At the beginning of the speech Patrick looked as worried as the others, but by the conclusion the corners of his mouth had lifted a fraction and the dancing light had returned to his eyes. "Well, now. My father, you say that the image which remains standing is the good spirit?"

The chief nodded.

"And the one which Jephthah destroyed is the evil spirit?"

Another nod.

"Then it seems to me that you and Black Coat are of the same mind in this matter. Only he is the stronger. Thus you placate the evil spirit with offerings and flowers, but Black Coat is so strong that he wanted to vanquish the evil spirit utterly and drive it out of your village. He was only trying to help!"

For a long moment the old chief's face was impassive while he considered this argument. Then the wrinkles around his mouth shook and spread into a smile. "There is merit in your argument. I will suggest it to my young warriors. Perhaps we can find a peaceful way out of this."

Marching outside, he hoisted himself up on the wooden platform in the center of the village and began making a speech in the Tuscarora language. It seemed to take him an extremely long time to repeat Patrick's simple argument.

"Why's he taking so long?" Hilary whispered.

"The more important the matter, the longer you talk about it," Patrick muttered under cover of the chief's peroration. "That much of their customs I do know . . . and faith, it's not so different from our own House of Burgesses, now that I come to think on it! You should hear my father going on about the tobacco duties!"

By the end of the chief's speech, the warriors who had clustered around to hear him were laughing and slapping one another on the back. Their merriment seemed to be enhanced by a brown earthenware jug they kept passing from hand to hand, each one taking a long pull at the contents before passing the jug on to his neighbor. One of the younger men, his face still smeared with the black and red circles of warpaint, staggered out of the crew and offered the jug to Jephthah. When Jephthah folded his arms and drew back, the man's laughter turned to a scowl.

"Here, friend, I'll have some, and grateful to you for it." Patrick's words might have been unintelligible to the Indian, but not the gesture. He took the jug and tilted it up to his lips for so long that the Indian grew impatient and snatched it back. Patrick wiped his lips and sighed as his host wandered unsteadily back to the group of laughing warriors.

"What was in it?" Hilary asked.

"Rum." Seeing her blank look, he added, "It's a kind of brandy made by fermenting sugar. They'll have stolen the jug from Ephraim's cabin, and a lucky thing for us. It's put them in a good mood."

Presently the warriors divided into two groups. Tasqui and the men of the hunting party sat down on the ground in the middle of the circle, still passing the jug around, and the returned warriors filed out of the palisade. As nobody seemed to be paying much attention to the white captives, Hilary took the chance to edge over to Bet and find out what had happened. Alice was resting on the ground, her back against one of the huts and her swollen belly sticking out in front of her, her eyes glazed with exhaustion. Ephraim knelt beside his wife and alternately fanned her with his hat and exhorted her to eat some of the boiled hominy that had been brought to the new arrivals.

Bet's story was much the same as Hilary's: a surprise attack, the firing of the cabins, and the survivors of the raid herded mercilessly down the forest trails to the Tuscarora village. Leon, she said, had died in the first rush of the Indians. "I'll miss him," Bet allowed. "He was good company, was Leon. Always cracking a joke. Kinda like Dickie, except he has—had—that cabin. They burned the cabin, I tell you that? First house I ever had to call me own, and they burned it."

She glowered at the braves in the center of the village, evidently resenting the loss of her cabin more than the loss of Leon.

Suddenly the warriors who had filed out of the village rushed back in through the open palisade gate with ferocious whoops and leaps. Their bodies were now painted to the waist with stripes of black and red, and their hair and loincloths were decorated with hanging beads,

squirrel tails, and feathers. Hilary saw one brave
who had tied a lady's hand mirror to the front
of his breechclout, where it dangled like a monstrous extra appendage, swaying in time to his
jumping, and banging against his knees with
every movement.

The men who had remained behind moved
aside and Hilary saw that they had lit a fire in
the open space between the wooden platform
and the medicine lodge. The painted warriors
filed around the fire while the other men stood
in a line before the medicine hut, chanting. The
two men on either end of the line held drums
covered with taut deerhide on which they beat
out a strange compelling rhythm.

Suddenly one of the warriors broke out of his
place in the dancing circle and ran toward them.
He seized Jephthah by the arm and tried to
draw him to the fire. Jephthah shook off his
grip and stood his ground, glowering at the
heathen spectacle. Two more warriors came out
of the circle and grabbed Jephthah by the arms,
followed by the chief.

"You must dance," he told Jephthah, staring
up unwavering into Jephthah's glowering face.
"You must show our spirits that you are well
disposed toward them."

"I am *not* well disposed toward them!"
Jephthah erupted. "They are evil abominations
upon the face of the earth, and I will not bow
down to Satan."

"But if you do not dance," the chief said
reasonably, "we will have to burn you to placate the spirits."

Jephthah leaned back against the tug of the

two warriors who had him by the arms. "Then burn me! I will accept my crown of martyrdom happily!"

Hilary had been frozen to the ground in horror when the warriors came out, thinking they meant to drag Jephthah to the fire. Now that worst fear was realized, and she darted forward. "He doesn't mean it," she cried, thrusting herself between Jephthah and the chief. "He'll dance. We'll all dance. Look, Jephthah, it's easy!" She hopped up and down in front of him.

One of the painted warriors knocked her sprawling into the dust with his open hand. Patrick picked her up, murder in his eye; Hilary leaned heavily on his arm to keep him from striking the warrior.

"It is not suitable for women to dance the victory dance," the chief said with a benign smile. He nodded at Patrick. "Take care of your woman, friend, lest my young men have to correct her again."

Hilary struggled vainly against Patrick's grip as the two warriors half-carried, half-dragged Jephthah to the base of the wooden platform. There they stripped off his clothes and tethered him to the platform by a rope around his waist. He was at least three feet from the fire and the rope gave him room to move several feet on either side. Hilary couldn't understand what they meant to do.

Jephthah neither resisted nor cooperated as the Indians stripped and tied him. He let them do what they would while he stared over their heads with a rapt expression that suggested he was already seeing his glorious reception above.

One of the Indians who had tied him backed away, picked up a burning brand from the campfire, and jabbed it at Jephthah. He remained immobile, though the red-hot glowing end of the stick passed within inches of his face. "Heathen ceremonies! Perverted orgies!" His deep voice rang out through the shrill monotonous chanting of the dance leaders and the excited cries of the women who had gathered to watch the spectacle. Another warrior approached Jephthah from behind and thrust a splinter through the calf of his leg. He did not flinch, even when one of the women darted up and set the splinter of resinous wood alight. The others were crowding closer now, and Hilary realized that Jephthah was to be killed by inches, not set in the fire where the smoke might bring him a mercifully quick death.

"Can't we *do* anything?" she cried to Patrick.

His only response was to gather her to him, holding her face against his shoulder so that she could not see what was going on. "Love, we've done all that we can. Try not to listen."

"The Lord shall smite you, and destroy you, and cast you into outer darkness, where there is weeping and gnashing of teeth! Behold, he that believeth shall be saved, and he that believeth not shall be cast away! Thou shalt not worship false idols! Thou shalt have no other Gods but only the one!"

The drums slowed to a heavy rhythmic beat that matched Jephthah's rolling voice, and the chanting died away. Hilary pushed herself away from Patrick and forced herself to look at the dreadful scene. The last thing she could do for Jephthah was to be with him during his death.

She was surprised to see that the Indians who had crowded about him were backing off. They still held wood splinters and burning sticks in their hands, but instead of using them, they were listening to Jephthah's speech. And he was just getting into his stride, arms waving and hair flying about as if he were addressing a church meeting. He seemed sublimely unconscious of his nakedness.

"For the Lord has spoken unto me, yea, even unto my unworthiness. and has lifted me up into his holy presence. And so shall he do even unto the least of you, miserable sinners, if you will but hear his word and turn away from the wickedness in your hearts."

Jephthah's arms went out as if to embrace his torturers. "Will you not hearken unto the word of salvation? Will you not drink of the water of life? Come unto me . . ."

His voice was low and pleading, infinitely gentle. The Indians who had been laughing as they jabbed burning splinters at Jephthah hung their heads and muttered uneasily as one of them translated what he could understand of the speech. The woman who had lighted the splinter in Jephthah's leg crawled forward on her hands and knees and pinched the glowing end with her fingers to extinguish it. Jephthah put one hand on her head without looking down and went on speaking.

Half an hour later they untied him and gave him back his pants. Jephthah stopped dressing with one leg in and one leg out of his pants to wave his hand in illustrating the story of the crossing of the Red Sea.

Sometime after that, when the sun was entirely down and Jephthah's face was lighted only by the flames of the campfire, the chief stood up and put a matchcoat of deerskins decorated with a fringe of glass beads around Jephthah's shoulders. The gesture did not interrupt the rhythm of the speech. He had just gotten to Sodom and Gomorrah. He seemed to find notable parallels between those sinful cities and London, Williamsburg, the Tuscarora village, and, in fact, everywhere except the now defunct New Community of Saints.

The chief backed away without altering his expression of grave interest. When he reached the edge of the circle of listeners, he casually wandered over to where the rest of the white captives sat.

"He talks well, your friend," he remarked. "I think my young men no longer wish to kill him." He gave Patrick a slight nod and drifted off, a stooped, frail figure in the darkness around the huts.

Patrick shrugged and grinned at Hilary. "Well, I did tell you they respect a man who can make long speeches . . . even if they don't understand him. For that matter, I don't understand him myself. But I think nobody's going to die tonight . . . and the longer he can keep it up, the better."

"Oh, he's just getting warmed up," Hilary told him. "He usually goes through the rest of the Old Testament for starters, including the minor prophets."

Patrick clapped one hand to his forehead. "You're kidding! I take it back. Those Indians are in serious danger. Jephthah is going to *talk* them all to death."

After a moment Hilary laughed with him. All these years she'd felt there was something wrong with her because she couldn't follow Ebenezer Graham's rolling, rambling sermons. But Jephthah talked the same way, and Patrick wasn't in the least repentant about not understanding him. And nobody was going to die tonight. And tomorrow they would all be ransomed, and then . . .

She shut her mind to the decision that would be forced upon her then. Not that there was any decision, really. She was Jephthah's lawful wedded wife, and there was nothing Patrick or anybody else could do about it. He would just have to go back to Moonshadows and forget her. It was the best thing for him really. She tried to recapture that certainty, the sense that she had left him for his own good; failed; and then forgot all about the morrow as an even more urgent problem confronted her.

A number of the young men who had been sharing the looted rum had fallen asleep during Jephthah's sermon, including Tasqui, who lay on the ground with his head pillowed on the jug. Their laughter aroused him and he slowly wandered over to where the whites sat, one finger hooked through the handle of the jug, swaying as he walked.

"Pretty," he mumbled, squatting before them

and reaching out to caress Hilary's head. She shrank back and he caught hold of a lock of Bet's reddish-brown hair instead. "Pretty Fire Hair, come to my lodge tonight."

Patrick's arms tensed around Hilary and she leaned back on him with all her weight, praying that he wouldn't start a fight. There was no telling what incident might change the Indians' drunken good humor into the lust for torture that they had all seen earlier. If she had to go with Tasqui to keep the peace, it was, she told herself, a small sacrifice to make. The thought did nothing to still the quivering cold fear in the pit of her stomach.

"Come!" Tasqui insisted. He yanked at the ribbon of shining red hair that he held, and Bet's tumbled head followed the motion. Her tangled hair hung down in front of her face, obscuring her features.

Tasqui stood up and tugged at the lock of hair like a leash, and Bet followed him. She managed to brush the tangles away from her eyes and gave Hilary a saucy wink as she was led away.

∾ 20 ∾

In the morning Hilary was relieved to see Bet emerge from Tasqui's lodge, flushed and disheveled but still grinning. They had heard cries and yelps coming from the lodge until late into the night; Hilary had wanted to go and make sure that Bet was all right, but Patrick and Mary refused to let her leave the guest lodge into which they had all been herded.

"She probably enjoys whatever that red savage is doing to her," Mary sniffed. "She looks like the kind of woman who would enjoy anything."

"Love, she did it for you. Don't spoil it by going over there and offering yourself to Tasqui now," Patrick advised, gripping her shoulder.

Ephraim and Alice contributed little to the discussion. Alice had been silent ever since they arrived in the village, drawn into a world of her own in which she hardly seemed to perceive what was going on around her, and Ephraim's only concern was to watch over his wife.

Jephthah stalked into the lodge in the middle of the night and told Hilary not to concern herself over the Whore of Babylon.

"I thought that was Rome," Hilary said.

"For once," Patrick told her, "the preacher and I are in complete accord. Don't worry over what you can't help. And try to get some rest. We'll all need to have our wits about us in the morning."

Finally, reluctantly, Hilary concluded that Patrick was right. But she had slept little that night, worrying about Bet, and the sight of her cocky grin the next morning was a great relief. She rushed over and took her by the hand.

"Bet, are you all right? I can't thank you enough—you sacrificed yourself for me . . . for all of us, really, because I think Patrick would have tried to kill him—"

Bet winked. "Anytime you want a sacrifice, dearie, just say the word. That Tasqui's the best set-up man I seen in a long time. Old Leon weren't good for much, despite all his dirty talk. One-two, one-two, that'll do! Now, Tasqui . . ." Her voice trailed off and her lips curved in a reminiscent smile. " 'Course, he was a bit angry when he'd sobered up a bit and realized he'd grabbed the wrong doxy," she admitted. "But I found a few ways to convince him he hadn't made that bad a bargain."

At that point Tasqui emerged from the lodge, stretching and smiling. Hilary thought he looked as contented as a cat in the sun. When he glanced at her and Bet, though, he sent a scowl in their general direction. As he stalked toward them, Hilary shrank back instinctively.

"Funny women," he said, letting one hand fall on Hilary's shoulder and one on Bet's. "Big joke on the drunk warrior, no?"

His hand felt like a weight of lead; Hilary was too frightened to speak. She admired the way Bet piped up cockily. "You got any complaints, big fellow, I'll take care of 'em tonight," she promised with a saucy wink.

"Too late," Tasqui said. A flicker of regret crossed his usually impassive features. "Today we ride to the treaty village to ransom you."

It was nearly a day's ride to the treaty village, not so much because of distance as because of the tortuous trail they must follow. Hilary rode before Patrick; the rest of the captives were mounted on sturdy little Indian ponies, with an escort of warriors before and behind to make sure that they didn't get any ideas about escaping. The chief brought up the rear of the procession, riding with a young boy whose presence no one bothered to explain to Hilary.

They went down and up the sides of deep ravines where a little clear water trickled through fallen leaves at the very bottom, skirted impenetrable thickets of thorny vines, and crossed a high stony ridge where Hilary suffered for the Indian horses with their unshod hooves. The metal horseshoes of Patrick's steed rang out on the granite outcrop and struck sparks from the bare rock at the top of the ridge.

From there she looked down upon a sea of red and orange autumn leaves, golden and fiery against the pure sweet blue of the sky. It was just an hour before sunset, and the autumn sun glowed through the trees and added an almost unearthly intensity to the colors of the turning leaves. The rolling hills flattened before them, and in the distance she could see the silver thread of a river. Between them and the river was a cleared circle surrounded by a high palisade of logs and earth.

As they came closer, Hilary thought that there was little to choose between this neutral village and the one in which she had been held captive. Inside the palisade was the same circle of houses made of woven branches and bark mats, the same arrangement of medicine lodge and storehouses and corn-grinding mortar at the far side of the circle. But more than half the men inside the palisade wore the fringed buckskins and coarse homespuns of frontier settlers, instead of Indian breechclouts. And on one short figure in a blue coat, brass buttons winked forth and caught the sunlight.

"Look, Bet!" Hilary leaned back and gestured the older woman to come up beside her as they entered the village. "Do you suppose that's—"

But before she could finish the sentence, Bet looked past her and her face lit up. "Dickie?" As if in a trance, she slipped off her pony and moved slowly over the ground toward the center of the village, where a little man in a blue coat stood, arms folded, tapping one foot. "I been an awful fool, Dickie," she murmured.

"That you 'ave," Dickie agreed. "Ought to beat yer, I should."

Instead he reached up to grab her by the shoulders and give her several smacking kisses. Hilary watched the reunion with wistful tears in her eyes, putting off the moment when she would have to face Jephthah. She slipped from Patrick's horse and pretended to fuss with straightening her clothes while the rest of the party dismounted and their horses were led off. Ephraim and Alice joined the frontiersmen; the Indians followed and the chief began discussing ransom terms with the whites.

When Hilary finally looked up, Jephthah was standing before her, an accusing figure in his shredded black coat. "Hilary, I have to talk to you before they settle the ransom," he said.

Before Hilary could reply, she felt hands falling lightly yet possessively on her shoulders. She didn't have to turn around to know who it was.

"Anything you want to say to *my betrothed*," Patrick said with hard emphasis on the words, "can be said before me. I'll not have you bullying her any longer, Preacher."

For the first time in Hilary's experience, Jephthah was speechless. His wide mouth opened and shut several times. "I didn't intend to bully her," he said finally, with surprising meekness.

"Well, you do," Patrick told him. "Now, listen to this, Preacher, and get it straight. You have no rights over Hilary. She is coming with me and we are going to be married."

"Patrick, *no*." The words broke from Hilary's lips like a moan of pain. "I can't marry you."

"You don't understand," Patrick said furiously, shaking her by the shoulders as he spoke. "Now, shut up and do what I tell—"

"You let me speak for myself, Patrick Lyle!" Hilary tore herself free from his grasp and whirled to face him, cheeks flaming. "You too,

Jephthah! This time you *men* aren't going to discuss it behind my back and decide what's to become of me without even giving me a choice in the matter!"

"Correct," Patrick said, folding his arms and glaring at her with eyes that sparkled like blue jewels in the glow of the council fire. "There is going to be no more discussion—behind your back or otherwise. And the decision has already been made. You are *mine*." He reached for her wrist, but Hilary ducked away before he could grab her.

"Oh, no, you don't," she shouted. Her hair was tumbling about her face and the overlong homespun gown threatened to trip her as she backed away. Patrick advanced slowly, half-crouching like an Indian, while Jephthah watched with something like a smile on his face. Hilary stepped back, fell against something hard and warm, turned and saw Tasqui grinning at her. In one hand he held one of the long poles used by the Indian guards to keep order at the council meetings.

"Thank you, Tasqui, that's just what I needed." She snatched the pole out of his hand and whirled it in a long semicircle. Patrick and Jephthah both instinctively stepped back.

"All right," Hilary said. "That's better." Patrick moved forward slightly and she jabbed at his chest. "Just stay there, both of you, while I tell you what I've decided."

Patrick threw up his hands with a disgusted expression. Jephthah looked at him and for a moment the two men seemed to share a masculine accord over the ridiculous whims of females. "All right. But I'm warning you, it'll make no difference. I'll not let you go with the preacher again, and that's that."

"I don't want—" Jephthah began.

"Stop!" This time Hilary jabbed the pole in Jephthah's direction, fearful that his deep resonant voice would hypnotize her into meekly following his orders once again. "I'll do the talking this time."

Jephthah shut his mouth, but his glowering eyes spoke volumes for him.

Now that Hilary had the floor, her mouth went dry and for a moment she couldn't think what to say. Her arms and wrists were trembling with the strain of holding up the long pole. She didn't know how long she could keep it up in the air. "Patrick," she repeated, "I can't marry you. I'm already married to Jephthah. Besides, it wouldn't be a good idea for you to marry me. Carruthers explained it all to me. Governor Spotswood—"

"To hell with the governor!" said Patrick between his teeth. "Hilary, darling girl, you don't understand. I've already—"

"But," Hilary went on, desperate to get it over with before her nerve and her wrists both failed her, "I will come back and live with you as your mistress."

Both men stared at her with horror-struck expressions.

"If . . . if you still want me, that is," Hilary added.

Patrick was still staring at her, so she babbled on while the long pole in her hands drooped closer and closer to the ground. "I've thought it all out very carefully. You see, Carruthers thought you would insist on marrying me if I stayed at Moonshadows, and he explained how that would ruin your life, so I had to run away. But it's different now, because you can't marry me even if you still want to, and I thought I could live very quietly, maybe in a little cottage somewhere on the estate, and you could come and visit me sometimes, and . . . and . . ."

Her benumbed hands gave way; the long pole thudded on the ground, and Hilary had to look away from Patrick's thunderstruck expression.

"You see, Jephthah"—she turned to her husband—"I do love you. And I always will. Because you were so kind to me when I was a child, and . . . well, because you're a good man. But it's not the same thing. I can't live without Patrick." She turned back to Patrick, hoping that he would say something. "If . . . will you have me that way?" It was what he'd wanted in the beginning. But so much had happened since then.

When she held out her hands to him, Patrick sprang forward and caught her in his arms, crushing her to him in the fierce intensity of his love. "Have you?" he repeated in wondering tones. "You darling, wonderful girl. Have you? You're damned right I will! But no, not as my mistress. We're going to be properly married, with banns and a church, and to hell with my family! Listen, Hilary. You aren't . . . I can't . . ."

He released her to yank at his thick black queue in frustration. "Oh hell. There's so much to explain. I don't know where to begin."

Around them the Indians of Tasqui's village were packing up their ransom goods and preparing to depart, while Colonel Quincy and his men retired to the guest lodge for the night. Now Jephthah stepped forward.

"If I may be allowed to get two or three words in before you begin these explanations," he said, "I have something of my own to say to Hilary."

Hilary looked up from the shelter of Patrick's arms, blinking back the tears on the ends of her lashes. Dear Jephthah! He was a good man, and courageous, and absolutely maddening—and she loved him like a brother. Would he ever understand?

"As I tried to tell you before you launched into this hysterical speech, Hilary," Jephthah said, "I have come to my own conclusions about our future."

She clutched the soft edge of Patrick's buckskin hunting shirt. "I'm not leaving Patrick. I'm sorry, Jephthah, and I hope you'll understand someday. But I've found out what's right for me, and I'm sticking to it."

"That," Jephthah said unexpectedly, "is entirely your concern. Hilary, when you arrived at the New Community, I felt responsible for you. In your youth and inexperience you were most unfit to go wandering about the American wilderness alone."

"Damn right," Patrick put in over Hilary's head. "But from now on she won't be alone. I'll be with her."

Jephthah's lips twitched at the corners. "An excellent decision. As I was saying, I felt that it

was my duty to marry Hilary at once, to keep
her safe. I hoped that with time, having begun
with the benefit of my father's godly tutoring,
she could become a fitting member of the New
Community of Saints. However, I have since
come to the conclusion that she is too light-
minded, worldly, and frivolous to belong among
us."

Light-minded. Worldly. Frivolous. Once those
words would have rolled over her as a crushing
condemnation, dooming Hilary to be just like
her mother, abandoning those she loved. Now
she clung tightly to the person she loved most
in the world and smiled sweetly at Jephthah.
"You're absolutely right."

"Certainly," he went on as though she had
not spoken, "you are not fit for the new task
which the Lord has laid upon me. The Community of Saints has been twice destroyed, in England and here. Clearly it is the Lord's will that
I should be a wanderer upon the face of the
earth, devoting my life to bringing the Word to
the ignorant heathen. The joys of domesticity
are not for me. I resign you into Patrick's care
and renounce our marriage, Hilary. You are
free to go with him."

He laid one hand on her head and looked
down at her. For a moment she could see the
loving kindness of the old Jephthah, the older
brother who'd protected her from his father's
stern rule in England. Then all tenderness vanished from his face and his eyes glowed with
the light of martyrdom. "Come, Mary. It is time
for us to go." Turning away from Patrick and

Hilary, he held out his hand to the gaunt Englishwoman.

"But where are you going?" Hilary cried as they walked toward the palisade gate. Jephthah was still limping slightly.

Jephthah looked back over his shoulder. "We are returning to Catechna to preach to the Indians there. They have shown a most encouraging willingness to listen to God's word, and the chief has invited us to remain among them as long as we like."

As he and Mary vanished into the darkness outside the palisade, Hilary felt her knees trembling with strain and fatigue. She swayed in the circle of Patrick's arms and would have fallen if he had not been supporting her. "My God. Is he serious? He'll do something to annoy them in a week and they'll burn him again. Patrick, you've got to stop him."

Patrick shook his head. "I don't think you or I or anybody else can stop Jephthah when he takes a notion of what the Lord wants him to do, Hilary. Besides, who's to say he's not right? I won't say I like him, but he's a damn brave man. They respect that. He may do all right. Besides"—his lips twitched—"don't you think he's better off among people who really respect long sermons?"

"You may be right," Hilary agreed. She looked wistfully back toward the palisade gate even as Patrick urged her toward the guest lodge where they were to spend the night. Jephthah had meant so much to her for so long. It didn't seem right that he should vanish from her life with those brief words of farewell.

"He'll be back," Patrick said as if reading her thoughts. "Just wait. Come spring, he'll be riding into Moonshadows again, telling us what miserable sinners we are and demanding a contribution of corn and cloth for his Indians from . . . from whoever owns Moonshadows," he finished, his voice trailing off as if he'd just remembered something unpleasant.

Hilary forgot about Jephthah when she heard the lonely note in Patrick's voice. "But can't anybody help? Your parents . . . the governor . . ." She bit her lip. She'd thought that if she didn't marry Patrick, but only lived with him as his mistress, she would be no barrier to his saving Moonshadows. But there was one source of help that he might be ruling out. "Patrick, if you married Cat Stilwell—"

"Hush." Patrick put his fingers over her lips. "I'm marrying you and nobody else. And as for Moonshadows, it's too late to worry about that, my darling girl." His smile was so tender, so full of joy, that only her intimate knowledge of him enabled her to read the slight tautness at the corners of his lips. to guess how much the smile cost him. "You've not been keeping track of the days lately. It's October, my love."

"October?"

"Yes. I've already missed my meeting with Governor Spotswood." Patrick's arm encircled her body like a statement that he would never let her go. "The news of the Indian uprising came the day before Spotswood was to come to Moonshadows. I couldn't wait. And I fear my disappearance will not have improved my position in the good governor's eyes. By now he may well have ordered Moonshadows sold by inch of candle to pay my taxes—having decided that I'm an irresponsible, frippery fellow after all." He squeezed her tight against him. "Incurably light-minded, in fact. We're a perfect match, Mistress Hilary . . . if you'll have a poor man?"

"I always said I'd rather marry a poor man than a rich one," Hilary said, striving to match Patrick's lightness of tone. She held up her callused palms for his inspection. "See, I'm already practiced at grinding corn. We'll have a little cabin, and . . . oh, how could I forget!" she cried. "Patrick, it's all your fault, you keep confusing me. I can't marry you! I'm already married to Jephthah!"

"I keep telling you to shut up and listen to me," Patrick said with mock sternness, "but damned little respect do I get! Bodes ill for our married life, my girl! You are not married to Jephthah, darling girl. In case you forget, you belong to me. As my bound servant. You can't legally marry anybody without my permission, not until the term of your indentures expires, and I do not—I most emphatically do not—give you permission to marry anybody but me!"

Colonel Quincy's blustering voice interrupted the kiss with which Patrick sealed this statement.

"Goddamn cheating Indians! Went off with the full ransom!"

Patrick released Hilary and gave the colonel a quizzical look. "And what's your objection to that?"

"Well, the preacher and that old spinster went back with them," the colonel pointed out. "That's two out of five. In common decency they should have given a third of the guns . . . er . . . trade goods back."

Patrick burst out laughing. "Seems to me it should be Kendall O'Leary who's complaining, not you, Colonel."

"Faith, and I'm not the man to quarrel over a pack or two," said Kendall, twirling his long mustache. "They left me personal pack on me little horse here. And if you've no objection, Colonel dear, I'll just take meself out of here in the morning and head south to see can I do a little business with the pitiful remnants of the trade stock you've left me."

"Hardly enough in that to be worth your time." Colonel Quincy gave a contemptuous glance at the bulging saddlebags on Kendall's horse.

"Oh, I don't know," Kendall said with a thoughtful smile. "There's a few small items they might find useful, once they've had time to examine the packs and look over their ransom goods."

"Like what?"

Still smiling, Kendall reached into the pack and drew out a small steel contraption that fitted easily into the palm of his hand. "The flintlocks for the muskets they just bought."

"My God!" The colonel exploded into a big harrumphing laugh that echoed off the walls of the palisade. "Put that away, you rascal. I didn't see it. As far as I know, you gave 'em—what did we say?—ax handles and cloth, and now you're heading south to sell 'em the ax heads."

"Whatever you say, Colonel dear." Kendall replaced the flintlock with a grin.

"If they don't scalp you first," the colonel muttered. "My God, man, those are going to be some seriously unhappy Indians when they unwrap their new toys. If we didn't have a hostage, I'd be afraid of their coming back here tonight and scalping the lot of us."

"Hostage?"

The colonel shoved forward a skinny boy who looked to be about eight years old. "The chief's grandson. He's coming with us as far as the Nottoway, then to Williamsburg as a hostage under Spotswood's eye."

"Very reassuring," agreed Patrick. He dropped to one knee and said a few words in halting Tuscarora. The boy's lips twitched as if he were trying to control a smile, but he raised his head proudly.

"What did you tell him?" Hilary asked.

"I tried to say that we were happy to be guarded by such a brave warrior on our journey home. But," Patrick admitted ruefully, "I'm afraid what made him smile was my accent. The Tuscarora language is quite a bit different from the Indian dialects I learned around my father's home."

His father. The proud old aristocrat, the cavalier who would surely look with scorn on his son's misalliance. Hilary felt guilty again at the havoc she was wreaking on Patrick's life. He had already lost his chance of favor with the governor by chasing off into the forest after her when he was supposed to be at Moonshadows; should she let him compound his troubles by defying his family? "Patrick, I don't think—" she began.

"So," Patrick interrupted her, "I have often observed. That's all right. I'll do the thinking for you. And I think we should get some sleep before the long journey tomorrow." He took her elbow and steered her into the guest lodge.

∽⟡ 21 ⟡∽

The long dark hut, the twin to the one in which they'd passed their ecstatic night of reunion at Catechna, was empty but for the low bedsteads. Patrick explained that Colonel Quincy and his men had insisted on sleeping outside, around the council fire, so that he and Hilary could have some privacy.

"What if it rains?" Ominous black clouds had been gathering overhead as the sun set, and Hilary had already experienced the torrential force of a Virginia summer storm. The men sleeping outside would be lying in a riverbed if the storm broke.

Patrick grinned. "They'll have to share some of the Indians' lodges. I made it very clear that they were not to bother us."

"I thought they insisted on giving us the privacy," Hilary teased. After her bold-faced confession of love outside, she felt almost shy of Patrick, afraid that she had forced him into some-

thing he did not really want. Talking about the
militiamen was one way to hold off the inevitable intimate confrontation.

Patrick's eyes were wide and innocent, gleaming blackly in the shadowed lodge. "That they
did . . . after I explained that I'd have the scalp
off anyone who tried to join us in here! After
all," he said with a wicked grin, "you need
your sleep. We've a long road to travel tomorrow. I was only trying to protect you, my darling girl."

"Are you sure sleep is what you had in mind?"

There had been a fire lit in the center of the
lodge to warm it, but the flames had long since
died down. Hilary shivered as she slipped her
homespun gown off and the chill night air struck
her flesh. Patrick knelt to blow the coals into
glowing warmth. Then he came to her and
loosed her coppery hair to tumble about her
shoulders, and she shivered from something
other than the cold as his lips and hands traced
the lines of her body through the flowing red
hair that crackled like flame over her arms and
breasts and clung to his fingers.

"Oh, Patrick," she whispered, putting her
hands on his shoulders, "I do truly love you."

His soft chuckle made his lips vibrate against
her. "It's about time you found that out. I've
known it a long time."

"Conceited," Hilary said. "Smug. Overconfident. What I haven't figured out yet is why I
truly love you."

"Haven't you, darling girl? Then let me
demonstrate."

"Oh!" Strong arms swung her off her feet

and lifted her onto the frame of saplings piled high with furs.

"Oh," she breathed again as Patrick's lips found the taut peak of her breast, warming her with the quivering lines of desire that radiated from that central point. He traced a line of kisses down the white valley between her breasts and up the other side while she shivered and clung to him.

"Speechless, my love?" he teased. The soft folds of his buckskin breeches caressed the inside of her thigh, and one hand molded the slender curves from her waist downward until his fingers brushed against the soft nest of curls. Hilary pressed her mouth against his shoulder as her body arched upward frantically, following the questing and retreating hand with a will of its own. She moaned with disappointment when the weight of him over her lifted for a moment, and cried out again when he settled against her, warm and naked, his flesh glowing darkly in the red light of the fire.

"*Now*, my darling girl," Patrick breathed, and his hands grasped her while they became one. Hilary opened to him, breathless with anticipation, and felt his love and strength flowing into her with the sweet joining of their bodies.

"Patrick . . ." She stroked the long hard planes of his body wonderingly, reveling in this treasure that lay between her palms, the supple length of bone and muscle and flesh that encased the quicksilver spirit she had come to love.

"Patrick," she cried out again as he moved within her, quickening the spark of desire to a molten heat that consumed her. "Patrick!" There was nothing but his body in her and holding her now, carrying them both away to someplace where only their love and their striving to become one had any meaning. She held him close with arms and legs and longed for him to come closer still, closer, to the very heart of her being, until the explosion that shook them both and freed her to drift gently down again into the warm soft pile of furs and the knowledge of Patrick lying beside her, his head pillowed on her breast, his rough uneven breathing echoing in her ear.

"Hilary, my love." One arm encircled her waist, holding her close against him. "Now do you know where you belong?"

"I think I have the general idea," she whispered. Her fingers traced the length of his body, daring in the semidarkness. "You might need to remind me from time to time." She felt him springing to new life under her hand and drew in her breath with surprise. His hand closed about her wrist before she could retreat.

"Don't stop . . . ah, my love!" He groaned with passion and his hand relaxed. He lay back on the furs, head thrown back, and she stroked long gentle fingers over him and felt a thrill of power at the evidence of her ability to rouse him. Throwing back the coverlet of soft tanned deerskins, she bent over him, letting the ends of her ringlets trail over his chest and flat stomach, until her lips daringly brushed him where her fingers had been.

"Enough!" Patrick's hands caught her about the waist with steely passion and lifted her bodily over him. "You must learn to finish what you've begun, my girl," he warned her, lowering her so that she could kneel astride him.

Hilary gripped his shoulders and an involuntary cry of passion broke from her own lips as he thrust into her from below, hips arching upward to join them again. His hands about her waist urged her into a rhythm that needed no teaching.

"Patrick, Patrick," she cried out as the rocking motion carried both of them away again. She felt as if she were riding the thunder and taking the lightning into her body. As the storm burst overhead, heavy droplets of water drumming against the roof of the lodge, she shuddered and fell forward over him, crying out in completion even as she felt him surging within her.

And she was right. Neither of them got much sleep that night. But in spite of that, she woke at dawn feeling as refreshed as if she'd rested for a sennight. She twined her arms about Patrick's naked shoulders, covering his tanned back with kisses, and he gave a sleepy murmur of protest as the furs slipped off his body, and then, awakened by the cool morning air, turned to her and returned her kisses with so much enthusiasm that they got a late start that morning, after all. Hilary endured Colonel Quincy's bluff, hearty teasing with good grace. For once she didn't even blush excessively.

It had rained heavily during the night and the trees dripped water down Hilary's back and onto her nose and into the gathered folds of her skirt. But the cloudy, damp day could not extinguish the glow of joy in her heart. The long ride back toward Moonshadows was an enchanted time of happiness for Hilary, marred only by her fear of what they would find when they arrived. Would the governor already have moved to auction off the house and strip Patrick of his possessions? Surely, she thought, he would not be so unjust. He would have to grant Patrick a hearing. There was still hope.

Patrick made it easy to believe in that hope. As he rode beside her, keeping a continuous undercurrent of jokes and flirtation and audacious double-entendres, he looked like a young man without a care in the world—not like somebody who might be going back to find his home put up at auction. And he was so handsome! If Hilary had admired him before, the aristocrat in charge of his plantation, she felt ten times prouder of him now. Dressed like the poorest of the militiamen in his old hunting buckskins, his curled wig put aside for raven-black hair pulled back in a queue, he still stood out among the rest of them. He didn't need the trappings of wealth and privilege to excel, Hilary thought, her heart swelling with pride. Wherever he was, whatever his station in life, he would be Patrick, her love, the finest man in Virginia—and to hell with that word *gentleman*, and all the grief it had caused them, one way and another. She straightened her back and rode proudly by his side, though by late afternoon when they reached the boundaries of Moonshadows plantation, every bone in her body was aching with weariness.

"I'll leave you here, Lyle," Colonel Quincy

said, reining in beside them at a fork in the path where they had to slow down as the horses picked their way through a muddy patch. Straight ahead lay Moonshadows, and Patrick's horses were pricking up their ears and sniffing the air as if they recognized the homeland and were eager to get back to their comfortable stables. "Be quicker for the rest of us to go by way of Martin's Ford. Servant, Lyle . . . Mistress Hilary—Mistress Lyle, I'll be saying from now on." He bowed from his saddle with a grace surprising in such a portly man, kissed Hilary's fingertips, and wheeled his horse to take the east-branching path down to Martin's Ford.

Patrick and Hilary rode on in silence. As the journey ended, Hilary felt her own apprehensions of what they would find at Moonshadows returning in full force, her hope that the governor would wait to give Patrick a hearing dwindling away. A glance at Patrick's serious countenance warned her that similar thoughts were troubling him.

When the path reached the riverbank, Patrick glanced downstream and jerked at his horse's reins. "What's that?"

A plume of smoke rose above the trees.

"I don't know," Hilary said, and then, as Patrick looked as if he wanted to investigate, "but whatever it is, it's the opposite way from Moonshadows."

Patrick frowned. "You're right. If it's a forest fire, we'd best ride to the great house and warn them. From the size of that smoke cloud, it's too late to stop it now."

An orange flame burst over the treetops, first

looking like an extension of the brightly colored autumn leaves, then forming a pointed tongue that darted upward three times, flickering with a life of its own, before it faded from sight again.

"Much too late." Patrick urged the tired horses into a canter along the river path. "But it's funny," he shouted over his shoulder to Hilary, "I'd have thought it's been too wet a season for forest fires."

"Maybe there's been a drought since you left," Hilary called back. The canter that Patrick mastered with easy movements of his muscular body, thighs tightly gripping the sides of his horse, was sheer bouncing torture to her. There might, she thought as she hung on with grim determination, be some compensations for her if Patrick lost Moonshadows. If she didn't marry into the gentry, she wouldn't have to learn to ride like a lady. One placid plowhorse would be their stable, and that would be more her speed. Thank goodness, here was Moonshadows at last.

"What the devil?" Patrick pulled his horse up at the edge of the cleared ground sloping from the river up to the great house and stared up at the house, a puzzled frown on his face. As Hilary caught her breath, she saw that the lower story of the great house was ablaze with candles. The sound of laughter and singing, the clink of punch cups, and a masculine voice raised in a toast drifted out the window—something about green Irish fields and gray-eyed girls.

At the sound of the toast Patrick's tense shoulders relaxed slightly. "Well, that settles one thing," he said, trying to smile. "It's not the servants up to high jinks while my back's turned, and they've not sold the house yet. That's my father's favorite toast. What a day, what a week," he muttered as they walked their horses up the last slope. "Forest fires in a dripping-wet forest, my father throwing a party in Moonshadows, my girl thinking I'd let her run off and marry somebody else. Doesn't anybody except me have any sense anymore? Come on, Hilary, we've got some explanations to hear. Oh, don't worry about your dress, you always look fine to me." Patrick lifted Hilary down from her horse and shouted for Hawkins to get a stable lad.

Men! Hilary tugged in vain at the hem of her lumpish, too-large, too-long homespun dress. She could feel that her hair had been pulled loose by every twig in the forest, so that she must look as blowsy a slut as Bet! Was this any way to introduce her to his rich, disapproving family?

"Patrick, I don't think—" she began.

"I know, I know," Patrick said under his breath as the door opened, "but could you possibly save your not thinking for later?" He straightened his arms with an impatient shake of his wrists that made the buckskin sleeves drape as elegantly as any London tailor's work. His arm went about her as excited people spilled out onto the portico, and Hilary realized that he too was nervous of this meeting. The knowledge stiffened her back so that she stood straight and proud beside him. Let Patrick's parents say what they liked of his bride's background, they should not have cause to complain of her behavior.

First through the door, after Hawkins, was a laughing, screeching long stick of a girl whose fine lace-trimmed gown was marred by a smudge of paint on one sleeve and a distinct smell of turpentine around her fingers. "Hilary! I knew he'd bring you back! Oh, I am glad to see you, and won't Aunt be furious!" Cat Stilwell embraced Hilary and rubbed some of the paint onto her dress. "Oh, sorry about the paint. I'm doing a picture of the furnace to celebrate . . . Oops, that's supposed to be a surprise. I didn't say anything!"

When Hilary disentangled herself from Cat's friendly, awkward embraces, she saw a man and a woman regarding Patrick and herself with curious expressions. The woman was tall and slender, with a regal crown of chestnut hair streaked with gray and wide gray eyes that met Hilary's with a question in their depths. The man was an inch or two shorter than Patrick, and his snowy white wig and turquoise-blue velvet coat set off his dark brows and sapphire eyes so that she had no question as to his identity.

"Well, Patrick," said Patrick Lyle Senior, "I see you've not changed. Out gallivanting while I take care of your affairs for you, eh?"

Patrick's tanned cheekbones flushed a dark red. "I do not recall requesting you to manage my affairs, sir. I am perfectly competent to do so myself."

His father cleared his throat. "That's not what Carruthers thinks. I had a letter from him. Is

this the young woman to whom he refers?"
Sapphire-blue eyes, the mates to Patrick's,
seemed to bore right through Hilary's skull to
read all her pitifully scurrying thoughts.

"Oh, to hell and back with Carruthers!" Patrick exploded. He put his arm around Hilary,
drawing her to his side. "Yes, Father, this lady
is Hilary Pembroke, my affianced bride—and I
don't care what you say about it!" he finished
with a sudden loss of dignity.

Patrick Lyle Senior laughed heartily while his
son's jaw dropped. "Faith, me boy, and it's
time you learned to stand up to the old man!
What the devil did you think I'd be saying,
except that she's the prettiest little girl this side
of the Rappahannock and it's about time you
settled down?" He bowed to Hilary with courtly
grace. "Your very humble servant, Mistress Pembroke, and you'll allow me the customary privilege of the father of the groom?" Strong hands
gripped her shoulders and Patrick's father kissed
her on the lips, then on each cheek, then let her
go with a regretful sigh.

"Patrick, I never heard of that privilege," his
wife said, "and you're embarrassing the poor
girl!"

"It's an old Irish custom, Mary my love,"
Patrick's father replied imperturbably. He bowed
again to Hilary. "Pembroke? And Carruthers
writes that you're from Cornwall. Any connection of Tremarthen Pembroke's?"

Hilary lifted her chin and met the blue eyes
with a steady gaze. "His daughter, sir," she
said, "but he is dead, and the family does not
recognize me."

Patrick Lyle Senior gave a satisfied nod. "Good for you! Neither does mine."

Patrick's jaw dropped another inch, a thing Hilary would not have thought possible. His father chuckled and put one arm around his tall son. "Ah, I can see your mother was right, all those years ago. She would have it you should know the truth, but I wanted you to feel as good as any of the other Virginia gentry. And you are, mind you," he added, rather obviously catching himself up in the middle of a thought, "for doesn't the blood of kings of Ireland flow in my veins? Not to mention my dear departed father, the Marquis of Clonmel that was. But that's just the rub, Paddy my boy. Didn't you ever wonder why I took Mary's name, instead of she mine? The fact is that my dear father didn't wish me to use his."

Patrick looked royally shaken up. "You're a bastard?"

"I've been called that," his father agreed, "but not in the sense you mean. No, the old gentleman was legally married to my mother. But there was a slight difference of opinion between us, and . . . well, to make a long story short, at the time I met your mother in England, I was living by my wits. A short time thereafter my wits failed me and I was transported to America as a common felon, which turned out to be a blessing in disguise, as I found my sweet Mary again, earned my pardon from Governor Berkeley, and began a new life in the New World."

He chuckled again at the dumbfounded look in his son's blue eyes. Hilary had the distinct impression that the story had been cut very short indeed; she found herself possessed of a most unladylike longing to know all the details.

"So, you see, Mistress Hilary," Patrick's father said with a bow to her, "I'm not likely to object to a lady who came to Virginia as an honest indentured servant. 'Twas a cut above me own arrival, so it was." His rich creamy chuckle rolled out like a friendly arm around her shoulders. "Indeed, you've been a distinct relief to me. For a while I feared I'd done too well by Patrick, raising him to be a damned snob like the rest of these jumped-up shop-owners. I can tell you'll be a grand counteracting influence on the boy." He winked and patted her hand. "And who knows? Maybe your family will wish to be reconciled someday? Mine did, once, but we came to grief again when I told my father I'd rather run a plantation in America than kick my heels in Ireland on his allowance."

Hilary felt that she herself was staring with much the same dumbfounded look of amazement that she'd seen on Patrick's face. After all her imaginings, the warmth of this greeting was the last thing she had expected. She put up one hand to check that her jaw wasn't hanging open and encountered the cool gray gaze of Patrick's mother.

"And you, ma'am?" she heard herself boldly asking Mary Lyle. "You've no objection to our marriage?"

She curtsied as she asked the question, and some blessed instinct told her to make it the simple bob and dip practiced in the colonies instead of the sweeping stage curtsy she'd learned from her own mother.

Mary Lyle broke into a warm smile that transformed her quiet face with its firm features. "I think you'll be very good for Patrick," she said. She leaned forward to give Hilary a kiss on the cheek. "He needs someone who will keep him in line, you know—just like his father!" She directed a stern glance at Patrick Lyle Senior, who responded with a wink and a kiss of his hand to the ladies. "A girl who can lead him such a merry chase as you've done," Mary Lyle concluded, "should be an admirable counter to all the lovesick damsels who've been swooning at the feet of my odiously conceited son since the day he was breeched."

Patrick laughed and put one arm around Hilary's waist, the other around his mother's. "And you first of all, Mama," he said with an impudent wink that mirrored his father's, "admit it, you're besotted by the boy!"

Mary's fond smile was confession enough.

"But we've guests inside," said Patrick, "or wasn't that a fiddle tuning up I heard a moment ago? And where Cat Stilwell is, there must be a couple of boys for her to flirt with in between artistic endeavors. Let's go inside. We're neglecting our company."

As he handed his mother up the steps of the back porch, Hilary lagged behind and turned to Patrick's father. "Then you'll . . . will you speak for Patrick to the governor?"

"No need. The governor's here himself, and I think you'll find he's very well pleased," said Patrick Lyle Senior. "Your countrymen were before me in working out a way to save the boy's neck. Iron mines!"

"The governor!" Everything else he'd said fled from her mind. As they entered the hall, Hilary had just a glimpse of a smiling gentleman in a curled brown wig and brown velvet coat, and then Mary Lyle gave a tiny shriek of dismay and whisked her away from the men.

"Whatever am I thinking of!" she exclaimed. "You can't possibly be presented to Governor Spotswood in that rag of a dress. Come upstairs, we must be able to fit you out better than that."

The delphinium chamber seemed to open welcoming arms to Hilary. The mahogany furniture was freshly waxed and polished, tall green bayberry candles stood on either side of the dressing table, and a spray of bright autumn leaves brightened a porcelain vase meant for fresh flowers. "Elspeth kept everything ready for your return," Mary explained, "being sure that my son wouldn't let you go like that." She threw open the wardrobe doors and came away from the shelves with her arms full, throwing a rainbow of gowns onto the bed. "Which of these do you think is most suitable for meeting a governor? Do you want to appear demure or dashing?"

Despite the question, Hilary found she had no choice at all in her toilette. Talking at top speed, Mary Lyle selected a gray silk gown with a lavender underdress, splashed her neck and wrists with lavender water, and piled her hair atop her head in a demure style redeemed only by two long coppery ringlets. In between instructions to hold her arms up, tilt her head to one side, and stop fidgeting, Hilary learned what Patrick's father had meant by his exclamation of "Iron mines!"

It seemed that the land where Patrick had started to build his furnace, although containing no silver, was rich in iron ore. The Cornish miners whom he'd accidentally bought in an attempt to get Hilary, led by Jer Polwhys, had discovered the iron-rich earth and had devoted their scanty free time to setting up a small test furnace out of the half-built one left behind when Patrick abandoned the project, and running a load of ore through it.

Iron mines, and the establishment of a local iron-working industry to rival the works in New England, were one of Governor Spotswood's pet projects. When he came to Moonshadows to find Patrick gone, he'd ridden around the plantation, noticed the furnace, and investigated. Mary Lyle and her husband, drawn by Carruthers' letter, had arrived to find Spotswood delighted by this effort at establishing local industry. Patrick's father had persuaded the governor to agree to a remittance of the taxes in light of the development of the mines and the fact that Patrick had settled three hundred new colonists on the land.

"It's too good to be true," Hilary sighed at the end of the story.

"Yes. Well," Mary Lyle said dryly, "it's not quite that good. Spotswood demanded a half interest in the mines." She stepped back and gave Hilary a searching, critical look. "Emeralds," she said. "Tell my son to give you emeralds when the mines start to pay off. They should be a wedding present, of course, but—"

"I wouldn't *dream* of letting him do anything that extravagant!" Hilary exclaimed. "When we're lucky to keep Moonshadows at all, and it'll be years before the mine gets anywhere, and—"

Mary Lyle smiled and kissed her on the cheek. "I knew you'd do for my boy. All the same, emeralds it should be, one of these days. Now, are you ready to be presented to the governor?"

Hilary's head was awhirl with all these new discoveries. The only person she really wanted to see was Patrick. If only they could be quiet and alone together for a little while, until she got accustomed to this new world! But as the master of Moonshadows, his place was downstairs entertaining guests—and her place was by his side.

She rose reluctantly and swayed as a sudden fit of dizziness attacked her.

"You look pale," said Mary with another searching, critical look. Her glance lingered at the waistline of the gray silk dress that had fit so perfectly a few weeks earlier. "Are you with child?"

The fires in Hilary's cheeks banished any suspicion of pallor. With child! She had never thought of that. Her lips moved, counting days, and she heard Mary Lyle's soft laugh. "Excellent. Tell that wild lad of mine not to delay the wedding too long. I've a fancy to see a grandson before the next year is out, and mind you, he had better be legitimate."

She pressed Hilary down onto the bed. "Lie there and rest for a moment. Don't come downstairs till you're fully recovered. We don't want you fainting at the governor's feet!"

Hilary's eyelids flew open. "I never faint," she protested.

"Good. Just keep on never fainting for another couple of days." There was a whisk of amber satin skirts, the soft sound of a gently closing door, and Hilary was alone in the blue-and-green room.

It seemed to her, as she lay there, that the whisper of satin skirts was repeated. A faint musky scent came to her nostrils, and she heard something like the echo of a laugh. I suppose my mother did the best she could for me, she thought drowsily, rocking back and forth on the edge of sleep. That's all any of us can do.

A vagrant draft shook the bed hangings and left her feeling as if something not quite there had brushed her cheek. Then the room was empty, and she drowsed in peace and stillness, finally at ease with herself.

She was not quite asleep when the door was thrown open with a bang and the sharp click of wooden heels crossing the wooden floor awakened her. "Hilary, darling girl," Patrick's voice called, "do you mean to sleep away your own party?"

Strong hands lifted her from the bed while she was still confused with the mists of sleep. His lips brushed hers and she returned the kiss with all her strength, wrapping her arms around his neck and clinging to him. "Patrick, I love you."

"I know." Patrick's eyes were alight with love and laughter as he gently disentangled himself from her embrace. "And faith, were it not for our guests, I'd keep you up here another hour or two and let you prove it! But if I must be downstairs, I'll have you by my side to sweeten the hours in company. Come and watch me teach Governor Spotswood the moccasin game."

He had changed into a clean white shirt whose full sleeves, bound at the wrists, billowed out from the confines of a deep blue velvet waistcoat. Freshly starched frills of lace brushed over his knuckles. Hilary looked at the fine clothes with suspicion.

"Only if you roll up your sleeves first," she said. "I don't think it would be tactful to win *too* much from the governor."

"Hilary!" The look of injured innocence was the one that had taken her in so many times before. "Don't you trust your very own husband-to-be?"

Laughing, Hilary took his arm. "Only when I can watch you. Which," she warned him, "I plan to do for the next fifty years or so."